Dedicated to the boys—and girls—of summer
(Because they asked!)

To Eddie Forehand, Suzanne Hance, Sean Meyers, Efrain Canellas, Big Serge and Little Serge, (Mehalichanco and McKenzie), Mike Anderson, Bobby Merrill, James Cintron, Matt, Mike and Danielle Marrache, Roger Lopez, Suzanne Medina, Alex Mehalichanco, Jamie, Tanya McKenzie, Nick McKenzie, Hector Hernandez, Johnny Mok, Eddie Hung, Aurora Muniz, Stephanie Smith. For the guys of Pariah—Brian Keller, Robert, Tony Rodriguez, Ben, and Jason Pozzessere—and the Hungry Sailor, where local music has a chance. For Shayne, Bryee-Annon, and Derek Pozzessere (and Chynna, even though she isn't quite old enough to hang out!).

And with special best wishes for Linda, Tom, and Andrew Dixon.

Dear Friends,

This book is a bit different, and a first for me. It's definitely a vampire book—with a touch of suspense, history, and romance. This book excited me very much to write, and I'm grateful for the enthusiasm that friends, readers, and booksellers have shown for the project. Meanwhile, I am still writing Shannon Drake historical novels. The Zebra paperback edition of *Come the Morning* will be out in February, followed by the second book in the Graham family series, *Conquer the Night,* in July. The third book, tentatively titled *The Lion Triumphant,* will appear early in 2001.

But back to this book . . .

When I first started writing, I sent my stories to *Black Cat, Twilight Zone,* and other magazines, and to the now-defunct *Miami News.* I wanted to be a twentieth-century Edgar Allan Poe! I've always been fascinated by the occult, and having grown up under the influence of a very Irish family on my mother's side, I learned early that just because we're not aware of something doesn't mean it doesn't exist. After all, banshees, pixies, and leprechauns are real.

And as to vampires—aren't they?

I hope my readers will want to come along with me in this new direction. This, too, is the first book in a series. The next book will be about a fellow you will meet in these pages. His name is Lucian, and he has an interesting history all his own. There's a chapter from ''his'' story at the end of this book.

Happy Hunting!
Shannon Drake

PROLOGUE

New Orleans
1840

"There is nothing wrong with Comte DeVereaux," Magdalena said. She sat upon the settee in the grand parlor of her father's great-columned plantation house in the city of New Orleans. Her feet were firmly on the floor, her back determinedly straight.

Watching his only child, Jason Montgomery sighed and shook his head sadly. He hated to hurt her, but the hurt was necessary. In fact, seeing her there, her rich dark hair with its glistening hint of red piled atop her head, only a few delicate tendrils escaping, he felt a sudden shudder of fear. He must be firm. She was his only child, and he saw her through a father's prejudiced eyes, but she *was* beautiful. She had the classic perfection of face and figure that belonged to legends. Her soft skin was as smooth and perfect as alabaster; her eyes were a flashing hazel-gold. She had incredible dignity, a will of steel, and a startling intelligence, yet she had the grace of a gazelle, her every movement was naturally elegant, and at unguarded moments, she could appear as soft and tender and sweetly seductive as the most naive of innocent lasses. She was young, impressionable, passionate. He had taught her to be strong; she was his daughter, his heiress, and she must be so. He, Jason Montgomery, was ruler of all that surrounded him here in their plantation world, and he was respected by all men in Louisiana, men who were now *Americans*—be their ancestry French or British. He was a wise man, a learned man, indeed a powerful man, and he had tried very hard to give his daughter all of the things that made up what he was.

Now, she used them all against him.

"You do not like the comte because he is French," Magdalena accused her father with quiet reproach.

"I do not like the comte, not because he is French, but because he is—" Jason broke off just in time. He would not have her thinking him a madman, he would have her respect his opinion and his dictates because he was her father.

"I have chosen to live in this place where my associates are most likely to be French!" he sputtered. Yes, he had chosen this place for just such a reason. There were men and women here of Colonial American descent; there were the French, the British. There were the islanders, the Creoles. There were people of mixed blood, coffee-colored ancients, younger, powerful dusky beauties who knew . . . about the darkness.

This would not do. He raised a fist before him, shaking it toward his daughter. "I am your father. You will not see Alec DeVereaux again. I have decided that you will marry Robert Canady and that you will do so in the next few months, as soon as a ceremony can be arranged."

"No!" Magdalena cried, leaping to her feet. Passion and fury filled her eyes. The beauty and grace of her motion were never more visible than when she was angry like this. "I'll not do it, Father." Suddenly she was choking, sobbing. "You have never treated me like this! You have taught me to think and feel—"

"But you are not thinking!" Jason cried. "If you were thinking, you would wonder about this man, Comte Alec DeVereaux. You would want to know his parents, you would want proof of who he is, of where he has come from—"

"Papa, you are sounding like such an arrogant fool!" Magdalena exclaimed. "Listen to yourself! You have told me that this is now the United States of America. We do not bow down to kings and queens, a man forges his own destiny—"

"And silly girls still swoon over mysterious men with high-sounding titles!"

"Papa, I am not a silly girl, I have never swooned, and I am not impressed with titles. Why, my own father is called Baron of the Bayou, and that is enough for me!" she tried to tease. But then she grew serious. "You don't know him, Father. Alec is so well read, Father! He opens the world to me. He makes me see faraway places, he makes me understand history and men and women, and things that have been, and things that will come. I am in love with him because—"

"No!" Jason gasped.

"I am in love with him because he is brave, because he is sometimes so serious. Because he can be fierce and so tender. Because—"

"He seeks to seduce you!"

"Papa, he is an honest man, he wishes to marry me."

"Never!" Jason vowed staunchly. "Never, do you hear me? Never!" Jason roared. "Tyrone! Come escort my daughter to her room. She is not to leave it!" he commanded, raising his voice to call the servant who hovered unhappily in the hallway, listening to the argument. Tyrone was an extraordinary black man, born in the bayou country, a free man. His parents had hailed from the islands, and before that, his ancestors had come from the far south section of Africa. He stood well over six feet tall and was pure sleek muscle from head to toe. He strode to Magdalena sadly. "I am sorry, Miss Magdalena," Tyrone told her.

Magdalena stared into the handsome, sorrowful face of her father's right-hand man. Tyrone's one fault was his absolute loyalty to her father. He would carry her bodily upstairs if need be.

She turned back to her father, still unable to believe his unwavering hatred for the young man she had come to love. "No kings, no queens, Father! No all-powerful men or women to command us, this is America. I will not bend down to another's will!''

She spun fiercely about, heading for the stairway with Tyrone close behind her.

''Magdalena!'' her father called.

He was her father. Before this, her darling, her best friend. She turned back.

''What about love, child? Would you bow to my will because it comes with a father's *love?*''

''I will love you all of my life, Papa. All of my life. But there must be other love, and it is for that I must defy you.''

''You will marry Robert Canady within the next two months.''

''Father, I will not.''

''Child, you will.''

She arched an elegant brow. ''Will you keep me in my room until then?''

''Indeed, Daughter, by the darkness of each night to come, I do so swear it!''

She watched him, still standing with incredible dignity. ''Don't call me daughter,'' she said softly, and started up the stairs again.

This time Magdalena did not look back. Her heart was breaking. She loved him so dearly—his trimmed, graying beard, his tall lean form. He had always been there for her. Bellowing at times, gentle most often. Loving his land, but loving his books more, spending time in his study, poring over his ancient texts, always looking and learning and sharing. He had his cronies, some of them funny, peculiar men who came upon occasion to closet themselves with Jason and his books. They were all gentle and kind and quick to greet her—to study her sometimes, as they did their ancient texts. All of her life they had offered her warmth, a reflection perhaps of her father's adoration. Her father and his friends had always encouraged her to learn, to think, to make her own decisions.

And now . . .

Tears seemed to well deep within her very being. Other fathers dictated their daughters' marriages. Not Jason. He had been parent and friend all her life. He had been everything to her.

How could it be that he did not understand now? He had known love once himself. He told her so often enough. He described her mother to her at times with such vivid detail that she could almost see the past. Jason had adored Marie d'Arbanville, had swept her off her feet, and brought her home. He had settled in New Orleans, Magdalena believed, to make Marie feel as if she were back at home with her people near Paris.

Well, it didn't seem to matter now. If he had known love, he had forgotten it. Her heart began to thunder in her chest. Robert Canady was a fine man, a good man, a handsome young widower with a blond mustache, tawny curls, and sensual blue eyes. He was thoughtful, charming, sometimes a bit too serious and wise, but she did care about him, very much so. She had almost loved him. She might have married him once; she could not do so now. Alec had touched her. She had felt his whisper, felt his eyes. She had even felt the love with which he could somehow envelop her. Since he had first come to New Orleans, since they had danced at the governor's ball, since they had laughed, chatted, ridden together, there could be no one else. No one else with eyes of fire, with a whisper to awaken such hunger within her.

She shivered, even as she stepped into her room and slammed the door, leaning against it. She had told him that she would come. That she would ride across the bayou, fly with the night, if need be, to reach him. She stared across the room to her balcony doors. She had to move quickly.

She tore apart her bed, making a body form out of the pillows, covering it with sheets and the bedspread. She tiptoed back to the hallway door and listened. She could hear Tyrone settling himself against the wall where he would stay to guard her, all through the night. She slipped her velvet cape from the hook by her bed and raced on a near-silent tread to the balcony doors.

"Magdalena!"

She paused, startled, for it was almost as if she had heard

his—*Alec's!*—pained whisper in her ear. As if he were near, calling to her. Beckoning her.

The night breeze brushed by her, lifting her hair and the soft blue silk of her gown.

"I am coming, my love!" she thought in return.

From the wrought-iron balcony she caught hold of an old oak branch. It had served her as a child when she slipped into the night. It would serve her now.

She climbed easily down the tree, leaping the last few feet to the ground. She could see her father in the great parlor still, head bent, shoulders hunched as he stood before the fire. Her heart cried out. He was so dear to her.

"My love, my love . . . "

She could hear the whisper again. Feel it caress her. She turned from the house, and hurried with soft footsteps away from the house and to the stables. Inside she slipped a bridle upon Demon, her favorite stallion, and led him out into the night.

A cloud shifted. The moon was full tonight. It rode the heavens, touched with a kiss of eerie red in the velvet night sky. Perhaps a storm was coming. It was beautiful; it was a bit frightening. It looked almost as if the moon had been bathed in blood.

Away from the house, she told herself that her love could know no fear. Once he was forced to realize that she loved Alec and had compromised herself with him, her father would relent. He would accept their marriage.

She leapt atop Demon and rode across fields, then picked her way more carefully through the swamp that hugged the shore. She knew the way, she knew the bayou. She had been born in it, and she did not fear it, nor any of the creatures of the night.

It seemed as if the reddened moonlight guided her well, as if Demon raced with winged hooves. Even as she worried with a heavy heart about her father, she burst upon Stone Manor, the old mansion off the bayou which Alec had bought upon his arrival in New Orleans. Beneath the eerie moon, it, too, seemed cast in a blood-red glow. The tall white columns were crimson with red shadow, and the smoke issuing from the chimney seemed touched with gold-red sparks.

He waited for her.

Waited . . .

From his bedroom window, Alec DeVereaux felt a quickening that steeled the length of his body and sent hot sweet shudders surging through him.

He had waited for her an eternity. Waited forever. And he had known, from the moment he saw her laughing far across the room, that he would love her. Then he had touched her. Held her while they danced. And he had wanted her. Wanted her with an anguish that surpassed desire. Wanted her so that he lay tormented in the night. He could take her, seduce her. He was a master of the craft. But she had to love him, as he loved her. And so he had waited.

Until tonight.

Tonight . . .

Tonight she had come. She appeared on a sudden rise, seated atop pitch-black Demon, bathed in the glow of the moon. She looked up at the house, and he longed to touch her face.

The dark horse began to race across the overgrown lawn to the house. Alec watched, mesmerized, as she leapt from the horse. He heard her speaking to Thomas below in the entry, and then he heard the soft fall of her footsteps as she raced up the stairs.

He threw open his bedroom door, and she was there. He lifted his hand to touch her at last, and the hood from her cape fell back. "You have come," he whispered, and stepping back, drew her into his domain. Her hand seemed so small within his own. Small, delicate, elegant. He lifted the cape from her, and let it fall to the floor, and his eyes devoured the length of her, the slender column of her throat, the rise of her breast, the slim grace of her body as she swirled into the room then, drawn to the red fire that burned in the hearth below the marble mantel. She stretched our her hands to feel the warmth from the fire and he followed her, gripping her shoulders both fiercely and gently, inhaling the scent of her hair.

"Where does your father think you are?" he asked.

"In bed, asleep," she responded.

He saw the pulse ticking furiously against her throat. He touched it with the lightest kiss.

She spun around, passionate, vivacious. "Alec, I could not lie! We fought dreadfully. I—"

"It's all right."

"I told him that we wished to marry."

"Ma belle, it is all right."

She sighed and then threw her arms around him. "He must accept us. For I love you."

"Do you? Can you really love me?" he whispered. "It means so much to me. You cannot begin to understand."

She drew back from him, puzzled, as she sometimes was. Dear God, but he was an extraordinary man. So tall, striking with his ink-dark hair and nearly black eyes. His shoulders were handsomely broad, his waist was whipcord lean, his jaw firm and square. There wasn't a woman in Louisiana who had danced with him who didn't consider him the most dangerously handsome man she had ever met. She knew a little bit about him from the things he had told her. Much of his family had perished in the French Revolution, but there had been survivors as well, defying the guillotine. He himself had fought at the Battle of New Orleans—as a boy, of course, a runaway in the employ of the pirate Jean Lafitte. He had traveled extensively, he had fought duels, he admitted, with pistols and swords. He was an excellent marksman. By the very nature of all that he was, all that he did, he was magnificent.

He turned his back on her suddenly and walked away from her. There was a silver tray holding a bottle of wine upon a small table. He poured two glasses, his back still to her. She looked around his room, his private abode. The spread had been pulled down from his bed. It was black satin, a startling contrast to the snow-white sheets beneath it. Numerous pillows had been laid high against the headboard. More wine chilled in a silver bucket by the bed. Champagne, she thought, French champagne. There was no pretense as to why he had wanted her here. He was clad in a floor-length black dressing gown with a red satin lining. She was sure he wore nothing else. Yet it seemed he pulled away from her.

"Perhaps your father is right. Perhaps you should not love me."

"Do you love me?" she whispered.

He turned to her, very solemn. "With all my heart. For all my—no, for all eternity."

"Then there can be no reason I should not love you."

"And what if I were a monster?" he inquired.

"For being a Frenchman?" she teased.

He smiled slightly, and she loved him all the more.

"For haunting the darkness," he said softly. "For haunting the night. I have killed—"

"Many men have killed!" she reminded him.

He smiled slightly again, watching her. She felt his eyes. *Felt* them. The fire of their touch seemed to seep into her, into her blood. She felt dizzy, hungry, delicious. She wanted him more than she had wanted anything in her life; more, she ached for him. Hurt. She had to feel him. His hands, on her body. His lips, kissing her everywhere. Himself. Inside her. A part of her.

She could barely breathe. She wet her lips. Her fingers seemed to rise and fall of their own volition to the buttons of her gown.

"Ma belle amie, ma petite chérie!" he whispered very softly. Sound on air. Sound that touched her. Sound that seemed to sweep around her like a soft red mist rising from the fire, falling from the moonlight. "You would not see evil in anyone."

"I know that there is no evil in you."

Button by button, she freed her bodice, letting the brocade garment fall to the floor, and stood shivering slightly in her corset and skirts. The red mist was like a balmy, soft whisper of breeze; she needed to feel it against her bare skin, just as she needed to feel the sweep of his eyes. *You are not thinking,* her father had told her, and it was true, she was not thinking.

Alec was strange tonight; it was almost as if he wanted to send her away. And she didn't seem to care. She knew right from wrong, and God help her, she wanted wrong. Yet, could it be wrong, to love so deeply?

He strode across the room to her, pressed a silver chalice of wine into her fingers. This close to him, she saw the torment in his eyes, the anguished passion. A stray lock of black hair fell upon his forehead. She stared into his eyes. He lifted her wine cup to her lips. She drank. The night breeze that seemed to swirl within the room rose and fell in waves of undulating red.

"What if I were evil?" he whispered.

"You are not."

"I never wished to be . . ."

The mist rose higher. The wine chalice was gone from her fingers. She couldn't remember setting it down. She blinked. His robe was gone as well. Against the soft, wisping swirls of smoke and moonglow that remained, he was naked. Hands outstretched, still staring at her with ebony eyes. A trembling began inside her, in her blood, her limbs, her soul, her being. She had longed for him and hungered, and she hadn't known just what she hungered for. Now she knew. His flesh was sleek, his chest was matted with dark hair. His body was perfect, powerful and strong. His legs were muscled hard, his waist and hips tapered lean and sleek from the breadth of his shoulders and torso. She stared from his eyes to the extent of his arousal, and she felt as if she spun and swirled with the mist that seemed to rise again.

"I don't care what you are!" she cried. "I do not care!"

"I could bring you to pain—"

"I stand in agony now," she swore. She could bear no more, and rushed forward, flinging her arms around him, bringing her lips to his. She had barely kissed before, yet she knew how to devour his mouth, to seek with her tongue, seduce, arouse. He lifted his arms, fought some fierce battle with himself, then crushed her against him. He lifted her chin. Kissed her. His tongue seemed to sweep down her throat, bathe her lips, her mouth, fill her with fire. She was up in his arms, flying with the night, with the velvet of the darkness. She lay upon the satin sheets, felt their coolness, felt his heat. His fingers, long, supple, tore at the strings of her corset, and it was freed from her body. She closed her eyes and felt him remove her shoes, her cumbersome petticoats, pantalettes, stockings. He ripped and tore at each with an urgency, yet she was so anxious for his touch that disrobing seemed to take an eternity. Each garment left more of her bare, naked to the heat of his whisper and caress. His fingers, so eloquently long, stroked her. Wet, hot, searing kisses followed each stroke. Touched her knee, her inner thigh. A drumbeat began within her. A pulse. It grew at a frantic pace. The red mist pervaded her flesh. She trembled, and was slightly afraid. She hungered too deeply, and ignored the fear. His palm moved erotically over the taut chestnut triangle between her legs. Wetness seared her. Then the excruciatingly intimate stroke of a finger . . .

The pulse quickened. She cried out. He was beside her again, dark eyes as red as the moonlight, words intense, anguished. "Can you love me?" he demanded. "Can you love a beast?"

"Oh, dear God, why can't you believe me? I love you, I love a man! A man who has made me laugh, made me feel alive, made me long for more than I know! A man who has lived, fought, learned. A man who commands, who listens, who is hard, who is tender. I love you!"

She couldn't understand him. She wanted him, wanted the mist and the promise of ecstasy that filled her. She wanted to hold him, to take the anguish from his eyes, assure him . . .

"Beast," he told her. "And I do not know if God remembers me!"

She pulled his head down, his mouth to hers, kissed his lips, aroused them. She brought his fingers to her breast, writhed to be even closer to him, a part of him.

"God taught us to love, and I love you. There is no evil I could not overcome! What is this, what is this beast you call yourself?"

*   *   *

"Vampyr!" Charles Godwin, the German professor, asserted. He had come to the Montgomery house that night along with Gene Courtemarch, the aging Creole doctor, and young Master Robert Canady, who so adored Jason Montgomery's beautiful young daughter.

Canady was new to this; a disbeliever. Godwin and Courtemarch had been touched by things of darkness before, and for many years they had kept up a vigil with Montgomery. Beautiful Marie was long gone, but darkness remained, and always would, and so, Magdalena had always been in danger.

"Yes, so I believe," Jason said, exhausted with worry and pain. He had sent for his friends soon after Magdalena had gone upstairs. He had feared the evil forever; he had known it existed. They had all waited and watched. They had prayed it would not come. And now . . .

"We must go for him with the dawn," Courtemarch said. "Then we may discover the truth."

"Gentlemen," Robert Canady said firmly, "I cannot condone this mad, rash action you propose! They will hang us all, one by one! And though I would gladly die for your daughter, Jason, I would have my death serve her well. The comte is newly arrived, mysterious if you will, but he has been a gentleman on all occasions—"

"Are you daft, young man?" Godwin, white-haired and white-mustachioed, exploded. "He takes the woman you love."

Robert exhaled slowly. "God help me, yes, I love her! But I cannot murder a man for loving the woman I would have—and having her love him in return."

"Don't you understand?" Jason Montgomery cried in exasperation.

They were disrupted as heavy footsteps came running hard down the stairs.

"Mr. Montgomery, Mr. Montgomery!" Tyrone shouted, black knuckles white as he gripped the stairway. "She tricked us, sir!"

"Tricked us—?"

"Her sheets cover her pillows; she is gone."

"Gone!" he gasped.

"We follow!" Godwin cried. "We follow! Tyrone, it is time. Bring the stakes, the swords. Quickly. God help us, let us be in time!"

"Gentlemen! Even if she chooses to love him, we still cannot commit murder!" Robert Canady said, trying in vain to reason with the other men. Dear God, didn't these old fools realize? No one felt this betrayal more than he did. He loved her, wanted her. She would have been his wife. The pain was like a knife twisting again and again inside him.

But she loved the Frenchman.

"Damn you, Robert!" Jason protested. "You do not listen!"

"To a bunch of old fools—"

"To the wind. To the moon, to the mist, to the sound of the surf! Have you looked above you? The sky itself cries tears of blood. You do not understand."

"And you must!" Godwin asserted.

"For the love of God, you must!" Courtemarch insisted.

"He is—" Jason began.

"Vampyr!" Courtemarch finished. "By all that is holy, you must realize. Her lover is *vampyr!*"

Her lover rose above her, straddled her. Sleek, powerful, beautiful, she thought, his features so masculine and yet defined and aligned, his eyes so dark they seemed to glitter with the strangest fire.

"Vampire," he said very softly.

She smiled slowly at first. Then she shook her head. "No. Someone has made you think that you are evil."

"I am a creature of darkness, of the night," he insisted.

A shivering began in her. He watched her so gravely. He trembled as he touched her face. "Perhaps love can set me free: that is the promise, the legend. And I love you so fiercely. As if I have waited a hundred years to hear your softest whisper, to taste this sweetness. You must understand, I'm afraid, afraid that the legend is a lie, that the promise is false. I could not bear to hurt you—''

''My love, I don't understand you, you must quit this!'' She sat up against him, pressing a finger to his lips. ''You cannot be evil, you cannot! I will not believe it, I will not!'' She pushed him from her; rose upon her knees to press herself against him. She kissed his face, his throat, his chest. Her fingertips fell upon him, adored the smooth feel of his flesh. An agonized groan escaped him; again he crushed her to himself.

''I may bring hell's fire, damnation—''

''Then bring them on, my love, for I will not leave you, I could not bear to leave you! They will not keep me from you, I care not what comes!''

She cared not . . .

No, she cared not. The world was gone with his harsh, ragged cry, and she was encompassed with the cool, sensual feel of the satin again as she was pressed back into it. Ah, dear God, the sweetness of his touch, as light as a breeze, a whisper, then fire. His arms, hard, demanding. His lips, everywhere, along her limbs, within the heart of her. Drumbeats tatted, pounded, escalated. Her blood grew molten. He touched her with intimacy until she shrieked and pleaded and swore she would love him forever and ever. Then, suddenly he rose above her, stared into her eyes, entered her body. Slowly. She shuddered against the pain, holding him, meeting his eyes, writhing with the wonder even as the knifing pain escalated . . . and subsided. ''Kiss me . . .'' she whispered.

He lowered his head, seized her lips. The sweet pulse began anew with his surging movement. His lips fell upon hers. He kissed her open mouth. His fingers threaded into her hair, his lips brushed across her cheek, down her throat.

The drumbeats were explosive. She soared in magic flight, she writhed in a strange anguish, wanting more. She could almost reach it, touch it. Each time he moved.

She felt his teeth against her throat. A sharp, shattering little pain . . .

A cry tore from her lips as she shuddered, gasped, convulsed. Pain and pleasure combined, and tempest reigned, sweet, delicious. So good that she saw velvet darkness, the red of the night sky, a burst of stars against it all. Everything went black for seconds, then the stars returned. The pain, the pleasure.

He had invaded her body, made it his own. Drawn hunger, drawn life, drawn blood.

Vampire . . . he had told her.

Vampire . . .

If she touched her throat, she would find blood. By God, perhaps . . .

He was not evil! her heart cried. Oh, God, she could still feel him, feel it, the wonder, the excitement, the fulfillment of the hunger. It swept her, it rocked her. It had brought her so high, cradled her downward in such a gentle, sublime caress. Shudder after shudder seized her. She felt him, his body, giving her heat, giving her life.

She had almost died of pleasure. She had reached such ecstasy that she had blacked out. She had tasted his searing fires of hell, and they were splendor. Sweet bliss had enwrapped her, shaken her, exploded in her. His whisper still seemed to be all around her, his weight and strength bore her down.

"I love you!" she whispered.

He started to reply. She saw his ebony eyes with their striking glitter, the handsome planes of his face, the slow, sweet, sensual curve of his smile . . .

Then he was silent, still.

Dead still.

She stared uncomprehending for long seconds, then saw the sharpened stake. It had been run into his back. It protruded through his chest. A crimson stain now spread across his flesh and dripped downward.

Upon her.

"*Vampyr!*" someone shouted.

Then the scream that had welled inside her wrenched hysterically from her, high, shrill. Alec had begun to crumble toward her; then he was stopped. From the corner of her eye she saw him wrenched backward. She saw the glitter of a broadsword, saw it swing.

They were decapitating him!

Mercifully, instinct warned her to close her eyes. She did so.

She felt his blood, hot and sticky, spill over her, and she began to scream again.

The body was pulled from her. She inched up against the bed in amazement, shocked, stunned, screaming in disbelief. Seeing now, unable to believe what she was seeing. Her father was there, with his funny little cronies—white-haired Godwin, tall, skinny Courtemarch. And Robert was there. Grave, sad, his heart in his eyes as he watched her. Robert, reaching for her now, arms strong, determined.

It was a nightmare, it could not be happening. But she could feel her lover's blood upon her breast, just as she could feel her own, trickling from the wound in her neck. This was too horrible to be comprehended; perhaps she wasn't comprehending. And yet the blood was real.

Alec's death was real.

"Magdalena, Magdalena!" Robert cried, pulling away to strip off his frockcoat to wrap around her, then draw her close once again. She was cold, so cold, but she couldn't accept his comfort. She kept screaming. He held her more tightly.

"She is *vampyr* now, too!" Godwin insisted, his hands tightening upon his broadsword.

"Leave her be!" Robert cried hoarsely, fiercely. "Damn you all, would you hurt her more?" His voice was a roar, powerful, like the sound of rushing water.

"She is my daughter, she is not dead, she is not *vampyr,* I can heal her!" Jason roared.

Heal her . . .

Nothing could ever heal her. Not after this night. She had known love, and now they were calling her lover a monster, and he lay dead just feet away, covered in blood, his head severed from his neck. They had slain him, and this awful little man Godwin, with the broadsword, meant to sever her head from her body as well, as soon as Courtemarch had impaled her with one of his stakes. She didn't know if she cared or not.

She had known such magic, and the magic lay dead. Life didn't matter . . .

In fact, it seemed to be flowing away. Flowing away in the trickle of red that seeped slowly down her neck. It was good. She was becoming numb. Only numbness, only death, could wash away the awful agony. She tried to rise, to push from Robert, tried to see her love one last time.

Her father came beside her as well, holding her. "No, Magdalena!" he whispered to her.

But she could see.

Oh, God.

There was no corpse. No corpse.

No body, no blood. Where her lover should have lain, the floor seemed burnt, with only black ash in the shape of a winged creature remaining.

She started to scream again.

And her scream faded away, and the world with it.

"She has died; she will become one of the creatures!" Godwin told them all firmly.

"She sleeps!" Jason protested.

"The sleep of death."

"She sleeps!" Robert Canady thundered.

"The sleep of life! She is my child, my flesh, my blood, I will heal her!"

He swept his daughter into his arms, taking her even from Robert.

And he carried her away. Walked away from the white manor made red by the glow of the moon. He stumbled, nearly fell. He rose and carried her again. The blood-red moonlight seemed blinding.

He looked up then, and realized that the moonlight was fading. It was a red streak of the sun beginning to burst forward that so plagued his eyesight.

The sun. The daylight was coming.

He began to run to his carriage.

* * *

*She lay in a strange, icy world of darkness. She knew that
she should fight the sensations of utter blackness and absolute
cold that settled upon her like an unearthly blanket. People
called to her; their voices seemed so far away. From somewhere
she could see a distant ray of light, but she could not seem to
reach it. Someone was holding her, she realized. She wanted
to cry out. She wanted to reach the light. She could not.* Let
me go! *she thought. But it was a soundless plea in the vast
darkness, in the void, in the loneliness beyond death . . .*

*Once again, there was sensation. So strange. She thought
that the chill that had settled upon her would never go away,
but there was something like warmth surrounding her, count-
ering the bone-deep chill. Even the blackness was different.
There were shades of gray within it.*

Time, she thought distantly.

Time . . .

Shadows, light, darkness, shadows, light, darkness . . .

The nights . . . they came and went.

*Finally, there came a moment when she felt her father's
hands, and knew that he was with her. She felt a liquid warmth
coming down her throat. Felt, yes she felt, and felt things that
were real, tangible.*

Time . . .

*It passed more easily. She grew stronger. She could lift her
head. Feel the texture of the cup from which she drank, touch
her father's fingers. She lay in her own bed. Its softness surrounded and embraced her. Candlelight flickered, gentle upon
her eyes. She kept drinking, not recognizing what strange potion
he had given her while she lay so sick, what warmth it was
that had summoned her back from the cold. At last, she found
the strength to become curious.*

"What is it?" *she whispered to her father.* "What is it that
I'm drinking?"

"Blood," *Jason said flatly.*

*She turned her head into her pillow. She cried, but tears
would not come.*

"For the love of God, Father!" she whispered.

"No," he said softly, *"for the love of my child. Hush, now, sleep."*

Her eyes closed again. She lay in a misery worse than death.

But in time, as he had gently commanded, she slept.

Jason rose with a heavy heart, pulled the covers high around her. She did need that warmth so desperately!

He walked downstairs to where his friends waited and strode to the mantel, pausing there, leaning upon the carved wood for support as he met their questioning stares.

He weighed his words carefully.

"I believe that she is going to live," he said very softly. Then he hesitated, knuckles white as he prayed that he was now making the right move in saying what he would say. He inhaled deeply. *"And I believe that she is going to have a child."*

CHAPTER 1

"Oh, Christ!" Jack Delaney swore, turning from the corpse into his partner's arms, his face a strange, pale shade of green. He was a young cop, just turned twenty-five, a good-looking fellow, six feet, with light-brown eyes and sandy red hair.

"Let the rookie by, guys, have a heart here," Sean Canady said, supporting his new partner for a moment.

"You gonna be all right?" he asked quickly, the question low and spoken for only Jack to hear. For a brief moment, Jack leaned on Sean, the older cop, two inches taller than he, and at forty a broad-shouldered, tautly muscled, impressive figure with ink-dark hair and sharp, dark-blue eyes. Sean usually kept a tight leash on his emotions, preferring to work out his frustrations at the gym.

Jack inhaled quickly, glad of the break. He drew strength from Sean, nodded, and knew that the teasing he took from the other men would be light because Sean had supported him.

"I'm fine," Jack said.

Sean nodded. "Make way there, fellows. Delaney needs to start asking some questions in the neighborhood. Make sure we've got men combing these streets; someone must have seen something!" Sean said firmly, making sure that his partner made it through the rows of cops out in their rain gear circling the stretch of narrow roadway where the body had been found. The area was now all nicely roped off with yellow crime tape. Jack had arrived at the scene just moments before Sean had reached the corpse, and turned away. Jack was new to homicide, only a few years on the force, a young Irishman turned over to Sean because, the captain had said, of his name. Put the ''Micks'' together, that had been Captain Daniels's comment. Sean didn't deny Irish roots—they were there somewhere— but the Irishman who had brought the Canady name to New Orleans had done so nearly two centuries ago, and Sean himself was a mixture of the many blends that made up the city. He had French blood, English, Cajun, and who knew? Probably a little Caribbean mixed in there, too. It didn't matter. Sean liked Jack Delaney, and knew the captain liked him, too. And that was why Jack had been assigned to Sean.

''Make way for the rookie,'' someone else called, and Jack was on through to the other side of the barricades. No matter what Jack had said, Sean was certain his partner was about to be sick.

''This was a tough one, kid,'' another fellow in uniform called out, and Sean was glad to see that the men were going to go easy on Jack.

There really was no such thing as a *good* body after a murder. Still, some were worse than others.

Sean strode on over to where Pierre LePont was bent over the body, intent on studying the corpse. He hunkered down beside the medical examiner, who was studying the corpse's fingers. He gave Pierre a brief nod of acknowledgment, then gave his attention to the corpse.

Unlike Jack, he'd seen his share of dead bodies. Too many of them—bodies bloated from the Mississippi, human bodies barely recognizable as such. The newly dead, the fresh kill, the form that bled into the pavement as well as the corpse that had managed to remain hidden until the unbearable smell had brought it to light and the corpse that had remained hidden so long that there was nothing left but bone.

And still, there was something incredibly strange about this one.

The man hadn't been dead long—hell, he couldn't have been, not right off Bourbon Street like this. The business day had started; it was just past nine, so the man might have been killed just before daybreak. The homeless did sleep on the street, so in the darkness he might not have been noticed. Nor was he a mess—no blood streaked over the pavement, no brains spattering the wall of the shop he lay before. This fellow was simply white—except for the line of red that circled his entire throat and neck. He wasn't just pale, nor was he grayish. He was white as a sheet. He almost looked like a caricature of life. The awful thing about him—that which had surely made Jack so green—was the fact that his eyes remained wide open, and they seemed to mirror an absolute terror. There was a look of such absolute horror in them that he was tempted to turn and try to see what those eyes had envisioned in the final minutes of life.

"God," Sean breathed.

"Yeah," Pierre agreed. "And you want to know the funny thing?"

"There's something funny here?"

Pierre made a face. "Peculiar, okay? There was no fight. This guy was scared, so damned scared he might have died from that alone. But he didn't put up a fight. Well, I've got some tests to do at the morgue, I can't give you guarantees right now, but it doesn't seem that he lifted a finger to ward off his attacker."

"Do you think he did die of fright?"

"He might have gone of cardiac arrest—but he didn't."

"He didn't? What was the mortal injury? The throat wound?" Sean shook his head even as he asked the question. A throat wound, obvious, if the pavement had been stained. But the way it looked, with no blood, the slashing of the throat should have come after death. "Where's the blood?"

Pierre, a slim, balding little man and one of the best in the business, shook his head as well. "There sure as hell isn't any blood here—and, by the way, it's not just a throat wound. This fellow has been decapitated." He carefully rolled the head just a shade, showing Sean that the head had been completely severed from the body.

Sean felt his stomach quiver.

He pulled out his notebook. "What's his age? Late twenties?"

Mike Hays, a uniformed officer, stepped closer to the two of them.

"His name was Anthony Beale, Lieutenant Canady. Native of New Orleans, twenty-nine years old. Had a record, petty, small-time stuff. Five arrests, three for robbery, one for home invasion, and one for the procurement of prostitutes. Only one of the robberies ever stuck, he served eighteen months for it. No visible means of support. He still seemed to be doing all right, eh, Lieutenant Canady? That's an Armani suit on him."

"Armani, huh?" Sean said, and shrugged. Not many of the homeless slept in Armani suits.

"Yeah, nice suit," Pierre commented dryly.

"Hey, Sean, I need a few more pictures," Bill Smith, the police photographer, called to him.

Sean and Pierre obligingly stood away.

Sean looked up and down the street. It was a decent section of the Vieux Carré, the famous French Quarter of New Orleans—if decent was a word that could be used for a street that housed dozens of sex shops. On these particular blocks, however, there were businesses and residences. Two expensive tourist hotels were just down the street from him on either side. Craft shops, antique stores, and boutiques lined the downstairs buildings here, beautiful window displays showing their goods. He stepped back. Offices, dance studios, a gym, and a tanning salon were advertised as being in some of the upstairs rooms. The street was lined with the type of structure that had made the French Quarter known around the world, handsome buildings with arched windows, wrought-iron balconies, buttresses, and other distinctive detail.

He stared at the body on the ground. New Orleans, *N'Awleans,* his city. He loved it. He'd been born right here in the city, literally in the lobby of one of the fine old residential hotels, since his mother had found it deplorable to whine about labor pains before it was necessary. He'd gone away to college, he'd tried to see the world. He'd come back. There was just something about the place. It was *his*. It was not crime-free. It was naughty, tawdry. It was jazz, it was beauty, it was dark waters of the mighty Mississippi. It was crawfish-etouffée, the best damned food in the entire world, a city riddled with ghost stories, tales of voodoo queens, and more. It had entered into contemporary times with the same woes and troubles ailing it as created hard times in other big cities—drugs, crime, home-lessness, inflation, unemployment. Some called it a city of the wicked, a city of the damned. Well, it might be, but it was his city, his city of the damned. Whatever he could accomplish to save it from the actual grips of hell, he was going to do.

This seemed pretty cut and dried. Anthony Beale, small-time hood, prosperous pimp. He'd messed with somebody bigger; he was a bad man come to a bad end. It should be one for the books.

"It does make me think of the cemetery stiff," Pierre said suddenly, even as the thought occurred to Sean.

"Woman's body," Sean said. "And cut to pieces." Even such a description was an understatement. "Jane Doe," female Caucasian, twenty-five to thirty years of age, five feet five, one hundred and twenty-five pounds, had been found in one of the old above-ground cemeteries outside the French Quarter just last week. She'd been found lying on top of one of the tombs, naked and disemboweled, almost as if a modern Jack the Ripper had taken a turn with her. Body parts and her internal organs had been neatly laid out beside her. The murder had sent the city reeling into shock; it was still *the* topic of conversation for residents and tourists alike. Naturally, such a crime—with no suspect under arrest—led to wild speculation and a great deal of fear.

"All that cutting, and almost no blood," Pierre said glumly, referring to their Jane Doe.

"Decapitated," Sean continued with a soft whistle. "Maybe we've got ourselves a connection here."

"A prostitute and a pimp," Pierre agreed. "We've got to

pray that there's only one guy evil enough to do such deeds in the city. Let me get this guy to the morgue, and see what else I can find.''

"You still have our Jane Doe on ice?" Sean asked.

Pierre nodded. "Yes, she's still with us."

"Maybe we can take a look at them both. Put our heads together on it."

"Sure thing," Pierre agreed. He shrugged. "Put *their* heads together on it," he said dryly, without humor. "I can tell you something right now."

"What's that?"

"Our murderer was a southpaw. Left-handed."

"What?"

"On both victims," Pierre continued. Again, he touched the severed head with a gloved finger. "See the way the throat was slashed? It had to have been an extremely sharp knife wielded with considerable strength. Actually, it is not easy to sever a human head."

"That's good to hear," Sean said.

Pierre nodded, rising. Sean rose along with him. "Gentlemen, are we done here?" Pierre asked Bill Smith and the other milling cops. "May I take this fellow on into the morgue?"

"Sean is senior homicide man here," Bill said. "I've got all my pictures, though, Sean. If you're set, LePont can have the corpse."

"He's all yours, Pierre," Sean said.

LePont made a motion to his assistants. A body bag was brought, and Pierre stepped away from Sean. "Give me a few hours, then come by and see me. I'll give you whatever I've got."

"Thanks," Sean told him.

"Days like this make me glad I'm the photographer," Bill said.

Sean arched a brow. "Nice pictures?" he queried skeptically.

Bill shook his head. "The pictures haunt you. Stay with you. You can wake up in the middle of the night seeing those damned pictures in front of you. But at least I don't have to find the wacko who did this."

"Wacko?" Sean echoed thoughtfully. "I hadn't thought of our guy in such a term, to tell you the truth."

Bill stared at him incredulously. "Okay, so you think someone quote unquote *normal* could have done something like this?"

Sean shrugged. "Define normal. My first instinct was that this guy crossed somebody bigger. It seems like a very methodical kill. The severing of the head is not an easy thing to do—Pierre has just assured me of this—and this head was not just severed, it was done so neatly. There's no blood. There should be pools of blood here. The obvious would be that the guy was killed elsewhere, and dumped here. The head was severed with a purpose, and put back in place so perfectly I didn't realize it wasn't attached until Pierre started moving it around. There's some system and reason here."

"Wackos do make use of system and reason," Bill reminded him. "You told me that yourself after you took that course on serial killers up at the FBI academy at Quantico. Remember?" Bill reminded him.

"My point is that we're not going to be looking for someone obvious—no drooling ghouls or the like haunting the city."

"This is damned scary. Right off Bourbon Street," Bill said, shaking his head with disgust. He dropped his voice to a whisper. "The girl in the cemetery had her throat so slit the head came off, too."

"Yep."

"Remember," Bill said, wagging a finger at Sean, "Jack the Ripper was supposedly extraordinarily methodical with body parts."

"Serial killers can be classified as organized or disorganized, or they can be a combination," Sean murmured. "An execution-style murder is usually preplanned, neat. Death is the ultimate goal. For some killers, it's the prelude to death that matters most. Jack the Ripper's body parts had blood on them," Sean mused. "At least some."

"Like I said, taking pictures is easier than going after the wackos." Again, Bill's voice lowered. "You gotta catch this one fast, buddy. My wife is scared out of her wits. Have you seen the headlines? Not just the *Times/Picayune*. The cemetery killing was so sensational, it's been picked up across the country.''

Sean exhaled a long sigh. He knew. The killing in the cemetery had been horrible, sensational, and—admittedly, Ripper-esque. The whole world saw it as a savage and terrifying event. What they didn't see was that the cops just didn't have anything to go on. The girl hadn't fought—there hadn't been a single cell of her killer's flesh beneath her nails, not a single hair or fiber had been found on her body. She'd had sex before her death, but according to Pierre, it hadn't been forced. They did have sperm samples, but not a single suspect with whom to compare sperm. DNA testing was being done by the FBI, but results might take days or weeks, and Sean was afraid now that their killer could strike many times before forensic science could help them.

There had been thousands of fingerprints on the tomb where the murdered prostitute was found. The same with footprints—there had been partials almost everywhere. There was nothing at all to go on except the pathetic and unmourned body of a dead whore no one had yet so much as offered to name.

''Serial killer, like you were saying,'' Bill suggested.

Sean had that uncomfortable feeling himself. ''I didn't exactly say that; we don't know that yet.'' Two decapitated corpses. A connection sure seemed probable.

''Hey, it doesn't make me happy.''

''Bill, we don't know anything yet for sure. There are still some differences here. When we get more verifiable information from Pierre—''

''Sean, you ain't a cop who goes by the book, you're a cop who goes by the gut. That's why you're a good cop. And you know that these killings are *different*.''

''We've got to watch what we're saying around the media,'' Sean insisted. ''New Orleans is going to go sky high over this one.'' He saw Jack over Bill's shoulder and managed a grin. ''There's my boy. I'm going to collect him and we'll do a door-to-door for witnesses ourselves. See you later, Bill. And remember, low profile on this, huh?''

Bill nodded glumly. "Sure."

Sean moved on. Jack was still ashen, but remarkably recovered—and embarrassed. "It was just the eyes," he told Sean. "I looked at him and felt that if I turned around and saw what was mirrored in his eyes, I'd see whatever monster had done this to him."

"That's all right, Jack. I've seen more dead men than I care to admit, but that guy is one to spook anyone. Did you get information on the street?"

Jack nodded. "Actually, I may not be very good with corpses, but I have made a discovery that might well interest you—and salvage a bit of my dignity," Jack told him.

"You don't need to salvage any dignity, but I'm intrigued by any discovery. What is it?"

"Follow me," Jack said.

Curiously, hopefully, Sean did so.

Maggie Montgomery looked out the window of her second-floor office. From her vantage point, she could see the area down the street which had been cordoned off by the police. She could see the dozens of police and citizens and tourists who were hovering on either side of the line. A little shiver snaked down her spine. It's not that New Orleans was crimeless—far from it!—and certainly not the Vieux Carré itself. But this had the look of something beyond the norm. Robberies were common enough; tourists were even warned by shopkeepers and hotel management to avoid certain streets. New Orleans hadn't avoided the drug crimes that plagued the country, and there was no way out of the fact that illegal delights, carnal and other, were readily for sale. Over the years, the area had seen murders that were bizarre, occult related, and more. And still . . .

"It's a body!" Angie Taylor, Maggie's assistant, said, her soft, drawling voice filled with both dread and fascination as she swept into the office, bringing Maggie a cup of rich, chicory-flavored coffee. "A *murdered* body," she added emphatically. Angie was a dynamo, five feet four in her highest heels, beautifully, compactly built. She was of Cajun descent, with dark, sweeping hair and huge, soulful, sensual eyes. She had a fascination for life, an energy that didn't quit. She was Maggie's best friend, as well as the most competent assistant in the world.

"Murder has happened here before," Maggie murmured, frowning as she tried to look through the crowd. Even from her point here above the street, there was little that she could see. The corpse was in a body bag on a gurney, being wheeled away to the ambulance that would bear it to the morgue. The crowd was just beginning to break up. Officers were still busy behind the crime tape, specialists, technicians, looking for clues.

"The rumor is already rampant on the streets. This body was *decapitated.*"

Maggie felt another little chill snake along her spine. "Male body or female body?"

"Male. A pimp, if the word at Café La Petite Fleur is right," Angie said slowly. The café was next door to them. Very convenient. It was new, but the husband-and-wife owner were Creoles with a family history that went back to the origins of the city. Their beignets and café au lait were out of this world.

Angie went on, speaking more slowly. "The murder victim was a young guy, handsome fellow. They say he was a pimp working the right kind of girls."

"It wasn't like the murder that filled the paper the other day?" Maggie asked, holding back the lace curtains to keep her vigil on the street.

"No, no. The body wasn't mutilated, just decapitated."

"Just decapitated," Maggie murmured.

Angie giggled nervously. "I suppose that is awful enough, isn't it? It was just the description of the way that poor girl was found in the cemetery . . . Well, she was a poor young girl. A fallen angel, if you will. Now this guy, it seemed, was living off the pain of others."

Maggie cast her a wry glance. "Angie, I don't think that all prostitutes are actually in pain. Some choose to do what they do because it can be what they consider good money." She shrugged. "Some women have even made media careers out of being madams!"

Angie wrinkled her nose. "Nobody goes to bed with yucky, hairy, disgusting or gross men without being in pain. My point here is that the fellow murdered last night—or whenever he was murdered—was selling someone else's flesh and making his money that way. I can't imagine anything more despicable." She looked at Maggie and sighed again. "Maggie, it's just a little bit better because he was bad, *evil* if you will. And maybe an evil thing happened to an evil person, and that's just a little bit more right than what happened to that poor young lost girl. Don't you think that evil pays to evil?"

"No, not always," Maggie said. Then she smiled, shaking her head. "Angie, you're looking for a perfect world. If there were a perfect world, wonderful, kind deserving people wouldn't be crippled and in wheelchairs. Babies wouldn't die of AIDS."

Angie sighed with vast impatience. "Just my point. Isn't it fitting when it's actually the bad person who has something bad happen to him?"

Maggie had to smile slightly. "What if he wasn't all bad? What if he had been abused or mistreated as a child? What if he had a deep-seated psychological hatred for women—"

"Maggie, he was bad!" Angie announced with impatience. "He prostituted women for money. An that's that!"

Maggie lifted her hands, still smiling. "Fine. He gets no excuses. You've made your point. Still . . ."

"Still what?"

"Two people decapitated in a week."

"You think it's the same murderer? One of the victims was a man, one was a woman. One was ripped to shreds and one merely lost his head."

Maggie hesitated. "Decapitation is not all that common," she said quietly. "And it's scary. New Orleans is going to be going insane. Tourists will start staying away if the police can't make an arrest quickly."

"Tourists are filling the shop downstairs right now despite the police. Or maybe because of them," Angie said with a crisp, businesslike warning.

"If Allie and Gema need help, they'll phone up," Maggie

assured her, leaving the window behind and returning to her desk, sinking somewhat wearily into the swivel chair behind it.

Allie and Gema were the saleswomen who manned the downstairs boutique section of Magdalena's. The business had been in Maggie's family for years. Since before the Civil War, Montgomery women had been designing fine fashion wear. It had been elegant ball gowns at first, and a great deal of the one-of-a-kind garments Maggie designed remained evening wear. But over the last few years. she had found herself working on resort wear and lingerie as well, going along with the times, she assumed. But along with her unique made-to-order designs, she kept a boutique where those without the pocketbooks for one-of-a-kind wear could also find unusual, special pieces. Along with Gema and Allie, she had a staff of twenty seamstresses, two supervisors with two assistants each, a receptionist and an accountant to deal with the goings-on of the business. She created the designs—lingerie, day wear, even jewelry— and she and Allie usually created the displays that showed through the windows in the downstairs store. Offices were on the second floor, production was on the third. The building was over one hundred and fifty years old, charming in its architecture, modernized just enough to make it comfortable and convenient, but retaining its character.

Cissy Spillane, the receptionist, a tall quadroon girl with a slim figure and stunning face, tapped lightly on Maggie's open door. "Maggie, there are two cops in the reception area. They want to speak with you."

"Me?" Maggie said, startled.

Cissy shrugged. "They asked me a few questions as well, and they want to talk with Angie. But they seem mostly interested in you."

"Why?"

"Because you own the building," Cissy said. "At least that's the way it appears to me."

Maggie glanced at her watch, disturbed that she felt such uneasiness. "I have an appointment at ten—" she murmured.

"It's Mrs. Rochfort. I'll hold the old battle-axe at bay!"
Angie promised.

There was no way she could refuse to see cops. They'd just
come back with deep suspicions and search warrants if she did
so.

"Fine. Show them in, please, Cissy," Maggie told her.

Angie slipped out the door to Maggie's office behind Cissy.
Less than thirty seconds later, Cissy stepped back in, followed
by two men. Neither was in uniform.

Maggie rose from her swivel chair and came around her
large oak desk, swiftly inspecting the two. They were an impressive pair. The younger man was a tall, well-built redhead with
a quick smile and warm brown eyes that seemed to deepen as
he watched her approach. He was handsome, in the prime of
life, Maggie thought, and wondered if his wife or girlfriend
feared for him at his job.

The second man appeared to be more of a veteran, definitely
older, yet incredibly attractive. For some strange reason, he
caused a little flutter to stir within her heart. He'd been around,
she thought, studying the sharp, intriguing blue eyes that studied
her so openly in return. He was a tall man, at least six two,
quite broad-shouldered, with very dark hair just beginning to
acquire a few silver streaks at the temples. His brows were
very dark, handsomely arched. His skin was bronzed from
exposure to the sun and there were fine lines about his mouth
and eyes. They added character to a face that was arresting,
more rugged than handsome, but cleanly, strongly sculpted.
There was a fluidity in his movements, something about his
eyes, and even the curve of his mouth that was elementally
sensual. There was a power about him, a strenth of will, that
was completely compelling.

"Miss Montgomery?" he asked. He had a deep voice. It
was resonant. She felt another little quiver deep inside her.

"Yes, how can I help you?"

"I'm Jack Delaney, Miss Montgomery," the younger man
began, quickly offering her a handshake. "This is my partner,
Sean Canady. We've—"

"Canady?" she repeated, her eyes falling back upon the older man. Sean.

He nodded, watching her in turn. He smiled. It was a nice smile, rueful, slashed across his bronzed face. It added charm and an even greater sensuality to his ruggedly hewn features. "Old-time name, I know. So is yours."

She nodded as well, and asked him, "Isn't there a statue of one of your ancestors on a corner not far from here?"

"A great-great-grandfather, I believe. Another Sean. He formed a cavalry company for Dixie and led many a gallant charge against the Yanks, so says the plaque beneath the statue."

"Ah, yes! I remember the stories about him. He could travel like lightning, so they say."

Canady smiled. "And I admit, I'm entranced to meet you. Magdalena's was here when Sean was defending his city."

Maggie nodded. "We've changed throughout the years, but yes, it all began back then."

"We're sorry to bother you," Jack said, "but unfortunately, we've a few questions we must ask you."

"Fine," Maggie told them. "Will you have a seat? Can I get you some coffee?"

"No—" Sean began.

"Yes—" Jack said. He looked at Sean. Maggie decided it was evident, though they hadn't introduced themselves with any rank, that Sean was the senior man here.

But Sean seemed completely at ease with his authority and needed to prove nothing. He grinned at Jack. "Sure. Coffee would be nice."

Maggie went back behind her desk and pressed the intercom, asking Cissy to bring coffee for the gentlemen. She sat then, sweeping a hand out to the richly upholstered Victorian armchairs that faced her handsomely carved desk. The men took the chairs, Sean in front of her to the left, Jack in front of her to her right.

"This is a business call, gentlemen?" she asked. She tried to look at them both. She found herself staring in Sean Canady's eyes.

He nodded grimly, watching her. She had a feeling in the few minutes they'd been together that he had done a total assessment of her—the way she looked, the way she moved, the way she spoke, the things she said. He would notice details. All the little details.

"You're aware there was another murder?" Jack said.

She managed to draw her gaze from Sean and look at Jack Delaney. "Another murder? Not to insult the efforts of the force, gentlemen, but I'm afraid there are many murders each year in New Orleans."

"Unfortunately, that's true," Sean said. He glanced at his partner, perhaps just a little irritated. "Let's rephrase the question. You're aware that a body was found on the street just about two blocks from here?"

She nodded. "A young man. A pimp—at least that's the word in the café next door."

There was a tapping, and Cissy stuck her head in. "Coffee. May I bring it in?"

Maggie nodded. "Thank you, Cissy, the desk will be fine."

Cissy set the tray on the table, swiftly showing the officers the sugar, cream, and artificial sweetener. Jack added cream. Sean took his black. Somehow, she knew that he would. He had the look of a dedicated man. One who would run out of his house (apartment?) with a muffin in one hand and mug of coffee—black—in the other. He wouldn't waste time eating when time was crucial, and though he'd need the caffeine often enough to keep going, he wouldn't spend the time to use cream or sugar. Jack might be like that one day—he just hadn't been around the block as many times as Sean.

She realized that Canady was returning her stare. She wondered if he was imagining her lifestyle, just as she was imagining his. Those dark-blue eyes of his were studying her. They were unsettling. She wondered with a shade of unease just what he saw. And strangely enough, she felt that little surge of a flutter within her breast again. He was the kind of man who could do that to a woman. She wondered if he was aware of his appeal. He was an attractive man. Hardened, no-nonsense, all grown up. And it was annoying to realize just how deeply she was attracted to him. Almost painfully so.

And his name was Canady.

She folded her fingers before her on her desk. What was the matter with her? She was all grown up, too.

"Gentlemen, I *am* aware that a corpse was found near here this morning. That of a young man."

"And he was a known pimp and petty criminal," Jack agreed.

"Yes, I heard that as well."

"Yeah?" Sean asked.

She shrugged. "You know that news travels fast—we've a little café just next door. Actually we've been wondering here this morning if there's any connection with the poor girl found last week."

"Obviously, we're wondering the same thing ourselves," Jack said.

Maggie lifted her hands. "How can I help you? Why have you come here?"

It was Sean who leaned forward, those sharp, deep blue eyes seeming to probe straight into her own. "Because, Miss Montgomery—it is Miss?"

She nodded. "Because—?"

"Because, oddly enough, our corpse seems to be missing most of its blood," Jack said.

"But," Sean told her softly, watching her, always watching her, "there was a little trail of blood drops, tiny, almost minute amounts. And they led back here. To the arched doorway leading up from the street to the second-floor offices of Montgomery Enterprises."

CHAPTER 2

"Now that," Jack stated with surety as they left the Montgomery Building behind, "is one beautiful woman."

Sean grunted.

Not that he didn't agree.

Maggie Montgomery was more than beautiful. She was tall and lithe, incredibly shaped, with ample breasts, a slim waist, and flaring hips; she had long, long legs, a headful of sexy auburn hair, and gold-flecked, intelligent hazel eyes. She moved with complete confidence and grace. She smelled provocatively of some sensual perfume. The moment he'd set eyes on her, he'd thought her the most unusual woman he'd ever met, the most alluring. Incredibly, he'd all but forgotten the corpse. There was just something about her. Something that brought out raw instinct. That made a man want to—

"I mean beautiful."

Sean grunted again.

"Really beautiful. Fantasy stuff. Movie star, model on a pedestal. Better yet, centerfold queen—"

"Jack, blood drops led right up to her place."

"She owns her own business. Big business. She must be as

rich as Midas. Did you see the outfits in those downstairs windows?''

"She's old money, Jack. The Montgomery name goes way, way back."

"Old money . . . but I wonder if she's closer to my age— or yours. Not that it matters. Wonder if she'd ever date a cop. Not me, of course. Despite the fact that I was drooling. In fact, it was so bad, I was afraid my tongue was going to fall right on the floor. But she was watching you. Whatever her age, she must like older men."

Sean drew to a halt at last, arching a brow to his young companion.

"Not that forty is actually old," Jack said quickly. "But I mean, hell, she just didn't seem interested in me at all."

"Jack, she could well be a murder suspect."

"Oh, come on, Sean! She's what? Maybe five feet eight and a hundred and thirty pounds, tops. Slender—but, man . . . nice shape. Even in that business suit. Great legs. I've always really liked a great set of legs. And hers . . . But she's just put together right all way around. Wonder if she works at it. I wonder if she goes to a gym. And if she does, I wonder which one. I'd like to see her in work-out clothes."

"Jack, I repeat, she could well prove to be a murder suspect."

"Give me a break! Can you imagine that elegant example of pure grace hacking a body to pieces and leaving the parts strewn on top of a tomb?"

"We don't have a definite link on the murders. We found a corpse this morning, and blood drops that create a trail to her door."

"There are several dozen people working in that office build- ing, Sean. And we've got forensic guys searching for more blood, and she didn't seem in the least disturbed that they were doing so. And if we find more blood in the building, that doesn't label her as the killer. It's absurd! I'm not as experienced as you are, but even I know that it takes some mean strength to sever a head that way! And if the guy was killed elsewhere and brought to the sidewalk, she'd have to be incredibly strong. With or without blood, that corpse was no lightweight.''

''So, if she didn't kill him, she may be shielding the person who did.''

''And a psychopath could have done in our corpse, and used her building as an escape route.''

''Could have—but we're going to have to follow every minute clue on this. A second killing of this kind in a few days' time—the press is going to butcher us.''

''Headless corpses . . . I guess it is a little unusual, even for New Orleans,'' Jack said glumly. ''But Maggie just has to be innocent.''

''Maggie?'' Sean inquired dryly.

''Miss Montgomery. Maggie fits her.''

''Because she's so warm and open and sweet?''

Jack grinned, shrugging. ''Go on, be a cynic.''

''Yeah, I can see you telling the chief, 'Sir, the woman is innocent, look at those gold eyes and long, wicked legs, and you'll know that in an instant!' ''

''Right. You looked at her eyes the whole time.''

''All right, so it seems she must have great breasts, too, though can't say that I could really judge beneath that suit.

''Sweet Jesus,'' Sean muttered.

''You've been around the block too many times, Sean— you're showing your age.''

''Yeah, maybe I am.''

''What's next?'' Jack asked more seriously.

''We put together a task force and have a meeting, and hope the guys on the beat might have learned something. Then we see Pierre, and hope he's on to something. Then, oh, hell, we're going to have to have some kind of a press conference.''

''Yeah, right. The press will be ready to sever our heads!'' Jack murmured.

Sean started to speak, then shrugged. Jack was right. The media would definitely be up for their own brand of decapitation, and if this situation couldn't be solved quickly, they'd all be bleeding.

*   *   *

Some of Maggie's employees were disturbed by the murder that had apparently taken place so close to the building.

Oddly enough, others weren't. Maggie had asked all her employees into the downstairs shop area just after five—quitting time for most, and when the doors of the shop closed for the night. She'd made arrangements to see that those who walked to homes in the Vieux Carré did so in pairs, and those who drove out of the old town area were escorted to their cars. In the end, however, a few of her girls remained with her, seeming untouched by the events.

"Honey," Cissy told her, "I don't have truck with lowlifes like that pimp and a prostitute. Now, this is N'Awleans, and I do keep careful, but I keep my nose clean, walk down the right streets, and if all the drug pushers and pimps in this city have the desire to decapitate one another, then so much the better! Now, you coming to watch Dean's band with us tonight or what?"

Dean, the twenty-five-year-old son of Chance Lebrow, one of her few male employees, and a supervisor in the sewing rooms, could play a mean jazz trumpet, along with a half dozen other instruments. He'd gone away to college and he'd just finished up his master's degree in architecture in New York and come home, and now, nights, he was playing in one of the popular local clubs on Bourbon Street.

"I'm not sure," Maggie told her. "I'm not in the party mood."

"Now, girl, you cannot let the murder of a no-good pimp get you down!" Cissy protested.

"It's not the murder of a no-good pimp so much as the fact that the no-good pimp managed to get murdered right by my door," Maggie admitted. "And then, somehow, he managed to get his little blood droplets leading right *to* my door."

"Honey, those cops dusting around the doors and hallways told me that they didn't find a thing inside the building," Marie assured her.

"And," Angie, who had stayed behind as well, assured her

dramatically, "Cissy should know. She spent the day flirting with a handsome young Adonis."

Maggie arched a brow. "A cop? You were flirting with one of the cops?"

"You have something against cops?" Cissy drawled.

"Only upon occasion."

Cissy grinned. "Well, honey, this fellow was an Adonis. Built like a brick. And he was tall. Being six-even for a woman is not easy. He was a good six three. I could date him, and wear heels."

"Marry him, and create Amazon children!" Angie quipped.

"Was this Adonis black or white?" Maggie asked.

"Black, honey, the only kind," Cissy assured her, and laughed. "It wasn't your lieutenant."

"*My* lieutenant."

"Best-looking white boy I've ever seen," Cissy assured her.

"A homicide detective investigating my building is not a good-looking white boy—he's a pain." But Maggie smiled suddenly. "I'm glad that your Adonis came along—at least it seems some good has come from the day. Did he ask you out?"

Angie snorted in an unladylike fashion. "Did he ask her out? She'd asked him before she'd found out if he spoke English!"

Maggie arched a brow to Cissy.

"I merely suggested that a man, weary after a day searching for clues which didn't exist, might enjoy an evening of jazz. So if you want to see this Adonis, you'd best come along with us tonight."

Maggie still hesitated. She'd been surrounded by people all day, and the visit from the police had been unnerving, to say the least. That blood drops led directly to her door was incredibly disturbing, and that she knew she'd be hounded by the police in the days to come was even more so. She needed a little time alone to gather her thoughts.

"We're not going to give you a chance to back out," Angie said determinedly. "We'll go right from here."

"Oh, I don't know, I'm not really dressed for a night at a jazz club—"

"It's summer in New Orleans, tourists are crawling around

in silly T-shirts and cut-off shorts, and you're worrying about what to wear?'' Cissy demanded.

"Especially when you only have to take your pick of clothing from any mannequin on the floor," Angie said.

"Heck, in some of these clubs lately, you could go naked with just a belly chain and be completely fashionable and go totally unnoticed," Angie said.

"Maggie, naked, unnoticed? I don't think so," Cissy protested.

"Well, you know darn well that I'm exaggerating!" Angie said with exasperation.

"Hey, hey! Okay, I'll go!" Maggie protested. "It will be good to hear Dean play."

"I'm changing first," Angie said determinedly. "If that's all right—I'd like to use your shower, Maggie, if I may."

"Sure. You go ahead," Maggie said. She had a private bath off her office—a rather extravagant luxury, she had told herself, but she loved it. She had a big, white marble bath with a whirlpool, a separate shower stall encircled with etched glass, and a marble vanity that stretched forever. Against the white marble, the floor and walls were in brilliant red, black, and gold. She reflected that it was just barely saved from looking as if it belonged in a high-class whorehouse by the delicate Venetian lace curtains that overlay the heavier gold draperies covering the windows that looked over the building's courtyard garden.

"Cissy, if you want, and you were planning on going straight from here, you can shower after Angie—"

"No way. I'm third. If we let you go last, you'll find some work you need to do and you'll try to bow out of joining us." She swung around, looking at the simple black sleeveless dress on the mannequin beside them. "Now this—is perfect."

"For you or me?" Maggie asked, laughing.

"Honey, I'm already perfectly beautiful in basic black. This is you, and you know it."

"I try not to design clothing I don't like," Maggie said. Cissy rewarded her with an exasperated glare.

"Black is your color. Your skin is so pure, just like marble.

And with your hair . . . why, honey, it's pure fire against black and white.''

Angie giggled. ''What an admiration society. Too bad we're all straight.''

''Men just forget to compliment women,'' Cissy said serenely. ''Sometimes we have to admire ourselves.''

''Since we're all so beautiful,'' Angie said, ''let's get dinner reservations.''

''I'll take care of it. You two get going,'' Cissy insisted.

Dinner.

Maggie was surprised to realize that her stomach was somewhat queasy.

A man had been viciously murdered just steps from her door. A pimp, a lowlife, a no-good SOB, most probably. And still . . .

''Dinner will be great,'' she said. ''A nice night out. We'll forget all about . . .''

''Dead people!'' Angie announced.

Maggie arched a brow, hesitating. ''Right. We'll forget all about dead people.''

Pierre LePont had been at his job well over twenty years. Though Sean knew many forensics men and women—and cops—who joked with graveyard humor, Pierre wasn't among them. He'd never seen Pierre munch his lunch while a stiff lay on a nearby table; the man maintained a respect for the dead that was sometimes humbling to those who worked with him.

Still, death could be a terribly humiliating state in itself. In life, Anthony Beale might have threatened and bullied, and defied dust and dirt in his Armani suit. Now, his body was naked and pasty white and his head lay in a separate stainless-steel receptacle on a gurney by the autopsy table.

No matter how antiseptic it might be, the morgue had a smell. Antiseptic death, but death all the same. ''What have you got for me?'' Sean asked Pierre, walking around the corpse, studying the pasty flesh. It was damned odd looking, worse than the skin on some of the corpses he'd seen dragged out of the Mississippi after days in the water.

"Not much blood," Pierre said, arms crossed over his chest as he stared at the corpse. Beale had already been autopsied, and sewn back up. He was ready to go back in the drawers. He looked somewhat like a replica of Frankenstein's monster, sutures holding together the Y cut done on his chest for the autopsy.

"So he was killed elsewhere and moved—"

"I didn't say that."

"What are you saying?"

"I'm saying he had damned little blood left in him. That's why he hasn't got any color."

"All right, so he was decapitated. Blood would have gushed out of the arteries ... unless he was killed before he was decapitated and ... hell, blood just doesn't disappear."

"I believe the blow to the throat at the time of death is what killed him. I'd thought maybe he'd died from a heart attack and then been decapitated, but that wasn't the case. Not enough trauma to the heart."

"Still, Pierre, he must have been killed elsewhere. Actually, he must have been killed in a similar fashion to the way we slaughter animals. Hung up and drained of his blood, then dumped where we found him."

Pierre shrugged.

"What does that mean?" Sean asked, aggravated.

"That's a possible scenario."

Sean threw up his hands.

Pierre stubbornly tightened his crossed arms over his chest. "I've taken our Jane Doe out again," he told Sean, indicating a sheet-covered corpse on a gurney a few feet away. "Jane Doe, decapitated, left on top of a tombstone, internal organs laid out around her. No blood. No damned blood."

Sean sighed, running his hands through his hair. "It looks like we've got some kind of ritualistic killings going on. Some voodoo cult or Santerias or the like. Killing for blood."

"Doing a damned good job of it," Pierre said.

"What have you got for me from the corpse?"

"Not much, I'm afraid. A left-handed killer with tremendous strength."

"Would it have to be a male?"

"Sean, that's a politically incorrect question these days."

"Oh, come on, Pierre—"

"A male, or a female, with tremendous strength. I would imagine that most persons with that kind of strength would be male. But there are no guarantees these days."

"So the killer is probably a left-handed male into ritualistic killing," Sean murmured. "You're right. That's not a hell of a lot to go on."

"Sorry," Pierre told him. "When we get the DNA reports back, we might have more. Computers have done a lot to help. Who knows, we might get a match-up with some bizarre crimes elsewhere."

"Pierre, we've weeks to go on the DNA," Sean said wearily.

"Yes, well . . . "

Sean took a step toward the corpse, shuddering as he looked at the neck—and the severed point where the head should lie. He hesitated, feeling his stomach lurch as he leaned closer to the dead man's throat. "What's this?"

"What?"

"That puncture point . . . there."

Pierre came around the corpse. Right next to the point where the head had been severed was a single, slight indentation that might have been a puncture wound.

"You know . . . damn, I hate to admit it. I'm not quite sure."

"Pierre . . ." Sean began, frowning.

"The way that the head is severed, there's so much trauma to the surrounding flesh that it's difficult to discover additional damage. If that is a puncture . . ."

"What?"

Pierre hesitated, unwilling to give information until he was certain. "Maybe he was bitten—either just before or directly after he was killed."

"Bitten—by a one-toothed creature?"

"Give me a break here, Sean. With the head having been severed, that small mark there is all that remains."

"Could it have been a dog?"

"I've taken all kinds of samples for analysis," Pierre told

him. "I told you, due to the head being severed, there's damage to all the surrounding flesh. I can't even venture a guess as to what caused that perforation mark, if it is a perforation. Hell, the killer could have bitten him—especially if we're dealing with something ritualistic. Or with a maniac. I don't know. As soon as the lab gets with me, I'll get back with you."

"I need every single little bit of help I can get," Sean reminded him.

"Hey, I know that. I'm on it." Pierre hesitated a minute. "Did you want to see Jane Doe again?" he asked.

Did he *want* to see Jane Doe again? Never. In a million years. But he suddenly realized he *needed* to see her again.

He nodded, taking a deep gulp of air.

"Good thing your new partner isn't here. Where is the young fellow, by the way? You let him out of the gruesome task of staring at corpses?"

"I gave him a more gruesome task."

"What's that?"

"Preparing a statement for the press," Sean said.

"Well, you're right there," Pierre agreed, walking over to the gurney that carried Jane Doe. "Poor boy. That was rather like feeding a good young Christian lad to the lions, wasn't it?"

"I should be with him in time to keep him from being completely devoured alive," Sean told him. "Just—just the head and neck, Pierre. That's all I need." "Jane" had been painstakingly sewn back together. She still made the bride of Frankenstein look like a beauty queen.

Pierre pulled the sheet back. Sean distanced himself and studied the cold, graying, decaying flesh of the poor girl. "Pierre . . .?" he murmured, pointing to what might have been a puncture, but what had become part of the severance at the throat.

"Possible . . ." Pierre murmured, sighing. "And I have to admit, I didn't see that possibility before."

"We didn't have a possible puncture to compare it with before," Sean reminded him. "And she was in several pieces when you picked her up. She was in so damned many pieces, and with her neck severed, there was no way you could have realized that this might be . . . not a part of the severance. I could be wrong. It might just be a jag where the knife tore at the flesh.''

''No, I don't think so. She wasn't attacked with a serrated blade; it was a smooth knife. A large, smooth-bladed weapon. Nine-inch blade, I'd say. I'll take more tissue samples for analysis,'' Pierre assured him. ''I wish I could have given you a few more definitive answers.''

''You've given me one.''

''What's that?''

''We definitely have a serial killer on our hands,'' Sean told him. ''And now . . .''

''Now what?''

''What to tell the press,'' Sean said unhappily.

''Glad that's your job. Well, whatever you decide to do, you'd best go rescue your Christian from the lions.''

''They will go right for the throat,'' Sean said.

''Lions, tigers—bears,'' Pierre mused. ''A dog—lots of dogs are trained to attack these days. Cat? Unlikely. Bat, rat? A bite that's not even there, that we're seeing because we're grasping at straws? I don't know. Good luck, Sean. I'll be talking with you as soon as I can.''

''Yep, thanks, Doc.''

Sean left the morgue.

He arrived at the station and reported to Captain Joe Daniels, head of homicide, a man dutifully referred to just as Chief by his subordinates. Daniels was a tall, rugged individual who had climbed his way to his position through hard work—he'd never kissed ass, and he still didn't play politics, which was one reason Sean had been glad to serve the city alongside him for so many years. Sean had never hesitated going to him; he didn't rant and rave and demand results and blame his officers for the fact that crime and criminals existed. If Joe called you out on the carpet, you deserved it. If you were a corrupt cop, you could expect the worst. New Orleans was a tough city. Joe was a tough cop.

''Tell me where we stand,'' Joe demanded bluntly. ''The truth. What you have, and what you don't have.''

"What we have, I believe, is a monstrous serial killer. What we don't have is a clue as to who it might be," Sean admitted, sitting in a chair in front of Joe's desk. He hesitated. "Due to the nature of the corpses, I believe we're dealing with a cultist or a serious psychopath."

"All right. I've heard everything on the corpse in the graveyard. Give me what you've got on this one."

Sean did. Joe listened gravely. He was of a mind that they did have a serial killer on their hands. That meant taking steps to go over the crime scenes with a fine-tooth comb and look for both tangible and psychological evidence. Since the seventies, when the FBI started profiling serial killers, police work on the behavior of criminals had come a long way. Sean had been to almost every class and discussion group offered to the New Orleans police on profiling, so he knew what he was up against—and he was more than willing to seek out advice from experienced criminologists.

A task force would be formed; Sean would head it. "We don't *know* that we've got a serial killer on our hands, but it darned sure looks that way," Joe said, and told Sean he'd deal with the city and state politicians, but since Sean was heading the local task force, the media was all his.

"And your boy is down there dealing with the vultures now," Joe warned him. "You might want to step in and help him out. Hey, if the lad survives this, he'll be a fine addition to the force."

Sean agreed, then quickly left Joe to join the media circus already in action. He reached the press conference just in time to step in behind Jack, who had been valiantly holding his own against a sea of shouting, but was beginning to grow frustrated.

"Ladies and gentlemen, we have no suspects at the moment, but we've a fine police department and some of the ablest forensic scientists in the business. Jack has given you everything that we have; when we know more, you'll know more. For the time—"

"What are the police doing to protect us?" demanded a young female reporter.

"Everything they can, ma'am. We're on double patrol around

the city, and the governor has asked for National Guard units to help keep a high profile. Now, you all know that in any big city, people just have to behave intelligently. Don't go down dark alleys, be careful when you're out late. Bear in mind that Jane Doe was engaging in dangerous and illicit behavior, and that Anthony Beale was equally engaged in illegal activities. Now, we're not quite sure what that means as yet, but it strengthens this piece of advice—keep out of dark alleys, try to go to and from work with co-workers, and be wary of strangers.''

''Great! Be wary of strangers in a tourist town!'' An aging reporter from the *Times/Picayune* cried out. ''What about our restaurant people, our hotel employees? How do they manage to be wary of strangers?''

''They use their intelligence and instincts to the best of their abilities,'' Sean said firmly. ''They stay aware, and report anything even slightly suspicious to the police. Now, no more questions; thank you very much.''

Sean ushered Jack out of the press room.

Uniformed officers closed in behind them, giving them a chance to escape.

Sean reflected dryly that the press would have liked to have devoured him and Jack—whole. Christians to the lions indeed.

''Oh, man,'' Jack groaned, leaning against the door. ''I'm not at all sure that being your partner is a good thing. What's next?''

''Next?'' Sean asked, then grinned. ''Well, I'm going to brief the night guys. Then I'm going home.''

''I'm glad to hear you can do that. That you can just eat dinner, get a good night's sleep.''

''I'm not too certain that I can eat dinner, *or* get a good night's sleep. I'm going to be as restless as a cat all night, but we've got another shift coming on, and they're good people. They'll get with me if there's anything else we can do. If there was something I could be doing, hell, I'd be doing it.''

Jack grinned suddenly. ''I know what you could do—if you wanted.''

''What's that?''

''You know Officer Mike Astin?''

Sean nodded. Astin was hard to miss. He'd spent a year in pro football, then mashed his knee so badly his career had been over. Astin, however, had always wanted to be a cop. He was good on the force—huge, nearly six feet four, and weighing in at nearly three hundred pounds of pure muscle. He was bright and even-tempered, an asset to any force.

"Yeah, I know Mike."

"Well, I think we should meet him at a jazz club."

"A jazz club—"

"Yeah, a jazz club. You know, a place where people go, have a few drinks, listen to some good music."

"Hell, Jack, the last thing I want—"

"Astin has a potential date with that tall, gorgeous receptionist who works at Montgomery Enterprises. Don't we need to know everything we can about the employees at Montgomery Enterprises?"

Sean opened his mouth, closed it. Lifted his hands, let them fall. Then he started to laugh. "God, I do love jazz. And it's been a hell of a long time since I've heard good music."

Jack was pleased. His partner had been covering for him all day, even saving his sorry ass at the press conference when the questions started coming a little too hard, fast, and furious.

But now . . . well, maybe, he'd get an opportunity for a little payback. "I'm going home to clean up," he said. "But you *are* joining Mike and me, right?"

"Oh, yes. Hell, yes. Bourbon Street in an hour," Sean told him, turning around to leave.

Jack watched him, grinning.

He guessed they weren't off for the night after all.

It was in Paris, not long after she first tasted blood, that she met Lucian.

And was told the rules.

She didn't know what was happening that first night; she thought she was dreaming. Indeed, it was *a dream, a nightmare of the most horrible proportions.*

She had only recently come to Paris. Her father had sent

her. Naturally, after her affair with Alec and its consequences, there was little to do but send a well-bred heiress to Europe.

And since she was a stranger in this beautiful old city, it was natural that she should sleep fitfully, restlessly.

And dream.

It seemed that the wind swept around her with a tremendous, dark force. The earth shook and quaked, the air was a tempest, the darkness was enwrapping. She felt that she lay still, teeth chattering against the strength of the force, and that she was lifted, lifted by the wind, by the very powers of the night, of darkness. She flew, compelled to soar through time and space.

Then, everything was still. The darkness remained around her, but slowly, a flickering red-and-ivory light brought the complete blackness slowly to shadow. She was down now upon something solid. She found herself on a rough fur rug before a hotly blazing fire. The flames kept the darkness at bay with an eerie red light.

She looked around, confused, disoriented.

She was not in her own bedroom, but rather in someone else's private domain. Near the fire was a huge four-postered bed with elaborate carvings and a black satin spread. There was a desk, a washstand, a swivel mirror.

And just ahead of her, sharing the fire's light and heat, sat a man in a large, wing-backed chair. He watched her, hands folded casually in his lap. Even though he was seated, she could see that he was a tall man, broad-shouldered. Regal, confident, arrogant even, in the way he sat. His hair was dark, rich, long to his shoulders. In the strange red-gold light that continued to press back the shadows, she made out his features. Sharp, severe, handsome in a curious way.

And frightening, for she could see his eyes.

Perhaps they should have been brown; that dark, dark brown that was nearly black in a Creole way.

But they weren't brown.

They were as red as the flames in the hearth.

She sat up, drawing her legs beneath her, trying very boldly to meet his stare. She tried to remind herself, convince herself that it was a dream. Dream. God, no! A nightmare, and she had fallen into the pits of despair to come upon the devil himself.

He stood, smiling. A wicked, pleased, smug smile, as if he had seen her eyes, as she had seen his; as if he had seen the fear within them, and was deeply delighted to realize that she was cowering there before him.

She tried to sit very tall and very straight upon her strange fur throne. Defiant. After all, if it was a nightmare, which surely it must be, it was right to defy the devil.

He wore a black shirt with stylishly frilled sleeves, open at the throat, skintight black breeches that hugged tightly muscled buttocks and thighs, and shiny black boots cuffed just above his knee. He wore no beard or mustache, his face was bare, further accentuating the sharp, striking lines of his features, the sensual fullness of his lips as he curled his mouth in a mocking smile.

He walked toward her, then around her, his smile deepening, his eyes, now suddenly as dark as they should have been, assessing her as if she was a surprise gift; a new pet perhaps, or a prize racehorse.

"Oh, mademoiselle, you are quite something! A creation beyond measure. I had heard that this was so. Alec was infatuated beyond all sense and reason, but Alec is dead, and you are with us—and you are to have a child! How rich, how droll! You are sent to Paris—your father is a clever man. A very clever man. You see—I know all about you. And you, my love, do you know who I am?" he asked her suddenly.

His voice was deep, masculine, yet husky as well, almost as if it were a part of the warm air still sweeping around her. It was a whisper that entered into her.

"The devil?" she queried in return.

His laughter was hearty; he seemed even more pleased.

"I am Lucian."

"The devil."

He shook his head, lashes lowering over his eyes, smile deepening with amusement. "Lucian DeVeau."

"The devil—"

He paused before her suddenly, capturing her hands, draw-

*ing her to her feet. She tried to wrench free, but could not.
Her bones would have snapped before his grasp would have
loosened. She had never felt such strength.*

*He smiled, mocking her efforts. His eyes burned into hers.
"Not the devil. The king. Your king. The king of your kind."*

*She shook her head vehemently. "No. You are a figure in a
nightmare. My kind, what kind? This is preposterous, you are
wrong, wrong, I am no kind—"*

*He began to laugh again, and she felt the force of him around
her. The power of the air and wind, and the power of the
darkness and night. The power of the strange storm that had
brought her. They were his power; in the strength of his arms,
in his eyes, in the laughter that was so rich, part of the tempest
that had swept her up, and cast her down.*

*"Denial, naturally. Ah, it is the sweetest, my little love, when
the good and innocent are so corrupted! But then, you're not
entirely an innocent anymore, are you? There was that young
fool with whom you fell in love! Poor Alec. He believed in the
old legends, that his love could save his mortal soul! Alas, but
your father murdered him!" he continued, still enjoying himself
tremendously. "But again, all in the name of love, eh? And so
you are here. One with us. My subject, as it were!" he taunted.*

*"This is a nightmare!" she declared. "You are a nightmare.
I won't stay here, I will wake up—"*

*"Oh, no, my sweet," he said, and his smile remained, but
it was subtle and tight. "Understand me. Life is now this
nightmare, and you will live it. And you will listen to me, and
learn. Because I am your king. And you need me. And oddly
enough, in my own wicked way, I am a just king."*

"Let me go—" she demanded, starting to struggle.

*"You have no strength. Strength comes with time, with prac-
tice. If the soul is what is stolen, the mind remains, and it is
the power of the mind with which we work. Pay me heed. No
one so lush as you has come along in a very long time, and I
will enjoy teaching you, and you will learn to listen. You are
mine, mademoiselle. And you will take care, chérie. Not many
are so willing to teach, and I do not always offer my wisdom
so generously, but then . . . you are unique. So pay heed, and*

learn well. You will hear many things, most of them myth, rumor. Trust me, not what you hear from others. Now, there are simple things. The sun will not kill you, yet the day is not your time of strength. You may function by light, yet your most restful sleep will come with the dawn. Wine will still taste sweet, yet it will not be enough. You can be hurt, but you can also heal. You can be hurt badly, and it may take years, decades more, to heal. You can be killed, but only if your head is severed from your neck, or your heart is pierced through.''

"This is hideous; I'll not listen—"

"You will listen, and you will remember—I rule. And we survive because I rule wisely and well, do you understand? My word, to you, mademoiselle, is law."

"I understand nothing; I will awaken—"

"Alas, you will not. Now, most importantly, you must always dine with the greatest care."

"I beg your pardon—"

"Beg nothing. You understand my every word. With most of us, one kill at the full moon is enough. If you wish to live in peace and avoid mortal hunters, you should choose those who live outside society. Seek those who wander, the homeless, the criminals, the prostitutes. Steal human cargo from ships at sea. Don't look so horrified. Oh, I suppose we do have a moralist or two among our number—and they choose to prey upon the prisons. Indeed, mademoiselle, you might be surprised to discover that even I have my code of ethics. If you're distressed by your hungers, rid the world more easily of those condemned already. Murderers rot in prisons, take them. It matters not. Method matters. Comprehend this. Dispose of all remains. Dispose of all remains properly, this is most important! A glut of our kind and we would definitely be done in. You must behead your victims, or sever the arteries, and if you don't, you will face trial and death by your peers. Yes! There is a law among us, for our survival! And our justice is swift. Take care with your actions. You may create just two more of our kind per century—"

"Create two more . . . per century! This is insane. I'm leaving!"

"You are not leaving!" he informed her.

"Rot in hell!"

"You are not leaving!"

Suddenly she felt as if she were flying once again. Seized by tempest, lifted, tossed. She landed upon the black satin expanse of the bed, breathless, stunned. And he was above her. His clothing cast aside now, his flesh as sleek as the satin, as hot as the blaze from the impossible fire, his eyes locking on to hers.

She shrieked and screamed, fought, gouged with her nails. He laughed throughout, amused, tearing away her gown. Where he did not touch her, it still seemed that he could force her to his will. His eyes commanded, her flesh obeyed. When he tired of the fight, he willed her to cease, to lie back. Her mind raged, her body was still. The fire of his eyes touched her and she shook with her rage, but she lay vulnerable. Naked. Limbs parted to his pleasure and amusement.

She was so angry that she wanted to kill . . .

But then . . .

The warmth began. Searing, permeating, invading her limbs. She heard his whisper, so coercive, soothing yet evocative. She felt his strange, sensual heat. The flickering liquid fire of tongue, his caress . . . about her, within her.

She fought then with her heart, her soul, her mind. Still, she fought a losing battle. And later, she was horrified to realize that he did have the power to force from her what he wanted. To demand, command, oh, God, to seduce. And worst of all, he could draw from her a hunger, a need, and the searing, explosive response he wanted. She was a sensual creature. Once she had loved, and so she had wanted, ached, longed, and the result had been beautiful. This was different. And still . . .

He had made her want him.

All to his vast amusement.

He was so pleased, lying at her side, touching her hair.

"You are exquisite. I am deeply sorry for our departed friend, who made you, and then perished! Poor Alec! He believed so deeply that his love might set him free! Poor fellow, so religious,

so aesthetic, believing in life, song, poetry, and myth. Beauty and the beast, and his beast could turn, if love were strong enough. Indeed, were I more familiar with such a sensation, I might love you myself. Perhaps I could learn to do so.''

''I could never learn to love you!''

''Ah, well, then it's a good thing that I truly don't give a damn—and that I do have the power. Nor am I ever content with just one lover. Still, you amuse me, please me, enchant me. And I will summon you when I choose—and you will come, because I demand it.''

''I will learn the power!'' she informed him.

Again, he laughed. His deep, husky, wickedly taunting laugh.

And then again, he touched her . . .

His whisper, like his sensuality, wrapped all around her. ''Ma belle, I do have the power . . .''

Her eyes opened slowly. She was in her own bed, listening to the church bells of Paris tolling the hour.

She lay in a fog as she struggled to awaken, thinking of her macabre nightmare. What a restless night; she still lay exhausted, the dream had been so very vivid!

She started to rise.

Then realized that her gown was in tatters, ripped and shredded. Her hands began to shake; tears stung her eyes. Oh, God, it couldn't be.

Oh, God, it was.

She fell back, wallowing in a cascade of tears and self-pity.

But then, when she had cried herself out, she rose. She walked to the window, and stared out at the day.

She would cry no more.

Lucian had power.

So be it.

She would have more.

CHAPTER 3

Angie, Cissy, and Maggie ate dinner at a new restaurant not far from the jazz club. While the other two girls ordered espressos, she excused herself to go to the ladies' room. On her return to the table, she passed through the bar area. At the far end of the elegant oak bar, there was a television. She was certain that it was frequently tuned to sporting events, but tonight, the stations were repeating segments of the six o'clock news. First, she saw the sincere young detective she had met that afternoon, Jack Delaney. The reporters asking questions began to grow surly. Then Canady stepped up to the podium. There was an air of authority about him that was assuring. When he said that the police intended to protect the city, his words were believable. It might even have had something to do with his physical presence, or the sound of his voice. Whatever his power, he managed to soothe the savage beasts ready to tear into the police force—fear did that to people, and, as she had overheard since she'd been out tonight, a lot of people in New Orleans were afraid. Still, people were vocal tonight, and she couldn't help hearing as well that there were those here who still seemed to believe—as much of the populace might have believed back in Jack the Ripper's day—that as long as their killer stuck to pimps and whores, decent people were safe. Still, such a killer had to be caught.

Maggie saw a shadow against the screen of the television. Someone very tall was standing behind her. She turned quickly, and saw that Sean Canady was right at her back. He'd changed. He was in a casual pinstripe jacket with a tieless silver gray shirt, just opened at the collar.

"How'd I do?" he asked her, and he sounded weary.

She watched him for a moment before answering. "Very well. There was a calm assurance about your words. Without actually saying anything of the like, you somehow conveyed to people that if they were careful and kept clear of underworld personalities, they'd probably be safe until the police caught the killer."

He arched a brow to her, a slight smile playing on his lips. "Now, is that a compliment, or are you mocking me completely?"

She didn't answer his question—but asked instead, "Did you follow me here?"

His smile deepened. He had one dimple, on the right side. Definite power. He had showered, and smelled pleasantly of soap and a subtle, woodsy after-shave. She swallowed hard, wishing she could look away from him, but she'd just asked him a question.

"No," he said. "I didn't follow you here. I was hoping to follow you to a jazz club this evening, and we just happened to come in here for dinner because it's close to the club."

Despite herself, she felt a smile tug at her lips. "Well, sir, you're honest."

"I try. Are *you* honest?"

"I do my best."

"Interesting reply."

"I didn't kill the pimp this afternoon. Or the girl in the cemetery."

"Did I accuse you?"

"You interrogated me this afternoon. And searched my building."

"You didn't have to allow me to do so."

"You would have gotten a search warrant."

"Yes, I would have."

"So . . . are you following me in the hopes of making an arrest soon?"

He didn't reply. Two seats had gone vacant at the bar and he took her elbow, directing her toward them. "Let me buy you a drink."

"Do you think I'll become intoxicated and spill the beans that I'm guilty?" she inquired.

He laughed, directing her onto one of the empty stools, taking another himself. The bartender was quickly before them and Maggie ordered wine while Sean asked for a Michelob.

"Are you allowed to drink on duty?" she asked him.

"I'm not on duty."

"Oh?"

"Oh."

"But you are following me."

He looked at her, amused. "Yes."

"But you don't plan on arresting me tonight?"

"You know that we didn't find a thing in your building."

"I was told that you hadn't found anything, that minute blood drops led to the side doorway but that there was nothing whatsoever discovered over the threshold."

"Still strange, don't you think?"

"I think a lot of things are quite strange. But apparently, you think that if those blood drops led to my door, there must be a connection to me. So, I ask again, are you planning to arrest me?"

He shrugged, shaking his head, then indicating the wineglass she held.

"You appear to be right-handed."

"So?"

"The killer is left-handed."

"I could be ambidextrous."

"You could be. What do you weigh?"

"I beg your pardon?"

He laughed softly. His laughter had a rich, husky tone to it. A tone that slipped sensuously beneath her skin. She took a long sip of her wine, determined to fight the feelings. He was a cop, after something!

"The killer is very powerful," he told her. "All implications suggest a heavily muscled man."

"Such as yourself?" she said pleasantly.

He arched a brow, a subtle smile still playing about his lips. He didn't reply to her question but said, "I just don't think that—at what your weight appears to be—you'd have the strength for these killings."

"Looks can be deceiving."

"Indeed, they can."

"So?"

"So—why are you following me?"

He drank from his beer, then set the glass down. "I'm not exactly sure. You're an intriguing woman."

"Intriguing?"

"And you've quite a presence."

"A presence?"

"All right, Miss Montgomery, fish for compliments. You're beautiful, a stunning woman."

She lifted her chin just slightly. "Are you allowed to hit on murder suspects, Lieutenant?"

"I don't suspect you of murder," he told her.

"Then what do you suspect?"

"Ah . . . well!" He lifted his glass to her. "All right, I suspect that someone in your building knows something. All the people in your building are your employees. You know all your employees. Maybe you know something that you don't want to admit, or maybe you even know something that you don't know you know."

"Oh, Lieutenant! What a way you have with flattering a woman. And there I thought for a moment that you were actually after me for my feminine appeal." She started to rise from the bar stool, ready to walk away.

But his hand landed on hers, pinning her where she stood, and his eyes were so dark a blue they were like a cobalt as he stared at her.

"You're not a fool, Miss Montgomery, nor are you inordinately modest. You know damn well that you have appeal."

She tried to tug her hand away. "What?" he demanded. "You wanted honesty, didn't you?"

"Yes, honesty is good," she said irritably. "Now, we don't have to play any games—"

"No games. I want to get to know you."

"What if I don't want to be known?"

"How about just sleeping with me then?"

"What?" she demanded, stunned and indignant.

But he smiled again, a deep, self-mocking smile. "Sorry, I couldn't help that one. And, of course, I could be joking. Look, you were insulted that my 'hitting on you' might have to do with police work. I told you exactly where I stand on that. I'm following you because you're so damned alluring I seem to have no choice. Our families do have a history together, you know. Give me a chance. Finish your drink. Let me stand somewhere near you at the jazz club."

"You know what's wrong with you, Canady?" she asked him.

"I'm sure there's a lot, but did you have something specific in mind?" he asked.

She didn't want to laugh or smile, or feel so fascinated by him and far too ready to comply with his wishes. Still, she did smile. "You're dangerous!" she told him.

"How so?"

"You're after something."

"I'm after a lot."

"You're also exasperating."

"Comes with the territory."

"Well, for the moment, my companions have just ordered dessert—"

"And you might want to notice that your companions have just been joined by mine."

Startled, Maggie swung around. He was right. She saw Cissy's Adonis—one of the tallest men Maggie had ever seen, black as ebony, handsome as could be—about to take the chair at Cissy's side. Jack Delaney was drawing up a chair beside

Angie, and the waiter was hovering to deliver various coffees to them all.

"They make handsome couples, don't you think?" Sean inquired.

She looked at him. "Your tall black friend is an Adonis. But it appears as if the law is descending en masse."

"My tall black friend's name is Mike. You met Jack earlier. And the only reason people are usually leery of the law is if they have something to hide. Do you?"

His gaze was piercing, eyes so dark. He looked at her as if he had a unique talent for reading human souls. She hesitated just briefly.

"I told you, I didn't murder the pimp or the girl."

"And I've told you—I don't think that you committed murder. I just wonder what you've got to hide."

"Ah, Lieutenant! What you see, sir, is what there is."

"So—will you go out with me?"

"I'm already out."

"But you wouldn't want to be a fifth wheel over there, would you?"

"I can be very independent."

"Ah, but look! They're all getting worried about us, see? Jack is straining his neck to see where I might have gotten to, and your cute little assistant is beginning to appear anxious. Maybe we should walk on over, sip espresso, and join them."

"And maybe I should just call it an evening," she told him.

"Well, of course we could slip away somewhere alone together. Tell me, are you living at Montgomery Plantation?"

She arched a brow. "I spend some time there. I have a complete set-up at the office as well." She hesitated, realizing that she should have gone home, but finding that she was growing more curious about him as well.

"Isn't there a plantation in the Canady family as well?"

He grinned, nodding. "Not what it used to be, I'm afraid, but still in the same place on the Mississippi, though there is a Burger King down the street now as well. The property isn't the same size as it used to be."

"A Burger King—right down the street?"

"Thank God I like Whoppers."

She laughed lightly. "But—"

"I'm exaggerating. We've still got a few acres left, and the house is beautiful. Hard to keep up, but beautiful. My little sister married an architect, so we get a lot of help with repairs through workmen who owe favors—the 'we' being my father and I."

"Your father's still living. How wonderful for you."

"Your family is . . .?"

"All deceased. We were never terribly procreative, I'm afraid."

"What a pity."

"Why?"

"Because you really are lovely. You should be cloned— community beautification and the like."

"You are a flatterer."

"Hmm. But I can't seem to say the right things so that you won't be so wary of me."

"You're a cop."

"And you're innocent—remember?"

She smiled, shaking her head slightly. "It's hard to understand just what you want."

He shrugged. "You're the one who's overly suspicious. I've been honest—and I'm an open book. I want you to think and then tell me truthfully if you might know anyone who has any idea of what is going on. And other than that . . . well, I've already said it."

"If there's anything I can think of to tell you, I will," she said after studying him carefully for a minute.

"So—do we join the others?"

"Umm . . . I suppose."

"You've opted out on spending the evening all alone with me, I take it. Sleeping together is out, as well? I'm going to have to be much more subtly flattering and cajoling and work far more slowly to get you into bed?"

She smiled, studying his handsome features once again, and the teasing light of cobalt fire in his eyes. "Don't under- or over-estimate my innocence, Lieutenant. I'm all grown up, old enough to know my mind. I've nothing against sleeping with a compelling man—if and when I decide he's what I want.''

With that, she turned quickly, leaving him still sitting on his bar stool while she threaded her way through the bar area, and back to her table.

Jane Doe had been killed on a Wednesday; Anthony Beale on a Friday. The city was in an uproar, but on Saturday morning, the front page of the newspaper didn't blast the police force half as badly as Sean had expected it might.

Instead, the article focused on the vice within the city of New Orleans, citing many bizarre crimes of the past. After all, New Orleans had always been *different*. Voodoo priestesses had practiced here, they still did. Cults remained, those who believed in aliens and people who believed themselves to be vampires roamed the streets, and the costumes of Mardi Gras had concealed many a criminal throughout the decades. This was the home of Marie Laveau, the most famous voodoo priestess of them all, above-ground cemeteries, and anything-goes sex clubs. There was an editorial bend in the story, suggesting that the entire city needed to be cleaned up.

Well, that might be true, Sean thought. But easier said than done.

He was sitting in the breakfast parlor at Oakville, his family ''plantation'' on the Mississippi.

Curiously enough, his Friday night had turned into something of a ''date.'' Maggie Montgomery had been charming, flirtatious, fun. They'd listened to jazz music, they'd even danced. And he'd seen her back to her office ''apartment''—and gotten a handshake at the doorway.

Fine. He hadn't pressed anything, even though his teasing words had held tremendous truths—she was quite simply the sexiest, most sensual woman he had ever encountered. Still, he had managed an incredibly casual and amused smile at her doorway—as if he could wait forever to get her with her clothes off—and then he'd driven around for an hour before deciding to come out of the heart of the city and sleep at the old family homestead.

After a very long, cold shower.

The term plantation had initially referred to a farm—and some plantations had been small, and some ostentatious. Oakville had originally been somewhere in between, yet definitely antebellum upscale. The woodwork in the house was worth a fortune itself, but Sean knew that any member of the Canady family would die a thousand deaths before allowing any of it to be cut out of the house. Oakville was typical of many a home built in the early years of the eighteenth century—a center breezeway opened to four rooms on the ground floor—now the kitchen, dining room, parlor and library—while there were five bedrooms upstairs. One was his father's bedroom, not changed a hair since his mother died five years ago. Two were guest rooms, while his room, like his father's, hadn't changed much since he had left the house to go away to college—many years ago now. And like his, his sister's room remained uniquely hers. The walls were still covered with posters of rock bands, and though Mary Canady O'Niall had been married now for eight years and had children of her own and a beautiful home in the Garden District, she still added new posters to her bedroom at Oakville now and then.

It seemed to mean a lot to his father that his children came home to Oakville.

For the first time in over fifty years, parts of the few remaining acres of property were being farmed once again. His father had a vegetable garden growing now, and he had proudly made Sean an omelette featuring his own onions and tomatoes.

Coffee here was always good as well. Bess Smith, who had been telling him what to do since he'd been in knee breeches, was still tending to the house for his father. She came Mondays, Wednesdays, Fridays, and Saturdays, and made the best cup of chicory-flavored coffee known to man. Sean had to admit, it was good to have his father's omelette and Bess's coffee as he read the newspaper.

His father, across the table from him, was studying him and shaking his head. Daniel Canady was perhaps a half inch shorter than Sean and in the last few years, had grown thin. At seventy, he had a distinguished appearance; he still stood as straight as an antebellum column. His hair remained thick and handsomely silver, and Sean had inherited his own deep blue eye color from Daniel. Daniel's investments had kept the family in decent financial shape, which was good, since for his chosen vocation, Daniel had been an historian. He'd taught at the university for several years, and dedicated himself to writing historical nonfiction. Thankfully, he'd managed to teach Sean about investments as well, since police work payed just about as poorly as the academic field.

"You're letting these murders get to you too much, Son," Daniel told him.

Sean set down the paper. "Dad—we're talking about people being decapitated."

"Well, decapitation is one way to assure death," Daniel said matter-of-factly. "But remember, Son, this is New Orleans. We've had pirate raiders, voodoo practices, zombies, and vampire cults over two hundred years of history. Hell, when I was a boy, we used to walk through some of the old graveyards on the way to school and play kick ball with the old skulls that would pop out of the broken tombs. This is a place where anything can happen—and has."

Sean nodded. "I appreciate the help, Dad. But the problem now is that I'm senior guy on these homicides and I have the entire city staring at me. I've even got the governor calling daily. I've got to stop this killer."

"You're senior man on the case," Daniel pointed out, "but you're not the only homicide cop in New Orleans. You've got good, competent help." Daniel shook his head. "Unfortunately, our city has had its share of very bad happenings. Think about La Maison Lalaurie. Madame Lalaurie and her physician husband kept a houseful of slaves chained to the walls and they performed the most horrible medical experiments on the poor people. They tortured, maimed, and murdered them—and they were only discovered at their grisly deeds when a fire brought in the city firemen who, in turn, in their horror, brought in the police. The house remains in the French Quarter today; the

Lalauries escaped. There was the butchery at the 'Sultan's' house, when the Turk and his entire household were found in pieces. In the late twenties, early thirties, we had the ax murderer. I'm sorry to say that the list goes on and on.''

"That was the past, Dad. And yes, it was horrible. But I'm responsible now. And I've got no leads.''

"You've got modern forensic science.''

"It doesn't seem to be helping. It's taking far too long. And all the modern miracles in the world won't help if I don't have a suspect to tie in with the evidence.''

Daniel was quiet for a minute. "Sean, for now you've got to quit beating your head against the wall. Unfortunately, lots of killers are never caught.''

Sean set the paper down. "Dad, I will get this guy. This is my city. Nobody kills and cuts up people like this in my city and gets away with it.''

Daniel grinned. "There's the fighting spirit. You got anything going that isn't in the papers?''

Sean shrugged. "Well, we didn't let it out in the papers that we found minute drops of blood—which proved to be the victim's—along the sidewalk. They led directly to the side door of Montgomery Enterprises—then stopped. I mean *completely.*''

"Did you investigate the building?''

"Of course.''

"Well?''

"Nothing. We scoured the place with a fine-tooth comb. Not another drop of blood. Nothing.''

"Interesting. Did you meet Miss Montgomery?''

"Yes, she was cooperative, and allowed us to search the premises.''

"And that's all? You asked to search her property and did so?''

Sean lowered his head, grinning. He'd spent about eight years of his life living with a girl named Sophie Holloway. Sophie was pretty, sweet, and vivacious, a Mardi Gras princess. They'd met when they were young, fought, broken up a few times, gotten back together. They'd finally planned to marry when Sophie had discovered she had uterine cancer, and no pleading on his part could convince her that they should marry for the time she had left.

Sophie had been gone nearly six years now. Sean dated. He liked women, liked sex—hell, it was a necessary fact of life, like breathing. But living with someone again was a big step; marriage even bigger. He hadn't found the right woman, and his father remained concerned that he was going to die a bachelor, and his illustrious line of Canadys would come to an end.

"Yes, Dad. I asked to search her property, and she gave her permission." He hesitated. "I also saw her at a jazz club last night, so we had something of a chance to talk. Why?"

Daniel smiled. "Oh, I'm curious, I guess."

"Right. Just curious."

"Honestly, just curious," Daniel insisted. "If you look in the old family records, way, way back, a Canady was engaged to a Montgomery. But the marriage never took place. The 'Miss' Montgomery involved went to Europe. Another 'Miss' Montgomery returned years later. The family has been interesting in that none of the women has taken on the surname of her husband. Daughters seem to be the only offspring each generation, and they cling to the Montgomery name."

"Now that *is* curious."

"Becoming more common these days, I'm afraid. Many professional women keep their surnames. Personally, I like the old concept, when a woman took her husband's name. And passed it on to her children. But then, the Montgomerys have been a little odd over the years." He paused, shrugging. "Downright snooty in a way."

Sean smiled. "How's that, Dad?"

"Well, they take off to Europe with their babies, then come back here to make American money."

"You can't arrest people for being snooty."

Daniel grinned. "I wouldn't suggest anything of the kind. But there have been interesting relationships between the families over the years. Sometime, I'll show you all the records I have. I wouldn't mind meeting your Miss Montgomery, though. Her ancestors have been fascinating women.'' Daniel hesitated again. ''She's not married, right?''

''No, Dad, she's not married.''

''Did you like her?''

Sean hesitated, seeing his father's hopeful expression. Then he relented.

''Yeah. I liked her.''

''Did you ask her out?''

''In a way.''

''Did she accept?''

''Not really.''

Daniel drummed his fingers on the table. ''You know, Montgomery Plantation isn't far from here. Since you're out, you should take a ride by the place.''

''She isn't there. I left her in the heart of the Vieux Carré last night.''

Daniel's brow shot up. ''You left her?''

Daniel sighed inwardly. ''Some of the guys and I escorted her and a few of her friends home. There was a wretched murder that took place yesterday, remember.''

''Ah. Still, you should go by and see Montgomery Plantation.''

''I've been by it. And I need to get some work in today.''

''It's the weekend, Son.''

''Murderers seldom recognize a Monday to Friday nine-to-five schedule. Cops don't get to, either.''

''But the blood drops led to Miss Montgomery's building.''

''That they did.''

''So she is at work. And, if I remember right, there's a smashing painting of one of her forebears right above the grand staircase. If anyone is in residence, you can take a look at the painting and see how the family resemblance has fared over the years. And then again, maybe Miss Montgomery herself is in residence. And if she is, maybe you can ask her out for a barbecue tonight. Then you can grill her in privacy.''

Sean shook his head. ''I left her in the city. But maybe I will go for a ride.''

''And if she happens to be there, you will ask her out for dinner, won't you? Do you know anything about her? What does she like? I do mean steaks on the grill. Maybe she's a vegetarian. So many women are vegetarians these days. Not that too much fat is good for you, but man was given the teeth to be a carnivore, and it seems to me a body needs a good piece of red meat now and then.''

''Sorry, Dad, when I was with her last night, she had wine and an espresso, so I don't know what she does and doesn't eat. But I will go to see her, and I will do my best to convince her she should come to dinner. How's that?''

''You do that. Try hard, huh?''

Sean arched a brow, somewhat disgruntled to realize that although his father spoke absently, it seemed he thought Sean would have to try very hard to convince a woman to go out with him.

Or maybe it was just because the woman was Maggie Montgomery.

He was suddenly very intent on seeing her himself.

The store officially opened at 10:00 A.M.: Allie Bouchet always came in by 9:30 at the latest. She made coffee, and spruced up any little thing that might have been left out of order. She was extremely proud of the shop.

Nearing fifty, she was an attractive woman, widowed four years now. Her hair had gone white at a very early age; she tinted it to a soft silver that went perfectly with her gray eyes and still-beautiful complexion. She was lean and trim, the result of a lifetime of moderation. She had been raised in a traditional mold, and was always a lady.

Therefore, though she was quite startled by the man who suddenly appeared—sitting on a corner of the rear oak desk that served as a cash station—she remembered her manners. Despite her annoyance.

''Why, sir! You did surprise me. I'm afraid that the store

hasn't opened yet. I'm sorry, foolish me. I usually do remember to lock the door while I'm preparing for the day to come. I do apologize if I've caused you any inconvenience, and I suppose you are welcome to stay—''

''Why, ma'am, I'm so sorry to have caused you distress,'' her visitor said, his voice a deep, soft drawl that was disturbingly . . . *sensual* . . . and yet lulling at the same time. He was young— somewhere right in a *manly* and mature prime of life. He wore black slacks and a fashionable black knit pullover. He was deeply tanned, had very dark hair, and fascinating gold eyes that were hypnotic and . . . snakelike. He was very handsome, but rugged and suave.

How rude, she told herself.

''Could I get you some coffee perhaps? My associate, Mrs. Gema Grayson, arrives soon, and then one of us can certainly help you with whatever you're looking for, sir.''

He smiled, a deep, inviting smile. He hadn't said a thing that wasn't just as polite as pie, and yet . . . it seemed as if he was somehow inviting her closer.

Silly old bat! she accused herself. He was probably fifteen years younger than she was, an eligible young cuss if she'd ever seen one, and it was most unlikely he was coming on to an older woman in her situation.

''Coffee . . . yes. Coffee would be nice,'' he told her.

''I do select and grind my own beans,'' she assured him briskly, glad of something to do, and aware that his eyes followed her to the little wicker table that sat center of the dressing rooms where she kept her coffee service. ''And I don't keep it on the heat—just as soon as it has properly perked, I see to it that my coffee goes into a carafe and is kept warm and just perfectly brewed.''

She poured a cup and turned around.

He was right behind her. Very tall. So close. Funny, she hadn't heard him move. Not a rustle, not a whisper of air.

He seemed to tower above her. He was definitely over six feet, lean, lithe, just like a black panther. Tall, smooth, so handsome, and with such a wicked, compelling smile.

Why, the way he was looking at her now . . . he was just riveting.

You devil, she thought.

He accepted the coffee from her.

"Why, actually, ma'am, I've come to inquire about your employer, Miss Montgomery. Would she be coming in today?"

"Oh, no, sir. Miss Montgomery takes her weekends. Unless, of course, we're in Mardi Gras season, or the like, which we're not."

"Oh, dear. I'm so sorry I've missed her."

"She'll be back in on Monday."

"Well . . . I can always find Miss Montgomery when I really need to do so . . . but she'll be here on Monday. I'm so glad."

He was incredibly close. She wondered how she could be so rude as to feel that he had "snake" eyes, and yet find his proximity to be such a pleasant thing.

"I'm so sorry that you've wasted your time."

She didn't exactly remember him drinking his coffee, but his cup was empty. He set it down, and took her hands. "Why, ma'am, I've not wasted my time. I've met you."

She was going to swoon. Get the vapors. She did, indeed, feel as if she was wearing a corset that was far too tight, when she wore no such apparel.

"Why, sir, you are a flatterer."

He smiled, and turned to leave, walking toward the front. She was so addled she didn't think to follow him, to lock the door when he had left.

She turned back to the coffee, still smiling to herself. Silly old thing, being so flattered and unnerved by a handsome *younger* man. Not that she didn't have pride in herself. She did, but he was so polite, such a charmer . . .

She turned about in a no-nonsense fashion to get back to work.

But she gasped in stunned surprise.

He was back. Right in front of her again.

Smiling . . . his eyes on hers.

"Why . . . sir!" she stuttered.

"Ah, well, there was just one more thing!" he told her, and

it seemed that his eyes drew her to him. "Just one more thing!" he said very softly.

And touched her . . .

CHAPTER 4

The Montgomery plantation was an extremely handsome picture of antebellum architecture.

Coming along the drive, Sean paused, staring at the beautiful old house. It had been built in an age of gracious living with a tremendous amount of money. He estimated that it probably contained about eight thousand square feet of living space. A semicircle of steps led to a deep grand porch with thick, white columns. The porch wrapped around the house, as did that on the second floor of the dwelling. He could well imagine that in decades gone past, guests escaped the heat of a Louisiana summer by opening their bedroom doors to the river breezes, and walking by night on that porch beneath the moonlight.

He had no idea how much property still remained to the house, but the lawn was meticulously manicured. The gravel drive left him right in front of the circular steps and he parked the car, again staring up at the facade of the Montgomery place and noting that it was freshly painted and in good repair.

Far better repair than Oakville, certainly. But then, it was larger than Oakville. Way back when, Sean thought with humor, there had been money—and then there had been *money*. The Montgomerys had managed to accrue the second kind.

He wasn't expecting to find Maggie Montgomery in, but he
had grown very curious, and since the place was in such great
shape, it didn't seem unlikely that there would be a full-time
housekeeper in residence. He strode up the steps and rang the
bell.

He wondered if the door might be opened by a Lurch-like
character right out of *The Addams Family*. At the very least,
he thought, the bell would be answered by a gaunt, dark-haired,
dour-faced woman—the housekeeper from a dozen Gothic-
type movies made back in the fifties.

His summons was answered by neither.

He was incredibly startled when a short, very round and very
cheerful woman of about fifty opened the door. She wore a
frilly apron over a simple flowered day dress. Her cheeks were
incredibly red, and her smile was quick and warm and trusting.
He hadn't come across Morticia Addams; he had stumbled
upon Missus Santa Claus.

"Hello. My name is Sean Canady. I'm looking for Miss
Montgomery. Is she in, by any chance?"

He offered her his warmest smile, his heart alive with
renewed hope that he might be asked in—even if Maggie
Montgomery wasn't here. His curiosity about her was growing
to obsessive bounds. He wanted to see her home.

"Mr. Canady, please step inside," the woman said. "The
heat today is just monstrous, and our brand-new air-conditioning system is pure heaven!"

To his pleased surprise, she stepped back. He entered through
a mud room to the grand foyer.

The house was spectacular. Typical of its time, it was built
with a great hall, or breezeway, with rooms opening symmetri-
cally to either side. The foyer itself was immense, and the
breezeway doors to the rear opened on either side of a grand
double staircase. A double set of stairs led from the ground
floor to a halfway landing point, then again to the floor above.
The wall in the center of the landing was covered with an
immense oil painting, pre-Civil War, Sean was certain, and to
each side, stained-glass windows brought the day's sunlight
streaming inside with rays of fantastic colors.

"Whoa!" he said.

"Isn't it just lovely!" the chubby housekeeper said.

Sean smiled at her. "Ma'am, it is."

"I'm Peggy, sir. You go right ahead and admire!"

He barely heard her. He was already walking deeper into the foyer, staring up at the oil painting.

It was a portrait of a woman—an exceptionally beautiful woman. Her red hair was swept up, with only a single ringlet left to curl against the expanse of her neck. She was dressed in a deep blue velvet ball gown, the neckline low, the skirt sweeping. She had been painted standing on the landing by a talented artist who had caught more than the form and grace of her beauty, but something of her inner soul as well. She was elegant, aloof, and yet there was a wistful quality within her eyes, something of wisdom, and something of innocence. The painting was breathtaking, and more. It was haunting.

All the more so, Sean thought dryly, because Maggie Montgomery was very like this painting.

"Magdalena," he heard someone say softly.

Startled, he spun around. He was amazed to see that the housekeeper had left the foyer—and that Maggie Montgomery was indeed in residence. He was annoyed to realize just how off guard he had been. All his years in the police force—and before that a stint in the army!—and she had come upon him as quietly as a puff of smoke.

He hated to be caught by surprise.

But Maggie Montgomery was smiling—amused to have so startled him.

"Why, what's the matter, Lieutenant? I'm assuming you did come here to see me."

"I was hoping to see you, but I doubted that I would find you in."

"Oh. Well, you could have called. I do have a telephone, you know."

"And the number is listed?" he inquired.

She shrugged. "You are an officer of the law," she reminded him. "Surely if you're seeking a phone number, it's easily enough done."

"I wanted to see you."

"Me, or the house?"

"The house is spectacular."

"Thank you."

"But you're more so."

She arched an amused brow. "You are incredibly good at flattery. What a glib tongue. But then . . ." She paused, looking him up and down with hazel eyes that seemed to glitter with pure golden color. She crossed her arms over her chest. She was dressed in black sandals, and a casual black knit halter dress. Her hair was swept up in a ponytail. She looked young, innocent . . . and almost at ease. "But then, you've come here to delve into my life, to search my house, and my past, and to try to discover if I might somehow be guilty of murdering a pimp a few feet from my office door. Since you've done so— invaded my premises, is that really legal these days?—it's a good thing that you're good at flattery as well."

He laughed aloud, amazed that any woman so beautiful could be so guarded—and convinced that a man might want anything but her.

"I have no evidence whatsoever against you. As to my being here, well, my father insisted I see if you were here. He's anxious to meet you."

"Oh?" He was glad to see that she seemed startled.

He nodded. "Oakville is not far from here."

"I know."

"Now I'm flattered that you know about the old Canady homestead. It's not, however, nearly so grand as this."

"Oakville is—I've heard—filled with exceptionally fine woodwork. Rumor has it that the house has been cherished by generations of thoughtful Canadys who have preserved it with exceptional care. I think you're being far too modest."

"I love Oakville, and it is outstanding."

"Ah."

"We've nothing like that, though," he assured her, pointing to the painting.

She came further into the foyer. He could see through an

open doorway that she had come from the library. Now she walked over to stand with him beneath the painting.

"Magdalena. She fell in love with the wrong man, and died young."

"How sad."

"Very," she agreed.

She turned to look at him, eyes glimmering with humor. "She was sent to Europe to bear her illegitimate child. Thankfully, though people talk, the world has always had a way of forgiving the sins of the very rich."

"Poor girl. She appears so vulnerable!"

"She was."

"Oh?" he inquired lightly. "You knew her well?" he teased.

Maggie Montgomery flushed, lowering her lashes, smiling. "I'm telling you about family lore. It was a very sad story. She fell in love with a Frenchman, a man her family didn't approve. He and his friends—a Canady among them, by the way—went after the lover. He was killed, but he had his just revenge. Magdalena was 'with child' as they said at the time, and so . . . well, she just couldn't make that proper marriage her father had intended."

Sean studied the painting. "Well, I would have to say that I'm grateful the man existed."

"Oh? Why is that?"

"Well, he must have been one of your ancestors. Without him, there couldn't have been—you."

"Flattery again, sir."

"I admit, I am obsessed."

"Umm, are you?" she murmured.

"I guarantee it."

"With sleeping with me?"

She was so challengingly blunt. He took a step back himself, arms crossed over his chest. Slowly, lingeringly, he allowed his eyes to travel the length of her body, pausing suggestively at all strategic locations. At length, he drew his eyes back to hers.

"Yes."

"You know, had we been living back in Magdalena's times,

I would have definitely been required to slap you in the face—
very hard—and demand that you leave and darken my door
no more.''

He laughed. ''Back then, I believe I might have been a
perfectly proper suitor. And, it seems, if Magdalena had it in
her hard little head to sleep with me, she would have done so.
Isn't that how the poor girl got in trouble to begin with?''

''Nothing so simple. She slept with a Frenchman. Canady.
Irish,'' she said.

Sean shrugged. ''Irish, yes, God alone knows what else.
Cajun, French, maybe even black and Hispanic. No pure blood-
lines left here anymore. In all fairness, you should know that.''

''Why?''

''You should know exactly whom you're sleeping with, don't
you think?''

''I imagine that this could be considered some kind of harass-
ment.''

''Really?''

''Are you trying to seduce information out of me?''

He shook his head. ''If information comes, all the better.
I'm trying to seduce you because . . .'' He paused, and suddenly
the bantering humor seemed to slip away from him. ''I'm trying
to seduce you,'' he told her quietly, ''because I've been on fire
since I met you.''

Her head and lashes lowered. She looked down at her folded
hands.

Sean thought they might have trembled.

''Well,'' she murmured, ''let's talk about your father. Would
you like iced tea, lemonade, a beer? Peggy will be happy to
serve us on the back porch. It's a beautiful view. Just the river.
You'd never know that there was a Burger King anywhere near
by.''

''Iced tea sounds great,'' he told her.

She nodded. ''Come on up. We'll go out to the den balcony
upstairs.''

He followed her as she started up the stairway. On the landing, he paused, startled to feel a strange dizziness. She paused,
looking back at him.

"Is something wrong?"

He shook his head. The odd sensation had already passed. He'd never felt faint in his life before—and that was a life that had seen its share of blood and guts.

"You looked as if . . ."

"As if what?" he demanded somewhat sharply. He wasn't about to falter in front of this incredibly independent woman.

"Oh . . . just as if . . . well, it is so damn hot outside. Sometimes, coming into the air . . . and then the stairs . . ."

"I'm fine!" he snapped.

She lifted her hands. "Sorry."

She turned again, continuing up the stairs and along the second-floor landing. He cursed himself. Any high school kid knew not to snap at the girl he's trying to get into the sack.

She led him to the first room on the left side of the second-story landing, a handsomely appointed office with landscape oils that must have been worth a fortune. An antique smoking stand sat next to a teak desk. Glass-covered bookshelves lined most of the walls, while much of the back of the room was taken up with French doors that stood open to the balcony beyond. A breeze lifted the rose-patterned curtains that had been halfway sashed to allow a view.

"Come on outside. I admit, I was just lazing around when you arrived."

He followed her out, thinking it seemed that she was royalty in this, her own domain. She was young to be head of a company like Montgomery Enterprises and rule such an estate as well.

The balcony looked over a manicured lawn that led down to the river. He had a feeling she owned the property on either side and even beyond the river.

Wicker lounges and chairs were set on the rear porch, along with a tea caddy. Maggie casually selected a lounge that had an open book lain on it. The latest John Grisham.

What had he expected? A copy of *Murder, Inc.?*

She sat, stretching out long, shapely legs. Golden tanned. Even as she did so, Peggy appeared, still smiling radiantly. She carried a tray with iced tea, little sandwiches, raw vegetables, and chips.

"It's so lovely to have company on a Saturday morning, isn't it, dear?" she asked Maggie.

Maggie looked at Sean, arching a brow. "Lovely. That looks wonderful, Peggy. Thanks so much."

"My pleasure, dear. Mr. Canady, enjoy."

"Thanks."

Peggy left. Sean's eyes followed her.

"She's charming," Sean said.

"Whom were you expecting as my housekeeper?" she inquired. "The ghost of Peter Lorre as Igor out of a Hammer production of *Frankenstein?*"

He grinned, taking a glass of tea and settling back himself. "Lurch—*The Addams Family,*" he admitted. It was nice here. The breeze off the river was great, cool and refreshing. He didn't just sit that often. Okay, so he worked a lot. Partied hard with the guys when he did go out.

"Peggy is wonderful. She's like a gift from heaven. I adore her."

"Has she been with you long?"

Maggie thought a moment, kicking off her sandals. "When she was very young, she worked for my mom. Then my mom did the Montgomery thing and went to Europe for a few years . . . I think I've been back now about seven years. And Peggy has been back with me since. I adore her. When I get rattled at work, she keeps things moving like clockwork here. If I travel, everything just keeps working."

"So she lives in?"

Maggie grinned. "What kind of a question is that? A prospective lover question—or a cop question? Could she have seen me wielding an axe or sword, coming home drenched in blood? Or could she possibly interrupt an intimate moment?"

He arched a brow to her, somewhat disturbed by her wariness regarding him. He could play it as nonchalant.

"Maybe the question regards both—then again, maybe it was an innocent question about your domestic situation. This is a massive place. It's amazing that even one little dynamo can keep it in such meticulous order."

She exhaled, looking out at the river, as if she might be just a little bit embarrassed she had jumped at him so quickly.

"Peggy has her own home; we remodeled the old carriage house. She lives on the property, but has her own life that way as well. Monday through Friday, she has two girls in from nine to five to help with the upkeep. Anything else?" she asked, and she looked at him, her eyes cool on his. "I'll do my best to answer what questions I can."

"Are your folks both—gone?"

"Yes. Let's see, you mentioned your father, so I assume he's alive. Your mother?"

"She died a while back. Now you—your father. He took the Montgomery name?"

"Used it daily," she said lightly.

"The men in your family don't seem to count for much," he observed.

"How rude."

"Well, your father—"

"I adored my father!" she assured him. "He was an incredible man. I can't tell you how much I loved him."

"I stand reproved!" he assured her softly.

She flushed. "Sorry. I cared for him a great deal."

"I'm glad. I'm sorry you lost him."

"He lived a full life."

"Well, I'm glad to hear that."

"Your father—what does he do?"

"He haunts me day and night—whenever he gets the chance."

She arched a brow.

"He was a professor at LSU. History. Now he reads, gardens, travels—and haunts me."

"Why?"

"He thinks I should be married, carrying on the family name."

"Ah . . . no siblings, eh?"

"One sister—who has married and procreated. Makes me look bad," he explained with a sigh.

She smiled. "Why haven't you married? Too busy following female suspects?"

He shrugged. "I almost married."

"What happened?"

"She died."

"Oh! I'm very sorry."

"So am I. But it's been a while now."

"Ah," she murmured, offering an understanding smile then. "So Dad wants you to get over it and get on in life, is that it?"

"More or less."

"So he sent you after me!" she murmured. "What a pity."

"Why?"

"I'm not the marrying kind."

"Oh?"

A smile remained about her lips. Her eyes were sparkling. They were very beautiful.

Barefoot, in her casual knit dress, her long legs stretched before her, red hair captured in a ponytail, she was stunningly, sweetly sensual.

Almost unbearably so . . .

"Well, I'm a businesswoman," she said.

"Ah. Just as well," he assured her lightly.

"Really? I'm so glad you're not distressed."

"Well, you see, I'd never give up the Canady name to father another Montgomery heiress."

"Ah!" she murmured thoughtfully, and he wondered if there wasn't just a trace of anger in her eyes. "Marriage is definitely out. Your dad will be disappointed. What about you, Lieutenant?"

He lifted his hands in teasing deliberation. "I don't know. Will you still sleep with me?"

"I don't know. Of course, you should give that some very careful consideration."

"Why?"

"Well, I could possibly conceive the next Montgomery heiress—without the blessing of the Church."

He leaned deliberately toward her, meeting her gold eyes.

"Hell, what's life without taking a few chances?" he asked her softly.

Maggie laughed out loud, shaking her head. Her cheeks were flushed, her eyes were bright. Sean made a mental note to thank his father for pressuring him into coming here.

Regretfully, he rose. There had been two gruesome murders in the parish. He had to spend some time at work.

She stood as he did, ready to see him out. He strode the few steps between them to reach her, taking her hands.

"Will you come to dinner?"

"Home to meet your dad?" she inquired.

He nodded.

"I . . ."

They had come very close. Her breath was a whisper against his lips. She was warm; she smelled intoxicatingly of a soft perfume. He hadn't meant to . . . not quite yet, but he lowered his head to hers, found her lips, and kissed her.

Gently at first. He hadn't meant to do it, and yet doing it beyond his conscious volition, he certainly didn't mean to touch her with more than the lightest brush . . .

But there was no way to kiss her lightly. She wasn't wearing a bra and the soft pressure of her breasts against his chest was alarmingly arousing. His lips molded to hers, he felt a savage thrust of passion tear into him, and he had to taste more, have more. His tongue forced entry into her mouth, ravaged, hungered. A pounding began in his temples, and he wrapped her to him, kissing, tasting, seeking. She wasn't fighting him. Her tongue played with his, lips molded to his, the length of her body seemed to supply flow against the hardness of his own. In seconds, he thought, he'd be ripping off her clothes, shoving her down to the floor . . .

He pulled away.

Just as she did.

Her lips were damp, slightly swollen. She brought shaking fingers to them, staring at him. But there was nothing accusing in her stare, nor did she seem angry.

Just shaken.

Still . . .

He knew suddenly that she was vulnerable, that a trace of innocence remained about her despite her elegance and worldliness.

And it seemed that she cast out webs that settled around his heart, drawing him ever more to her.

Madness. Obsession. He was falling in . . .

Lust.

He cleared his throat and stepped back.

"Can I pick you up at about seven?"

"I . . . I don't know—"

"All right, how about seven-thirty?"

She arched a brow. Her lashes swept her cheeks, and she smiled again. She stared up at him gravely, searching out his eyes. She seemed to come to some important inner decision.

"Seven-thirty," she said.

"Good."

"I'm anxious to meet Dad."

He nodded, and turned around quickly to leave her. He didn't want to give her a chance to change her mind.

Seven-thirty.

Dinner.

And then he was sleeping with her.

In 1860, there was life at the old Montgomery plantation again. The heiress came home from Europe; she was called Meg. She was a beautiful woman, sophisticated, confident, sure of herself, serene.

Meg was ecstatic to be in New Orleans, but she had come in the midst of tempest and turmoil. Though sane heads were trying desperately to keep the country together, war was brewing. Most Louisiana plantation owners were avidly vocal and furious against the North. Militia units formed right and left; Louisiana quickly became famous for its colorful Zouave regiments, and men and boys alike cried out that they were going to whomp the Yankees within a few weeks.

Mr. Sean Canady wasn't so sure of victory. Meg met Sean, son of Robert by his first wife, Deirdre, the very week she returned. Since he held property not far away along the river, it was fitting that he call on her, offer his condolences on the recent death of her grandfather, and welcome her home. Though he was charming and good-looking, she wasn't instantly smitten. Or so she told herself. She'd traveled, she'd seen Rome, Paris, London, Madrid. She was not easily swayed, impressed, or subdued; she was sophisticated, knowledgeable. It wasn't until he left her house that she realized she was anxious to see him again. Anxious to hear his deep, resonant voice, even his ideas, his concern that the South might have a few difficulties "whomping" the Yankees.

His mind fascinated her. As did his dedication, his passion. His underlying strength.

When John Brown was hanged for his insurrection at Harpers Ferry, most Northerners were irate, and most Southerners were elated—after all, the man had hoped to arm slaves to murder their masters in their beds, not to mention the fact that he had cold-bloodedly murdered men in the Kansas/Nebraska arena unrest, dragging them from their homes to kill them right in front of their families. John Brown might have held some lofty ideals, but in practice, he'd been a murderer, and the Northerners couldn't change that fact! But as the strife within the country increased, Sean was neither irate nor elated; he took the matter quite gravely. Yes, John Brown had deserved to hang; he had committed murder. But what had happened was an American tragedy, because they were coming closer and closer to war, and what too many Southerners couldn't see was that they had no production in the South, and that the North had an endless supply of another factor—manpower.

Every time they talked, Meg fell just a little bit more in love. She loved his light eyes, his dark hair, the way it curled over his forehead. She loved the sound of his voice, the breadth of his shoulders, his laughter. Mostly, she loved him for what he was inside, loved his soul, his intelligence, the way he thought things out, the sincere way he cared for people.

He asked her to marry him.

She turned him down. She couldn't marry. She wasn't the marrying kind. But she was enchanted with him. He said he would wait, she told him again that she couldn't marry, and yet . . . she admitted she had no desire to be with anyone else.

"I'm not the proper bride; trust me, I'm not the proper young lady for you, I can't be—"

"You are all that I want."

"But I can't marry you."

"Why?"

"I—I can't."

"You will," he promised her.

Southern boys whooped and hollered and carried on at barbecues and balls. Meg and Sean went everywhere together.

It was at the elegant Wynn town house in the French Quarter that she first met Aaron Carter.

He appeared to be a handsome young man, tall, lean, blond, and dark-eyed. He claimed to be a distant cousin of the deceased Mrs. Wynn. Meg politely acknowledged her introduction to the young man, but paid him little more attention. She had eyes for no one but Sean. Yet, as she stood at the punch table, Aaron approached her. "Miss Montgomery, you are delightful. I would call upon you, if I may?"

Startled, she met his gaze. She smiled ruefully, realizing his pursuit. "Sir, you are welcome to call, but I must inform you . . . I am nearly engaged, sir."

"Ah. To the Canady."

She nodded. "But you must be aware, we've many lovely young ladies here, and many who would enjoy—"

He stepped closer. "I would have you."

She shook her head, backing away. "I have just told you, sir—"

"It doesn't matter what you're telling me. I know who you are, I know what you are, and we are one and the same, and I will have you."

Her smile was brittle. She was furious, but determined. "I don't know what you're talking about; we are not the same in any way. And you can go to hell."

As she turned to leave him, she felt a force drawing on her. And then she knew. Knew what he was. She gritted her teeth together, and spun on him. "We are not the same. And this is my city. You, sir, would perhaps be happier living elsewhere."

"I warn you, Miss Montgomery—"

"No. I warn you. Leave this place. There is no room for you here."

"So, my dear, you assume it's your territory."

"I am fiercely fond of my family's home, Mr. Carter. You cannot imagine with what strength I can defend all that I hold sacred."

She waited.

He kept smiling. "I understand that you are a favorite with men in high places."

"Now, sir, I really don't know what you mean."

He shrugged. "Lucian, mademoiselle. I understand that you are among his . . . chosen."

"How dare you imply—"

"I imply nothing. You are favored, my beauty. But I understand as well that you seek your independence in all things, and so, trust me, his protection will only go so far. I would protect you, my dear."

"I don't want your protection. I have told you that I am nearly engaged to Mr. Canady—"

"Nearly. He is not such a man as I."

She smiled. "Thank God."

"Watch yourself, my beauty. There are rules."

"And I abide by them. I pay heed, and I bother no one else. This is my home. Understand that. You will leave?"

"You are magnificent. A challenge."

"I have told you that my interest lies elsewhere."

"I will change that."

"You refuse to listen, and you are becoming a bore, sir, and . . ."

"And?"

"Don't underestimate my power. I can destroy you."

He bowed deeply, smiling.

"See that you leave."

She had come across others in her travels across Europe and America. They had acknowledged one another, and moved on. They had never threatened. Sometimes they had talked, and almost been friends. There were the rules, of course. The rules, which kept them surviving. They must respect one another.

She stared hard at Aaron Carter, then spun again, away from him, and walked on. She met Sean in the ballroom, and danced with him, but she watched Aaron Carter.

At last, as he bid good-bye to their host, he looked for her. His eyes met hers across the room. He saluted her, again bowing deeply, taking his leave.

"What's wrong? You seem distracted," Sean said.

She cast back her head and smiled at him. "No more, Sean. No more." She felt a tremendous relief. Aaron was gone.

He had believed her; he had recognized her strength, and he had left. Thank God (if God still heard her). Life was torment enough without creatures like Aaron Carter to make matters worse.

That night, young Lilly Wynn awoke. She felt as if her name were being whispered upon the air, as if the beautiful winter's night were calling to her.

It wasn't the night. It was him. He had said that he would come to her when she had met him at the soiree. He was kin, she thought, giggling. But no matter. He was distant kin. She had warned him about Papa, and he had said that he would come in the night, and her father would never know. It was so secretive, so romantic . . . Yes, she could hear her name, he called her name.

She rose, feeling as if the air itself enwrapped her with a strange, sensual embrace. She wanted to hurry to the courtyard, to dance beneath the magical light of the stars and the moon. She was very nearly eighteen, well in a marriageable age, and anxious that her papa should give her permission to wed. Other girls her age were long married. Papa was so strict! Tonight she dreamed of a lover, of a man to come, to touch her, make her feel more of this elusive magic.

The Wynn yard was deep. Wrought-iron chairs and tables sat along tile paths. Fountains bubbled. In the far corner of the property, ornate graves and mausoleums housed the Wynn dead. She ignored them, having seen them all her life. They were but a part of her home. She looked up to the moon, to the stars. Her soft blond hair blanketed her shoulders like a cape as she spun about, and yet then . . .

She paused, suddenly frightened. Behind her . . . there was something.

No . . .

She spun about. Again. Again.

She looked to the house. It was so far away. And when she turned again, it seemed . . .

It seemed that shadows had come alive. Shadows . . . writhing, dancing among graves and mausoleums, casting darkness upon the face of an angel here, a Madonna there. The shadows twisted and curved . . .

And inched forward.

A scream rose in her throat. She had to reach the house; she had to come to her papa.

She turned, and slammed against a man. She backed away, looking upward into his face. His eyes fell upon her with a light like fire. Warmth invaded her. Yet she remained too frightened to speak.

"My little beauty!" he breathed.

She wanted to feel sensual again, as if the breeze stroked her, as if there were magic on the air.

The fear continued to choke her.

"Little one . . ."

He lifted her gown so that it fell from her shoulders. She stood naked in the moonlight. Captured by his eyes. In terror, yet unable to move. His hands brushed over her, slid over the down at her pubis, between her thighs, over her breasts again, to her throat.

"I . . . I must go in!" she managed to whisper.

"Of course."

"I must." She was vaguely aware that she was still standing there before him, naked.

"Yes."

He stepped aside. She started to walk. She felt the darkness

behind her. Felt as if shadows and evil breathed down her
neck. She quickened her pace. The air, the wicked air! Now it
felt as if it touched her with a stroke of evil, down her back,
against her neck . . .

Yet evil was tempting. So tempting.

Evil felt good.

No . . .

The breath of air against her bare flesh was erotic. The
whisper of it seemed warm against the winter, like a blaze
stoked within her soul . . .

Oh, God, oh, God, she was far too fanciful . . .

She turned, wanting to scream . . .

But no sound left her lips.

For he touched her, drew her to him, seduced; and the
warmth of her life's blood flowed between them, and the chill
of winter became the fires of hell.

Eighteen sixty-one came along, and Louisiana seceded from
the Union. Sean came to Meg's house, bursting through the
front door in a fury. Her household servants scattered, silently
disappearing. They were alone on the beautiful broad staircase
of Montgomery Plantation. He was in a rare passion, all but
breathing fire, and Meg felt a momentary unease.

"I have to go," he told her. Having money, he'd formed a
cavalry unit with himself as captain. It hadn't mattered that
he wasn't at all sure that war was right, or that the South could
win a war. This was his home; these were his people. His unit
was now being called to war, and he'd be riding away. "I
have to go, and damn you, damn you. I love you. Marry me."

"I can't!" she whispered, heartbroken.

He shook his head, his frustration and fury greater. He strode
the three steps to reach her, and swept her into his arms. He
kissed her deeply, ravaging her mouth. His hands were tearing
into her clothing, touching her, touching her more, demanding
greater and greater intimacy. Her clothing tore away, lay scattered across the stairs. His mouth moved with an urgent hunger
over her flesh until she was shivering and shaking and in a

tempest to match his own. She kissed him furiously in return, nails raking his back. She very nearly bit into his shoulder . . .

She felt the Persian stairway runner against her back, the hardness of the wood beneath it. He made love with a reckless, desperate passion, and when he was done, she found that she was sobbing, clinging to him, whispering that she loved him but that she could not marry him. Puzzled, he demanded to know why. And at last she told him that if they both survived the war, she'd explain. But marriage didn't matter. She'd be here, she'd be here waiting, and she'd love him until the end of time. That would have to be enough.

It wasn't enough, he told her, but it was all that he had. And he made love to her a second time, more gently, and yet with the same searing passion that all but stole thought and reason from her.

Then he rode away.

CHAPTER 5

Sean read and reread the police reports taken by the officers who had thus far worked the homicides. On Monday morning he'd be having his first meeting with the task force assigned to the murders, and he wanted to make sure he hadn't missed important details in any phase of the investigation.

A tourist couple had first come upon the body of Jane Doe in the cemetery. The husband's rueful statement read: "Okay, so we were warned that the cemeteries were in a dangerous neighborhood, but we weren't expecting anything like this. I'd even heard that there were bones sticking out of the graves now and then, but, oh, God, nothing like this. Nothing like this."

Pierre had made an interesting comment in his medical report: Jane Doe, laid out on a tomb as if on a bed, had been left in a very similar position and appearance to Jack the Ripper's fifth victim, Mary Kelly. Jane Doe's head had been completely severed, and though Mary Kelly's hadn't, the body mutilations were incredibly similar, down to the way that parts removed had been arranged around the body.

The photos were enough to make even the most street-hardened cop sick for a week. Luckily, the discovery of the body had been early and the young couple in the cemetery had been so shocked and horrified that they hadn't looked long before hysterically hailing a police car on the street. No one but cops—and the murderer (murderers?)—had seen the body. The police had been honest with the press regarding the fact that she had been decapitated and mutilated, but the police had carefully guarded details of that mutilation. The young couple had returned to their home—in Alaska, thank God for small favors—that very night. The wife had been sedated, and both she and her husband begged not to be identified to the press. She was hysterical, anxious not to be associated with the murder in any way. So much for tourism; Sean doubted they'd be returning to New Orleans. Still, it had been a break for the cops. Too many people wanted the sensationalism of a press interview. The young couple from Alaska had been far too afraid of the murderer.

Sean picked up Pierre's forensic report. The list of trauma to the poor, savaged body was endless. The good seemed to be that most of the wounds were postmortem. He didn't need the medical report to remember the autopsy. He'd stood by Pierre while the medical examiner cut into what was left of the body, speaking his findings to the microphone suspended above the body in an even, enunciated voice. It wasn't something he'd forget.

He set the report down, and dragged his fingers through his hair. Jane Doe, decapitated, destroyed. A pimp out on Bourbon Street. Decapitated, not mutilated. Did the killer only mutilate women? Was it even the same killer, or did they have a pair of maniacs with similar method roaming the streets. It wouldn't be the first time unrelated murders had occurred with fearfully close timing in New Orleans.

He looked over at the computer screen on his desk, then pushed the exit button with an aggravated sigh.

It wasn't that he couldn't find similar homicides across the country. The problem was that he could find far too many. The microchip had done amazing things. He'd described their recent murders for the computer, and it had seemed that the information returned to him scrolled endlessly.

He'd pushed the wrong keys, he told himself morosely. Crimes, solved and unsolved, from more than a century past had appeared. Jack the Ripper appeared on the screen, along with the New Orleans Axeman, Jeffrey Dahmer, and Theodore Bundy. He needed to try again, entering—for the time being— only the past few years' worth of unsolved crimes.

"Voodoo, hoodoo," Jack said, arriving by the side of his desk and plopping down a stack of books.

Sean looked up at him.

"Read the morning papers?"

Sean shrugged. "Under the circumstances, I think the press has been kind. Did I tell you that you had to come in here today?"

Jack grinned. "I knew you'd be in."

"Ah. Well, you're a good kid, Jack."

"I've been trying a few angles. Doing a lot of reading. What do you think of voodoo?"

Sean leaned back, arching a brow. "What do I think of voodoo? Let me see . . . okay, back a few centuries ago, slave traders dragged men out of Africa. Those guys brought pieces of an old religion with them here. For instance, a snake is important in many of the voodoo rites; it is referred to as the great Zombi. Their 'voodoo' was something they could use against their masters. Then Marie Laveau came along and made voodoo into big business. She worked as a hairdresser and used the gossip she heard to make the populace believe she knew the deep, dark secrets and desires of her clients, and had the power to 'see.' Today, voodoo is still a major source of income for many shop folk in the Quarter."

"All right, all right. Scoff, but I've been reading."

Sean arched a brow, grinning as he waited. He wasn't scoffing at the concept. Voodoo was like any other cult or magic. Sometimes, those with homicidal tendencies were influenced by the practices. And gris-gris, voodoo magic, could work off the power of the mind, just like any other so called "magic."

"The Marquis de Vaudreuil made a ruling, back in 17-something, that any slave master who allowed his slaves to congregate would be fined heavily. Slaves caught congregating could be whipped, branded with a fleur-de-lis, or even put to death.''

''Ouch,'' Sean said, and shuddered.

''So even back then, folks were damned afraid of what voodoo could do. After 1803, when the Americans took hold of New Orleans, things changed. Lots of West Indian slaves had been brought here—and naturally, we Americans were more enlightened. Slaves began to congregrate, and practice voodoo. Okay, so to some, it was an innocent form of religion.''

''Umm,'' Sean agreed. ''Lots of dancing, drinking of *tafia*—stuff nice and strong in alcoholic content. Enough people together in a frenzy and an energy is created—psychologists have studied the results of group energy among voodoos—and ye olde Shakers, too-who, incidentally, were never accused of much black magic. You can get a similar level of excitement in a good Baptist tent meeting.''

''Right. But there are documented cases where voodoos practiced a lot of different sacrifices.''

''Drinking the blood of a kid—or a black cat. Black cats can give a good voodoo some serious power,'' Sean said.

Jack cast him a serious frown in return. Sean shrugged. ''Go on, prove your point here.''

''Sean, in 1881, a pair of voodoos were arrested when they tied their son across a fire and beat him to death with a stick. In 1863, half a human torso was found in the home of a woman suspected to be a priestess.''

''Anybody can do anything in the name of religion. Look at the tortures of the Inquisition.''

''This is New Orleans, today—'' Jack protested.

''And Jack, I'm damned proud of you. You've done some good reading, and since we don't know what will turn up in this investigation, anything you've learned may prove to be important. Now, what have you learned about Jack the Ripper?''

''He was never caught, and there are a million theories as to his identity. Some Ripperologists are convinced that he might have been attached to the British Royals, and others believe he was a menial Polish worker—known as Leather Apron. Some believe he was Montagu Druit, and some believe that the Maybrick diary is true. Had the police only had today's scientific knowledge, some of the truth might easily have been proven—either to exonerate or condemn those suspected and arrested. Some say the police wanted a cover-up—especially if the murders involved the Royals in any way. However, had they had modern technology and used it, dozens of speculative books might not have been written, and the Ripper Tour in London might not be nearly so popular.''

"Helpful, very helpful," Sean said.

Jack shrugged. "There are books on Jack the Ripper in that pile as well.''

Sean leaned back. "You don't seem to think we have a copycat killer.''

Jack shrugged. "Jane Doe—ripped to shreds. Like the Ripper's last victim, not his first. I think our killer was playing. He had plenty of time with his victim, knew about Jack the Ripper's crimes, and meant to send us scurrying for books and coming up with profiles and deeply pondering the issue. Then again, this killer likes attention. We're a big, busy, multi-ethnic city. To get attention, a murderer has to go for sensationalism. This guy doesn't want a few lines in the press and a three-minute spot on the local news. He's going for the spotlight.''

Sean was silent.

"Well, what do you think?''

Sean grinned. "I think you're going to make a damn good homicide detective.''

"As soon as I quit getting sick over the corpses," Jack said.

Sean shook his head, studying the forensic reports once again. "You've got to have heart and soul for the job, kid. Trust me. Guys like Pierre give us a hell of a lot to work with, but half the battle still comes down to gut instinct. Like your last comment on the killer. He wants his crimes known. He wants to puzzle us. Play games. Keep us unnerved—which we are. We have no idea how, where, when, or who he'll strike next. God knows, so far we've been lucky. Not too many of the details on our Jane Doe are known, and people still see a pimp and a prostitute.''

"Well . . . I hate to say it, but . . .''

"But what?"

"I mean, I really hate to say it because . . ."

"Because what?" Sean demanded, exasperated.

"I happen to think she's the most exciting creature I've ever happened upon, but . . ."

"Could we be referring to Maggie Montgomery?"

"Well, frankly, we've got nothing. Not a damned thing from the cemetery—poor Jane Doe slashed to bits—and nothing that even resembles a lead. The girl died without scratching a microscopic piece of flesh from her killer. Then we've got our pimp. Dead in his Armani suit. And nothing—except a trail of minute blood drops leading directly to Miss Montgomery's building."

"And stopping at the door."

"But going *to* the door."

Sean nodded slowly, watching Jack. "Tell me, in your study of the voodoos, did you come across a cult that siphoned human blood from corpses?"

"There are lots of stories of blood lust. *Dracula*, by Bram Stoker, written in the late eighteen hundreds, was based mainly upon the legends of Vlad Dracul, the Impaler. Naturally, there are more historical tales of incredible blood lust. Take the case of Elizabeth Bathory of Hungary, late fifteen hundreds into the early sixteen hundreds, who bathed in the blood of hundreds of young virgins, searching for eternal youth and life everlasting. We had the bizarre case here of the killers who tied their victims up and drank a little blood from them day after day—and were only caught when one hysterical young man escaped. There are more. In fact, the list is probably endless. Just because we now have created phrases and descriptions for serial and mass murderers, we can't discount the historical cases of madmen and -women who were vicious criminals before we came up with modern concepts of psychology. Then remember, we are in New Orleans. We have voodoo, magic, and we also have our share of vampire cultists here as well. Last Mardi Gras, I must have seen dozens of men—and women dressed in white flowing shirts with the dark capes—and fangs, of course."

"Elizabeth Bathory, huh?" Sean said. "You have gone back in time, for sure!"

Jack flushed. "Yeah, well, I was kind of a horror fanatic as a kid. I've got all kinds of books, tapes, and CDs on vampires, werewolves, ghosts, mummies, and the like."

Sean nodded gravely. "We may need them in this one. Tell me, where does Maggie fit in with your reading material?"

Jack grinned broadly. "*Playboy*—I wish."

Sean grunted.

"I had a great time last night. In fact, I woke up feeling guilty. We're investigating two horrible murders, and I'm having one hell of a time at a jazz club."

Sean leaned back, studying Jack. "Kid, if you're going to stay in homicide, you have to learn to live in spite of the murder victims. Pierre manages to have a life despite all that he deals with. We're the only hope for justice for the victims. He can be their voice, and we can be their justice."

"That's good. A damned good thought. Not that I feel too bad for Anthony Beale—it seems that what he got might have been justice. But our little Jane Doe . . ."

"You've got a good background for her?"

"Yeah. Poor kid, needed to do something to get ahead in the world. Maybe just to eat."

"There's a soft side to you, Jack. Take care."

Jack nodded gravely, then grinned. "Yeah, and it seems there's a soft, lascivious side to you as well. You seeing Miss Montgomery again?"

Sean nodded, watching Jack. "I'm bringing her home to dinner tonight."

"Oh, yeah, no kidding? Hey, can I come? It's sure to be great conversation with your dad doing the grilling."

"He's not going to grill her; she's not under arrest."

"He's going to grill her—he's going to try to fix you up with a woman who'll be more than a pit stop for you."

"She is under suspicion, and no, you can't come."

"What if I were to bring her friend?"

"The little Creole?"

"Umm. Angie. Her name is Angie. Angie Taylor. She's one

of Maggie Montgomery's best friends, has the keys to the place, and probably knows your woman better than anyone else.''

''Is that so?''

''It's a fact.''

''And you know she'll come?''

Jack grinned. ''I do.'' He folded his arms over his chest and gave Sean a superior, king-of-the-beasts grin. ''When some of us meet a woman, we know what we're doing.''

''You slept with her already?''

''No,'' Jack admitted. ''But I did pass out on her couch. Can I bring her to dinner?''

Sean hesitated. It might make for an interesting evening. Maggie Montgomery was their only lead—however fragile that lead might be.

He didn't want her to think they considered her a lead. If she was involved, it was without her knowledge. If her building was being used, surely it was without her knowledge or consent. And yet . . .

As much as he didn't want her to be a lead, he had a strange feeling that somehow, she was involved.

No proof.

Gut instinct.

And it didn't really matter. He had to get closer to her, one way or another. He had to know.

''Bring Angie. Seven-thirty. Dad's going to barcecue out on the lawn. Make sure she isn't a vegetarian.''

It was noon when Gema Grayson called Maggie.

Gema was thirty, happily married, the young mother of two. She and Allie were a wonderful team as saleswomen and best friends. Allie was as pale as moonlight, and Gema was pure ebony. Gema had lost her own mom just before her tenth birthday. Allie filled a nice place in her life.

Gema tried not to sound concerned.

''Maggie, I hate to beother you on a Saturday, but I'm worried.''

''What's the matter?''

"It's Allie."

"What about her?"

"She isn't here."

"She didn't come in? Have you called her?"

"Well, she did come in. Coffee was on and everything was neat as a pin when I arrived. The door was unlocked. I thought maybe she'd gone next door for beignets or croissants, but Hal, behind the counter, hadn't seen her."

"Did you call her house?"

"No answer."

"Did you call the police?"

"They said they couldn't fill out reports on every woman who wandered away for a few hours."

"Did you remind them that we had a homicide just outside our doors hours earlier?"

"I did. Didn't help."

Maggie hesitated. "Gema, don't worry. I'll call the cop who came in yesterday. Are you all right there?"

"Yes, I'm fine."

"Is it busy?"

"Yes, but I'm glad to be busy."

"I'll call Lieutenant Canady and be right in myself."

"Oh, Maggie, I'm sorry, you don't have to—"

"I'm not doing anything but lying around on the porch in the sun. Allie is special, and I don't care what they say—if she isn't at work, something is wrong."

"Okay. Thanks, Maggie."

"I'll be right there."

Maggie hung up and stared at the phone. She felt a deep-seated fear, and she wanted to shake it off. She closed her eyes tightly, wondering if she wasn't making an awful mistake.

Sean's card was in her handbag. She dug around for it, stared at the numbers, then dialed. He answered with a curt "hello" on the first ring. "Sean?"

"Maggie?"

"Sean, I'm sorry to bother you now, but it seems that one of my employees has . . . disappeared. She's only been missing a few hours—we think—but she's incredibly conscientious and I'm worried. Could you—could you possibly meet me at the shop?''

"I'll be there," he said briefly.

The line was dead. Maggie stared at it, then quickly hung it up. She called out to Peggy that she was leaving, grabbed her handbag, hopped into her sandals, and hurried out of the house.

Gema tried to talk with a slim teenage girl who was asking about a custom dress for a special party she was having. She kept watching the door.

She sighed with relief as she saw the tall, handsome cop from yesterday coming toward the door, followed by his younger apprentice. She apologized to the teenager, asking her if she could come in on Monday or Tuesday when Maggie Montgomery would be in. She barely noticed whether the girl paid any attention to her or not; she hurried toward Lieutenant Canady.

Instinctively, she reached out. He took her hands. "Maggie must have called you. Thank you so much for coming. I understand that you don't usually worry about a missing person so quickly, but if you knew Allie—"

"Hey, it's all right, we have to worry about all missing persons—it's just that when they haven't been missing too long, they sometimes reappear on their own," he told her. He had a great smile. Flashing eyes that could be both stern and strangely assuring. He had a strange power, she thought. It came from within. From knowing right and wrong, from a confidence that dwelt deeply in his soul.

"Still, thanks—"

"There's an officer coming behind me who will take down information about your friend, and we'll put out an APB on her right away."

"I wouldn't want you to do anything . . . wrong."

He flashed her another smile. "One of the perks of being an underpaid and overworked cop. I can break a few rules when I want."

She already felt better.

"Maggie's on her way as well. I'm so flustered myself, I'm afraid I'll forget something important."

Canady turned to the young man standing slightly behind him. "Radio Carl in the car. Find out if he's reached Allie's home address yet."

"I'm on it," the young man said, and turned around.

"Gema, can we get you something to help you feel a little calmer. A cup of tea?" Canady asked. His smile flashed again. "Maybe a spiked café au lait? Valium?"

She smiled in return, shaking her head. "No, I'm keeping the shop open regular hours. And I'm too unnerved to calm down."

He arched a brow. "Ah, well. Good girl. So, tell me about Allie. I know I spoke with her yesterday. She's a very attractive woman, charming. Silver hair, silver eyes, slim, personable. She must be excellent at sales."

"Oh, she's wonderful! And she loves our line of clothing. We both do. Maggie's so talented."

"Yes, she is," he murmured, looking around the shop. Mannequins modeled a number of the garments. Maggie knew how to cut a dress, shirt, skirt or jacket to complement a feminine form. Even mannequins looked good in her clothing.

He turned back to Gema, still smiling. He was like the Rock of Gibraltar. She felt as if she had been drowning, and someone had thrown her a rope.

"Now . . . Allie's just never late for work, huh?"

Gema shook her head. "She was here. That's the point. She'd already made coffee. She's very proud of her coffee. Buying clothing here isn't just shopping. It's a social experience. We're in all the travel guides, you know."

"No, I didn't know. But good for you. So you believe that Allie came in and made coffee—"

"I know she did. Who else would open the doors, spruce up, and make the coffee?"

"You're probably right. It's just good to separate the 'probable' from absolute fact."

"Oh, certainly. Yes, I can see . . . ."

Gema broke off, because he was staring past her. She turned

around. A little cry escaped her. To her amazement, she saw Allie hurrying back toward the front door of the shop.

"It's Allie, right?" he asked gently.

Gema nodded. She awkwardly moved past him, hurrying to meet her co-worker as Allie burst through the door, looking very nervous and fidgety.

"Allie! I was so worried, just worried sick!" Gema said. She plowed into Allie, hugging her tightly, then pulling away.

"Oh, I know, I'm just so distraught!" Allie said, smoothing back her silver hair, then noticing that Sean stood just beyond Gema. "Oh, dear, no! You've called the police!"

"It's all right, Mrs. Bouchet," Canady assured Allie. "No harm done."

"Oh . . . of course, after yesterday . . ." Allie murmured. "I'm just so . . . so embarrassed!"

"Well . . . what happened? Where were you?" Gema demanded.

Even as she asked the question, Gema saw that Maggie Montgomery had arrived, wearing a casual black knit dress and sandals.

"Allie!" she cried, pushing quickly through the shop doorway.

"Oh, Maggie, I am so sorry—" Allie began with distress.

She didn't finish. Maggie was hugging her, stepping away, looking at her, looking at Lieutenant Canady. Something flashed through her eyes. "Did you find her?" She didn't wait for an answer, but looked back to Allie. "Oh, thank God, you're okay!"

"Quite fine," Allie said.

"No, I didn't find her," Canady informed Maggie.

"Then what—" Maggie began with concern.

"Oh, I was just about to explain!" Allie said with distress. "And I'm so sorry to have disturbed the police when we have such awful things going on in the city!"

"Maybe we should let her tell her story," Canady suggested.

Maggie glanced at the cop, biting lightly into her lower lip as she looked from him worriedly back to Allie once again. "Of course. We should have waited, except that . . ."

"Hey. We're all on edge. A man was murdered near here," Canady finished.

Gema noted that her boss was looking at the cop with both appreciation—and wariness.

"Oh, dear! And my explanation is so senseless!" Allie murmured.

"Allie, whatever it is, we're all going to be quiet now until we hear it," Canady said firmly.

Maggie cast him a fiery glance but remained silent.

Allie sighed.

"The pitiful thing is that . . . Oh, Lord! The explanation is that I don't really have an explanation. I remember being in here, making the coffee, and then . . . I think I remember going out to bring in some croissants, beignets, muffins . . . rolls. The next thing I knew, I was standing in the Square, watching a juggler! Oh, it was just awful. I remember opening the door to the place, and thinking I was just stepping down the street . . . Oh, Maggie, you should just fire me here on the spot. I must be going senile. I had a complete lapse of memory!"

"I'm certainly not going to fire you!" Maggie assured her.

"Oh, thank you, dear. I've never had anything of the like happen to me before, and I don't know at all what could have triggered such an incident, but . . ."

"Are you sure you're all right now?" Canady asked her carefully.

"She looks fine!" Gema said quickly.

"I think we should take you to the hospital."

"The hospital!" Alarmed, Allie looked quickly to Gema for help. Gema smiled encouragingly.

"Allie, maybe you were bumped on the head somehow!" Maggie said. "We need to get you checked out—"

"And have them tell us all that I'm a senile old lady?" Allie protested.

"You're not old at all," Canady told her, laughing. "Don't even say that—you'll have the rest of us catching hives if we start thinking of you as old!"

Allie flashed him a grateful smile. "I just don't know—"

"Allie, please!" Maggie insisted softly. "Please, let us bring you in. I'm not going to fire you, and I'm absolutely convinced that you're not senile. But I am worried, and I do want to make sure that you're well. And we put a drastic sum into our health care program each month, so let's make them give us a little back, huh?''

"Well, dear," Allie said, further distressed, "I don't like leaving Gema here all alone—"

"Gema is fine!" Gema insisted firmly.

The young cop had come in and he was standing quietly at the back of the store.

"Let's get Allie some health care, huh?" Canady asked. "Jack, we'll drive."

"All right," Maggie said. "She looked back to Gema. You can call Angie or Cissy now. In fact, I need you to call Angie— she called me just as I was leaving, and she's concerned. She's—she's planning on being with me tonight anyway, and I'll have to come back for my car."

"Hey! Allie is back and okay. I'm just peaches with the world," Gema assured Maggie.

Maggie flashed her a beautiful smile. Gema smiled back, thinking how she loved her boss.

Within a few minutes, the cops, Maggie, and Allie had left for the hospital.

Giddy with relief, Gema went back to work.

Darkness fell at about eight P.M.

That, not midnight, was the witching hour, Bessie Giroue thought dryly.

Kook time.

She was a working girl. She was used to crazies. Most of the time, however, she got fairly straightforward stuff. She worked through a woman with a handsome bar and restaurant on Prince Street. The place was legit—on every tourist map of the parish. Mamie Johnson just supplied a few things on the side—to the people who knew to ask.

The johns got a clean girl, regularly checked by a physician. In turn, Bessie got guys with real cash. No quick sex in a back alley for her. Well, sex was still as quick as she could make it, but she used grade-C hotels and rooming houses. Spartan but clean, with no one paying too close attention to what was going on.

Mostly, guys wanted fairly straight sex. Or oral sex. Or both. She didn't mind. She charged big time for going down on a guy, and she made 'em all wash up good first. If taking strangers into her mouth had once been repulsive, she had long gotten over that. Sometimes she came across a real nervous married man who just wanted a single doubles fling with his wife or girlfriend. Those occasions she usually found amusing. The guys usually lost it just watching her come on to their women— she was good at it. If you could take a stranger into your mouth, it was no big deal doing a woman. Women tended to be cleaner than guys. It was just a job. Work. Paid so much better than filing in an office or waitressing.

Every once in a rare while, she hit a real kook. Some pathetic case who wanted her putting him in handcuffs, spanking his bottom, and calling him Big Daddy. And every once in a while, she got ahold of a john who wanted to spank her.

There were clubs in New Orleans that offered just about everything. Those into the stuff that really hurt usually knew where to go to get it.

So business was pretty much usual.

She was a working girl. She had a kid to support. A great kid; he was just four now. Her one venture into "true love." True love had sucked. She'd done everything for him, and anything. Great at first. Then he'd used her, and left her. She'd learned a good lesson. Might as well get paid for all the things she'd already done. And another good thing had come out of it, though she'd almost starved until she'd gotten going in the trade. Her son. She adored her baby boy. And if she worked things right and saved her money, she could quit the business and move to Iowa or something before he got old enough to know how she was supporting him.

She was so tired that night. She nearly called Mamie, ready to beg off, saying she was ill. But if she called in, Mamie would remember when the big spenders were in town.

So she was taking the john. And as she hurried toward the hotel, she was shaking her head, looking at the sky. Queer sky tonight. It wasn't quite dark—it would be any minute. The sky was blood red. The moon was already out. Great. The guy was going to be a kook.

She tried to cheer herself up by reminding herself that kooks often paid damned well.

When she reached the hotel, the sky was still red, but darkening. A jazz trumpet was blaring from somewhere nearby. The music in the neighborhood got louder and louder, the later it got. She wondered how anyone ever slept in the hotel.

She made her way through the lobby. The guy on duty at the desk didn't even look up. Either he didn't hear her, or he just didn't give a damn.

As Mamie had instructed, she opened the door to room number 13. It was dark inside. As she reached for the light, she heard a husky voice.

"Leave it."

"Hey, it's really dark," she protested.

"There's light from the window."

"Sugar, you don't need to be shy. I'm here to make your fantasy, and it don't matter to me if you're beautiful or not," she purred. She was startled to realize that she wanted to see this guy. He had a great voice.

He moved slightly. She saw his silhouette in front of the window. He was tall, lean, seemed to have all the right body parts. "Move on in. Where I can see you," he told her.

She did so, setting her handbag down on the floor. She was a medium tall brunette with a good, firm body. Nice breasts, tight butt. Worth what she charged, she had determined.

Now he was in the shadows again. She felt the red light from the strange sky and a dozen glaring neon lights blazing in on her. "Well . . . let me see more of you."

"Sure, sugar, sure," she said huskily. She liked his look, and she liked his tone. He might not be so bad. There was even something about him that seemed erotically, *dangerously,* sexy. Hmm. She hadn't felt like this about a john in a long time.

No, never.

She was wearing a blouse with ties in the front, a short skirt, garter, bra, stockings, and four-inch heels. She untied the blouse slowly, imagining that she probably looked pretty damned good in the weird light. Business, she reminded herself. She always got it over with first.

"Sugar, let's just get the paperwork out of the way, huh? A straight shot is one hundred. Double it if you want a little tongue. And if there's anything else . . ."

"Baby, I assure you, I'm a straight shooter," he told her.

She shimmied out of the blouse. Then the skirt. Then she tossed off the shoes. Hell. She wasn't bad at all at this part. She should have been a stripper with johns on the side.

"That's fine, honey . . . just fine."

She leaned forward, freeing her stockings from her garters, doing so in a way that pressed her breasts high, together. One and then the other. She shed the stockings. Straightened.

She nearly gasped out loud. He was behind her. Close behind her. Up against her, his fingers feathering over her, her thighs, belly, breasts, throat. For a moment, she closed her eyes. It was almost like making love. God, she had sex every day, but she could barely remember *making love.*

Then he moved, suddenly, violently. Her panties were ripped away. Hot kisses seared her back. His hands were savage. All over her. He was within her, without.

They were down upon the floor. She was writhing, jack-knifing, desperate for more of him.

Ridiculous. She was the whore. The professional, she told herself. She was panting like a schoolgirl, soaking wet, reaching pinnacle after pinnacle. She was hot, dripping, and his kisses continued along her neck and spine, delicious, just a little hurtful as he nipped against her flesh, bathed it again with kisses . . .

Harder. Liquid heat streamed down her back. She moaned, feeling delicious.

Then a curious, recognizable scent came to her nostrils. She felt sticky.

Then she realized what it was . . .

Blood, her own blood, pouring from her while he lapped it

up. He was licking it from her flesh, as he'd lick an ice-cream cone.

She froze, not alarmed at first, she still felt so euphoric, there was no pain . . .

But there was so much blood. She tried to scream.

She had no voice, no strength, and he was laughing huskily.

She saw him open his mouth. Saw the glitter of white.

Then his eerie kiss touched her again, and for just a split second, she was aware that blood bubbled from her throat and that . . . and that he was thirstily drinking it . . .

Then, mercifully, she knew no more.

CHAPTER 6

Sean was both pleased and curious to see the way Maggie worried about Allie Bouchet. Even after the doctors had examined Allie and proclaimed her quite all right, Maggie continued to fuss over her, insisting that she stay overnight in the hospital for observation. One of the young physicians on duty, a Dr. Garcia, seemed to think that Allie's blackout might have been due to too much sun, and he agreed with Maggie that a night in the hospital might be a good thing, just to keep Allie under observation. If she was really concerned with her memory loss, however, it might be a good thing if she made an appointment with a specialist.

Maggie smoothed back Allie's hair, gently took her chin, and surveyed her face from every angle, still appearing worried. But at last, she seemed satisfied that the older woman was going to be all right. She allowed Sean and Jack to lead her from the hospital. And, seated next to Sean in his unmarked police car, she apologized for bothering him.

''I suppose that's why the police want a 'missing person' to prove to be really missing before becoming involved in stacks of paperwork. I am sorry, Sean, Jack. I suppose you two had much better things to do than spend your afternoon on a woman with a touch of sunstroke!''

"It's all right," Jack told her, leaning forward.

"But you have two serious homicides—and I'm sure there are more crimes in New Orleans—''

"There are," Sean said, looking at Jack through the rearview mirror. "But Jack and I have been assigned especially to these two cases." He shrugged. "There's really not nearly so much work when a drug pusher kills a middleman who won't pay up, or when a husband freaks out and shoots his wife for shrinking his favorite bowling shirt in the dryer. We have a number of homicide detectives as well, so don't worry about taking up our time."

Grinning, Jack leaned his chin on the seat as he spoke to Maggie who turned around to smile and listen to him. "What Sean is trying to say is that we really haven't any viable clues, and so we may as well spend our time harassing you. We've a lot of stuff out at labs, but nothing back in from them yet. Sean has stared at dead bodies just about as long as is humanly possible, and it's Saturday, and we've both put in almost seventy hours already. And they gave us both titular promotions to keep from paying overtime, so hey, this was an okay way to spend the afternoon. And you know what?''

"No, what?" Maggie asked him, grinning.

"I invited myself to Sean's house, and your friend, Angie, is going to come along with me."

"Is she? Great. She didn't tell me."

Sean met her eyes in the mirror. "Want to just come along home with me now?" he asked.

She hesitated, then shook her head. "Hot day. I think I'll shower and wear jeans tonight—bugs like barbecues, too.''

Sean shrugged. "As you wish.''

He left her in front of her shop, watching as she waved, then went in to talk to Gema, giving the younger woman a report on her friend. Gema seemed relieved. She was picking up the coffee pot and cups. It seemed that Maggie Montgomery was going to give her a hand in closing.

"What are you waiting for, what do you think we'll see?"
Jack asked.

Sean shook his head. "I don't know. I don't know anything
at all that's going on, but . . ."

"But what? One of those 'gut' things?" Jack asked.

"Yeah," Sean said quietly. "Yeah." He put the car back
into gear.

Gut reaction. Jack had been right. He was actually doing the
only thing he could do as a good cop. He was spending as
much of his time as he could with Maggie Montgomery.

Dinner was delightful. Jack had indeed invited both himself
and Angie, and apparently, Maggie thought, Sean must have
decided that he should take it a step further and make it the
same group they'd had the night before. The incredibly tall,
black, and handsome Mike Astin had been invited, along with
Cissy Spillane. It was comfortable for her to be with her friends.

Maggie wondered if it was comfortable for Sean to have two
extra police officers on hand.

Sean's father, Daniel, was nearly as tall, broad-shouldered,
and striking as his son. His hair was just dusting with dignified
gray; the creases at the corners of his eyes added a depth of
character. He'd invited a friend as well, Anne-Marie Hunting-
ton. She was perhaps fifty or fifty-five—a one-time flower
child, so it seemed, for her light hair had aged to a soft platinum,
and she wore it parted in the middle and long and straight down
her back. She was dressed in a soft, flowered, ankle-length
gown in a flowing material, and was slim and pretty. She
seemed exceptionally at peace with herself, a pleasant quality.
They talked while Cissy and Angie took a walk down by the
river and the men drank beer and hung around the barbecue.
Maggie learned that Daniel's lady was a librarian, and that she
had a love for both the classics and modern fiction. Maggie
could well imagine that an academician like Daniel would get
along well indeed with the serene librarian.

"I must admit," Anne-Marie told Maggie, sitting across a
picnic table from her on the back lawn of Oakville, "I jumped

at the chance to meet you. Oh, not that I don't enjoy Saturday nights with Daniel as it is, but ..." She paused, shrugging ruefully and sipping her wine cooler. "Well, we do have a great deal of literature on your family. I've always wanted to meet you."

Maggie lifted her hands, smiling in return. She was puzzled, and just a bit uneasy wondering what literature the library might have on her family.

"Well, I'm in business right in the French Quarter," Maggie reminded her. "You could have come by and introduced yourself."

Anne-Marie laughed softly. "Oh, dear, no! I couldn't do such a thing. I'm from an old Southern family, and my mama would have slapped my hand had I ever thought to do anything so rude as to walk in anywhere and introduce myself—for the sake of my curiosity."

"Well, we've been introduced. And please, you're welcome to come by anytime. You might enjoy my offices. We've got design sketches that are decades old, fashion magazines from the eighteen hundreds . . ."

Daniel Canady slid onto the wooden bench alongside Anne-Marie. "I hope I'm included in that invitation."

"Naturally."

"Thank God," Sean murmured, setting a massive platter of ribs, chicken, burgers, and hot dogs on the table. "He'd be asking me to come up with a search warrant to get in, now that he knows we've met."

"Children," Daniel said to Maggie, flashing her a warm smile. "They can be so annoying."

Anne-Marie hopped up. "Let me go for the bread and the salads."

"I'll help," Maggie said.

By the time she came from the kitchen, bearing a tray of potato salad from the refrigerator, Cissy and Angie had returned, and were ready to help bring out the side dishes while the meat remained smoky warm. For the next several minutes, they all fixed their plates, reaching across one another.

Despite the fact that the sun had set, Oakville's lawn area

seemed remarkably free from bugs. The moon was full, big, and strangely, beautifully red in the night sky—it was because the sun took a while to set on these late-summer nights, Daniel explained. Sean argued the point with him lightly, and the two bantered back and forth. It seemed a nice relationship, and it gave Maggie a moment of nostalgic pain. She missed that kind of love.

They avoided talk of the murders, the guests all compliment-ing Daniel on his barbecue. "My own sauce," he assured them modestly, smiling across the table at Maggie over a rib, "Thank God you're not one of those will-o'-the-wisp women with no flesh on her bones!"

"Dad!" Sean laughed in protest. "It sounds as if you're implying—"

"That she does have meat on her bones. In all the right places, naturally. Although Americans do need to cut down on their consumption of red meat, meat is important to most diets. We are carnivorous creatures; we need only study the teeth God gave us. But young ladies are so diet conscious these days! I was afraid you'd be a vegetarian!"

Maggie smiled, arching a brow to Sean. Looking back at Daniel, she shook her head. "Oh, no. I love meat. I truly enjoy a good steak, the rarer the better."

"Ah, well, good, good for you!"

By the time they had finished eating, the bugs were beginning to come out, and they moved inside for coffee and the crème brulée Anne-Marie had made. They sat around Oakville's library, a beautiful room with hand-carved shelving and cozy window seats. Sean sat beside Maggie on one of the love seats, sipping strong coffee. She was amazed at how natural it felt to be with him. How warm. He'd showered, and he smelled invitingly of soap and after-shave. He wore cut-off jeans and a tank top, and though he was completely casual, his clothing emphasized the sleek strength of his body. She was alarmed by the strength of the sexual urges that burned through her each time his shoulder brushed hers, or his knee touched hers, or just when he looked at her and smiled, a slow-burning fire subtly glowing deep within his eyes.

She swallowed, looking across the room to the great oak desk where Daniel had been poring through some of his very old books, giving them all bits and pieces of Louisiana and New Orleans trivia through the decades.

"Here, Son, not that the tragedies of times gone past give you any pleasure, but here's a piece on the New Orleans Axe Man. They think he killed thirteen people, and though the relative of one of the victims claimed to have shot and killed the killer, the police never knew the truth." He looked across the room at Sean, his eyes bright over the rim of his reading glasses.

"Dad, they didn't have half the techniques we have now," Sean reminded him.

Daniel shook his head. "Some crimes are never solved. You know that. You have open cases on your books. These murders have just occurred. It takes time to catch criminals. Weeks, months—years, in some instances."

"Yeah, but we've got to solve these murders quickly!" Jack said.

"We'll be victims of the good citizens of New Orleans if we don't," Mike Astin agreed.

"Hmm. Are there good citizens in New Orleans, do you think, Miss Montgomery?" Daniel queried her lightly.

"Oh, definitely! And like good citizens everywhere, they battle the crime beneath their noses and try to make it a better city," Maggie assured him.

Daniel sat in the swivel chair behind the desk. "Now, it all depends on what we see as crimes, right?"

"Well, naturally," Maggie agreed.

"Okay, Dad, what's the moral dilemma we're getting to now?" Sean asked.

Daniel stretched out a hand, indicating the book. "All right, let's ponder this. In 1862, New Orleans is taken by the Yankees. Now, we all know that there were lots and lots of good, moral Yankees, men of character and concern. Unfortunately, one of the men taking charge of New Orleans under martial law definitely did not seem to be among their number. I refer to—"

"Beast Butler!" Jack interrupted.

"Precisely! Now, the Southern ladies of New Orleans still have kin out on the battlefields—brothers, fathers, husbands, lovers . . . so they're not friendly to the invading soldiers. All right, they are downright rude, stepping off sidewalks if the soldiers are on them, spitting upon occasion. Still, nothing that an invading soldier wouldn't understand. But old Beast Butler puts out an order about the behavior of Southern women. Any lady acting so rudely to the Yankees was to be considered a prostitute, and treated as such."

"Now, that's rude," Angie murmured.

Daniel smiled. "There was a Yank soldier who took Butler's order to heart. He was most probably guilty of several rapes before he picked up a young girl named Sandra Hill. She most probably put up quite a fuss and gave the soldier one fierce battle. In his efforts to quiet her, he killed her."

"Poor thing. How awful!" Cissy said. "Back then, I assume he was executed right away."

Daniel shook his head. "No. The Yank was arrested, but an investigation determined Sandra to be a woman of loose morals—since she had been rude to the soldiers. The soldier was chastised and given a dishonorable discharge while poor little Sandra lay rotting away."

"That's horrible, pure and simple. So what is the moral dilemma here?" Jack asked.

"What happens next," Anne-Marie advised.

"While the Yank soldier is being held, some good citizen of New Orleans took the law into his—or her—own hands. The room where he was being kept was broken into late at night. He was found the next morning—beheaded by a broadsword stolen off his sleeping guard."

"Grisly," Cissy said, shuddering.

"But was it justice?" Sean asked softly.

"My point. Was his murder a crime, or was it justice? Naturally, that's a debate we go through continually here in the States. When we execute a criminal, are we equally guilty of murder? And if not, was the Yankee soldier's death murder—or justice?"

"Was the killer ever found?" Maggie asked.

Daniel looked at her, smiling, shaking his head. "Never. If the good citizens of New Orleans knew anything about the killing, they never breathed a word. The whole incident was kept hushed, Beast Butler was finally removed from New Orleans. Naturally, we've other such interesting cases. One involves your family, Maggie."

"Really?" Sean turned toward her. "Do you know what he's up to now?"

Maggie nodded, smiling at Daniel. "I think so." She laughed, realizing that the light in the library was low, only the desk lamp giving any real illumination. Outside the handsomely draped windows, the night sky still seemed to be glowing with deep red overtones. All eyes were on her.

"One of my great-great—I'm not sure how many greats— grandfathers—was accused of murdering a French nobleman." She grimaced. "Apparently, he thought the man was a vampire."

"Really?" Jack laughed. "Oh, well, this is New Orleans."

"Did he kill the nobleman?" Jack asked.

"I'm not sure. He was very rich, and had a lot of power in the community. If he killed the man, he had the sense to get rid of the body."

"Nothing was ever proven against Jason Montgomery," Daniel informed them. "It seems that the young nobleman was after Montgomery's daughter, Magdalena."

"Ah! The lady on the stairway landing!" Sean said, looking at Maggie with an even greater interest.

Maggie smiled. "The very one."

"Some say that despite the fact Jason Montgomery lived and worked here, he didn't trust Frenchmen in the least. And the Frenchman most probably seduced young Magdalena. She did disappear to Europe soon after and bore a child, so rumor goes."

"There is, of course, the possibility that the Frenchman merely returned to France—and that Magdalena later joined him, and that the whole thing is nothing but a great, late-night story," Maggie said dryly.

"But it is a good story. The young lover slain by the young

beauty's father . . . the girl leaving, never to return. Perhaps she never forgave her poor father for slaying her lover. Who knows?'' Anne-Marie mused.

''There's another little twist to that story,'' Daniel said, winking at Maggie.

''Oh, yeah?'' Sean asked, his eyes alight with amusement.

''I think,'' Maggie said slowly, ''that your father is referring to the fact that Jason Montgomery wanted to have his daughter married to a Canady.''

''Well, it's a good thing they didn't marry,'' Sean stated, watching her with a warmth that was absurdly arousing. ''We'd be related.''

''Well, there was another occasion when a Canady nearly married a Montgomery. During the war. Apparently, our family hero—he with the statue in the Quarter—was deeply in love with the Montgomery heiress. And she adored him, so the story went.''

''What happened there?'' Angie asked.

''Well, now, Angie, surely, you know the answer to that one! That's why there's a statue to the man—he was a valiant soldier who supplied his own company with arms and horses, helped supply the city, defended his men at great risk to his own life—and was finally killed trying to defend the city.''

''How sad. How tragic,'' Cissy said.

''How strange. How did the family name continue? Ugh. Are you two related?'' Angie asked Maggie.

''No!'' Maggie protested.

''Sean had been married several years before he'd met Miss Montgomery. His wife died of smallpox, but left him with a son.''

The room seemed very silent. Then the breeze knocked one of Daniel's books off the desk. The thud caused everyone in the room to jump. Except Sean. Maggie felt his fingers squeeze around hers and rest on her knee as the others laughed, suddenly aware that they'd been sitting and listening like children around a campfire while a counselor told ghost stories.

''Maggie, honey, I just never knew how interesting your family was!'' Cissy informed her.

"I imagine all families are just as interesting," Maggie said. "The Montgomerys kept coming back to New Orleans, so it's easy to find all the skeletons in our closets."

"Now, Miss Cissy Spillane, you had an ancestress who was extremely close to the old voodoo queen, Marie Laveau," Daniel said.

"I know!" Cissy said, wincing.

"Was she a good voodoo?" Angie asked.

"I think she was a spy for Marie Laveau. Marie's power was in what she knew about people—she knew things about them because she kept their servants busy listening and watching what was going on! Supposedly, though, my great-great— I don't know how many greats!—grandmother was a power in herself. She danced wickedly with the great Zombi, the snake, and she could threaten and cajole a great deal of money from her own followers. Supposedly, she cursed a man to death. And she nearly hanged for it, except that the magistrate didn't believe in voodoo, so she was set free. Thank God. Or else I wouldn't be here. The man she married was one of the witnesses who testified on her behalf."

"Now, that's a good story," Maggie stated. "Wonderfully romantic."

"The Montgomery women sound nicely romantic," Sean teased.

"Kind of hell on the Canadys, though," Jack observed dryly.

Sean smiled at Maggie. "I'm willing to take my chances."

She smiled back.

Uneasily.

She asked him in for a drink once they reached her house.

Sean wasn't sure she really wanted him to come in. She seemed uncomfortable.

Inside the plantation house, she led him through one of the right side doors, through a large formal dining room to what had become a huge kitchen in contemporary times. There was a window seat half the length of one wall with a patterned yellow seat cushion that matched the cheerful draperies. Copper utensils hung from wooden rafters above an island work station. It was an attractive, warm, friendly room that would have done any cook proud. The kitchen table was a butcher-block affair, as unostentatious as the rest of the room. Maggie bid him draw a chair at the table while she searched through her refrigerator and cabinets.

"I should offer you something to eat, despite the fact that your father served a feast! Let's see, cookies . . . grapes? And what can I get you? Coffee? Or a drink? Maybe spiked coffee would be in order . . . I can make a great café au lait."

She was ducked down with her head in the refrigerator. Sean eschewed the chair she had offered, and came around to stand behind her. He set his hands on her hips. She froze, straightening. For a moment, he felt the pulse of her blood, felt as if he touched the fire racing through her. Then she slipped from his arms.

"Sombreros," she stated, taking glasses from a cabinet. She reached to the rear of a counter where there were several bottles of liquor, and she dashed a splash of Kahlúa into each glass. "Sean, could you get the milk, please?"

He obliged, handing her the carton. She topped off their drinks, handing him one.

He remained close by her, watching her. She swallowed down her drink in a gulp. He set his on the counter, reached for her determinedly, and kissed her.

No holds barred. He slipped his hands down around her buttocks, pressing her against his growing arousal. He moved his hand up her back to the nape of her neck, fingers threading into her hair and cupping her head while he pressed his tongue deeper and deeper into her mouth. She tasted sweetly of Kahlúa. The subtle aroma of her perfumed flesh was intoxicating. Her nipples seemed to burn through all the fabric between them and press into his chest. He felt her soften, weaken, melt against him. Felt her fingers in his hair, down the length of his back. Her mouth met his hungry kiss. Tongue plundered along with his. Hot, wet, sweet. She trembled. He slid his fingers into the waistband of her jeans, drawing them around the front, where he loosed the button and tugged on her zipper.

She pulled back, her head lowered. "I . . . I think you should go now."

He didn't force her. "Why?" he asked.

She looked up at him. Her beautiful eyes were strangely glistening with a hint of tears. "Jack warned you," she said flippantly. "Montgomery women are hell on the Canadys."

"Though I pity my poor ancestors, I thank God."

"Really, Sean—"

"I've stated that I'm willing to take my chances."

"You just can't expect too much!" she whispered. "You can't want too much!"

She spun away from him, walking through the house. He followed her. She was already headed up the stairway. "You can see yourself out," she called to him.

He watched her for a moment, then swore. "No!" he told her angrily, striding up the stairs as well. He caught her on the center landing, gripping her by the shoulders. "Damn you, no! There's something here between us, something different, something special, and I'm not going to let you throw it away— because I'm a cop!"

Her eyes lowered. She tried to wrench free from him, but he held her tightly. She looked up at him again, eyes now a gold fire of both anger and pain. "That's not—"

He didn't let her finish. He kissed her again. Kissed her so that she couldn't speak. Cupped her jaw, stroked her cheek, her throat. Forced her against him. Once more, she seemed to melt against his body. Grow weak. He pressed his advantage. The few buttons on her tailored shirt gave easily. He was good at bra hooks. Her breast spilled into his hands and he worked her nipple until she was whimpering against the force of his kiss. Once again, he thrust his hand into her pants, forcing her jeans down, rubbing, probing. He stroked through pubic hair, finding the warm center of her with his fingers.

He thought that it might have been a long, long time since she'd had sex. She seemed on fire, despite her protest. Hot, a million degrees hot, wet, falling against him. His lips broke from hers at last as he eased her down upon the stairway landing, fleetingly glad of the rich Persian runner as he hastily slid off her sandals and pulled down her jeans and exotic lace panties. He rose over her, seeing her eyes again, listening to her feeble protest.

"Sean, really . . ."

He touched her lips again, licking, nibbling, tasting, teasing as he briefly struggled to discard her already opened blouse and bra. When she was naked on the exotic carpet, he paused, looking at her. God, she was stunning. Tiny waist, flaring hips, flat belly, deep, fire-red pubis, long, long legs. Her breasts were full, her nipples large and deep rouge, hardened now to little peaks. Again he lowered himself over her, tasting each nipple, tugging with his lips, grating with his teeth. Her arms came around him. He found her lips again, but then lowered himself against her body. He spread her legs, settling between them. He licked, kissed and caressed her sweetness while she writhed and gasped out unintelligible words . . . then shrieked, trembling with a wild force as she climaxed.

He hastily ripped open his button-fly jeans, and settled on top of her, thrusting into her wet warmth, so aroused by then that he moved with blind hunger and the speed of a jackrabbit. Yet her legs wrapped around his waist, her hands fell against him, and she arched and twisted with abandon to meet him, her passion rising again to meet his. God. Oh, God. Friction was ecstasy. Her heat spilled all around him. He came with a violent force, jerking spasmodically into her again and again. Empty, as sated as a drunk, he fell to her side, somewhat stunned by the sheer, volatile force of the passion they'd shared.

She lay at his side, trembling slightly. He thought that she might be cold. Then he realized that he'd rather forced the issue on her stairway. He turned to her. She seemed somewhat stunned herself, almost like an innocent who had just discovered the secret so many grown-ups shared—that sex could be a sensation like no other. Her eyes were still so shimmering, liquid gold. Her body was bathed in a fine sheen of sweat. Damn, so perfect. Even after everything, he looked at her breasts, her waist, the sleek ivory perfection of her belly, the fire red triangle at her thighs, and felt arousal beginning all over again.

"I'm not sure whether to say 'wow!' or 'I'm sorry,' Maggie,'' he told her softly, and he was glad when she smiled. She reached out and stroked his cheek.

"Wow!" she told him in a husky whisper.

"Good!" he murmured, feeling a rich contentment seep into him.

Her smile deepened. "No, that was my wow! You can come up with your own again anytime you want."

He laughed, rising on an elbow, pulling her against him. He kissed her lips, her forehead. "God," he breathed. "Just touching you, seeing you . . ."

"I do have a bedroom," she told him.

"Now I am sorry. Rug burn?" he asked her.

"Worth it," she told him solemnly.

He rose, halfway buttoning his jeans so he wouldn't trip and make an ass of himself on the stairway. Then he reached down for her, glad that police work forced a man to stay in shape. He lifted her effortlessly into his arms, keeping his eyes on hers as he started up the rest of the steps.

"Which way?" he asked.

She pointed to the left side of the house, smiling, her arms around him. "Second door, right side of the hallway," she told him.

He pushed open the appropriate door. Red moonlight spilled into her room from the balcony windows. He saw the shadows of furniture against the walls, a small table before the windows, a large four-poster bed against the rear wall. He ripped down the elegant satin spread and laid her upon the sheets in a field of pillows. He shed his own clothing quickly. She watched him.

Then he came to her, and she rose to her knees to meet him. Her kisses bathed his chest, his shoulders. Her fingers feathered over his flesh. He had thought that he'd been aroused before . . .

Her hands closed over his sex. Stroked. She pressed him back. She bathed the length of him with the delicate lap of her tongue. Took him deeply into her mouth. He shouted hoarsely, grabbed her roughly, dragged her beneath him, surged into her. And while he moved, they kissed. Embraced. Her lips teased his shoulders. Her nails raked his back as she cried out.

Her teeth just grazed his flesh . . .

They spent the majority of the night awake, tiring, then awakening, becoming sated, glutted, then aroused again and again.

Then, limbs tangled together, they slept.

When Sean awoke, she was gone.

He rose quickly, stumbled around for his jeans, calling her name.

There was no answer. He looked through the house, noting that she had collected her own clothing from the stairway. Paused up on the landing, he looked up again at the magnificent painting of Magdalena. They'd made love that first time beneath the painting. On a strange note of whimsey, he hoped that her long-dead ancestress had approved. He saluted the painting.

"Ridiculous, but I am in love, you know?" he said lightly. He hurried on to the kitchen. Still no sight of her. Coffee had been made. He poured himself a cup.

He looked out the rear window and at last saw her, standing down by the river, wearing an ankle-length, sleeveless dress. The material floated softly around her in the breeze. Her hair was loose, and as she sipped coffee, she stared thoughtfully at the water.

He let himself out, walking quickly along the porch and across the lawn to the water.

"Maggie?"

She turned to him, a smile curving her lips, but a worried expression on her face.

"What's wrong?" he asked her.

She shook her head. "It's not that anything is wrong, it's just that . . ."

"Maggie, please, if you think there is a Montgomery curse on the Canadys or the like, please—quit thinking."

She looked out across the water. "I'm just afraid that we've rushed things. I think I need to step back. I . . . I'd appreciate if you would leave now."

It was the last thing he'd expected after the night they'd spent together. "Maggie, something is really right here—"

"Sean, I think we've rushed it. And I'd like a little space. Please."

He nodded, amazed that he could be so hurt—and probably not taking it very well. In fact, his attitude was sadly immature. "Hey, fine. Whatever you say. Sex is sex, right? Well, thanks for a few damned good fu—"

"Sean, don't, this is not easy for me!" she whispered.

"Sorry. I still may have to call on you in the murder investigation. The blood drops did lead to your door. Anyway, thanks for a fun night. And by the way—if you should realize that what we had was really damned good, you call me. If I'm available, we'll do it again."

He turned around, striding angrily away from her.

"Sean . . .!"

He thought that she might have called his name. Softly. But his male ego was fiercely wounded.

And he kept walking.

1862

Captain Sean Canady was perplexed, irate, and sickened.

War was one thing.

Murder was another.

War was ugly. It was blood and bullets, and tattered, ragged flesh. It was the tragic waste of human life, the defilement of youth and beauty. It was the stench of blood, the screams of the dying and wounded. It was ugly and horrible, a travesty, and still, it wasn't so chilling as what had been happening lately.

The Union meant to take New Orleans. The Mississippi was like a great artery to the South, pumping life's blood throughout the land, supplying the populace and soldiers alike with food, medicine, and arms, and New Orleans near the great mouth of the mighty river. Take New Orleans, and break the back of the South. Cripple her.

It was an awful concept.

It was happening.

While much of the fight was being waged upon the water,

*and the Rebs fought valiantly against Union naval strength,
there were pockets of fierce fighting on land.*

*Fierce . . . indeed. He had lived for those few precious times
when he dared steal a few hours to be with her. He loved her,
adored her, survived for her. She wasn't just succor against
the storm; she listened, she understood, she seemed to have
the wisdom of the ancients. She understood his battle strategy,
and though he heard her cry soft tears when he left, she never
begged him to stay.*

*With New Orleans precariously close to falling, he had hid-
den nothing from her. He had poured out his heart to her,
telling her even about . . . the hideousness of the murders.*

*Over the last few months, each time the desperate fighting
around the city let up, and each time they were able to come
for the wounded, they found that the wounded had been killed.
Slashed to death with a saber. Horribly hacked and mutilated.*

*"I've tried to discover what is happening. I came upon one
poor boy once . . ."*

*He lay with his head against her pillow, staring at the ceiling.
She was at his side, on an elbow, close and offering comfort,
not touching him, listening so gravely.*

*"He told me that the colonel had come. That was all he
could say. 'The colonel came.' Doc Jenkins, our company surgeon, told me that they'd had something of the like happening
farther north on the western edge of the fighting. He thinks
maybe we've got ourselves some kind of a fanatical traitor on
our own side . . . you know, a high-ranking officer who really
supports the North. My father's old boyhood friend, Elijah
Wynn, commanding Company B, said he heard something of
the like occurring along other fields of battle. Oh, Jesus. A
madman, fighting on our side. Then killing our boys. But, oh,
God, my love, you should see what he's doing to them . . ."*

*"Sean, dear God, hush, hush, for now!" she told him, slip-
ping down to encompass him in her embrace, her cheek against
his chest as she held him. "My love, you must take care—"*

*"I must find out what is happening. My men are willing
to die for a cause; I'm not willing to see them senselessly
murdered."*

"Yes, but you must be careful. Your men cannot spare you."

"I won't die," he told her, smiling crookedly. "I have to live. For you. For us."

When he kissed her good-bye, Sean was suddenly, strangely afraid. For her. She had an unsettling look of determination about her.

"You should go into the city," he told her.

"I'm afraid the Yankees might be there too soon," she said, wrinkling her nose.

He laughed. "There are some good Yanks, you know."

She shrugged. "Maybe."

"There are. We both know it."

"Yes, we both know it. But I'm a Southern girl. In love with a Southern boy."

"Promise me that you'll take care, you'll not be caught unawares when the bloodshed comes too close!"

"I swear it, my love."

He kissed her again.

"I'll be watching over you!" she whispered.

He pulled away, eyes narrowing. "What?"

She shook her head.

"You're always in my heart," she told him.

Dusk.

Pale light dying against the horizon, being subdued by the colors of night. Darkness came slowly, fighting the strange shades that streaked across the sky, pastel pinks, soft yellows, streaks of crimson like the blood that flowed upon the ground and made rivers run red.

The fighting had been fierce, but it had ended, and the Yanks had withdrawn, and, God help him, Sean meant to save his wounded.

He rode ahead of the horse-drawn ambulance that ventured into the field of death to bring the wounded men deep into the woods, to the church converted into a hospital. Coming upon a clump of bodies, he dismounted, looked at the fallen, and felt his temper soar.

Dead, all dead. Slain viciously.

He mounted quickly, spurred his horse, and rose on hard ahead. There, in the falling shadows, he saw movement. A silhouette.

He heard a scream.

And he knew. A killer walked among the wounded.

"No, bastard!" he raged, and drawing his own cavalry sword, he rode hard upon the man posed with a saber high, ready to slash down upon the piteously wounded man on the ground. The fallen soldier screamed in mortal terror. Sean bore down on the madman ready to slaughter him.

In the nick of time, the silhouette swung around, ready to face Sean and defend himself rather than slay the wounded soldier. Swords clashed with a tremendous strength. Sean was nearly unhorsed. Nearly.

He rode back, bearing down again.

Surprise caused him to hesitate as he saw the identity of their murderer.

Confederate Colonel Elijah Wynn. His father's old friend. A man whose home he had visited time and time again.

"Come, take me, Sean!" Elijah cried, loud, challenging, heedless that Sean now knew he was a cold-blooded killer.

"Elijah," Sean said, reining in, staring at the man. Anger simmered and seethed with the enormity of the pain he felt, a pain of deepest betrayal. Here stood the man who had sympathized with him, who had worried with him over the other wounded. "What madness is this? Sir, you're a leader, not a killer! By God, end this madness!" Sean cried. "For the love of God, sir, why have you done this? What has caused you to inflict this incredible cruelty?"

"They are fiends, boy. Monsters, don't you know?"

"They're soldiers, sir, fighting for a cause. You're murdering them. My God, you're mad, sir."

"It's not murder, it's survival for us, for humanity! They are not decent young men but fiends of darkness, out of the hellhole of New Orleans! Bastard sons of voodoo whores, perhaps, and they must die. They are tainted! One seduced my dear Lilly. You know, you saw, she was taken by a spawn of

Satan, and she perished, died of his rotting disease, and he must now die.''

Sean shook his head. All this for poor Lilly! Elijah Wynn was speaking of his daughter, who had died just after Christmas, wasting away of a consumptive disease. But Elijah himself now seemed diseased. His daughter's death had cost him his mind. ''Elijah! You cannot find the man who seduced your daughter! You can't make scores of fine young soldiers pay for her death. These poor men are not monsters. We are at war, Elijah, fighting to form a new nation—''

Elijah shook his head sadly. He ignored Sean, turning again to the wounded man. ''One of them is a monster. A monster so horrible that he must be destroyed. Sean, I tell you the truth. I met the monster, I saw him, but I did not see his face. I felt his touch, but did not see his face. He gave me strength, and I must use it to destroy him, before he finishes with me!'' He drew his saber high.

''Elijah, no!'' Sean roared, and he rushed toward the colonel.

He had fought in dozens of battles and skirmishes. He had dodged bullets, dueled in hand-to-hand combat again and again for his life with his sword. He was well trained, agile, an expert with his weapons, and even his fists. God knew, war gave a man such talents.

He fought Elijah, a man twenty years his senior, old and maddened. Sean thought he could easily best the man, but Elijah had an incredible strength, that of his madness.

''Elijah, damn you . . .''

He had a chance to pierce his enemy through. Kill Elijah. A strike straight through the heart. He didn't take it.

Perhaps he didn't believe that Elijah would kill him, despite the man's savage strength. He had known Elijah far too long. Elijah's grief had made him insane. Despite the things he had done, Sean didn't want to kill him. He threw himself on Elijah, and attempted to grapple the man to the ground. The old colonel might well hang once he was judged in a military court, but Sean meant to do his damned best to bring him in alive.

But Elijah was clever—and by God, he had amazing power,

*the strength of a good ten men. Despite Sean's well-honed
abilities, Elijah threw him off with incredible vigor, then
dropped his sword, drawing his pistol.*

*"Jesus, Elijah, no, damn you!" Sean roared, springing at
him to wrest the pistol from him. But even as Sean fell against
him, a bullet burst from Elijah's Colt, and ripped into Sean.
Gut wound. The pain was staggering. Stunning. He wondered
if he was going to die, or if the bullet had pierced cleanly
through him, missing vital organs. He tried to stay on his feet.*

He couldn't die. He'd promised he wouldn't.

*He saw Elijah's face. The old man was raising his saber to
slash him now, to make sure that he didn't lie wounded. To
make sure that he died.*

*Yet, he couldn't stand on his own. As he began to fall, he
felt a strange cold rise with the breeze. The air seemed to twist
and writhe, and he heard a shrieking like the wail of a banshee
on the wind. Elijah, ready to bear down on him with the death
knell of his steel, was suddenly torn away from him. He heard
the old man shriek and cry out.*

*Someone was fighting with Elijah Wynn. Oh, God. The world
was in a strange gray mist. He had no strength. He couldn't
focus, couldn't fight. Slipping away. A taste of death. Death
he could bear; helplessness he could not. He was so afraid.
For her. Meg! It was madness, but oh, God, he had to be
delirious, seeing things. It was Meg who fought with Wynn.*

*Willpower alone brought Sean back to his feet. Fury caused
him to set his hands around Wynn's throat, and with a strength
born of love and fury and desperation, he wrenched Wynn away
from Meg.*

*Yet, even as he did so, a force came from behind him, with
a power like thunder. He in turn was seized, thrown back.*

*There was another man in the midst of their fray, with them
now on this desperate field of battle. He was reaching for Meg,
trying to bring her down . . .*

*Elijah was rising as well. Not dead, he was rising, with
renewed strength . . .*

*But it was the newcomer who had seized Meg. Sean threw
himself at the man's back.*

The newcomer turned, grappling Sean. His strength was uncanny. Sean was slammed down to the ground. His head struck rock. Black crystals seemed to burst into shards around him.

He was blinded, yet he heard fighting. There was shouting, the sound of fighting, fists flying, connecting. Yes, there was a fight being waged, fast and fierce. He heard a groaning, a bubbling sound . . .

As if someone choked on his own blood.

Sean's vision began to clear. There was someone by him. Meg.

No.

He looked up into dark eyes. Someone else . . . the man, the newcomer, the bastard who had touched Meg. He had a vaguely familiar face. Sean couldn't quite place him. A man he had met casually somewhere before. As he stared at the face in confusion, the man smiled.

"You're hard to kill, Canady! Half dead, but you're still trying to fight me," the man said. "But by God, you will die!"

He swiftly drew a knife from a sheath at his side. Sean managed to pull his own weapon, but even as he felt his knife make contact with flesh, he felt his opponent's blade slice into him. It became buried in his chest.

With a cry, his opponent fell to his side.

But too late. Meg, where was Meg?

Pain . . . and numbness. Meg, dear God, Meg . . .

There was a shrieking. A cry of fury on the wind. The man at his side, his murderer, was wrenched away. Gone. Taken. Dead? No matter, he couldn't rise again, couldn't touch Meg.

Sean felt death's cold touch upon him. Fingers of ice, caressing him, squeezing around his heart. He was falling through light and shadow. Death was coming. He saw it, felt it, tasted it. Oddly, death seemed to take so long.

Yet, then he felt a gentle touch. He found himself cradled in tender arms, and as he looked up, he thought himself already dead. Because she was with him. His dear precious Meg. Eyes burning with a strange fire. Shedding a rain of tears. Her touch was so infinitely tender. Her beautiful face was twisted in anguish.

"My love. Oh, God, Sean, I must get a surgeon—"

"No surgeon. Ah, love, too late for a surgeon. Meg, my God, you must flee, save yourself. Damn me for a fool, I cannot protect you—"

"I'm safe—"

"No, there's another killer here—"

"No, Sean, I'm safe, I must get a surgeon—"

"No. Hold me. Hold me against the cold. Tell me you love me. Tell me you would have married me. Tell me that you'll love me for all time."

"Oh, God, Sean, I love you, for all time, yes, for all time, you can't be dying, I can—"

"I love you," he told her. "So much. Oh, God, I love you. I love you. I would die for you, time and time again."

"Sean, no . . . oh, God, I will kiss you with life. Give warmth to your lips . . ."

Desperately, she leaned over him. Kissed him.

But too late. For life was gone.

She let out a cry of the greatest grief. She had come too late, too late. Too late to even offer up a last kiss . . .

She held him, sobbing. The dead lay strewn around her. She heard voices in the far distance; the men in Sean's medical party were seeking out his lead to find the wounded. There were so many, it would take the doctors and orderlies a very long time to cross the field.

Exhausted, she was shaking as she looked to where Wynn lay fallen in a pool of blood. The old man had been tainted. She looked further. And there he was. Despite Sean's blow, he was standing again, staring at her in triumph.

Aaron Carter.

He strode to her. To where she held her beloved Sean.

"You bastard!" she raged, and tenderly set Sean aside to rise to her feet.

"I told you that I would have you. We are one and the same. You will come to understand—"

"I despise you and loathe you and I will find a way to rip

you to shreds! I told you to leave, and you took that innocent girl. You killed her slowly, and when her father was insane with his grief, you added to his madness by taking just a little of his blood. You gave him greater strength, and caused him to mete out his justice on men innocent of the murder you committed.''

''I seduced an innocent! Dear me! Yes, my sweet, that is the nature of the beast, mademoiselle!''

He was smug, amused.

''I will kill you!'' she raged, and she flew at him with tremendous strength. Even he was startled by her power, his smugness gone as he raised his arms to defend himself. All she could feel was her grief and hatred. She tore into him with such force and power that she ripped flesh from his bones, tearing into his face, his throat, doing real damage.

''Bitch!'' he roared.

The wind seemed suddenly to roar, to rage between them. She stepped back, spent, acknowledging the higher power that was coming between them. Heedless of all else, she fell to her knees beside her lover once again.

Oh, God . . . oh, God, she had meant to watch over him! She had hovered too far in the distance, and she hadn't seen what was happening, she hadn't realized that . . .

Carter. Aaron Carter. She'd thought him gone. He'd played his game subtly. And taken his revenge.

She eased back against the bullet-riddled trunk of a thick old oak that had somehow survived the battle. She closed her eyes, in agony. She would gladly tear Aaron Carter from limb to limb, and yet she was horrified, wishing that by closing her eyes she could vanish what lay before her—the blood of war, and the blood she had wrought herself. She wished she could make death itself disappear.

Either that . . .

Or know its embrace.

But there was a miasma to death as well. Death had a stench. Even with her eyes closed, she could smell death.

Then she heard the wind again, an angry sound, a rustling against the trees, a thunder in her soul.

Judgment was coming.

She opened her eyes. Lucian was there, standing in the midst of the field of strewn corpses, staring down at the body of Confederate Colonel Elijah Wynn. Looking from her—to Aaron Carter.

"What have we here?" Lucian demanded.

"A traitor to our kind! She has mauled me! She must be made to pay. She doesn't understand that there are rules, that we abide by our own laws. She is dangerous, she must be taught. She will get our kind killed again and again."

"Ah!" Lucian murmured, studying the damage Meg had done to Aaron.

"You are the ruler; you owe me justice. Give her to me. I will mete out the right punishment."

Lucian looked at Meg, arching a brow. Momentarily, he appeared amused. "Well, well, well!" he said, and his eyes had a touch of fire, and his mouth was curved into a smile. "How intriguing. Just what happened here?"

He reached down, plucking up Wynn by the neck. The heavy man might have been weightless. Lucian gazed around at the other bodies, then saw the way she knelt by Sean Canady. His smile faltered for a minute, and his eyes fixed hard upon hers once again. She didn't care.

"Ah . . . goodness and evil both have their prices, don't they? Everything in life—and death—has its price. A lesson learned here, I think? Meg, my poor Meg. Well, indeed, you will perhaps learn not to lose your heart to mortal lovers. You forget who you are, Meg Montgomery! What you are. Child of dark forces, daughter of sin." His face hardened, and for a moment she was certain that he was being deliberately cruel, insistent on her believing that she had brought this pain on herself. "For pity's sake! You must learn to finish your meals!" he exclaimed.

With that, he took Elijah Wynn as if he were a doll, twisted his hand, and broke Wynn's head from his body with one powerful, clean movement. He let the man fall to the ground.

"He was not my meal!" she protested. "He was Aaron Carter's game, his experiment in cruelty! He killed the man's

daughter, then tainted him. He bled him, but neither killed nor gifted him. He simply destroyed human lives for the fun of it, he is the one who is dangerous, who will expose us all with his carelessness and cruelty. No hunger drove him to this! That creature," she spat, indicating Aaron, "is a true abomination even among us!"

Lucian shook his head, eyes narrowed. "That creature—as you refer to Mr. Carter—is not my doing, my dear sweet. But I'm afraid that he is one of us, and we are beasts of a like nature. And you know the rules, that you are not to kill your own kind."

"I didn't try to kill him. The bastard—"

"The gallant old colonel had a very beautiful and luscious daughter, so I've heard."

"Quite luscious," Aaron Carter said, grinning with lascivious pleasure.

"I believe she now walks among us," Lucian said.

"Indeed! And you allowed it—" Meg accused.

"My love, you forget yourself! It is his right, as it is yours, to choose to whom he will bestow the gift of this life."

"He seduced the man's only child, and turned a mortal into a madman who went wild killing injured soldiers on a battlefield—"

"And the madman killed your precious mortal. I'm afraid there is no crime against our kind in that. The rules by which we live are for our survival, not that of mortals. We must survive, my love, and you must understand that. Ours is a harsh and brutal world. We must survive. We are all alike, we are of a kind. Do you think you can change what you are by dining only upon evil men? Thank the Lord—or the devil—that the world is peopled with score upon score of vicious mortals— and that you can indeed grow fat upon them! You defy what you are, and choose not to accept the companionship that is offered you, or to make a companion of a man. My dear moral beauty, alas, just think on this! There lies your just and good Captain Canady—a man you would not taint—in mortal death. You had the power to save him."

"Perhaps I don't believe that being 'gifted' with this life is being saved!" she choked out.

Lucian hunkered down at her side, shaking his head sadly. "What an amusing pair you might have made. You who believe so deeply in the soul! You and your ethical young man! They tell me you attend church services!" He shivered at the very concept, then smiled, an attempt at humor and even empathy, she thought. "Imagine the two of you—the newspaper headlines rising above those of battles won and lost—Heroic Spawn of Satan Join the Temperance League! Welcome our latest members to the Salvation Army effort!"

Then Lucian's smile faded. He reached out a hand to her. "Come, Meg, with me."

Aaron was enraged. "No! You will not forgive her and comfort her. Give her to me! She has wounded me, she must care for me, she must be mine, she owes me—"

"No! He had no right! No right! He knew that—that—" Meg choked out.

"That you loved your mortal?" Lucian voiced.

"Give her to me! It's justice, I demand it!" Aaron persisted.

"No," Lucian said quietly, standing, still watching Meg. "This is her place, Carter. You were wrong to come here."

"She has maimed me. You stand up for her because she—because she entertains you!"

"You are maimed because you coveted her yourself. Go. Time will heal your wounds."

"I'll not!"

"You will."

"You think that you can claim her because you are king; you can do what you will—"

"Yes," Lucian interrupted impatiently, "I can do what I wish because I am king, because I have the power, and the strength, and if I choose to find you in the wrong, I have the power to destroy you. Unless you can best me. Which you cannot do. So you will go. I have commanded it."

Aaron Carter stared at Meg. "Lucian will not always be with you. I am powerful. I will be stronger. You have not heard the last of me. I am what I am, and I have my rights, and even our mighty king admits those rights! My beauty, you will pay in time!''

"Aaron, go to Europe," Lucian advised. "There's a season of tremendous debauchery on the Côte d'Azur, so I've heard. Go—before I forget that I must defend all that we are and maim you myself."

Aaron let out a hissing, snakelike sound of fury. But he was gone.

And Lucian, oddly quiet, hunkered down by Meg again. He reached out a hand once more. "I'm sorry, Meg. Honestly. Come. I command that you come."

"No."

He arched a brow. She wondered why she so stubbornly fought him, except that she was in such terrible pain. She had been existing in a sad delusion. She had told Aaron to leave; she had thought he had done so. She had so foolishly believed in her own power.

But Lucian was the king of their kind. She could fight Aaron and win. She could only hope to fight Lucian. She had learned strength from him. But he was older, stronger, still.

"My dear . . ."

When he touched her that time, she allowed him, for a moment, to comfort her. There was something about Lucian. In his strength and power there was ego and a sense of absolute right, but he was not like Aaron. She clung to him, and shook with a long flow of heaving sobs.

Then she pulled away.

Lucian could force her, take her, bring her to him at his will. And she didn't hate Lucian. He didn't expect their kind to be moralistic or ethical any more than he would expect a tiger to refuse meat. But, no, he was not like Aaron Carter. He had the wisdom of the ancients. He knew there must be rules. He had known about Sean, and he had allowed her the dilemma of loving a man she refused to turn into their kind, and so now, had lost. No, she despised Aaron, but she didn't hate Lucian.

Still, she defied him. Because drawing from him, she saw the mortal remains of Sean, and she didn't give a damn. All

she wanted to do was cry. And hold Sean Canady while his
life's warmth remained, and dream of what might have been.

"Come," Lucian persisted.

"No, I will not leave him now—"

"He's dead!"

"I will not leave him."

"Fine, foolish girl. Mourn your weak, pathetic, human
remains. You'll come back to me." Lucian lifted her chin. She
stared into his eyes, and her own came alive with a stubborn
fire. "You'll come back to me," he continued, "because I have
the power, I am the power. I am the god of your world. And
you'll come back to me, whether you admit it or not, because
you're a sensual little beast, and you need me."

She was angry and she jerked from his touch. "You don't
begin to understand love!"

He arched a brow, but allowed her the freedom. "You speak
of love, but you play with fire," he warned. "I repeat, ma
chérie, I am your god, king within our world. I know the rules,
and I see that they are kept. By right, you acted against one
of our kind. I should have given you to Carter. Remember
our rules. Break too many of them, and you will suffer the
consequences."

"Because I refuse you when I want to die!" she whispered.

Curiously enough, she realized that Lucian was hurt as well
as angry. "Maybe," he told her quietly. "Careful, my love,
don't push me too far! I will damn you and do my best to
see to it that you have a life so long you will beg for my
forgiveness."

She leaned back against the tree, real tears raining down
her cheeks.

There was another whisper in the air.

Another rustle of sound.

The smell of the bloody battlefield rose all around her. She
was alone with her dead human lover.

Aaron Carter was gone. He would not have her.

And Lucian was gone. He had defended her, but now, he
might not forgive her. It didn't matter. Nothing mattered.

Because Sean was gone.

CHAPTER 7

The third body wasn't found until Thursday.

Pierre estimated that the poor creature had been dead nearly a week, which seemed to mean that their killer had spent last Wednesday, Thursday, and Friday on a spree.

"Nights of the almost-full and full moon," Pierre noted glumly, which caused Sean to nod reflectively. Nights when the moon had glowed strangely red over river and bayou alike.

This time, the victim had been found in the bayou. Water and animals alike had done damage to her ravaged body.

Her torso had been found in the morning.

Her head in the early afternoon.

Parts of her would probably remain missing forever, consumed by wild beasts, the muck of the swamp—or even her killer. The savagery with which this killer was mutilating bodies was growing disturbingly more reminiscent of Jack the Ripper.

The good thing about standing with Pierre over the gurney as he pointed out his findings was that the victim's grotesquely ruined face was so grossly swollen and gnawed that it was hardly recognizable as human.

Poor Jack. He'd been determined. He'd come down to the morgue with Sean. He'd lasted ten minutes before he'd gone off to throw up. As Pierre explained that the tear marks on the neck indicated the same method of dispatching the head that they had seen before, Jack returned. He was nearly as pasty as the corpse. But he stood beside Sean, listening to the series of mutilations, what Pierre did know, and what Pierre didn't know.

"Oh, man. We definitely have a big-time madman on our hands," Jack said.

"Pure lunatic, I'd say—off the record, of course."

Sean nodded, feeling ill himself. Monday, they'd enlarged the task force and had a two-hour meeting. He and the chief and his men had welcomed the addition of two FBI men, a profiler and a physical evidence man, but not even FBI prowess was helping them. All leads had simply been exhausted.

Even the Maggie Montgomery lead. Both FBI men had interviewed her—and every person in her employ. Polygraphs had been given. No one knew anything.

Now, with this new murder, the tenuous link with Montgomery Enterprises seemed to be fading. There were no known possible witnesses. They believed they knew the victim's identity, though her fingerprints and dental records were still being checked. She was a prostitute—with a child. Her neighbor had reported her missing when she hadn't come for her four-year-old boy by midnight last Friday, as planned.

Poor Bessie. At some time, she must have been an attractive woman with a heart full of dreams. According to the neighbor, yes, she had been in the business, but only with high-class clientele. She had wanted to make money and get out to raise her son elsewhere. She had worked through someone, though the neighbor didn't know who. Bessie hadn't been a two-bit hooker but a hundred-dollar-a-shot call girl.

Right now, it didn't matter what she had charged her last john. She'd been the one to pay.

"What else can I tell you?" Pierre asked.

"Nothing, now. Cover her up, huh?" Pierre obliged. Once again, they'd be doing all matter of tissue and secretion samples. With any luck, despite the way the bodies had been destroyed, they could at least match sperm from the two female victims. Hopefully, they'd have a lot more.

As Pierre covered the corpse, Sean turned to Jack. "Get the guys together. I want everyone out on the streets. We're going to keep this as controlled as possible, but there's no way to exclude the press. Everyone is to be very careful regarding what is said. I want meetings with the undercover guys in the French Quarter, I want the names of all known pimps and madams in the area, and I want the names of anyone even remotely suspected of supplying sexual services or escorts on the side, all right?"

"Gotcha," Jack said, only too glad to leave the morgue.

"So, what are you going to do now?"

"I'm going to head out and interview the neighbor myself," Sean said. "Maybe there's some little piece of information that was missed. And when I'm done there, I'm going to find any possible—remote!—infractions and start combing the under-belly of our fair city for those dealing in human flesh."

"Have fun," Pierre told him.

"Yeah, right."

The dead girl's neighbor was a pretty, petite brunette, a fresh-faced young woman who admitted "dabbling in the trade" herself. She had cried real tears for Bessie, Sean thought, and he felt an anguish he couldn't quite help for the poor dead girl when he met her little boy. Four years old, shy and hesitant, he told Sean solemnly that "Auntie" Jeanne had told him Mommy had been called to heaven, and that she was safe and happy living with God. She just couldn't be with him anymore. Auntie Jeanne Montaine then sent the little platinum-haired child into the den to watch a Disney video while she sat down with Sean, offering him coffee.

Jeanne smoked nervously and puffed on a cigarette. "God, I wish I could help you! How can anyone do such things to other human beings? It's so horrible . . . and poor Isaac! Oh, I know, lots of people will just think that Bessie was a whore and she deserved what she got, but . . . well, most of what she made, she put away. She dreamed of moving away from here one day. We used to lie around and try to think about the most remote place possible—a city big enough to blend in, small enough so that it was still rural America, you know? Somewhere to lead a new life. She might have been what some folks call immoral you know, but good folk, bad folk, black folk, white folk, I've almost never seen anybody love somebody like Bessie loved her boy.''

"Miss Montaine, I'm afraid I didn't know Bessie, and I surely wouldn't presume to judge her. We all do what we've got to do in life.''

Jeanne brightened. She looked at him, sighing, and with her sigh, she lost some of her defensiveness.

"Yeah, we do. I want to keep her boy, you know.''

"If there's anything I can do to help, let me know.''

"I may make you keep your word on that," Jeanne told him.

Sean folded his hands together, leaning seriously toward her. "Jeanne, I don't judge Bessie, and I can't help her now, but if I can help her son, I promise I will. And I may be able to help some other poor girl. But I'm desperate. This horrible thing was done to her, and I've got just about nothing to go on. Can you think of anything, anything at all to tell me?''

Jeanne thought about it, then shook her head with frustration. "I know she had a pimp . . . and that's it. I don't know where she was supposed to meet the john she had that night or anything. She just called me, told me she'd be late. I told her, sure, I never mind having Isaac. But when she didn't come home, I knew something was wrong. She just wouldn't have left her baby, you know?''

Sean nodded. "Has anybody called you about Bessie or her son?''

"No.''

He produced his business card. "Well, if you come up with anything at all, anything—you know the routine—please, call me. That's my direct line at the office, the other is my home— and there's my beeper number. If you don't get me at either phone, please leave a message, and I'll get back to you.''

Jeanne nodded. "Of course. Of course. I'd do anything to help. Anything at all.''

"Thanks," Sean told her. As he got up to leave, she let out a little squeal. "Wait!"

"What?"

"It's nothing that big, I'm sorry!"

"Whatever it is—"

"Well, I was just thinking, maybe it is something. I think that her johns were acquired for her through a woman. A woman who owns a restaurant."

Sean's heart was thundering. *Dear God, something! At long last, something!*

"What makes you think so?"

"When she called about my keeping Isaac, she said something about a 'she' who had made arrangements. And Bessie had said she knew she'd be home by midnight, but she wasn't exactly sure how long she needed to be available because there were so many dishes clanking in the background when the arrangements were being made."

Sean nodded. "Good. Great. Miss Montaine, I could kiss you. I *am* going to kiss you."

He drew her close, pressing his lips to her forehead. She was excited, flushed, pleased.

"Thanks!" he told her.

"Is it a good clue?"

"A great clue. I'll keep you posted."

He hurried out to his car, and quickly radioed Jack.

Jack sounded frustrated. Combing the city was turning up too many pimps. "It's like going through the hair for bugs in the head of a kid with lice," Jack told him.

"Never mind. Get a car over to the Creole place, Le Bon Marché, on Prince Street. Arrest Mamie Johnson."

"All right," Jack said slowly. "Sean, I do need to have a specific reason to arrest her, you know."

Sean hesitated. "Bring her in for accessory to murder. That should help get her talking."

"Will do."

Thirty minutes later, Mamie Johnson, a tall, regal, copper-colored woman, sat in a conference room with Sean and Jack and Gyn Elfin, one of the two women in his task force. Gyn reminded Mamie of her rights, but despite her elegant appearance and confident ways, Mamie seemed ready to talk. She knew the cops weren't interested in busting her chops for her little side line—she ran a clean show. There was far too much that was really low-down and dirty in New Orleans for them to be bothering with her little piece of the action.

"Bessie Girou was certainly a friend of mine," Mamie said. "And I did try to steer her toward a certain caliber of men when she was looking for a date. May I have a cigarette?"

"There's no smoking in this building—" Gyn began. Sean looked at her and she grimaced. "A cigarette. Sure. You fussy on kind?"

"Anything menthol. And I'll take some coffee, too. I haven't had much sleep lately."

Gyn hurried out on her quest for coffee and cigarettes.

"Okay, Mamie, so you arranged for Bessie to meet a gentleman on Friday night," Sean said.

"I did."

"Who was the gentleman?"

"A tall, handsome, smooth talker. I'd never seen him before. He came into my place in a fine-looking leisure suit, smelling of expensive cologne. He ordered the most expensive meal in the house, steak au poivre with lobster au gratin. He ordered a hundred-year-old bottle of wine, and we got to talking, and he asked me if I was interested in a date, and I knew what kind of date he meant, and he was so smooth and good-looking that I almost said yes, except that my business sense got to me—it was a Friday night, when I make most of my income—and so I told him I knew a few really fine ladies who might want to enjoy a quiet night with him. He agreed. I gave him a time and place."

Sean nodded as Gyn returned with coffee and cigarettes. "So, you can tell me where they met?" he asked her.

"Sure. The Blue Pontchartrain. Room number eight. Just two blocks from my place, right off Prince." Mamie took a long sip of her coffee. "Why, Lieutenant, you need to talk to this girl. Honey, there should have been something stronger than coffee in this coffee."

"Oh!" Gyn declared, startled.

Sean almost smiled, looking at Gyn, assuring her that it was okay, and she'd learn eventually just how to deal with whom. Spiked coffee was *not* actually required for questioning.

"It doesn't matter anymore, Mamie. Listen, I'm calling an artist. I want you to give him a description of the man who came into your place and made arrangements for, er, feminine companionship. When we've got a drawing of this fellow, I'll take you for a drink myself."

"Why, Lieutenant, that would be fine."

"Jack, get a crew over to the Blue Pontchartrain. Mamie, you're with me."

"Sure thing, honey," Mamie drawled, tawny eyes raking him.

"Gyn!"

"Yes, sir!"

"You come along, too. I think we could all use a drink."

Back in the very beginning, she had learned. Learned about herself, learned about others. That there was good, and there was evil, but not just black and white; the world was filled with all kinds of shades of gray. Therein she lived. Her world was not darkness, it was gray. Back. Way back.

She awoke hungry. So hungry it hurt. So hungry she felt as if long, taloned nails dug into her stomach, clawed at her insides, ripped into her heart and soul.

Night. Naturally, she couldn't sleep.

She had tried so hard to refrain. To prove that what was couldn't be. In weeks now, she'd had nothing but a sewer rat here and there, seized with revulsion when she couldn't bear the cold . . .

Then, of course, there had been the morgue. But in the last few days, she'd not allowed herself any real sustenance.

And now . . .

The pain. Agony.

A full moon. Night. The hunter's time.

She prowled the city. Like her, it seemed that Paris seldom

slept. Prostitutes walked along the Seine, hawking their avail-
ability with sensual invitations, softly spoken, almost melodies
on the breeze. Men walked by; dock workers, drunks, the occa-
sional aristocratic college student, out on a lark, young, eager
to be taken . . .

She could hear the pulse of so many hearts! Young hearts,
wild hearts. The men stopped her, thinking that a woman alone,
she, too, was plying her trade.

Veins . . .

From a distance it seemed that she could see the blood
vessels of the people around her. All of them huge, all of them
popping from their necks . . .

No, no, she could not kill . . .

So she had hunted out the Paris morgue, but unbelievably,
in this city of so many, there were no fresh corpses. She had
learned early from her father that she would not sicken and
die from the blood of one already dead—her dear father! He
had done so much research, so much to keep her alive. He had
defied his friends, who all thought she'd be better off dead.
She had wanted death herself. Her father had told her it would
be suicide—a sin to the Catholic church. She had told him she
was already dead; he had refused to believe her. What could
the Church matter, when she was among the damned? But he
didn't believe her, damnation was only in the soul, and in her
soul, she had sinned only in her determination to trust and
love, and those were sins God easily forgave.

But her father had never prepared her for this kind of
hunger . . .

"Ma belle!" *A lady of the night called to her.* "Come, come
with us, we can show you a different way to pleasure."

She found herself smiling. "No, m'amie! I'm afraid that I
would show you a different kind of pleasure!"

She hurried by. There . . . on the ground. A drunken old sod.
But his pulse, oh, his pulse!

No, walk by, he is drunk, he is pathetic . . .

"Whoa, there's a lively one!" *the drunk called, reaching*
out for her skirt. "Come, ma belle, *entertain old François!"*

"Let go!"

"I will have your purse, and your love, mademoiselle!"

"And what will I have?"

"Your life!" he snapped out.

She shook her head. He reached for her. His vein, oh, God, his vein, there, pulsing so rampantly in his throat! The bastard had threatened to kill her . . . she could almost taste the life-sustaining blood.

He whimpered as he saw her lips contract, her feeding teeth appear. She suddenly felt pity, but it wouldn't have been enough to stop her if not for . . .

The garlic. His breath. The scent of it sickened her. She threw him down, and ran, and ran . . .

On the outskirts of the city, she heard a strange sound. It came again, and again.

Cows . . .

She walked out into a field of them. Even the blessed cows had such big, brown, trusting eyes . . . but she realized that this field where she had come was on the outskirts of a large slaughterhouse. She chose an animal. It stared at her. Oh, those eyes! She stared back. Slowly, the creature closed its eyes and stumbled down. Gently, she petted the beast. Then she bit into it . . .

She glutted. And glutted. When she was done, she looked at herself. She was covered in the blood. The edge of her hunger had abated. She lay atop the animal she had drained.

"Now that's lovely, really lovely."

Startled, she looked up. Lucian, immaculate in black frockcoat, top hat, and sweeping cape, stood over her, amused. "The morgue was empty, eh?" he mocked.

She stood, tottering to her feet, smoothing back her hair. It did her little good. Her face was smeared, her hair bloodied.

"The morgue was empty," she agreed, embarrassed, and not at all sure why.

"And you are still in pain," he said softly.

"No," she lied.

"Come with me."

"No."

But he led her to a pond, where she washed, and while she did so, she heard him hacking off the head of the beast she had chosen. He came back to her, covering her with his cloak. "I nearly killed a drunkard tonight," she told him tonelessly.

"But you did not. So . . . when such a night comes again, there are, of course, more cows. And when you cannot bear what is happening to you . . ."

His hand came around hers. She felt the swirl of mist that had transported her once before. She found herself in a foul place with a stench even worse than that of the slaughterhouse. Filthy straw littered the floor. Men and women, as dirty as the straw, lay listlessly about behind barred sections. "The prison," Lucian said softly. "And there, Jean LeBeau, the killer of thirteen women. He goes to the guillotine tomorrow at dawn. There, a more pathetic fellow. Hector Roderigo, a Spaniard convicted of killing his young wife in a rage. He is repentant, but too late, for she lies dead and buried. He cries, you see . . . there are more, but there you have it, if you must be a moralistic demon, choose a worthy—or unworthy—victim."

"Who am I to judge them?"

"My dear, they are already judged. Their death sentences have been given them. Take LeBeau—who deserves the worst death. The guillotine is too good for him. Then there is poor Roderigo . . . so afraid. He could be taken so much more gently from this life!"

He waited, watching her.

"I will take Roderigo," she said after a moment, hanging her head. "I will be gentle," she said softly.

"Your kiss will be far more tender than that of Madame Guillotine," he assured her.

Lucian left her.

And she heard Roderigo, sobbing, praying to the Virgin, bemoaning his wife, despising himself, praying that he would not show his fear before the masses when he was forced to walk to meet the blade of the guillotine.

And so she went to Roderigo, and she soothed him as he cried, smoothing his hair, touching him, and she promised him that there was more to life, that there was a God, and that she believed He forgave.

Then she drank . . .

The week had been long.

And painful.

Maggie hadn't realized that she'd been moping around most of the week until first Cissy, then Angie, commented on her quiet mood.

"Hey! Is there life in there?" Cissy asked, playfully tapping her on the head as closing time rolled around on Friday.

"Yeah."

"We haven't talked about dinner," Angie said, taking a seat on the corner of Maggie's desk.

"Did you want to go somewhere for dinner?" Maggie asked.

"No, I have a date," Angie informed her, crossing her arms over her chest.

"Good for you. The cop?"

Angie nodded.

"Well, boss lady," Cissy drawled, "I'd love to accompany you somewhere to get you out of your funk, but I have a date as well."

"Good for you. Another cop?"

"Yep. Adonis."

"If you both have dates for dinner, why are you bringing it up to me?" Maggie asked.

"Because you, Miss Montgomery," Angie chastised, "should have taken better care of the lieutenant."

"Really?" Maggie tapped her pencil on her desk, arching a brow imperiously. She wished she could have taken better care of him. She was just so afraid of getting involved. With a Canady, with a cop.

But fear hadn't helped the anguish that had plagued her all week. God, it had been wonderful. Wonderful. Lying alone and awake at night, she could almost feel his touch again. She had silently railed against herself, telling herself that she couldn't be such a fool regarding a *physical* relationship, except that it had been more than physical. Even if it had been wildly, wickedly, incredibly physical, it had been more.

And she'd sent him away. And now she was grieving. It was the only right thing to do. She didn't want an involvement. The minute his eyes touched hers, it was an involvement.

"Back to the dinner thing, honey! You know, Angie and I are double dating and you're more than welcome to join us," Cissy told her.

"No . . . but thanks. And hey, since you ladies do have plans this evening, go on, get out of here."

"Really, I was just teasing you before—you should come with us," Angie pleaded.

"Angie, honest, I think I know what I'm doing," Maggie assured her.

"No, you don't," Angie said stubbornly.

"Well, I'll have to live with my own foolishness then," she said, rising. She brushed past them and out into the hallway where a small spiral stairway led down to the shop below. When she reached the ground floor, it was just five-thirty. The store was empty, and though Gema and Allie hadn't yet locked the door, Allie was in the back at the register desk, working on the day's receipts.

"Hey, lady, how are you doing?" Maggie asked her.

Allie flashed her a warm smile. "I'm doing just fine."

"You're sure you feel well?"

"I feel great. And I'm so glad to have worked the last two days. I feel . . . normal. That's most important."

"Definitely. And I'm so glad you're back as well. But, listen, it's been a long day, why don't you go ahead on home? I'll finish up here."

"That would be nice, because I'm meeting a friend for dinner. But Gema was going to give me a ride—"

"That's fine. Gema can take off now, too. I don't have a thing to do tonight, and I'm a little restless. You two get moving."

Gema, straightening out the folds of a ball gown on a mannequin, looked up. "You sure, Maggie?"

"I'm positive. Out with you both."

Gema shrugged. "Okay, Allie. Get our purses, will you? Thanks, Maggie."

"Hey, you guys stay late for me all the time."

Gema laughed, a happy woman with Allie back in the store with her. "Right. But overtime is great as well."

"Don't worry, you're not being docked. Get out of here."

Waving good-bye, the two left. Maggie frowned once they were gone, trying to concentrate on one of the receipts she couldn't quite read. When she heard the light tinkling of the bell at the front door, she was startled, and realized she had forgotten to lock up.

"I'm so sorry, we're closed—" she began, calling out. But then she saw the man standing just inside the doorway.

Tall, slim, he had a strong, wiry build. He was dressed in casual black pants and a soft silk shirt. His features were classical and arresting, his eyes were a curious gold-hazel, almost like a serpent's eyes. He was a good-looking man with a startlingly sensual appeal. Immaculate, charming.

"Hello—Maggie," he said.

"Oh, God!" she breathed.

She set down her receipts.

"Maggie, you don't look happy to see an old friend. I tried to warn you that I was in town. I came by to see the pretty old lady the other day. Didn't she tell you?"

Her mouth was dry. "No, no, she didn't tell me. She had a blackout, a memory loss. She spent the night in the hospital."

"I'm so sorry to hear that; she was a right charming old bird."

"You didn't—you didn't hurt her—"

"Now, Maggie! I wouldn't have hurt the old darling for the world. I did wind up taking her out for café au lait—she does know her coffees. We had a lovely walk, and I brought her back here, safe and sound."

Maggie hesitated a long moment, trying to control both her fear and her temper. "Thank you."

"My pleasure."

"And what have you been doing?" she demanded somewhat

nervously, her heart seeming to sink in her chest. "You haven't come to New Orleans to be kind to old ladies."

He studied his nails. They were long, neatly manicured, buffed to a shine.

"No. It's absolutely perfect at the ski resorts in Switzerland, this time of year."

She dreaded her next question.

"Then why—why are you here?"

By then, he had reached the rear desk. He leaned against it, smiling. "For the sake of old times!" he said softly. He touched her cheek. "I care about you, Maggie. I wouldn't want anything to happen to you."

"It's been over between us for a long time!" she reminded him.

"Umm. Maybe. That's what you believe. There is, however, always the future, isn't there?"

"No."

"Well, of course I can just leave . . ."

"Wait!"

"What was that?" he inquired, arching a brow.

Maggie gritted her teeth. *"Please* wait," she said.

"Ah?"

He perched upon the desk, crossing his arms over his chest. He smiled like a well-fed cat.

"Please, tell me why you're here," she said. "Oh, God, you haven't been . . ."

"Excuse me?"

"Lucian, I—"

"No! I haven't been."

"Then . . .?"

His smile faded. His eyes touched her in a way that brought a trembling to her limbs. He did care about her. In his way.

"I've come to warn you," he told her softly.

By the time Angie and Cissy came down from upstairs, showered and ready for their dates, Maggie was alone again, staring at the front door, seeing nothing.

"Is everything all right?" Angie asked her.

She nodded, not looking at either of them.

"Hey, girl! Snap out of it!" Cissy said, coming around in front of her. "Are you alone here? I thought I heard voices."

"I'm—I'm alone," Maggie said at last. She shrugged. "Last-minute customer."

Angie had walked to the door. "Whoa! Good-looking boy. Wonder who he was shopping for?"

"His newest love, I imagine," Maggie murmured.

"Who?"

"Who does a man buy nice clothing for?" Maggie said, forcing her voice to be casual. "The love of his life, I imagine. Except that he didn't buy anything."

"Oh, well. Hey, are you sure you won't come with us?" Angie asked her.

Maggie narrowed her eyes at her friend. "Is Sean going to be with them?"

"No, honey. Sorry," Cissy said.

"Maybe I'll come with you then," she said. "I won't stay too long, I'll just get something to eat with you guys."

"You'll be good company," Angie said. "The guys are kinda glum tonight."

"How come?"

Cissy looked at Angie. Angie looked at Cissy, then at Maggie. "You haven't heard the news yet, huh?" She tapped her temples. "How dumb of me—Angie and I just heard the report upstairs. Another body has been found."

Another body. Maggie felt as if she was choking.

"Oh?" she murmured.

"Another hooker. Pretty girl, the newscaster was saying. Had a little boy. What a shame, huh? We really need to stick together. We can't be letting you wander around alone, no matter what's going on in your love life."

"And this girl was . . . mutilated?" Maggie asked.

"They're not saying a lot, just warning single women to be very careful and not go anywhere alone."

"Well, I won't go to dinner with you if you don't let me leave."

"We're going to be with two cops," Cissy said. "We'll have dinner and see Maggie home."

"I'll just stay in the city tonight. You can walk me right back here, how's that?"

Cissy and Angie looked at each other and shrugged.

"Sure," Angie agreed.

It was true. Though they tried to be decent dates, both Mike the Adonis and Jack the charmer were down. The body had actually been found yesterday, but they'd kept it out of the news until the evening, trying to ascertain an identity on this one in order to notify next of kin before getting involved with the barrage the press was sure to put on them as soon as the news was out.

Angie reminded the two of them that although they were cops, they couldn't expect to cure all the ills in the world. Mike agreed, but said, "It's just this case. It's just so damn bad."

"All killings are bad," Maggie reminded him.

"Yeah. You're right. It's just Sean is getting heat on this one. It's tearing him up. We've got something of a break on the case, though."

"Oh?" Maggie asked.

"Well, we're not supposed to say too much. But we may have something of a description of the killer. That's going to help a hell of a lot. It may actually be the break we need."

"A description?" Maggie murmured.

"Hey, Maggie, sorry, we really can't say more, you know?" Jack said.

"I know. It's all right," she told him.

When they finished eating, they all walked back to the shop.

"Go on up and lock yourself in," Jack told her gruffly.

"I will. Thanks, guys. Good night."

She entered the building, and knew they were waiting to hear her twist the bolts. Dutifully, she did so. Then she leaned against the ground floor door to the upstairs offices. She bit into her lower lip, and thought again that missing Sean, even if they'd really only had one night, was like missing a limb. And she was scared. Unnerved.

She suddenly ran upstairs, determined to act, and drew out her phone book, looking up street addresses. Then she hurried back downstairs, and let herself out of the building.

The night was dark. The full moon had waned.

She started walking down the street quickly, searching out faces as she went.

CHAPTER 8

He was dreaming, and he knew he was dreaming, but it was damned real. He tried to fight it; to wake up.

He was riding a horse. A handsome gray gelding that moved with the speed of lightning.

All around him, he could hear the thunder of hoofbeats. He rode hard, knowing that everything hinged on his ability to find and defeat his enemy. He felt the horse, felt the heat of the day, felt sweat trickling down his neck. He was wearing wool, and the sun was merciless.

Then he heard himself. He was hurtling out some kind of loud, shrill yell, a sound that was fierce and savage, and startled him so badly that . . .

He woke up, fighting left-over vestiges of the dream. Oh, wow. He'd just been riding. He hadn't known where he was going, only that he was searching for an enemy.

Great. Maybe he could go galloping through the streets of New Orleans and catch the killer.

He stretched, aware that he had dozed off on the sofa, staring at his television screen. He should have been dreaming about murder victims. Thankfully, however, the news about the latest find had been carefully doled out to the press, and by some miracle, the newscasters were being responsible and panic might be kept down to a minimum.

At the moment, though, it was two prostitutes and a pimp who had been killed. The moral majority liked to believe that such a killer would never be a threat to decent people. Maybe that was helping to keep the panic down, to keep much of the city halfway sane. Then again, New Orleans was a city fond of sin, the forgivable kind of sin. And God knew, soon enough, the populace would see the victims as humans, and not as sinners. Soon enough, the entire city would be up in arms.

He tensed, stretching, reminding himself that he just might have a chance at the killer now. He had an artist's rendering of the man's face, and he had Mamie back at work, waiting, watching.

He rose, walked into the kitchen, and got himself a bottle of beer. He looked around, feeling bleary-eyed.

Sean owned the hundred-and-fifty-year-old building he lived in on Conte Street in the heart of the city. It was in good repair, not so much because he was able to put any time or effort into it, but because he rented the ground floor to a friend of his sister's who ran one of the finest Cajun restaurants in the city. Grateful to Sean who had given her six months free rent when she started her business, Danielle Bonet now made sure that the place was painted, reroofed, and repaired at the slightest hint of trouble. She also sent her own cleaning woman in twice a week, sent up delectable things to eat, and saw to it that his shutters, drapes, and upholstery were kept in good form. Due to her, his living quarters in the city were consistently pleasant, and home was a haven from the office and the world.

He lifted his beer bottle. "To you, Danielle. Thanks."

He chugged down a few long swallows of beer, feeling restless. There were things he could do. He'd already been to the hotel room where the most recent victim had been killed. It had appeared spotless. Evidence experts had, however, lifted numerous prints, and they were sifting through them.

They'd also found minute quantities of blood, and a veritable rain of semen. Still, it was difficult to imagine that such a

violent murder could have occurred there, and been cleaned up
so well.

There were other things he could do. He could go hang out
at Mamie's bar, watch, and wait. He could interview more
employees at the hotel. But he had felt that he was spinning
wheels, that he was exhausted, that he needed a night's rest.

Now, he was wishing he was at a bar.

He was startled when his bell rang. In a lousy mood for
company, he answered the door as he was—shirtless, barefoot,
his beer bottle in his hand, his hair in disarray, the first two
buttons on his button-fly jeans unbuttoned.

He was absolutely amazed to throw the door open and find
Maggie Montgomery standing at his doorway.

His brow arched.

She flushed.

"I . . . just came by to say that I'm sorry."

"Oh?"

He didn't open the door for her to come in. He felt very
wary. Still hurt.

"I heard about the third victim. I'm so sorry."

"Did you do it?"

"What?"

"Did you do it?"

"No, of course not!"

"Then why are you sorry?"

She threw up her hands, apparently at a loss. It looked as if
she was about to turn away. "I'm sorry for the human loss,
and I'm sorry that it makes life even harder for you."

She looked like a million bucks. She was in white tonight,
a sleeveless white dress that showed off her perfect tan and
her long legs. Her hair was like dark fire against it. She smelled
delicious. She started to turn.

She was going to walk away.

"Why are you really here?" he demanded curtly.

"What?"

She spun back around.

"Why are you really here?"

"How nice, how pleasant. Why not, 'Please come in, can I get you some wine, a bottle of beer, how have you been—' "

"No niceties—I wouldn't want to get too involved," he told her dryly. "You asked me to leave your house, remember? So, what are you doing here?"

"If you're going to be rude and unobliging—"

"I never said I'd be unobliging. I just want it up front, out loud. What are you doing here?"

She hesitated, then it seemed that she saw no other choice than to be as blunt and callous as he.

"Well, frankly, the sex. It was really great. But if you're busy . . . or happy with your beer bottle, I can always come back at a better time."

"There's no time like the present," he told her. Then he reached out, and pulled her into the apartment. He fumbled for the hall table so that he could set down his beer bottle. Then he dragged her into his arms.

She returned his eagerness, fumbling with his pants. Her hands closed around him. He staggered, they came down to the floor together. He'd never felt so desperate. She was incredible. He ran his hands up and down her length, lifted her skirt.

She was bare beneath the white dress. The feel of her naked skin was incredibly erotic. His erection surged painfully against the cup of her hand.

He fell back, and she was on top of him. He caught her hips, guiding her.

He closed his eyes as the urgency of their passion rode with them.

Later, as he held her, he wondered how he had survived the days without her.

London
Fall, 1888

Having recently arrived in London, the American heiress Megan Montgomery was living in an apartment at St. James's Place. The next apartments were occupied by a young doctor and his wife, Peter and Laura Austin.

They were charming, and welcoming, and Megan found her-self spending more and more time with them. As spring passed, she and Laura became the best of friends. She told Laura about her ancestral home in New Orleans and how all Montgomery heiresses spent time abroad studying fashion until returning to New Orleans to take over the reins of the family business. Her mother had left New Orleans during the American Civil War because of the death of a close friend, and met Megan's father on a holiday in York. Megan had been to New York City and Chicago and even San Francisco, but she'd not yet been back to her family inheritance in New Orleans. With both her parents gone now, she would soon return to the States for good.

Laura, in turn, told Megan about her own life. Peter had been born to a wealthy and aristocratic family who had never forgiven him for marrying her, the daughter of a poor church rector. She had grown up without money but with lots of love; Peter had grown up with money and expectations. Having met Laura while he tended to her father on his deathbed, Peter had opted for love.

A friend who was traveling on the Continent had given the St. James's Place apartments to the Austins for their use for the next three years, so, despite their apparent affluence, they were poor as churchmice. "Peter is an excellent doctor, but he is even a more excellent man," Laura assured her proudly. Then she sighed. "He is desperately determined to help those who are so terribly down and out in the wretched slums of London. He believes that something must be done, there's such terrible poverty, especially in the East End."

Megan's heart immediately went out to Peter and Laura. She had seen a great deal. War, poverty, suffering . . . but in the rigid society of Victorian England, she saw a sadness unlike anything she had ever seen before.

Laura often accompanied her husband on his charitable trips into the tawdry filth of the East End. But come summer, she was heavy with her first pregnancy, and Megan insisted on taking over for her friend. "Ask Peter! The place is ripe with infestations and disease. Laura, for your health, for the baby, you must stay away," Megan told her.

So Megan began accompanying Peter.

In the East End she found a pathetic horror unlike anything she had seen in America or France or anywhere else she had traveled. Not that she had been blind to poverty and suffering before, but here, mothers with children slept ten and twelve to a tiny, rat-infested room. Broken windows went unmended, raw sewage was cast to the streets, and women turned desperately to prostitution for the few pence needed just to have a room in a doss, or flophouse, off the street.

Men and women alike drank away the hours. Although drink stole the money needed for a bed, gin was comparatively cheap. Gin could take the edges off the misery of life, tone down the dirt and decay, make people forget, if just for a spell, that they lived with no hope.

Peter was a saint, Megan determined. He worked office hours at the Austin apartment during the days, and he worked all hours of the night, leaving the apartment quite late sometimes to tend to the children, the alcoholics, and the expecting mothers of the East End. He tended to the men and women cut up in drunken bar fights, the battered women, and the whores. He did so without judgment, quietly giving the name of a friend who might need domestic help to a man or woman if it seemed he or she was really trying to find a way to make a new life off the street. He gave away clothing and toys which were left at his apartment by paying patients who knew about his double life.

Laura's pregnancy was a difficult one. Peter started spending more time at home, but that merely served to upset Laura. Peter must keep busy, she said, and Megan promised her that she would keep on helping out; she was glad to be busy.

One night in the midst of a wet, cool summer, Megan found herself sitting at a pub table with Peter, talking. "For me . . . I am drawn here," he told her. "I'm a physician, with a gift to heal, I believe. I feel I must do something. But Megan, you're rich and beautiful and young! You need to find a life with a good man who will love you. You will not find such a man here."

She smiled. "I've been in love."

"And?"

"He died," she said softly.

"There will be another—"

"No, never. He can never come again."

"Ah, but perhaps—"

"I've no desire to be in love, thank you. I'm older than you, trust me. I know my own mind, and I'm happy to work with you, and to help Laura—"

He lowered his head. And he broke down and cried. He was so worried about Laura. Megan tried to soothe and assure him. He got control of himself, swallowed down a pint of stout, and apologized. *"And here I've got you drinking with a man in such a mean establishment! You say you don't want to find a proper man, but I shall ruin your reputation, nonetheless."*

"I'm not at all worried about my reputation; I am a rich American," she told him, laughing. Then she added quite seriously, *"Peter, truly, I don't give a damn—see, I'm not a Victorian lady, I can cuss if I so choose!—and I find this loathsome! You've made me feel so passionate about reform. So much is expected in the behavior of the people, the nobility and royalty have their great balls, and people speak just so, and tea is served just so—and all this suffering goes on! I swear to you that I am happy to work with you, delighted to have Laura for a friend."*

"Yes, it is possible for us to be the best of friends," Peter said gravely after a moment.

"Yes, it is."

They squeezed each other's hands. Peter went for one more pint.

Megan was suddenly seized by a strange draw. Frowning, she rose slowly, not at all of her own volition. She wandered outside the public house, and across the road. There, she saw a man. Mist swirled low on the ground; the streetlights were dim here, the shadows were vast.

He appeared elegantly tall and slim, much like Peter in a tall hat and black cape. He carried a black medical bag. From a distance, it might have been Peter. She knew immediately that it was not.

His hair was tawny, and he had grown face-concealing, reddish whiskers—very fashionable here these days. He laughed when he saw her staring at him, and seemed to close the distance between them without actually walking to her.

"Why, 'tis an angel, angel of mercy," he said, touching her cheek. His fingers had tremendous strength.

She felt cold. Colder than death. But she was strong, too, and she pulled away.

"Come with me."

"You are a fool. I despise you, I will always despise you. Go haunt some other place."

"Taking a married lover, Megan—is it?"

"He is a friend, a concept you know nothing about."

"The concept you do not comprehend is what you are."

She inhaled and exhaled. Slowly. "No, you are wrong. I have a perfect concept of what I am. I know my strengths, and I know my weaknesses. What you are is not at all necessary."

He shook his head. "Wolves hunt and kill to survive. Lions in Africa stalk their prey. We are no different."

"We are different; we are not animals."

"I beg to differ. We are."

"You are a cruel being, and I will never have anything to do with you."

She started to turn, he caught her arm, dragging her back. "Maybe you could change me. Damn you, we could rule the world together. We could have hundreds quaking in fear, we could change history, events—"

"No, we could bring about the death of all our kind. And I don't want to rule the world. I—"

She broke off, suddenly pained.

"You what?"

"All I ever wanted was a normal life," she whispered. "A family, a home."

She turned and started walking away.

"Get back here, I am talking to you!"

She ignored him. In a rage, he was suddenly before her, pushing her back against the wall with tremendous strength. She fought him, but he was very powerful. Flush against the wall, she suddenly discovered that he had a very sharp knife against her throat. "What is it? What is it about me? Lucian forced you to him, and you remain friends. Should I not do the same? Force you with the superior strength of a multitude of decades? Force you to learn, to see what you are! To see that we are as necessary as hyenas, vultures, buzzards, wolves? Look around you—the world is a cesspool, and there are many who would welcome a kiss of death!"

"Let me go, now."

"I could kill you. Sever your head."

"Then Lucian and others would be forced to destroy you."

"Lucian is king now, but I grow more and more powerful! Lucian has lost his blood lust, and thinks that he can form us into a society of scholarly intellectuals! Hah! Lucian will fall from his mighty pedestal, because we are animals. As men seek cattle, we seek men."

"Let me go!"

At that moment, Peter came out of the pub, calling her name. "Megan?"

She was suddenly alone in the swirling fog. She hurried to Peter, explaining that she had thought she heard a cry in the streets, but she had been mistaken. They started walking, seeking a cab. They heard the clip-clop of horses' hooves, but the fog had risen so high they couldn't see. "I'll just look around the corner . . ." Peter said.

Megan waited. Waited and waited. Peter didn't come. In terror she began to look for him.

Forty-five minutes later, she found him, slumped against a building.

She instantly looked at his throat, and leaned back, breathing far more easily. He was clean. She was about to seek assistance when he groaned and came to. "Megan . . . sweet Lord, Megan, I left you alone in this awful place and I . . . I just blacked out! What is wrong with me? Too many hours? Am I losing my mind?"

"It was a blackout, Peter, nothing more. Come on, it's nearly morning. If Laura wakens, she'll be worried."

They went home. The light had come. It was early morning;

the sun rose. She slept deeply, then felt a summons with a power unlike anything she had experienced in years. And she suddenly found herself before Lucian, who was in a cool, regal fury. Aaron Carter was there as well. She was grateful to realize that Lucian's fury was directed at Aaron. "You tempt fate with the games you play, Carter. Throughout the centuries we have made our rules, and the first is that we let each other live our lives as we choose—and keep our distances. Leave her be. The world is a vast place when we realize that we are perhaps no more than a few thousand, and the world is so very large."

"We could be so many more!" Aaron argued.

Lucian shook his head. "If there were no rules, there would be no food!"

"Lucian! You are a fool, thinking you can turn lions to lambs!" Aaron told him.

"The lions perish if they eat all the lambs! We are prey to the balance of life like all creatures; the laws were written by the ancients, creatures before even my time! And my preferences are none of your concern, except that you are the fool if you can't see that the world is changing. Perhaps not this decade or the next, but each year the world inches closer to a higher technology, and if we do not learn to live with it, we are doomed. I warn you, don't let this quarrel affect our world. And remember! If either of you truly seeks to destroy the other, you will be condemned by your peers en masse, and hell will be all that awaits you—should those fires indeed exist."

Aaron lashed out furiously. "You took what you wanted, Lucian! Why can't I?"

"Each new being must have a teacher; I was that with Megan. She has learned. She has made her choices; she is an entity in her own right."

"Indeed? Because you have had what you want, Lucian? Because you call yourself king?"

"I am king, because I know the difference between desire and excess. I have survived, because I know that there are boundaries of sanity, even in our world. Would you test me, Aaron? Would you come after me? Come—come take me on!"

Lucian spoke quietly. He lifted his hands, his lip curling, and he invited Aaron to provoke battle between the two.

"The day will come, Lucian, I swear it."

"The day will come when your sadistic excesses bring about your destruction."

Aaron swore vociferously, and stared at Megan. He pointed a finger. "You, too, will have your day!" he promised, and he disappeared then, into a swirl of spiraling mist.

Lucian shrugged.

"Well, he is gone. For the time."

"Thank you," she said softly.

He nodded. "I have a soft spot for you, you know. Even if you so foolishly prefer mortals. The time will come when you realize it isn't to be. And then I'll be there. Waiting."

She laughed softly. "Waiting—with your harem."

"Ouch, not fair."

"Absolutely fair."

"I still love you, you know."

"Lucian, in your own words, you don't believe in love. You lust for me—but only for the seconds it takes you to find new entertainment."

Lucian laughed. "Perhaps. Still, I do have that fondness for you."

She hesitated. "Lucian . . ."

"What?"

"Alec . . ."

Lucian arched a brow. It had been a very long time since she had mentioned Alec.

"Yes?"

"Alec did believe in love. Before . . . before I was changed, it was as if he believed we could have a life—"

"You do have a life."

"No. A normal life. With death at the end. He told me that love was the greatest power on earth, that the only true freedom on earth was in love."

"He was romantic. A believer in fairy tales. A beautiful,

*poetic young man. And he is dead. There lies your legend. Take
care with Aaron. He is powerful,'' he warned.*

"Perhaps,'' she told Lucian. "But then, so am I. So am I.''

They awoke Saturday morning together. Maggie put the coffee on before she showered, and it was ready when Sean finally dragged himself up. It was delicious. While he sipped it, he watched Maggie digging around in his refrigerator. She was wearing nothing but one of his tailored shirts. The tails came to her midthighs. Her hair was wild, she looked great. He leaned against the refrigerator, just watching her.

She let out a sigh of pleasure, then stared at him, quite surprised.

"I just can't believe it.''

"What?''

"Your refrigerator is so well supplied.''

"Oh, that,'' he murmured, then shrugged. "Danielle sees to my refrigerator.''

"Danielle?'' she queried.

He nodded. "A friend. She owns the restaurant downstairs. She went to school with my sister.''

"Oh,'' Maggie murmured, studying him. He decided not to tell her that although Danielle had grown into a very beautiful woman, she had been friends with his little sister Mary for so long that he'd feel incestuous if he ever gave her more than a brotherly hug.

"Well.'' Maggie turned back to the refrigerator. "Mind if I cook? Kitchen-sink omelettes, grits, and English muffins?''

"It will be a slice of heaven,'' he assured her. He wanted to watch her, but he finished his coffee and set down his cup. "I'm going to shower,'' he told her. "I'm not sure what today will bring.''

"Do you have to go to the office—or the morgue?''

He shook his head. "I think I'm going to go spend the day in a bar.''

"Oh?''

"I'll tell you about it while we eat.''

Shaved, showered, and in jeans and a denim shirt with rolled-up sleeves, Sean told her about their latest victim while he sat across the kitchen table from her and munched on an omelette. "Anyway, I've finally got a real clue, a rendering of what this man looks like."

Maggie was staring at him, a piece of toast in her hand. "A rendering?"

"Well, I told you, the guy had dinner at Mamie's place and asked about an escort. Mamie made the arrangements. It does appear that Bessie Girou was killed in that hotel room, and then her body was dumped out in the bayou."

"How do you think the killer managed to get out of the hotel room with a body dripping blood?" Maggie asked.

"I don't know."

"Maybe the guy in the bar wasn't her killer. Maybe she had a visitor after he left."

"Maybe. Maggie, what are you trying to do? Dash my fragile straw of hope?" he demanded. What she was saying was possible; he knew it well enough. Didn't matter. They had a suspect, and he'd be damned if he wouldn't comb the city, trying to find him.

Her eyes were on her food. "I guess I'm just trying to keep an eye on perspective," she said softly. "Have you got a copy of your sketch of this suspect?"

"Yes, the whole city should have a copy."

"What?"

"Hang on," he said.

He left the table and opened the apartment door. His newspaper was sitting just outside and he brought it in. The headlines read: *Possible Big Break in Ripper Case: Have You Seen This Man?*

He cast the paper down in front of Maggie. She stared at it. He couldn't see her eyes, but for some reason, the way she looked down at the paper disturbed him.

"Someone you know?" he demanded.

She shook her head, not looking up at him.

"No . . . no."

"Ah. Well, anyway, I thought maybe you'd like to spend a casual day with me."

She looked up at last. There was something carefully guarded in her expression. "A casual day? I thought that—"

"Let's just take a long, leisurely stroll around the Vieux Carré. You know. Enjoy the architecture. Grab a café au lait, smell the flowers, sit down by the river. After noon, we can go to Mamie's and have a drink in the bar. Catch a bit of a preseason game on the bar TV, and then have a long, elegant dinner. How's that sound?"

She nodded. "I take it we're going to be watching for this man?"

"Yes."

She tapped the newspaper. "You know, once he sees this likeness of himself, he might turn tail and run to another city."

"I don't think so."

"Why?"

"I think he's the type who enjoys taunting the police. Half the thrill is knowing that we should be right on his tail, but that we're stumbling around like idiots in the dark. We can walk to the hotel as well, take a look at the room, talk to a few more employees. You game? I don't have any right to drag you along, you know. You can go back out to your plantation for the day and soak in some sun. But I would enjoy your company."

"Umm, I'm not really a sun lover. And I hate the idea of you just walking around without my company."

"Oh?"

"Well," she said lightly, "I get the impression that there are other women who wouldn't find the task too challenging . . . and frankly, as I said . . ."—her eyes touched his over the rim of her coffee cup—"the sex is just really too good to jeopardize."

"Ah."

He reached out across the table, finding her fingers, curling his own around them.

Then suddenly he was up, drawing her to him. She was naked beneath the tailored shirt. The buttons gave easily. His hands were all over her flesh.

They made it to the sofa in the parlor. She tugged at the buttons on his jeans. His erection jackknifed from the spread of his clothing. It was just great sex.

God help him, it was so much more.

Later, with her curled on his chest, he stared at the ceiling and wondered again how he had survived the days without her.

Well, now he had her.

Just how the hell did he keep her? Even in his arms, she seemed elusive. And mysterious.

"I'm hopping into the shower," she murmured against his flesh. "Just for a minute."

With grace and agility, she rose and was gone. He heard the water running. In a few minutes, she was back out, wearing her white dress, her tanned flesh glowing beautifully, her red hair loose over her shoulders.

"Ready?"

"Give me two minutes," he told her.

"Two minutes?"

"Okay, five."

But he really did wash and dress that quickly. He was afraid to let her out of his sight for long.

Afraid she would disappear. Into thin air. Into mist.

CHAPTER 9

They wandered around for an hour, down narrow streets beneath overhanging balconies. They stopped for rich café au lait on Prince Street, and ambled to Jackson Square to throw breadcrumbs to the birds.

They talked mostly about New Orleans, about its rich and varied history—avoiding the topic of murder. As they kept wandering, Sean became involved in their discussion regarding Andrew Jackson, and he didn't realize that they had come to the statue of his Civil War ancestor until they were standing right beneath it.

He looked up.

Another Sean, a different time, and a far different world.

Captain Sean Canady stood in the military frockcoat of his day, plumed slouch hat low over his forehead, scabbard and sword at his side, one booted foot set atop a rock as he looked out over the city he loved with handsomely chiseled marble eyes. A plaque at the statue's base mentioned the dates of his birth and his death, and his valiant achievements. He had died in his attempt to save the city of New Orleans; he was a hero who defended his men to his own tragic death, and he would live on forever in history as a seeker of justice.

"Quite an impressive fellow, eh?" Sean inquired.

Maggie looked at him a trifle strangely, he thought. She seemed a little pale. "You look just like him."

"Do I?" Sean stared up at the statue—carved with beard and collar-length hair. "Hard to tell. I need the frockcoat and the stance, don't you think?"

She seemed to be shivering. He slipped an arm around her. "Hey, you don't believe in ghosts, do you? Not a sophisticate such as yourself!"

She withdrew slightly from him, studying his eyes. "Don't *you* believe in ghosts?" she asked.

He frowned, amused. He shook his head. "No. I don't believe in ghosts. Or haunts. And hey, he was supposedly a good guy— if he came back to haunt us, he'd be a benevolent spirit, right?"

She shrugged. "He would be a benevolent spirit."

"Meaning . . .?" Sean queried, bemused. She was usually just so damned matter-of-fact.

"Don't you ever think sometimes that . . ."

"That what?"

"I . . ." She looked at him, then moistened her lips. "I don't know. That there's evil in the air sometimes, I suppose."

"I don't believe in ghosts at all, that's for certain."

She looked at him, shaking her head. "If you don't believe in ghosts, haunts, spirits—or the like—how do you explain the murders?"

"Explain them? People were viciously killed."

"How?"

His eyes narrowed and he frowned. "What do you mean?"

"Well, you know, just exactly how? How do you explain the lack of blood, or the body of a butchered victim being moved from a hotel room without witnesses noticing a thing?"

He crossed his arms over his chest. "Jesus, Maggie, if only that could be my answer! Spirits. I don't believe in evil spirits. People commit evil. There's an evil man killing people, and I'm going to find him and turn him over to the due process of the law."

She shook her head suddenly. "I don't think it's going to be that easy, Sean. I . . ."

She broke off, interrupted as a bloodcurdling scream suddenly filled the air.

Sean backed away, frowning, quickly looking down the street. A young blond woman had emerged from one of the dusky, side-street jazz clubs. She wore sandals, a halter top, and a short skirt. Blood dripped from her hand as she backed away from the door, staring in horror at the burly, dark-haired and bearded fellow who followed her out. The man cast back his head and began laughing. The sound was strangely demonic, and the man seemed heedless of witnesses as he came after the young woman, wielding a broken bottle.

"Hell!" Sean muttered. "Shit! Maggie, stay here, please, wait for me."

"Sean . . ."

He left Maggie by the statue, tearing across the street, drawing his police .38 special, which remained his weapon of choice.

The man was almost atop the shrieking girl. By now, another fellow, staggering—an unbroken whiskey bottle in his casual grasp—had followed the first one out.

"Cut her, cut her, cut the bitch!" yelled the second fellow. He was skinny, and had rotten teeth. "Cut her, Ray, come on, she called us both cocksuckers, cut her up, let her see . . . hey, Ray, come on, my man, you done got the pow-er!"

Passersby around them came to a halt, rooted to the ground with horror and fear as they watched the husky one called Ray as he quickened his pace, staring at the terror-stricken girl, laughing at her as he moved like a bird of prey ready to pounce upon a quivering mouse.

"Stop!" Sean commanded.

Old Ray ignored him.

"Mind your own business, eh, sucker?" the skinny fellow with the bad teeth yelled. "She's my woman, been doing a lot of wrong. Ray here's gonna carve her up—just a few words of description on her face—and her cheatin' tits, maybe, too!"

Tears streaked down the girl's face. She had been pretty once; Sean noted she was now far too thin and frazzled. He noted the veins in her arms. Drugs. A lot of drugs. Drugs cost money. Maybe she belonged to old rotten-teeth with the skinny butt over there—egging the big man on—but she was probably working the streets for the money to keep up her habit.

She stared at Sean, fear in her huge blue eyes. She didn't trust anyone. Poor little creature. She wasn't a mouse. Just a sad little street-rat.

"Come on. It's all right!" Sean said quietly to the girl.

She was so terrified, she still didn't seem to hear him.

Ray was closing the distance between them.

Sean caught her arm, drawing her slightly behind him. He stared at Ray, who returned his stare. Ray's eyes didn't look crazed, but his laughter continued to ring with chilling effect.

"Shoot me—you're going to shoot me? I'll kill you deader than a door nail, copper!" the man cried.

"Copper, copper, he's a freakin' copper?" the skinny one cried.

"Shut up, Rutger!" Ray snapped. "Well, well, a copper!" he continued, his eyes on Sean. "Chop, chop, chop up the cop, eh?"

"Another foot and I shoot you—asshole!" Sean said with a polite smile. His gun was aimed dead on Ray's heart.

To Sean's amazement, Ray kept coming forward. Sean fired a warning shot.

"Halt! Stand still and drop that bottle!"

"Little man, little man, get out of my way!" the man bellowed, casting his head back.

"Tell him who you are, Ray, tell him what you told me—then cut up that *cunt!*" Rutger called to him.

Ray grinned.

Just like the devil.

"So good, Ray. Go on, tell me who you are," Sean encouraged.

"Don't you know me? I am God, I am Satan, I am invincible."

"Oh, yeah, well, I'm Lieutenant Canady. And what you are is dead if you don't do what I say!"

"Tough boy, tough boy, eh?" Ray said, and his voice was deep and husky, somehow getting beneath Sean's skin. "I want the girl, copper. Just get out of my way. I want the precious little dove, want to play ..." He made a strangely obscene gesture with his tongue. "Drink her all up, all up." He made a licking motion. "Carve her ... like a little roast piglet!"

The girl remained behind Sean, clinging to his arm, shaking like a leaf blown in winter. "It's all right," he said quietly to her.

"But—"

The man let out a roaring sound. "I want the girl!" He started forward.

"Get her, Ray!" Rutger cheered.

No more warning shots. Sean was tempted to go for the heart. He aimed for the leg.

His shot was true, striking the kneecap. The man should have fallen in almost unendurable pain. He jolted, but kept coming forward. Near, nearer.

"Damn you, last chance. Halt!" Sean shouted himself.

The streets came alive with the man's startling laughter again. No choice. Sean fired directly into the man's chest.

The fellow fell against him, clawing to reach the girl, who began to shriek again. Sean was amazed by the tremendous force with which the man grappled with him. They went crashing down to the sidewalk together. The man still held his broken beer bottle. Dark eyes malevolent, he tried to slash at Sean's neck. Sean rolled, dragging the man with him, at last pinioning the fellow to the ground.

The dark eyes looked up at him. Rolled so that the whites were all that eerily remained visible.

Ray's eyes closed.

Sean put his fingers to the man's throat. No pulse. He was cold. Cold as ice.

Listening to the sound of police sirens, Sean eased back, exhausted, amazed. Where the hell had the fellow come up with such strength?

He staggered to his feet, faltering. Ray had taken a toll on him. He tried to shake it off, and somewhat succeeded. The girl stood behind him, sobbing softly, stuttering out words. "Ray's gone, but Rutger's going to kill me now, oh, God, I don't stand a chance, I don't stand a chance. You'd think he couldn't hurt me 'cause he's so skinny and scrawny . . . he's nearly choked me before!'' she ended on a whimper.

Sean turned around and looked at her. She was so sad; such a young, pathetic wreck of humanity.

''You've got to get off the stuff,'' he told her quietly, ''or else it will be a mercy for you if he strangles you.''

Her eyes were huge and blue and filling with tears. ''I want to . . . he won't let me. Oh, God, he's already coming for me!''

She shrank back against Sean, clinging to his arm. He could see that Rutger stood about ten feet away, on the edge of the crowd. He was looking from Ray on the ground to the girl. Admittedly, he looked as if he was already planning her murder. For a moment, his hands clenched into fists at his sides. Instinctively, Sean stepped forward.

Rutger held still. Sean could see the tension knotting his neck, the veins bulging against his skinny throat. Then Rutger eased back, giving Sean a thumbs-up sign and a mocking smile.

By then, several uniformed men were running up around him. ''The one on the ground isn't going to give you much more trouble—but haul that son-of-a-bitch over there down to the lock up!'' Sean commanded, pointing at Rutger, who was now looking for a place to run.

''Arrest me for what, free speech?'' Rutger taunted.

''Inciting a riot,'' Sean snapped. ''Hell, I'll give you any additional paperwork you need—just read him his rights and arrest him!''

Luckily, the first uniforms on the scene were toughly muscled guys, two of whom were quickly on either side of Rutger. While a crew-cut, six-footer in his prime recited Rutger's rights, Rutger shouted out explicit instructions as to what Sean should be doing with himself. Sean ignored Rutger, glad to see that Heidi Branson, a capable young policewoman, had arrived on the scene and was taking the girl in hand.

Blood still dripped from the young woman's hand. Heidi was calmly asking her just how she'd been cut, and assuring her that the medics would be arriving any second. The girl quietly insisted she was all right, then burst into tears.

Sean felt hands on his shoulders. He swirled around. Maggie. Sweet Jesus. Maggie. Eyes dark and worried, flesh pale.

She was staring at the corpse. With a strange dread. Finally, her eyes touched his.

"Are you all right?"

"I'm fine. I'll have to go to the office for a bit."

"I'll tag along."

"Thanks. You're a good kid."

She smiled, moistened her lips, looked at the corpse again. "What about him?"

"He's dead."

"You're certain."

"Maggie, of course I'm certain."

"Where will they take him?"

He frowned. "To the morgue, of course."

"Oh." She hesitated. "Autopsy?"

"Naturally. He died an unnatural death."

"But everyone on the street saw—"

"Maggie, honey, you know that there's always an autopsy."

She nodded.

He tugged lightly on her arm, wanting to draw her away from the man he'd been forced to kill. But she resisted, looking at the girl now. "Is she going to be all right?"

"Heidi is great with battered women."

"Is she a junkie?"

"Yes."

"Give me a minute. Just a minute."

Maggie eluded his hold upon her arm, stepping past Heidi, touching the girl lightly on the cheek. The girl looked at her. "Don't be afraid," Maggie told her. "This is your chance, your real chance to break away."

The girl stared at her. Tears welled in her eyes again. "I can't help it. I'm scared to death!"

Maggie shook her head, smiling. "The cops won't let that scum near you now. It's your chance. Get clean. Get to another city if you have to. This is it. Don't be afraid, take your chance, run with it."

To Sean's amazement, the blonde offered Maggie a tenuous smile and inhaled on a ragged breath. ''I'm going to try.''

''You'll make it.''

''I always wanted to believe that we had angels. You know, like guardian angels. Maybe mine will watch out for me now.''

''Believe in yourself. That's more important.''

''Are you a cop? Will I see you later?'' the girl asked anxiously.

Maggie shook her head. ''No, I'm not a cop, but I'm friends with some great cops. And I'm sure we'll see each other again.''

She left the girl to Heidi then, joining Sean once again.

''We'll get my car,'' he told her. ''Sorry, but I do have to do a report on this one.''

''How long can you hold Rutger? All he did was egg on the other guy.''

''I'm going to have to get the girl to file charges. I can hold him long enough to give her a break, at any rate.''

Maggie nodded. She frowned, looking at a streak of blood on her finger. ''Must have jabbed it on something,'' she murmured, staring at it. She shuddered suddenly, bringing her finger toward her lips.

''No!'' he cried, grabbing her hand.

Startled, she stared at him.

''Honey, I don't think that's your blood. And,'' he added softly, ''Blondie there is definitely a junkie. We're talking serious communicative diseases here.''

''Oh . . .''

''Come on.''

The afternoon was wretchedly long. Maggie did hang around, meeting a lot of the cops who were in the station, chatting, laughing with them softly as he worked—making him more and more distracted. Paperwork. He hated it—it had to be right. He wanted charges brought against Rutger, and he wanted them to stick.

The young blonde's name was Callie Sewell. She was twenty; she'd run away from an abusive father to an abusive lover. Patterns were hard to break. She needed help—and self-esteem. Somehow, it seemed that Maggie had given her the latter.

She was in the hospital now. The gash on her hand had been severe enough for her to lose a lot of blood. Between that and her fragile physical condition, they'd determined to keep her overnight.

Dr. Larson Petrie had been the man to see the blonde. Sean knew Larson, and that he did his best to get around rules and regulations to help people. He was probably keeping Callie Sewell to see her through a rough night.

The dead man—Ray Shere—was in the morgue, scheduled for autopsy the following morning. Sean was sure they'd find that he'd been pumped through with drugs as well as alcohol. Something had to explain his walking as far as he had after being shot in the chest.

At four o'clock, Sean was finished with desk work at last. Jack had come in—for moral support, he told Sean, but it seemed to be Maggie he was supporting rather than Sean. When Sean finished up, Maggie was seated on the edge of Jack's desk, and the two of them had been laughing and chatting away. "Where to, boss?" Jack asked.

Sean arched a brow.

"Ole Mamie's bar?" Jack suggested.

"We were going alone," Sean said.

Maggie grinned. "Naturally, you're invited."

"What the hell difference does it make?" Sean muttered. He rubbed his jaw. Five o'clock shadow. Well, hell. He felt as if he'd been dragged through the mud. An arm muscle ached and he was beginning to feel the spot in his ribs where he'd hit the pavement when he went down with Ray. "I need a drink. Let's go."

Maggie still looked fresh, bright and beautiful. The concept of being alone with her had been a nice one—even if being alone meant keeping an eye on every customer in Mamie's place.

The hell with it. This was better. He could sit back with Maggie and relax. And Jack could do the looking.

Maggie slipped off the desk, setting her hands on his shoulders, brushing his lips with a kiss. She was about to escape. He caught her by the waist.

"As long as I get you alone later."

She tensed slightly.

"I'll have to go home tonight—"

"No."

She stiffened.

"Please. I want you with me tonight." He hesitated. "I need you with me."

He met her eyes. She seemed to be working something out in her mind.

"Maggie . . ."

She nodded after a moment. "All right. I'll . . . I'll stay tonight."

Maggie was startled by the elegance of Mamie's establishment. It wasn't ostentatious, just quiet and nice. In both the restaurant area and the bar, soft lighting spilled over fine carved light-wood booths, tables, and chairs. Watercolors lined the walls, and several large tropical fish tanks were attractively set around the rooms. The bar was a deeper wood, finely polished. Table settings were spotless, glasses sparkled, the linen was snowy white.

They were seated in a booth in the bar, Sean taking the rear— so that he could see everyone who came and went, Maggie was certain—even though he had told Jack that Jack was "on" and he was "off."

Maggie was equally amazed when she met Mamie, who was as elegant as her decor—even though she could slip into street language at the drop of a hat. But Mamie seemed decent and down to earth—not at all like she had expected a female pimp to be.

And the wine list was incredibly extensive. She ordered a 1976 California burgundy which was excellent. Sean ordered a beer and Jack did the same.

Sean drank half the beer on his first swallow, and eased back in the booth somewhat. Maggie couldn't help studying his face. He was tired; sore. He looked worn, and yet even the weariness seemed to add to his character, and she was frightened by the force of the emotions that pulsed through her. He hadn't hesitated. When there was trouble, he instinctively ran into the fray. He hadn't been stupid, he'd done his damned best not to kill. And when the drunken perp had assaulted him, he'd fought back with strength and determination. And Ray had fallen.

She bit lightly into her lower lip, staring down into her wine.

Ray had fallen. Dead. But not until after he had come after Sean while surely almost half dead.

She shook.

She looked back to Sean, alarmed to feel tears of gratitude welling in her eyes. Jack excused himself for a trip to the men's room.

Sean's fingers closed over hers. He smiled. A rueful, tired, half-smile.

"What are you thinking?"

"I . . . I was thinking that it's amazing that Mamie is a woman who sells human flesh," she said. It was only a lie in that it wasn't her present thought.

Sean shrugged. "Mamie isn't evil in what she's doing," he murmured. He lifted his hands, then drew a finger around the rim of his beer glass. "Mamie doesn't make arrangements for anyone to do anything he or she isn't about to do already. She takes a very small commission from women who would be walking the street one way or another."

Maggie arched a brow to him, curiously amused. "You're a cop condoning prostitution?"

"I'm a cop aware that he can't stop prostitution—Jesus himself wasn't quite able to manage that feat. Remember, we're talking about the oldest profession. In a city like New Orleans— where we do have some of the wildest sex clubs in the nation— the best I can hope to do is keep it down at its seediest."

"But shouldn't you be arresting Mamie?"

"I already arrested Mamie—I needed her to talk."

"Ah . . . the lesser of two evils."

"I think Mamie is definitely the lesser of two evils—when you consider this murderer."

Maggie nodded. Oh, yes. Definitely.

"Well, Mamie also carries excellent wine. Would you order me another glass? I'm off to powder my nose," she said.

Sean's mouth curled into a wry smile and he lifted his hands as if in defeat. "Here I am, the hard-working and worn-out cop—deserted by my friend and lover alike."

"I will be right back," she assured him, then frowned. "Jack has been gone a while."

"He's probably calling in to see what's going on. The guy with the rotten teeth today—skinny old Rutger—was squawking away about his lawyer coming in. I want to make sure we've got him locked up for at least one night."

"The girl—Callie—is in the hospital?"

Sean nodded gravely. "I'd like to figure out somewhere to whisk her away to before Rutger hits the streets—and her— again."

"Can't you get a restraining order?"

"The chief is working on it."

"Good. I'm glad. Poor kid."

"We'll see if we can't get her a break somewhere," he said lightly, and offered her a sexy smile. "Hurry back. We supposedly have a great appetizer tray on the way."

Maggie felt a compelling warmth sweeping through her as he smiled. He had a great smile. His dimples showed, his eyes became blue fire. The rugged lines of his face softened, making him both very handsome and very masculine. She moistened her lips, tempted to pause and just whisper the words . . .

She was falling in love with him. She didn't want to do so, of course, but still . . .

He was Sean.

She turned quickly, and headed for the ladies' room.

Yet along the way, she paused and scrutinized the clientele in Mamie's herself. Each and every face.

She checked her watch, and nervously wondered just how late Sean intended to stay. The evening seemed to be passing far too quickly.

Dusk had come and gone . . .

And there was a full moon rising.

* * *

London
Late Summer, 1888

Murder wasn't at all unusual in the East End.

Fights broke out in bars.

Husbands beat their wives.

Drunks came at one another with knives and broken bottles.

Still, even in the East End, there was usually motive for murder.

Robbery. Hate, jealousy, passion.

Whores sometimes died, abused by their clientele. But by August 1888, London was already prey to a number of strange events.

Several female torsos had been discovered in the Thames.

One East End prostitute died, the victim of a gang rape by three men, terrible damage done to her genitals by a blunt object.

Two women plying their trade had been threatened by men with knives.

Then, in the wee hours of the morning after the Bank Holiday of August 6, 1888, the body of a woman was found in George Yard. She had been savagely stabbed thirty-nine times.

There was no real panic at that point. The murder made the papers; she wasn't identified at first except as a woman of middle age and height, with black hair and a round face—apparently belonging to the lowest classes. The newspapers did comment on the way that she had been "butchered," and that a sense of insecurity was being felt. She was soon identified as Martha Tabrum, and since she had last been seen walking the streets with a soldier, soldiers were paraded before possible witnesses, all to no avail.

Peter was deeply disturbed by the murder; he didn't want Megan accompanying him into the East End anymore. She assured him, trying to be light, that she wouldn't be soliciting soldiers while helping him with his work. She won the argument, but Peter still seemed disturbed.

Then, on August 31, the body of another woman was found. She was identified within twenty-four hours as being Mary Ann or—as she was known to her friends—Polly Nichols. Her throat had been violently slashed, and worse. She had been savagely mutilated. Her throat had been slit so that her head was nearly detached, and her stomach had been ripped open, her intestines exposed.

Police and surgeons argued; newspapers speculated. Most believed that this new murder was different from that of Martha Tabrum, though the victims were equally sad women who had led sad lives, falling to the depths of doss houses, prostituting for the few coins to buy a bed in a public house, and sometimes—as Polly had done that night—spending bed earnings on liquor several times before actually attempting to buy a bed for a night.

Peter was again worried about Megan accompanying him on his rounds into the dark underbelly of the East End. "There is such wretched horror there!" he insisted.

Megan again insisted that she would be fine; she was assisting a doctor, not prostituting. Laura argued with her husband; Megan insisted that Peter himself could be in danger, and Laura quit arguing with her—maybe there was safety in two of them working together.

Peter worked the doss houses, warning the women away from prostitution. Working among the women, Megan began to find the murders all the more tragic. The dirty, mist laden streets of the East End had created some fast friendships and she learned about the murder victims. Once upon a time, Polly had been respectably married. She had borne five children. Her marriage had failed. Some blamed the breakup on the nurse who had lived in her house during her last confinement; her husband blamed it on her penchant for drink, and claimed that she had deserted him several times. Polly had wandered, living at workhouses, returning home to her father for a spell, moving on to more workhouses and doss houses. Not long before her death, she had taken work as a domestic servant, and she had tried to make contact with her family again, writing to her father that she was employed and doing well. On the night she died, Polly had been pathetically proud of her new black bonnet. She had been cheerful despite her alcoholism and the sad state of her life, and those friends she had made on the streets had been very fond of her.

From the very beginning, there was an argument as to whether the same killer had done in both Martha and Polly. They were both middle-aged women, sad to extreme, with broken marriages and problems with alcohol. They were poor, pathetic creatures, who prostituted on the streets.

With Polly's death, political upheaval began, people riding hard on the police, and the politics of the Home Office coming hard under attack as well. The respectable citizens of Victorian England began to scream that something must be done, and the lives of many who had been like dust swept under a carpet were suddenly exposed.

Megan was passionate about her work with Peter. There were so many children who needed help, so many women who might be turned to a better life with just a little nudge. The killer made it all the more important that they not desert a people who needed all the charity that they could get.

On Saturday, September 8, the body of Annie Chapman was found.

Dark Annie. Poor Annie. Megan learned from her contemporaries, sitting with the huddling women in a public house one morning, that Annie was perhaps the most pathetic victim so far. She'd married a coachman named John Chapman, and borne three children. Her son was born a cripple. Her precious Emily Ruth died of meningitis at the age of twelve. Her second daughter was with a traveling troupe or circus in France, and her boy was taken into the care of a charitable school. Her marriage became frayed, and snapped. Her husband gave her a small allowance, then died. Despite the breakup and her arrangements with other men, she was shattered by the news, and was left destitute.

Making her way in the East End.

Until she met her killer.

The papers talked of a man named "Leather Apron," a

slipper maker who bullied prostitutes with a knife. Leather Apron could not be found.

Peter grew morose. And coming home with him in the very early morning hours, Megan found out why. "Have you noticed that you haven't seen me when these vicious crimes have taken place?" he demanded.

Incredulous, Megan stared at him. "What are you saying, Peter?"

"I'm wondering if I haven't lost my mind. I keep having the strangest blackouts. Something attracts my attention while on the streets, or even inside, and suddenly, I've blacked out again. I awaken, in a different place, and don't know where I am, or where I've been."

"But, Peter—"

"The first murder, I was here alone. The second murder, you were with me, but you stayed in the Remington house, if you'll recall, while I said I was going to see to old Mr. Throgmorton below. The third murder . . . you were in the public house trying to educate the whores."

"Oh, come, Peter! You'd be drenched in blood, you'd be—"

"Twice it seems there was not the blood on the victims where it should have been. And all the medical experts agree that the victims were most probably partially strangled before death at least, and that the blood soaked backward and did not spray."

"Peter, you can't really believe this! Why should you suddenly slay prostitutes?"

"I don't know, I don't know!" he moaned, and he suddenly stopped, and leaned against the building they were passing, slumping to the ground. He pressed his skull between his hands. "Megan, I last awoke with a bloodied knife by my side. And blood on my cloak. I panicked, and washed in a butcher's yard, and left the knife atop his work aprons. If that man should become suspect—"

"I've heard nothing, Peter. But you are not doing this. I promise you."

He shook his head. "What if I am losing my mind? What if I have looked at those poor, rotten-toothed, drink-laden old hags so long that I can't bear it anymore and feel that they must be better off dead?''

''Oh, Peter! If you thought them better off dead, you'd shoot them in the heart and be done with it. And you're far too moral to consider yourself the judge of who should live and who should die to begin with. And if you ever lost your mind and started killing prostitutes, you'd not be ripping them up in such a macabre and ghastly manner! Please, Peter, this is insanity.''

''Megan, I'm scared.''

''Peter—rumors abound, I do assure you. Everyone is accused, from immigrants to midwives to royalty. The police can't give the newspapers too much information or they'll have nothing to work with, and so the press takes what it can and invents the rest from speculation among frightened women in the public houses. You listen to me, Peter. You're a good doctor—and a good man. You are not a killer. That is fact!''

He nodded after a moment. ''But what is happening to me? What is happening?''

She smiled at him. ''I guess we'll have to consult another physician!'' she told him, smiling. And he smiled as well at last.

She helped him up. She was suddenly determined that she had to keep going to the East End. At first, it had been to help the women.

Now she was determined to catch a killer. She loved both Peter and Laura. She couldn't bear to see them hurt. And with Peter's desperate confession, she had realized that she just might be the only female in the East End with the power to catch the killer.

CHAPTER 10

Mamie bustled over with the appetizer herself. Sean arched a brow as she set the plate on the table, sliding beside him at the booth as she made a presentation.

"Honey, there you have some of the finest steamed crawfish in all Louisiana. Escargot in butter and wine sauce, the little fried triangles there are the alligator tail, umm, let's see, shrimp, onion strings, and Cajun potato poppers. Guaranteed to make you need another beer," she said with a wink.

"Ah . . . looks great," Sean said.

"Where are your friends?"

"Rest rooms. Have you seen our fellow? I've seen a few guys in nice suits around. Slim, dark."

Mamie shook her head. "He isn't here. And I have the oddest feeling that I'd know, that I'd feel him watching me if he were to show . . . rest assured, Lieutenant. I do intend to help you get this guy."

"Good. Thanks, Mamie. You know, we ran the sketch in the paper. Hopefully, it will keep women away from the bastard."

"Whores, you mean," Mamie said lightly.

"Women. And men, for that matter. Victim number two was a—"

"Pimp."

"I was going to say man."

"He was a pimp," Mamie said matter-of-factly.

Sean shrugged. "All right. He was a real son-of-a-bitch, and maybe he deserved to die."

Mamie smiled. "I like you, Lieutenant, you know that?"

"Thanks."

"In fact," she said, lowering her voice, "I'm concerned about you."

He arched a brow.

"This is New Orleans." Mamie said it the native way. It flowed off her tongue. *Naw-leans.*

He smiled, thinking of the conversation he'd had with Maggie that day. They were all getting spooked. It did seem a bit more natural that a woman like Mamie would be more attuned to occultism than Maggie.

"Go on."

"Honey, whether you like it or not, there is good air—and bad. The world is filled with all kinds of vibes, and it don't matter if you're white, black, French, English, or anything in between. There's bad in this city right now. And I'm worried about you."

"Mamie—I'm a cop. I carry a gun. I look after myself."

"And you're not stupid, and you're no fool. But I want you to go see a woman named Marie Lescarre," Mamie told him very seriously.

"Why?" he asked, a half-smile curving into his lips.

"Because she's got the vision."

"She's a voodoo and she's going to want to milk me for a bunch of money?"

Mamie sat back, shaking her head sadly. "Boy, you need some help, and it's simply beyond me to give it. Take your girlfriend."

"Maggie?" he said, surprised. His eyes narrowed and he was startled to hear how defensive his voice sounded. "Excuse me, you're saying there's something bad about Maggie?"

"Oh, no! Why, she is one beautiful woman with a gentle voice and way, either despite her self-confidence or because of it."

"Okay, then—"

"Don't go getting mad. I repeat, I'm not saying that the girl is evil or anything of the like. In fact, honey, she seems to have some kind of a good aura circling round her pretty little head. But something's not right, and that I can tell you."

"Mamie, you were the one who gave me my lead, my best clue yet. You saw a flesh and blood man, so we both know that at the very least. There's a bad man out there, an evil man, if you will. And that's who we're after."

"You should still see Marie Lescarre." Mamie was suddenly talking fast, and he could see that Jack was returning at last. Apparently, Mamie didn't want Jack hearing. "You can find her at Jackson Square most of the time right at dusk, selling her 'oils.' She's got a license—she's all legal. I'm not looking for police favors for anyone here, I just think you should see her!"

Mamie turned just as Jack arrived, offering him a big smile. "Sugar, you sit down and start eating! I'll see that your waiter brings you more wine and beer."

Mamie slipped away. Jack sat down, stuffing an alligator tail into his mouth as he did so. "Two things," he muttered around the food, then chewed, looking at Sean unhappily.

"What?"

Jack winced slightly. "Rutger's out already."

"What?" Sean snapped, leaning forward.

"His lawyer pitched such a fit, promised to sue the department, civil rights, the whole nine yards. But don't worry—we've got armed protection on the girl."

Sean stared at him, leaning back. "How the hell did we manage that at this time? I'd have thought we'd get a no on that with what's going on in the city. How can the department afford more overtime?"

"Off-duty guys doing it for free," Jack said, smiling. "You never know, huh?"

"I think I'll still take a side trip by the hospital on the way home."

Jack nodded. "Sure."

"Well?"

"Yeah?"

"You said *two* things."

"Oh, yeah . . ."

"Well?"

"Maggie . . ."

"What about Maggie?"

"I don't know. You might want to caution her to be careful, huh?"

"Why? What's going on?" Sean asked, frowning.

Jack shrugged. "Well, she seemed to be scouting the place out herself, looking for this guy."

"What do you mean? She was on her way to the rest room."

"Yeah, well, she was walking in that general direction. But she didn't see me on the phone. And she was looking. Looking hard. You've got to emphasize to her that this guy is dangerous."

Sean sipped his beer. "Yeah. Yeah, I will."

Maggie returned and sat down next to him. His head was suddenly pounding as he looked at her. She smiled at him. Angelically.

"See anything?" he asked her.

She frowned, beautiful eyes grave. "Like . . .?"

"It seemed you were looking around," he said, taking care not to say that Jack was the one who had been noting her movements.

"Oh . . . well, naturally, I was looking for the man your artists sketched."

Naturally. Was he being ridiculously sensitive to every movement, every look . . .

He felt uneasy, spooked.

Why not?

Mamie had said that Maggie had an aura.

Since when had he listened to voodoo mumbo jumbo?

Blood drops had led to her doorway . . .

"Maggie, when we're through here, we're going to stop by the hospital, do you mind?"

"Something else happened to Callie?"

"No, but Rutger's out," Sean said.

"Rutger's *out?*" she repeated.

Jack laid a hand on hers. "Some off-duty guys are watching over her. She'll be all right."

"It's just infuriating that—" She broke off, shaking her head. "What am I saying? You guys put your lives on the line, and then . . ."

"The bad guys walk," Sean said. "Sometimes it stinks. But I still believe in the law." He sipped his beer, staring at Maggie. "Don't you?"

She smiled. "Most of the time."

"We've got this great appetizer tray and now everyone is depressed," Jack said. "Alligator tail?" he offered Maggie.

"Don't mind if I do," she said.

She dipped the little triangle into cocktail sauce.

Sean realized that it looked as if they were all dipping into a little pot of blood.

Rutger Leon swaggered down the street, arms swinging at his sides. He patted his pocket, making sure he carried his knife.

The cop had brought him down.

His lawyer had set him free. Old Iggy—*Esquire,* as he liked to call himself—couldn't make it without Rutger's kind of money. Drug money. Blood money.

Rutger felt like laughing again.

The bitch was going to get hers. That damned Callie. Coming to him whining, begging for another pop when she wasn't pulling her own weight in any shape or form. Once, she'd been a pretty little thing, good in bed, eager to please. Man, she'd do anything for a fix—anything. He liked the taste he got in his mouth, just thinking about it. Still, she'd caused this, caused him to get arrested—and Ray killed. Of course, Ray had gone off the deep end—*charging* an armed cop, but it was still her damned fault, and now she was going to get hers.

The cops assumed the bitch was safe. But there were always leaks. So now little Callie was in the hospital, shaking away by now, he was certain, facing withdrawal. Poor baby.

He walked around the corner, looking up at the building. He

had the room number, the floor number, and his hospital greens. Callie was going to have the words "whore" and "bitch" carved into her back cheeks before the cops on duty ever suspected trouble.

Maybe it was a good thing Ray got killed. Rutger wanted Callie back. Wanted her when she was in one of those moods to do anything—*anything*—at all that he wanted. And she wouldn't be too quick to make it with anyone other than a john he'd picked out for her—not with her butt all carved up with his signature descriptions. Actually, she wasn't going to get much punishment—not half of what she deserved.

He smiled, thinking about her expression while he told her what he meant to do . . .

Hospitals—no matter how the administration tried to modernize them—smelled like hospitals. Maggie didn't mind visiting, but she was always glad to leave.

She was glad she and Sean had come. It was good to see Callie all scrubbed up, pale and wan and hurting still, but sedated to get through the night.

Callie smiled when she saw them.

"You guys really came."

"Sure," Sean said, sitting at the foot of her bed.

Callie twitched. She'd probably twitch now and then for a long time to come, Maggie thought. Drugs were a disease like no other.

Callie looked at Maggie shyly. "You're not even a cop."

Maggie shook her head. "We just wanted to see how you're doing."

"Hand's all wrapped up," Callie said. She winced suddenly, and closed her eyes, groaning. "Oh, God, I don't know, I don't know . . ."

Maggie reached out suddenly, squeezing her hand. "Fight it. Think that you're going to be clean, you're going to start over. Hell, Callie, think about that guy's teeth! That's enough to keep you off the street."

Callie had been in hellish pain. It was evident in her ashen coloring. Still, she smiled. ''His teeth do just suck, don't they? Thank God, Rutger's in jail. I hope they throw away the key!''

Sean glanced at Maggie, then back to Callie. ''Actually, Callie, they let Rutger out.''

''Oh, God, I'm a dead woman!'' Callie breathed.

''No, you're not,'' Maggie said firmly.

''You have two cops out in the hall, Callie. Friends of mine— good guys. Two more cops will spell them in a while. You're going to be fine.''

Tears pooled in Callie's eyes. She looked like a little girl lost, so small against the white expanse of her hospital bed, frail beneath the worn hospital gown. ''I wish I could believe you!''

''Well, you'll believe me come the morning. I'll be back in about ten.''

''Nine,'' Maggie corrected.

Sean looked at her.

''We'll come before you take me into work, and I really need to be in by ten. A Monday morning, you know.''

Sean offered her the half-smile she loved so much, and touched Callie's cheek. ''Try to get some rest. They're going to give you another shot. Help you along a little, okay?''

Callie tried to smile.

''You're going to be all right,'' Sean assured her. His voice was determined, gentle.

He rose, and took Maggie's hand. They paused to talk to the two cops outside Callie's door.

''Maggie, Jimmy Cross, Angus Canham—guys, Maggie Montgomery,'' Sean said, introducing them. Jimmy was about thirty, crinkly brown hair, friendly hazel eyes. Angus was older, white-haired, with pale-blue sparkling eyes. They both shook her hand, acknowledging her with a speculation Sean ignored.

''I understand you guys have all managed to be here on your own time. It's great, and I really appreciate it.''

''Hey, Sean, it's a tough time for all of us,'' Jimmy said. ''The last weeks have been brutal. If we can help the little waif in there, all the better.''

Angus nodded. ''Sean, now, ye're a man puttin' in his own

fair share of hours, and we heard ye were afraid fer the wee lass,'' he said. Obviously, Maggie thought, Angus was as Scottish as his name. He smiled at her. "He's a right fine fellow there, eh, Ms. Montgomery? We'd do a lot fer the likes of him, we would.''

"That's great!'' she assured him. Impulsively, she kissed his cheek. "Thanks.''

"Hey!'' Sean protested, laughing. "Angus, you're stealing my girl. It's that accent. Women are suckers for an accent!''

"Hey, Angus, want to teach me an accent?'' Jimmy queried hopefully.

" 'Tis me charm, and not me accent, young whippersnapper!'' Angus claimed.

They all laughed, bidding one another good night. When they reached Sean's place, Maggie immediately turned into his arms as he closed the door, throwing her arms around him, kissing him hungrily, with passion, need—and tenderness.

"Hey!'' he murmured softly against her lips, tugging at her zipper, and then her hemline. "What did I do to deserve this?''

"You're just you!'' she whispered against his mouth, kissing him again. "You're just . . . you . . .''

He kissed her back. Their clothing was strewn. She was up in his arms, feeling his strength, his warmth. Naked, he crawled over her in his bed. He threaded his fingers through her hair. She studied his face. Loved his eyes. The planes of his cheeks. His dimples. His smile. Loved the strength that lay within his heart.

"Sean . . .'' she whispered.

"What?''

"I . . .''

"Yesss . . .?'' he teased softly, nuzzling her lower lip with his own, planting a kiss between her breasts.

"I'm falling in love with you,'' she whispered.

He stiffened slightly; stared at her. Smiled very slowly, and then his smile faded and his eyes were dead serious. "I fell the moment I met you,'' he told her.

And his teasing attitude was dropped.

And he made love to her with a wild, wicked passion that exceeded her every expectation.

He dwelt in darkness. A strange darkness.

Then he was aware of noise, and of a moving sensation.

He felt as if he were very slowly struggling awake after a long and incredibly deep sleep.

He was cold; he shivered.

No wonder. He was sleeping on something very hard, and very cold. He was aware suddenly of unyielding . . . steel? . . . beneath his body. He inhaled suddenly, sharply. Something was sucked into his mouth. In panic, he pawed at it. A sheet. He'd drawn his sheet all the way over his head.

He became aware of light then; light, pools of piercing light that fought back the shadows that hovered over most of the room.

He began to hear a trickling of water.

Up. He needed to get up. It seemed so hard. He was accustomed to doing whatever the hell he damned pleased. He was a strong man. Hell, he cracked heads when he felt like it.

But he'd had that fight, though. With the cop. The asshole had shot him, that was it, he was in the hospital, he was . . .

Hungry.

Hungry in a way he'd never imagined. Desperately hungry for meat. Red meat. Raw meat. No, no, no . . .

Something red, but . . .

Oh, yeah. Real raw.

Blood.

He managed to sit up. He looked around. Hospital room. Sterile tile. Water running. Shadows of night still in the room, yet a brilliant pool of light over his bed. He squinted. Something else up there. A microphone?

And the bedside table . . .

It wasn't quite right.

He scratched his hairy abdomen and looked down at his

round belly and flaccid penis. Shit. He was sleeping naked in the hospital?

He grinned. Maybe it was a Catholic hospital. And maybe he could stir up an erection before a nun showed up.

He felt great all of a sudden. Strong as an ox. And still, so damned . . . thirsty.

Hungry.

Desperate for something . . .

Red.

Strange. Everything was strange. Some hospital. He looked at the bedside table again. There were surgical instruments on it. Something that looked like a damned bone saw. Scalpels, things that looked like forceps . . .

A doorway was open. He was distracted from the bedside table as he saw someone walk by. A woman in a lab coat. Pretty, young. Short, dark hair, nice, clean-scrubbed face. She looked like a med student, maybe. He found himself staring at her throat. Amazing. He could hear her heartbeat. He could see the veins in her neck . . . pulsing. He wanted to touch her. Kiss her. Suck her neck. Bite down, see blood gushing all around her.

Ah, yes . . .

Bite, rip, break, tear . . .

Drink.

He heard a whir of movement and turned. He blinked, wondering if he was dreaming up the hospital, if he wasn't already dead, and if—strangely—he hadn't arrived in heaven. There was an angel moving toward him. Moving in smoke, in clouds, or in mist, coming toward him. Naked. Whoa.

But there was something in the angel's eyes, something angry. The angel had read his mind. But he was feeling powerful. So powerful. More powerful even than he had begun to feel before . . .

Before his fight with the cop.

"All right, baby. Come my way!" he urged. His voice was husky, strange. "Baby, the other looked sweet, but now you . . ." He let out a howling sound, staring at the elegant length of her neck. "I'm about to glut—and dine."

The angel had a strangely determined voice as well. "I don't think so—you vicious brute."

He'd been feeling powerful. Incredibly strong, powerful.

But she was strong as well.

And faster.

Before he could move, she'd plucked up the bone saw.

She was so fast, indeed, that he was pitched into the true darkness of hellfire and damnation even as he realized just what she meant to do . . .

Rutger took his time.

He sauntered into the hospital at midnight, making his way to the maternity ward.

No one noticed a nervous man in the waiting room.

He drank coffee, watched cable news. He wished he knew the killer who ruled the news. Now, there was a man who knew how to deal with lying, cheating, no-good women.

In the wee hours of the morning, just before dawn, he slipped into a maintenance closet and unfolded his hospital greens, covering his head and hair, and half tying a mask around his lower face. He walked through the hospital, acknowledging the few nurses and aides who greeted him in the hall with a return wave.

At one of the nurses' stations, he helped himself to a prepared shot of some old geezer's nighttime sedative and hurried onward again.

As he'd suspected, there was only one guard on Callie's door by that time. A tall, slim, good-looking dark-haired dude, maybe thirty, thirty-five. His head was leaned against the wall; he was dozing.

Rutger walked briskly toward Callie's door—finding her room had been a simple matter of asking at a different nurses' station.

Then again, the plainclothes cop—still obviously a cop— was a dead giveaway as well.

"Hello, Doctor," the cop said, standing to greet him.

What luck. He could pin the cop with the sedative so easily now.

"Hello, there. How's my patient doing?" Rutger asked cheerfully, approaching the cop. His hand in his pocket, he fingered the needle and syringe, drawing it out and holding it against his side.

"Seems to be doing fine, Doctor."

"Well, good. And it's good to have you out here!" Rutger beamed.

In a flash, he raised the syringe, and jabbed it into the cop's arm.

Good cop.

He slumped back against the wall, fell to his rear, his head bowed over.

Rutger stepped over him.

All right. He had to work fast. Didn't know when some real members of the hospital staff might be coming by. Close the door first. Then get a gag around Callie's mouth. Didn't want her to let out a scream that might alert someone . . .

She was sleeping restlessly. He stood over her, gently picked up one wrist, and then the other, tying them to the bedposts with surgical tape he had pilfered from the nurses' station along with the syringe. Callie was so sedated, she didn't awaken at first. He pulled a sock from his pocket to gag her. As he stuffed it into her mouth, he slapped her cheeks.

It was time for her to wake up.

She did. Her eyes widened like saucers. She tried to scream, but choked as he taped her lips, forcing the sock more deeply into her mouth. She was powerless, and terrified. He pulled his knife out, smiling at her. "Yeah, baby. I'm here. Oh, yeah, you betcha. But guess what? I'm not going to kill you. I'm just going to make you wish you were dead."

Her eyes closed; to his vast dismay, she slumped against the bed in a dead faint.

"No way!" he muttered furiously, stepping forward again. Let's see how she'd sleep if he slashed her right in the face!

A cold suddenly settled over him. He froze, sensing someone behind him. He managed to turn.

The cop was behind him.

Couldn't be! He'd knocked the damn cop out. But there he was, smiling pleasantly.

"Doc, now, is that any way to treat a patient?" the cop demanded.

"Man, you should have stayed down!" Rutger muttered, but he still felt the cold. "You should have stayed passed out, because now I'm going to have to stick you in the gut, pig!"

The cop smiled, shaking his head. "You've got it all wrong, Rutger. Now I'm going to have to stick you."

Rutger saw the hands descending upon his shoulders. He was lifted, drawn forward. Just as if he weighed no more than five pounds.

The pig was opening his mouth!

Ah, hell, just what he needed, a gay cop. The guy was going for his damned neck.

Rutger almost managed to scream.

But his scream was nothing more than a gurgle. His vein was instantly, expertly punctured.

He was unconscious in a matter of seconds.

The room was filled with a complacent slurping sound.

Rutger was drained. Dry. The "cop" let him fall to the floor.

Callie began to awaken with a growing sense of panic, remembering that Rutger was in the room. She wrenched at the tapes holding her wrists, choking on the gag, trying desperately to get some sound out.

Then she froze. Rutger was on the floor. A cop was in the room with her, seated across from her, in the visitor's chair.

The cop belched, then drew a hand to his lips, looking slightly embarrassed. "Excuse me!" he said. He rose, stretched, and nudged Rutger with a toe. He plucked him up from the floor then, holding him easily, as if he was no more than an ashen rag doll.

Then, with a powerful movement, the cop ripped Rutger's head from his body.

Once again, Callie passed out cold.

The cop took a step toward her.

*   *   *

He was riding again, his horse's hooves pounding the earth, spraying dirt over the length of the field.

A . . . battlefield.

The boom of a cannon sounded, as loud as a thunder clap. He was blinded by the powder that filled the air around him. He inhaled the smoke, the powder, the smell of death. From somewhere, a horse screamed.

"Hold up, hold up!" he commanded. "Take to the far cove of trees!"

Men rode with him. He looked at their faces, and he knew them, yet, for some reason, he couldn't remember their names. They were dependent on him, and he knew that danger came from everywhere, and still . . .

God, but he was anxious for the day to end. Come hell or high water, he would ride to her. He had to see her, had to reach her, touch her, feel her. He could endure it all, when he heard her voice . . .

But again, he heard the explosion of cannon fire, and the dirt and trees before him suddenly exploded and . . .

Sean awoke. His eyes flew wide open, and he stared at his ceiling. He was vaguely aware of the dream—nightmare?— that had so recently plagued him. It had been so real, but now it faded quickly away, and it just seemed a silly dream. He lay, breathing deeply, mentally shaking his head at the fine sheen of perspiration that lay over his body. He was like a kid, surely, wanting to play soldier.

How long had he dreamed? He suddenly worried that he might have awakened Maggie. He reached out for her.

She was gone.

He bolted up, anxious. Gone. Gone where? Had she tried to make it back to her office, wanting to awake in her own place to shower and dress for work. God, no. There was a maniac at large in New Orleans.

"Maggie!"

He almost shouted her name; his voice was hoarse.

"Sean?"

He swung around, blinking. She was standing in the bathroom doorway, lithe and naked, a glass of water in her hand, red hair falling around her slim shoulders like a crimson cloak in the muted night light.

"Oh, man, Maggie!" Shaking with relief, he buried his head in his hands.

She walked to the bed, silent and graceful, setting her glass on the bedside table.

"Sean?" she repeated softly.

"Oh, God, Maggie, you scared the hell out of me!" he told her.

"I'm here, Sean."

He pulled her down to the bed. She slipped easily into his arms, and he held her tightly, tenderly against him. She threaded her fingers through his hair, her eyes on his, soft, liquid gold.

"You know I lied earlier," she told him.

"Oh?"

"I'm not . . . falling in love with you."

"You're not?"

He felt the jagged slam of his own heart.

"I do love you, Sean," she whispered. And he smiled, and held her closer. Her free hand fell against his chest. "But I'm afraid, Sean!" she added on a barely audible breath. "I'm so damned scared!"

"Don't be afraid. I'm with you, Maggie. I love you, Maggie."

She was quiet as he sat in the darkness and shadows, rocking with her.

Yet he was strangely convinced that was exactly *why* she was afraid . . .

But he couldn't begin to fathom her reasoning.

All he knew was that he was afraid himself.

Afraid that he would lose her.

So he held her all the more tightly, and told himself that he simply wouldn't let her go.

* * *

London
September, 1888

Newspapers were wild with speculation.

And information came to the streets through the inquests into the deaths of the murdered women. Dr. George Baxter Phillips, the divisional police surgeon, believed that Dark Annie's killer must have had some surgical skill or anatomical knowledge to have mutilated and removed organs in the manner done—and in the time the murderer must have had.

Papers spoke of a monster. A creature with the ability to melt into the shadows and mist of the night.

More rational people whispered of some manner of a slaughterhouse worker—or a surgeon. Perhaps there was a madman out there procuring human organs for medical schools—killing for gain.

The police had a number of suspects, but no investigations seemed to pan out. "Leather Apron," or George Pizer, an immigrant accused of threatening whores with a knife, was found and taken in, but he had an alibi for each murder, and it turned out he had been hiding out in fear of what the maddened throngs might do.

Several suspects were saved by the police from lynch mobs.

At first, after the Chapman killing, people lived in terror. The streets of Whitechapel were deserted in the late-night hours.

Then the days began to pass, and despite the fact that the outcry remained in the papers and the vigilante committees continued to function, women began to move about again. They had to survive.

Robert Louis Stevenson's Dr. Jekyll and Mr. Hyde *was showing in London; Peter took Laura and Megan to see the play, and they enjoyed the fine acting. Yet, after the play, Peter discovered that even the actors—due to the nature of the play— had been interviewed by the police, and that seemed to cause him a melancholy that deeply disturbed Megan. No word of Peter's fears had ever been whispered to Laura, but she was a loving and devoted wife who saw his depression. She thought he was working too hard, and she encouraged him to stay home. Peter obligingly remained put for a week, but then grew restless. He had to continue his work.*

Megan would not think of allowing him to do so without her.

As September passed, she began to breathe more easily. The murderer had moved on elsewhere, many believed. She knew that Peter was innocent, and on a more personal note, she was relieved to assume that Aaron had found greener pastures to haunt and had opted to leave her alone.

Then the killer struck again.

Twice, in the early morning hours of September 30.

At a time when Peter had gone out to seek a cab, only to disappear.

They had been attending a sick child at the home of Melville and Ana Charlton; she was a laundress, he a carman. They and their four children lived in the bottom floor of a three-story dwelling off Providence Street. Peter went out, and did not return.

Megan chatted reassuringly with Ana, who rocked her sick baby, then, as the time passed, she grew increasingly nervous. Peter did not come back for her to tell her that their hansom had arrived, and at last, she excused herself to Ana and went out in search of him.

Fog swirled low on the ground. The lamps offered little illumination against the shadows in the night. "Peter!" she shrieked his name, and she began to run.

The streets began to look alike. Narrow here, wide there, dark shadows that seemed to live and breathe with lives all their own haunted every nook and cranny. "Peter!" she cried again, and began to run. And run. It seemed she ran throughout the night, from street to street, shadow to shadow.

Along Berner Street, she first heard the cry of "Murder!" And slowing her gait, she drew her cloak about her and came closer and closer until she heard the murmurs of workers and neighbors who had come to gawk as the police stood guard over the body.

"Another one!" cried a raggedly dressed woman.

"A woman dead," sighed a carman, shaking his head.

"Slain!" said the young woman at his side.

"Throat slit!" clucked an old man.

"Still warm, poor creature, when they found her!" whispered the elderly woman at his side.

"A monster, surely, for she was murdered in just minutes, so say the police patrolling the area!" said the carman.

"Poor thing isn't butchered at least!" murmured the old woman.

The old man stared down at her. *"Like as not, he didn't have time."*

Megan turned away. Stumbling down the street, she worried desperately about Peter, wondering at her own sanity. Could he be right? Could he be doing these terrible things?

No, she told herself, no! She knew Peter. She had come to know good and evil. Peter was good.

But where was he?

CHAPTER 11

There was a rustling sound. Sean awoke instantly. He slept with his .38 special on the night stand, within split-second reach, and he had always prided himself on his ability to awaken in a flash.

Lately he hadn't been doing so good on the "flash" part. He was sleeping more deeply. He had never been plagued by nightmares before. Maybe he did need to go see the old voodoo woman as Mamie had suggested.

The sound was Maggie, slipping from bed. He lay back for a minute, watching her, trying to warn his anatomy not to get too excited at the sight—it was morning, and they needed to get going. But Maggie was beautiful, and the mind cannot always rule the body.

She left the bed, unaware that he watched her, and she stretched, arching her back, and he was reminded of an elegant Lladro statuette. He pulled down on the sheets. No good. They continued to tent.

She turned and caught his eyes, smiling. "You wake at the drop of a pin. I wanted to get coffee on."

"I used to wake at the drop of a pin. I'm not quite so good at it anymore. Getting old."

"Oh, come now. You're nearly a spring chicken."

"Honey, I'd be one tough spring chicken," he assured her.

Then he saw that her gold-tinted hazel eyes fell along the sheet, and she smiled with a small shrug, meeting his eyes again. "Well, you look wide awake."

He grinned back. "You just seem to have an eloquent way of saying, 'Rise and shine, boys.' "

Maggie laughed. He kept watching her, his eyes grave. "Of course, it is morning, and time is limited, and I wouldn't want to coerce you or anything."

"I do have to get to work, and—"

"We both want to go by to see Callie. Not to mention that I am in charge of the most bizarre homicide mystery to hit New Orleans in decades. Still . . ."

"When someone is so very wide awake . . . well, it would just be a shame to waste what's . . . so awake," she said huskily. She came around the bed. He eased up on an elbow, pulling her against him. He nuzzled her belly. Teased its softness. His tongue flickered over her flesh. Her fingers threaded into his hair. He nuzzled lower. She groaned, body arching.

"How long do you need?"

He paused. "Well, I think I'm supposed to exaggerate— only slightly, of course—and say, 'Honey, I could last all day and all night.' But at this particular minute, I think . . . about two, three minutes. If I'm lucky, five."

"Damned good, 'cause five is all we've got!" she whispered.

She was incredibly sexy, straddling over him. He cupped the globes of her breasts with his hands and felt the violent rush of pleasure as her body gloved his. Sexy or no, though, he suddenly wanted the upper hand, he felt a strange need to be the aggressor. He caught her waist, rolled them both without breaking contact, and took top position, impaling her deeply with a searing flash of nearly violent desire. Then her arms were around him and he groaned, and let nature itself take its course.

Afterward, they both lay dead still for several seconds, weak, spent. Then they both bolted up, making a mad dash for the shower.

"Hey!" Sean protested.

"I'm the guest. And you were the one who was so . . . wide awake."

"Oh, like you weren't willing."

"I try to be obliging."

"What are we arguing about? I can solve this."

"How?"

"We shower together."

She shrugged. "Don't go asking me to soap things for you. We really are out of time now."

They were out of time, so they quickly showered and dressed and grabbed paper cups of coffee down on the street.

The closer they came to the hospital, the more nervous Sean found himself becoming. Sure, there had been guards on, and long ago, he had learned to trust his fellow officers. If anything had gone wrong, he would have been called.

As they walked to Callie's room, he kept quickening his pace. "Is there a reason we're running?" Maggie asked.

"No." But he didn't slow down.

Frank Ducevny, a young beat cop, was sitting in the chair in front of Callie's door, chatting with a nurse's aide as he accepted coffee from her.

"Hey, Frank. This is Maggie Montgomery. Maggie, Frank. How's it going, how is the patient?"

"She had a rough night. Nightmares, tossing and turning."

"Withdrawal," Sean said briefly. "But how—?"

"Oh, she seems to be fine this morning. I popped in when I took over from the five-to-seven A.M. guy. She was sweet, a little rueful, and told me she dreamed she was wrestling with all kinds of demons last night."

"She's still got a long way to go," Sean said. He and Maggie entered Callie's room together. She was propped up in her bed. Her face remained pale, but her eyes were clear and sparkling when she acknowledged the two of them. "Hey, you guys!" she said weakly, but with pleasure. "Thanks. Really. Thanks for coming back."

"Of course we came back," Maggie said, taking her hand and sitting by her side. "We said we would."

"So, how's it going?" Sean asked.

"It's tough," she admitted. "You wouldn't believe the

dreams.'' She shivered, and looked at Sean. ''Rutger was in them. He was into some kind of a bondage thing.''

''Rutger?'' Sean said worriedly.

''Don't be so concerned—apparently, I was dreaming. Or hallucinating. The doc said I might have trouble with stuff like that for a while. I mean, if Rutger had been here, I'd be dead, right?''

''And there was a guard on your door all night, a cop, right?'' Maggie said.

Callie nodded complacently. ''Oh, yeah. One of them was a good-looking son of a gun. I had a few weird dreams about him, too. I mean *weird,* and I'm not sharing!'' She laughed. A pretty sound. A young sound. Then she sobered, looking from Sean to Maggie. ''Guess what?''

''What?'' Sean asked.

''My—my mom called. Apparently, there were some news cameras out there yesterday. She's going to come for me this afternoon, and she's going to go with me to a special clinic out West and pay for me to go through a rehab.'' Tears sprang into her eyes, and she tried to smile at Maggie. ''My mom. My mom is coming for me.''

''Oh, Callie, that's great!'' Maggie said.

Callie had leaned forward. Maggie hugged her, patting her back, soothing her, congratulating her. Sean watched, leaning against the wall. He thought about what Mamie had said about Maggie. She had a good aura. But something wasn't quite right.

A nurse popped her head into the room. ''Lieutenant Canady?''

''Yeah?''

''I've got a call for you at my station.''

''Oh?'' He arched a brow, then straightened, shrugging to Maggie. ''I'll be right back.''

''Who is it?'' he asked the nurse as he stepped into the hallway.

''Doctor LePont. Pierre LePont. From the morgue.''

She left him at the phone. Sean was dimly aware of dieticians bustling about with breakfast trays, doctors droning on as they made their rounds, and nurses pushing about their medicine carts.

He felt a heaviness in his heart.

"Pierre, please don't tell me we've got another body."

"No—no new ghastly murders."

"Then . . ."

"Well, I do have a ghastly scene on my hands."

"All right, Pierre, damn it, what—"

"I've got a guy killed twice here."

"What?"

"Early, early morning, the guy you shot yesterday was being pulled out for autopsy. He was lying on a gurney nice and quiet."

"They usually do, don't they?"

"Usually, yeah."

"But . . ."

"Well, someone came in here and killed the guy all over again."

"You're not making sense."

"Nothing makes sense. Sean, someone came in and cut the guy's head off. He's been decapitated, Lieutenant. How soon can you get down here?"

"Fifteen minutes."

Maggie wanted to go with him. She was insistent.

He was equally determined, and left her at the hospital with Frank, who was going to drive Maggie to Montgomery Enterprises, since he was being replaced by another cop in a few minutes.

Sean didn't know why he was so determined not to take Maggie with him, he just was. He was head over heels in love with her, she was the best thing that had ever happened to him, but Mamie was right: Something wasn't just right. Maybe she knew the murderer and was protecting him. Maybe she knew the murderer and didn't even realize that she knew him. He reasoned that he'd be better off keeping Maggie a little in the dark about developments.

At the morgue, Pierre showed him the body.

They both stared in a grim silence that became drawn out.

"I don't get it," Sean said.

"I wish I had some answers for you."

"You sure he was dead when he came in here?" Sean asked.

"Oh, come on, you're a cop! You killed him. You know damned well he was dead."

"Yeah, I suppose." Sean lifted his hands. "Maybe we're missing something. Maybe the decapitation is some part of a Satanic ritual, a religious thing . . . I don't know." He sighed. "Well, let me speak to your employees who were at hand. Then I'll get back with my task force and the FBI and see if we can't begin to make some sense of it all."

He spent two hours talking with everyone in the place. Jenson, the night guard, swore he'd been in front of the door without moving between the hours of two and seven. The skeletal night force had moved about as usual without seeing a stranger in the building.

Guys from the evidence lab arrived and tried to lift finger and footprints. None could be found. The bone saw, which apparently had been utilized for the grisly deed, was wiped clean. Gil, the specialist, warned Sean, "We've got prints from other items in the autopsy room, but I have a feeling we'll find they belong to the docs and the technicians. I'll keep you posted."

Pierre walked back out to Sean's car with him. "Not that it was impossible for anyone to come in," he said, "but . . . it's unlikely. I mean, suppose the guard did take a bathroom break. Suppose my employees were all in different labs. It's just bizarre."

Sean agreed. Bizarre.

"Thanks, and do keep me posted," Sean told him. He paused, slipping behind the driver's seat of his car. It was a beautiful day. Blue sky, little puffing clouds. The sun beamed down magnanimously. It didn't seem to be the right atmosphere for such macabre happenings.

But then again, night did come. Darkness, mist, fog, and shadows. He gave himself a shake. He was late for his task-force meeting.

Within an hour, he was seated in a conference room with

his people, and on their "what we have" board, he added the beheading of the corpse in the morgue.

"So, at this moment," he said, addressing the men and the one woman gathered before him, "we think we have three actual victims. Jane Doe, found in the cemetery, suspected to be a local prostitute. Anthony Beale, known pimp and petty criminal. Bessie Girou, high-paid call girl. Now we have a beheaded corpse as well."

"There was another prostitute, Shelley Mathews, killed down near Jackson Square," Gyn Elfin reminded him.

He nodded. "But no decapitation. Gerry," he said, addressing one of the other men, "aren't we about to make an arrest on an old boyfriend on that one?"

Gerry nodded. "The guy confessed. Not that confessions are always true."

"Right, but that has to be a different case, what do you say, Manny?"

Manny Garcia was the FBI profiler.

He shrugged. "I'd say definitely." He looked around at the cops, aware that FBI men could be resented by local law enforcement. "Profiling is coming along but it's still no guarantee. The Boston Strangler, Albert DiSalvo, was profiled as being a loner—he turned out to be a family man. Still, I'd say that there is a reason for the decapitations, and that we need to find out what it is. And our killer is a sociopath rather than a psychopath—meaning he's a man who is sane in that he does know what rational behavior should be, he merely flouts it and considers himself to be a cut above normal men, and therefore entitled to his excesses." He hesitated, looking at Sean. "He is a sexual killer, evidenced by the semen found, and by his method of mutilation—he slashed his female victims from the pubic area upward, attacking the genitals. I do believe, however, that either the killer himself beheaded the corpse, or else there are copycats in the city already, or a group of cultists. Why Beale was killed, I don't know. I tend to believe he stepped into the middle of our killer's fixation on prostitutes. And why the corpse was beheaded . . . I haven't a clue."

Sean sat back, flushing slightly as the others stared at him.

"All right, then, let's get moving on what we've got going. Gentlemen—and Gyn!'' he said, nodding his acknowledgment to their female member with an encouraging smile, "let's get out on the streets and see what we can find out. We need a connection between the corpse and the murder victims. We need to keep our eyes open for any sign of the man in the sketch Mamie helped us create. You all know your individual tasks. Let's get to it, before the city starts to take us apart."

The others filed from the room. Only Jack and Manny stayed behind.

"You got anything else for me, Manny? Anything at all?"

"Nothing tangible," Manny said.

"But . . ." Sean said hopefully.

"Just some comparisons," Manny said. He flipped open the screen on the state-of-the-art laptop computer he had with him at almost all times. He punched a few keys, and had Sean look over his shoulder. "Read this."

It was an autopsy report. Sean scanned it quickly.

. . . body was found on its back, head turned to left shoulder . . . intestines drawn out to a large extent and placed over the right shoulder . . . piece of about two feet was quite detached from the body and placed between the body and the left arm, apparently by design . . .

Sean straightened, frowning. It sounded like the report on Jane Doe, found in the cemetery.

Yet, it wasn't the language Pierre would have used.

"Okay, Manny, what is it?"

"The Ripper," Jack said.

Sean looked at him quickly. "Jack the Ripper, London, 1888. Modern day 'Ripperologists' believe that he actually killed five prostitutes in Whitechapel and Spitalfields, although as many as seven to nine murders have been attributed to him."

Sean arched a brow to Manny.

"I think our fellow is a copycat, all right."

"Where does Beale come in, and how about the beheading of the dead man in the morgue?"

Manny shrugged. "I don't know. It's quite possible that the beheading of the corpse had nothing to do with the killings.

Ask Pierre about medical students—it might have been a prank.
A bit sick, but those kids have to learn to deal with death, and
sometimes, that's the way they do it. Beale—he was a pimp.
I'd say he got in the way. It appears we have a serial killer on
our hands who studies serial killers. Say, any information I
have on Jack the Ripper can be acquired by anyone out there.
Old records are public domain, and books on serial killers are
plentiful. You might be dealing with a modern-day killer with
an old-fashioned sense for the dramatic. You have kooks all
over the country who like to dress up in cloaks and top hats,
play vampire, ghoul, ghost, and ripper. And this is New Orleans,
land of Anne Rice and sanctioned vampire tours. The city is
like one big invitation to weirdos. I just thought you should be
aware of how similar the discovery of Jane Doe's body was
to that of Catherine Eddowes, as reported by Dr. Frederick
Brown.''

"Like I said, Manny, anything helps. Anything. But correct
me if I'm wrong.''

"About what?'' Manny asked.

"It's been a while since I've read much about Jack the
Ripper's victims, but I think there are two main differences,''
Sean said.

"Right. Our victims have been beheaded,'' Manny said.
"But—the Ripper's victims had their throats so severely
slashed that they were *nearly* beheaded.''

"So close . . . with our guy going all the way.''

"What do you see as the other main difference?'' Jack asked.

"There was blood, lots of blood, pools of congealed blood
when Jack the Ripper killed. Our guy seems to be . . . lapping
it all up.''

"In some instances, the medical personnel at the time of the
Ripper killings were quoted as noting that there wasn't really
as much blood about the victims as there should have been,''
Manny said.

"And hell, like we already noted . . .'' Jack murmured.

"What?'' Sean asked.

"It *is* New Orleans,'' Jack said dryly.

* * *

Maggie was nervous about Sean's having insisted she go to work, and she knew he would go to the morgue. She changed her clothing, straightened out her personal quarters at the office, and sat down and tried to get something done, but she couldn't concentrate. Angie came in on her while she was supposedly sketching out a ball gown for the wife of a senator. When Angie looked over her shoulder and gasped at what she was drawing, Maggie knew she was in trouble.

"What's that, my God!" Angie breathed.

Maggie looked down at her paper, and frowned. Her fingers started shaking.

She'd been drawing a street. A darkened, shadowy street, with the figure of a woman lying so crumpled and sprawled upon it that she could only be dead.

She pushed away from her desk, horrified.

Angie quickly came behind her, hugging her shoulders. "All right, so I like Sean Canady, he's as sexy as they come, and I've encouraged you to see him, but, honey! You've got to get away from cops and crime for a while!"

"No, no, it can't be Sean," Maggie protested.

"You're getting too involved in this. Just because a no-good pimp decided to get himself murdered too close to this building!"

Angie was wonderful; she and Cissy were Maggie's best friends, but right now, Maggie didn't want to be told that her association with Sean was wearing on her well-being.

The murders had to be solved, and until they were solved—one way or another—she was involved.

She sprang up, trying to sound calm, rational, and natural. "You know what, Angie? I think I do need a walk. Clear my head. Or fuzz it up. I'm going out for a drink. I'm not sure yet if it will be coffee or something chock full of alcohol, but when I come back, I'm going to get the design sketched out for Mrs. Smith."

"Maggie, you shouldn't go out alone—"

"Angie, it's broad daylight. I'll be fine."

Maggie gave Angie an impulsive squeeze and hurried down the inside stairway, waving to Gema and Allie—who were both busy with customers—before hurrying on out to the street. She wasn't sure where she was going until she realized that she was walking in the direction of Le Bon Marché—Mamie Johnson's place.

It was afternoon, nearly four, so there wasn't anything strange about crawling up on a bar stool and ordering a Manhattan. She felt the stares of a few of the men in the place, but she was capable of returning a look with one so frosty that even a polar bear would have kept his distance. Still, she had been there less than five minutes when the stool next to her was taken. She knew before she turned that Mamie herself had come to sit beside her.

"I expected you," Mamie said.

"Did you? Why?"

"I don't know."

Maggie smiled, sipping her drink. "Well, that's good. Because I don't know exactly why I'm here."

Mamie lifted a hand. "I've promised to watch for the killer, but I don't think he will come back here. He reads the paper. He sees. He knows that I know him, and that I will be watching for him. And it isn't his way to walk in here with so many people about and kill me."

"So . . . if he is looking for a certain kind of woman, he'll have to go somewhere else."

Mamie nodded.

"Where?"

Mamie smiled. She was a very attractive woman, her flesh a true copper, her teeth so white against it. Her features were arresting, her movement smooth. "Honey, there are a hundred places he could go."

"Yes, but . . . I think he liked what he got from you. A touch of class."

Mamie shrugged. "There are—naturally—others like me. We don't hire out whores, we provide escorts. Companionship in a lonely place."

Maggie didn't comment. It was all the same. Rich or poor.

Sometimes, high-class call girls were asked to do nothing but sip champagne and listen to a fellow's woes. With a street-girl, she got to drink beer or cheap wine while she cradled a man's ego. And sometimes, rich or poor, she met with perversion . . . or brutality.

"Sean wants to know what you learn," Maggie said. She sipped her drink, then took a deep breath. "I'm sure they're going to set up a policewoman—or even a policeman—if the killer approaches a—er, procurer of escorts—again."

"So I would think," Mamie agreed.

Maggie took another deep breath. "Mamie, would you call me first?"

As she had expected, Mamie frowned. "What you got in your pretty little mind, chile? Haven't you heard how these women are being found? Why, you're as slim as a ribbon, honey—"

"I'm stronger than I look."

"Oh, honey!" Mamie protested, horrified, shaking her head.

"Mamie, please." Maggie set her hand over Mamie's copper one. "Mamie, please, look at me." She hesitated. "I don't want anyone else to be hurt. I—"

"Just whores, honey, hadn't you heard?" Mamie asked wearily.

"Mamie, come on, you sound so bitter! I don't judge whores, I don't judge anyone. We all do what we've got to do to get by. Mamie, please, I want to help. I want to save lives. I may know who is doing this. And he may have a grudge against me in particular—"

"Oh, no! No, no, no, no! You are not going to sacrifice yourself because you're on some kind of a guilt trip, Ms. Maggie Montgomery. What happened? Were you turning tricks somewhere? Why would this guy who is so brutal to whores want to get even with you?"

"I wasn't turning tricks, Mamie. I just have an enemy."

"Tell Sean about it."

"I can't."

"Why?"

"He wouldn't understand."

Mamie sighed. "Then you've got to tell me."

Maggie shook her head. "If I did, you wouldn't believe me anyway."

Mamie stared at her a long while. She reached over for Maggie's Manhattan and drank it down herself, signaling to the bartender to make them each another drink.

"I come from the bayou, honey. I got some voodoo in my blood, even though I've not got the sight like some others. Talk to me. You want my help, talk."

"At this point of my life, I really wish I could make you believe me," Maggie said softly.

"Like I told you, my mind is open."

"But can you keep your mouth shut?" Maggie asked. "Mamie, I will really, really need your help, and your confidence."

"Talk to me, honey. I may be an old whore at the core, but I swear to you, I'm one with the old heart of gold."

Maggie exhaled on a long breath.

She started talking.

The afternoon wore on.

Mamie listened and listened. Disbelief faded to simple doubt. And then wonder.

CHAPTER 12

Callie's mother had indeed come for her and she was now on her way to a clinic in Denver. Rutger had apparently gotten out of jail and crawled under a rock somewhere, but wherever he was, it didn't matter anymore. He couldn't touch Callie.

One good point, Sean told himself. Thank God. He needed one.

With his leads getting him nowhere, he decided again that walking the city was just as useful as any other enterprise. And so he walked down by Jackson Square, and there, among a dozen other vendors, he saw a woman he was instantly convinced had to be Mamie's friend, the voodoo, Marie Lescarre.

He wandered over to her.

Two giggling young tourists were asking her about love potions. As old as Methuselah, brown as a gnarled oak, Marie still had a pleasant, lilting voice, touched with old Southern overtones along with a hint of Island-French dialect. She told the girls her potions were just herbal oils, but it was no fault of hers if the smell was so sweet that the right men came running.

The girls bought the potions while Sean studied her supply

of incense burners, stones, herbs, and the like. When the girls disappeared, the woman looked gravely at Sean.

"Captain Canady."

"Mamie told you about me?"

"I knew you were coming," she answered, rheumy old eyes focused hard on his. Right. She knew. Mamie hadn't told her; she had just known.

"So you are Marie Lescarre?"

"You know it," the old woman answered, smiling. For an old bird, she had fabulous teeth. He wondered what gris-gris, what magic, gave her such a good calcium retention.

He smiled. "Real name—or stage name?" he inquired, adding politely, "Your name is very similar to that of the voodoos who became so famous here—Marie Laveau and her daughter."

The old woman smiled. "Marie—it is a common enough name for any woman of French, Catholic, or Island descent. Lescarre—my late husband's name."

Sean felt uncomfortably reprieved. As if he had been mocking her. He felt as if he were behaving like a child—and as if she were behaving in a far more mature manner.

"You don't need to blush, Lieutenant. You're a good man."

He shrugged. "Thanks." If Mamie hadn't talked to her, how did she know his name and rank—or even that he was a cop? Foolish. His name and face had been on the news and in the papers often enough.

"So you have come to me," Marie Lescarre said then.

He shrugged again. "Mamie Johnson suggested I do so."

"Ah. So have you come to a voodoo to mock me?"

He shook his head, realizing the sober truth. "I've come because I'm willing to try anything to stop these killings."

She seemed pleased, nodding. But then her voice carried a worried tone. "You are in danger, you know."

"I'm a cop. I'm always in danger."

Marie shook her head. "You are an old soul, Lieutenant, a very old soul."

"Now, Marie—"

"Hear me out, Lieutenant," she said quietly, raising a bony

hand. "We see that there is black, and there is white. There is night, and there is day. There is evil, and there is good, just the same, even if 'evil' is not always seen, nor can we always touch 'good.' There are forces in the city now; good and evil. There is a fight."

He hesitated, not quite believing what he was about to ask. "Is Maggie Montgomery evil?"

To his relief she shook her head. "But guard yourself! Guard yourself well. She is not what she seems."

"Is she a voodoo?"

Marie smiled, as if she laughed inwardly. She shook her head. "Pay heed to the nights, Lieutenant."

"Now, Marie—"

"There is nothing more I can tell you. There has always been gris-gris in this place. Magic. Good and evil. Guard yourself, take care. Look to the beast, and think of what weapons you will need. Open your mind. That is the most important. Legends are usually based on fact. You believe in God, Lieutenant, right?"

"Yes, I'm from an old Catholic family myself—"

"You don't see Him, you don't know Him, but you believe He exists. Faith is believing in what you cannot see. We think that faith is something shared by intelligent men. Then know that there is more in this world than we can see with the naked eyes, that we can find in what is known and accepted. The world is not flat; men have walked on the moon. All things are possible. Look to the earth, the sky, the night. The black and the white. Remember, the red that flows throughout veins is our life's blood. And take this magic that I give you."

She reached for his hand, her bony one clenched around something she held.

She dropped it into his palm, curling his fingers around it.

"I can't just take something from you—" He began to protest. She was old. Maybe she was a voodoo quack—she still needed an income.

"You take this."

"Come on, now, what do I owe you?"

After all, this could even be a con between Mamie Johnson

and Marie. Mamie procured ''escorts'' for those who needed them; perhaps she procured magic as well for a cut of the proceeds.

''You owe me nothing. Nothing at all. It is a gift. Because there is darkness and light. Good and evil. You are good. I am good. And we are all one. That is what matters.''

She studied his eyes intently, then she turned quickly away from him, hobbling over to a young couple going through her vials of scented love oils and lotions.

He shook his head. He already felt foolish. Listening to a voodoo! What the hell had she given him? Some kind of a talisman, a rabbit's foot, a chicken claw?

There was a cross in his hand. Nothing more occult than a cross, silver, about two inches in length, and strung from a long chain.

He smiled. Well, she had mentioned that those of French, Catholic, or Island descent bore her name.

He started to turn away, and walk through the scattered tourists.

''Lieutenant!''

He turned. Old Marie Lescarre had called him back.

''Wear it!'' she urged him.

She was so sincere. He had to smile back at her, nod.

And slip the chain around his neck. She hadn't given him some silly amulet. It was a cross. He could live with that. If it had been some kind of an amulet . . .

Well, he was a cop. Okay, and he had a bit of an ego-macho thing.

But a cross . . .

Actually—and quite oddly—he had to admit that he did feel more secure wearing the thing. What the hell. Couldn't hurt.

Leaving Jackson Square, he was surprised to find himself venturing toward Mamie's place.

He ordered a Coke and a sandwich, and when Mamie came to sit at the bar next to him, she assured him that she hadn't seen the man again.

''I don't think he'll come back here.''

Sean shrugged. ''He may.''

"He's surely seen his face in the newspapers."

"But he may think himself too good to get caught. If so, he might want to show you his face again. Challenge you. See if we can get to him fast enough. You're not scared, are you?"

"Maybe. Just a little. Can *you* help me fast enough if he comes for me?"

He chewed roast beef on wheat and smiled at her. "You've got cops here all the time now, you do know?"

"I suspected. You're ruining my trade."

"I'm a cop. I'm supposed to be arresting you for your trade, you know."

Mamie grinned. "Thank God my chef is good."

"I saw your friend in Jackson Square."

"You went to see Marie?"

He nodded. "You told her I was coming?"

Mamie shook her head. "No."

He half smiled. "She knew me."

"She's voodoo."

"Come on, Mamie."

"There's good, there's evil. There's religion, there's hocus-hocus. All the same."

She sounded disturbingly like Marie. "Well, I'm wearing the cross she gave me, how's that?"

"You're going to need it," Mamie assured him.

"A cross?"

Mamie nodded.

"Crosses scare away bad voodoo?"

"Now, boy, you had best learn to believe that there are forces beyond man. You want some garlic bread?"

He stared at her, frowning. "Mamie, I'm eating a roast beef sandwich."

"Garlic bread would be good for you."

"Mamie, I don't want any garlic bread. I—"

"You should take her out tonight."

"What?"

"Your girl. Take her out tonight. Nice Italian restaurant. Eat a lot of garlic."

"Do you dislike Maggie, Mamie?"

"No, I like her just fine."

"Then why do you want me to go spoiling a good relationship with breath to kill?"

Mamie shook her head. "Like I said . . ."

But she didn't say. Her voice trailed away.

"Garlic?"

She shrugged.

"Mamie, we've been talking about good and evil. Voodoo. Now crosses and garlic. I saw lots of Hammer films with Peter Cushing and Christopher Lee when I was a kid. It's starting to sound as if you think the city is infested with vampires."

"Who are we to know?" Mamie asked innocently.

"Mamie, come on, we're talking about a flesh and blood killer here. Don't go getting sidetracked." He slipped off his stool, reaching into his wallet for his money.

"On the house," Mamie said.

"I think I should probably pay," he said with a wink.

"Don't pay me. It may be your last meal."

He shook his head, leaning toward her, surprised that she was regarding him with such concern and affection. He kissed her cheek. "I'll be okay. I'm wearing your friend's cross."

"Sure," she said.

"Okay, now, Mamie, have some faith! I'm wearing Marie's cross, right? I went to see a voodoo because you wanted me to."

"Right. So?"

Mamie had nice eyes. Wide, dark brown with gold specks. "I want you to wear something for me."

"What?"

He shrugged a bit sheepishly. "I got it from the FBI guy helping out down here. It's a watch, but if you're in trouble, you just push down on the face. It's better than calling me, or paging me, or having anybody get me on the radio. It's like a beeper, only it's private, between you and me. You buzz, and it will vibrate on my end."

Mamie laughed, delighted. "Oh, honey, I could buzz you and make things really vibrate, if you gave me half a chance.

But then, you're vibratin' enough as it is, aren't you?'' she demanded. "She's something special, isn't she? Your girl?''

"She's different from anyone else, and that's a fact.''

"Don't go falling too deeply in love, Lieutenant,'' Mamie warned.

"You keep your nose clean,'' Sean warned her, leaving her at last. "Don't forget, if you're in trouble . . .''

Mamie grinned again. "I'll be glad to buzz you, sir!'' she said, and saluted playfully.

Leaving Mamie's, Sean put in a call to Maggie's office from his car. She was concerned, and wanted to know what had been happening. He told her that Callie was gone, and that Rutger had made no appearances to stop her from leaving. "Thankfully, he's one bad penny that didn't turn up again.''

"What happened at the morgue?''

"Oh, you know the morgue. It's just full of dead bodies.''

"I know, but . . .''

He liked the sound of her voice. He missed her. They'd only been apart a few hours, but he missed her. Still, he suddenly felt that it was important to keep a certain distance from her.

Voodoo.

He didn't believe in voodoo.

Of course, he'd often gone on gut feeling . . .

"I'm going to be out kind of late tonight,'' he told her.

"Oh.''

He hesitated, damning himself. "But then again, if you happen to be a night owl . . .''

A night owl. Hmm. The city crawled with night owls, people up at all hours. He grinned. Mamie was suggesting the city was filled with vampires along with voodoos. Well, they liked the night, didn't they?

The murderer certainly did.

"Call me at any time,'' Maggie said. "I mean it, Sean, any time.''

"Great,'' he said.

"Sean?''

"Yeah?''

"I love you,'' she said softly.

Everything inside him seemed to melt a little bit. "I love you, too."

He clicked off, and kept driving. He hadn't even been sure at first where he was going, but he found himself on his way to Oakville Plantation. When he drove into the driveway, he saw that his father was sitting on the porch, slowly listing back and forth in the big old whitewashed swing.

"Hey, Dad."

"Hey, Son. Glad to see you. What brings you out in the middle of the week like this?"

He joined his father.

"Beer?" Daniel asked, watching him curiously.

"Sure."

His father reached into the ice chest at his side and produced his newest, self-bottled microbrew. Sean grinned, and swigged. It tasted damn good.

"Okay, so what's the problem?" Daniel said.

"I need answers."

"You need fingerprint experts, technologists, those new high-tech lights that show sperm all over like in that Sharon Stone ice-pick movie—"

"I've got all that, Dad. Guess what else I have?"

"Don't know. Tell me."

He told Daniel about the corpse that had been beheaded, and he kept talking, describing Mamie, and even admitting he'd gone down to Jackson Square and that Marie Lescarre had given him a cross to wear.

"Interesting," Daniel said.

"Yeah, it is, isn't it? Can you give me anything out of history even remotely like what's going on here?"

"Sure."

"What? Great! Help me."

"Jack the Ripper."

Sean sighed. "Dad, Jack the Ripper's last murder was in November of 1888—so say the leading Ripperologists, even if a few more victims are thrown in the heap now and then."

"You've been reading," Daniel said solemnly.

Sean shrugged. "There's a task force on this, Dad. Everyone's been reading."

"All right, so you know about the murders . . . dwell on the suspects. Some say Montague John Druitt, an affluent young man who didn't quite make it through med school, died in the Thames soon after the last murder. Then there was a fellow named Ostrog, wound up in an insane asylum. There's the school of thought convinced that there might have been a Jill the Ripper—probably a bitter midwife or the like, you know?— and there's the Royal theory—either the Duke of Clarence himself, Victoria's grandson, or a court physician, William Gull. There's the latest, stemming out of the *Jack the Ripper Diary,* written by Maybrick, who died of gastroenteritis not long after the murder. Now, that was a sad case! Not for Maybrick, but his wife. Poor thing. She was condemned for murder without much proof, but it *was* Victorian England and the poor dear had been having an affair while her husband ran around all over the place. I think the chap's family had a lot to do with the wife winding up condemned. She was to hang— got reprieved at the last minute."

"Dad—none of these people is in New Orleans ripping up hookers and beheading corpses!"

Daniel shrugged, offering him a half-smile. "Well, then, there's the theory that Jack the Ripper was a true monster. Made out of the mists and dirt and the tawdry poverty of the East End. True evil."

"Great. I can just tell the chief—and the newspapers—that I'm looking for an evil mist."

Daniel grinned. "Tell them you're looking for a monster. Men are quite capable of being monsters. You asked."

"Is that all you can give me?"

Daniel thought a minute. "Well, it is New Orleans. Supposedly, zombies have walked in the shadows of the old plantations—and in the French Quarter, too, I would imagine."

Sean grunted.

"Then there was that case in the prison in 1909 . . ."

Sean frowned. "What case?"

"An interesting one. All the beheadings reminded me of it."

"Well?"

"A retarded boy, Josh Jurgen, was condemned to death for the murder of a playmate. Josh—and his mother—claimed during the trial that a drifter had killed the little girl. Apparently, a lot of folk thought the boy was telling the truth, but you know how cruel some people can be ... wouldn't have happened now, I can tell you, but back then ... well, anyway, the mother was hysterical, the boy terrified, crying and carrying on during the days before his execution. He was kept in solitary, waiting for the big day, then—I'm not sure I've got this just right."

"Dad! Damn, now, tell me what you know."

"Probably has nothing to do with anything. The night before he's due to hang, the boy kills himself."

"Strange," Sean said slowly.

Daniel grinned. "Strange—but why am I telling you this, huh? He hanged himself. And managed somehow to hang himself so tightly and with such force that ... well, that, he managed to pop his head right off. Beheaded himself."

"Whoa—now that is one for the books," Sean admitted.

"There's a little more to it—as far as your interest in the story might go," Daniel said.

"Yeah?" Sean said.

Daniel took a long swig of his microbrew. "Good batch, this, wouldn't you say?"

"Dad, are you trying to provoke violence?"

Daniel grinned. "The kid's mother was best friends with Mary Montgomery—who must have been your girl's great-great-grandmother, maybe. Mary pleaded for the boy at the trial. Despite her prestige, the boy was condemned. They say that she was the last one with him before he killed himself."

"Interesting, indeed," Sean said. What was it with everyone? Trying to make Maggie's family out to be cursed or the like.

So then why did he feel himself as if there were something so damned strange about her?

"The bayou is full of ghost stories," Daniel reminded him.

"Thanks."

"Full moons bring out werewolves. Naturally, there is basis in such legends. The gravitational pull of the moon causes physiological responses. Luna—lunatic. Anyone working in the emergency ward of a hospital can tell you that violence escalates during the full moon.''

"What a help," Sean said dryly.

"I'm doing my best. Then, the city is big on vampire cults, you know."

"Yeah, yeah."

Daniel grinned. "Your cross is silver. Wonder if old Marie was worried about werewolves or vampires."

"Dad—"

"The Montgomerys—and a Canady, come to think of it—supposedly killed a man once, suspecting him of such foul habits. Remember? We were talking about it the other night. Some say they killed him just for being French, but that's a little drastic, don't you think, especially in a city like New Orleans? Then, of course, that gave rise to legends that the Montgomerys popped out a vampire now and then, every other generation or so—something in the genes, I imagine. There have been strange rumors about the Canadys as well."

Sean groaned.

"Well, hell, we couldn't all be heroes. Though, of course, it's nice to have a few in the family line, don't you think?"

"Sure, Dad. Nice."

"Honest to God," Daniel said, "I wish I could be more helpful." He shrugged. "As far as Jack the Ripper goes, we'll probably never know. We didn't have the technology then that we have now. But there were truly those back then who believed that the very air in the East End was so rank with poverty, cruelty, and crime that evil actually lived there. You've been there, remember the trip we took to Europe your senior year of high school? You've toured the Ripper's haunts, and you know that there are still areas that desperately need renovation, where mist still hides murder, and where you can really believe in evil. Not just in London. In most cities. And throughout history—across the world—there have been reports of super-natural creatures. Some people today are convinced that angels guard them. And in the Middle Ages, well, men thought they had reason to believe in haunts and vampires. There are dozens of cases, legally documented by sane officials, of outbreaks of vampirism. Some of it can be explained. Sadly, people were sometimes buried alive, and so, if dug up, their corpses appeared fresh. Also, even after death, some bodily functions continue, and so corpses have 'sat up' after death. As for vampires, blood pools to the downward position of the body after death, leaving the face extremely pale.''

''So, uneducated men believed natural phenomena created vampires,'' Sean said.

Daniel shrugged. ''Ah, but there are other historically documented cases as well. Many in Europe, not so many in the United States. There was a New England family who lost a daughter who then began to appear at night to her sisters. Five children died before the father determined to dig up the offspring he had buried, stake their hearts, cut them out, and burn them to ash. The deaths then stopped.''

''The children probably had a contagious disease they passed to one another.''

''But the four remaining children survived—after the five had been disinterred, dealt with, and reburied.''

''So, a vampire is doing all this?''

''There have been those who historically *think* they are vampires. Countess Bathory took the lives of hundreds of young women, believing that their blood would give her youth. There was a case here in the early twenties when several people were murdered by men who drank their blood. Real or imagined, you need to look at every angle, and study what you're up against.''

Sean stood, patting his father on the shoulder. ''Thanks, Dad. You were a big help. Honest to God.''

Daniel smiled. ''I try. You leaving already?''

''Have to—there are just so damned many corpses around these days, I don't seem to have a choice.''

His father waved, and he did the same, returning to his car.

As he drove, he replayed all the conversations of the day in his mind.

He'd just reached the French Quarter when he realized that

his end of the pager he'd given Mamie was vibrating in his pocket.

He pulled out the device, and scanned the neon lights that platted out the city. He frowned for a minute, getting his bearings. She was in an alley, off Bourbon Street.

He flipped mental pages to see the area with his mind's eye.

He floored the car. He sweated every moment of the drive.

The alley was dark, dingy, flanked by ancient structures that were nearly all condemned. There were a few shops on the street, a few poverty-level homes.

In fact . . .

The alley was remarkably like many a street . . .

In old London. Whitechapel, Spitalfields.

The Ripper's old haunt.

London
November 9, 1888

Megan didn't find Peter until nearly five in the morning, in the dark shadows of an alley, fallen against the wall of a tenement. He sat, his hands bloodied in front of him, his eyes on his hands. She called his name, hurrying to him and enveloping him in her arms.

"You didn't do it, you didn't do it!" she assured him. "You didn't kill her, Peter."

"How do you know I'm not a monster?"

"I know."

"How can you?"

"Because I know. I've seen monsters, Peter, and you're not one. You didn't kill her."

"Her?" Peter said, and he began to laugh hoarsely, but in a way that frightened her, for he verged on hysteria. "Haven't you heard? It's been a double slaying tonight. Two women dead. Two. One at George's Yard, the other in Mitre Square. And, ah, you should hear what they already whisper about the second. The things that were done to her, the violence! She was mutilated beyond recognition!" He started to laugh again, and then to cry. Megan shook him fiercely. "Peter, you are

stronger than this!'' She forced him to his feet, and then, when he continued to seem to have no will of his own, she slapped his cheek. ''You have not done this! Understand the truth. You could not have done this!''

''No, no, I don't believe that I could have done such a thing, but I don't know where I was, or what I have done. The time is gone, the past is gone, there is nothing but this blackness and the blood. Oh, God, look at the blood on my hands, look at the blood . . .''

She maneuvered him home. They slipped through the remaining darkness of night. Daylight came at last to wash away the shadows.

But no amount of light could take away the new terror. The first victim, eventually identified as Liz Stride, or Long Liz, was a Swedish prostitute. She had been spared mutilation.

The killer made up for it with Catherine, or Kate, Eddowes. She had been even more cruelly ripped and torn than Polly Chapman. ''Butchered like a pig,'' one witness to the finding of the body reported. Stomach slashed open, organs removed . . . organs gone. Though killed within a mile of each other, Liz had died in the jurisdiction of the Metropolitan Police; Kate had been killed in that of the City Police. Massive manhunts by both forces were instantly underway. A piece of bloodied apron was found, and written in white chalk on the fascia of black bricks at the edge of the nearby doorway were the words, ''The Juwes are The men That Will not be Blamed for nothing.''

What was written came to the people through word of mouth, for Sir Charles Warren, afraid that the words might cause anti-Semitic riots, immediately ordered them erased. And so began the pondering on exactly what the words meant—and if they had even been written by the killer.

Once again, the city went berserk. Peter was at first ill with fear, then he began to believe Megan's assurances, and he became determined that he would prove to himself that he was not guilty of the heinous crimes.

Immediately after the killings, a major newspaper let out the information that a letter had been received—prior to the latest killings—written by a man claiming to be the murderer. It was addressed *"Dear Boss,"* talked about the foolish police and the sharpness of his knife, promised to send a lady's ears in next, and was signed, *"Jack the Ripper."* Another letter had been received soon after by the same author—promising a double event.

And more awful offerings were to arrive in the mail.

George Lusk, chairman of the Mile End Vigilance Committee, received a small brown parcel. It contained half a kidney, and a message from the killer that he had *"prasarved it"* for Lusk— while he fried and ate the other half.

The foremost pathologists were approached by the police and the consensus confirmed that the kidney was human, most probably female.

London went wild with fury and panic.

Peter spent hours staring into space.

Megan took to the streets alone, seeking Jack the Ripper.

October passed. Laura became ill, and Peter tried to rouse himself from his lethargy and fear. He tended to his wife, and as she seemed to recover somewhat from the influenza that plagued her along with her pregnancy, he began to notice that Megan left night after night.

He followed her, demanding to know what she was doing. *"Saving your sanity!"* she told him.

"At the cost of your own life, little fool!" he charged her. *"If you're about on this fool notion, I must be with you."*

"Who can I solicit if you're with me?" she inquired.

Peter became angry, warning her that she dared not taunt such a killer. She tried to assure him she was in no danger, she was young and strong and seldom drank.

Still, that night, she shared a pint with him. And they commiserated together that rumors grew more absurd daily. Doctors were suspected, butchers, tradesmen, foreigners—even members of the Royal household, despite the fact that Queen Victoria herself was appalled and demanding answers from the police. *"Since the letters have been published, the police have received more confessions than they can count!"* Megan reminded Peter, and he was much better.

They made a pact that night. Peter would work again, and believe in himself. And they would hunt the killer together.

Throughout October, the killer lay dormant. Yet, like the police, Megan and Peter hunted the streets. It was easy enough for them to do so; Peter had legitimate business among his patients.

Friday, the ninth of November, was to be the day of the Lord Mayor's Show. The new Lord Mayor of London would drive in state with tremendous pageantry down the streets of the city to take his oath of office at the Royal Courts of Justice in the Strand.

Peter and Megan talked about the pageantry as they walked through Whitechapel that night.

It was a strange night, the temperature growing chill, and yet, a fog swirling in the darkness and shadows. As they walked, they suddenly heard a soft cry.

"Murder!"

"My God!" Peter cried. "Stay close!"

And he ran forward.

Yet somehow, in the darkness and the shadows and the relentless swirling of the fog, Megan lost him. She cried his name, running through the night. She ran, and ran, and ran. When dawn came, she had still not found him. She kept walking, and realized at last that morning had come, and she had walked home.

She was alarmed to see that Peter's and Laura's door stood open. With dread filling her heart, she hurried forward. She hesitated just briefly, then heard the sound of a wretched sobbing so deep it was unbearable. She rushed in then, and found Peter on his knees by the side of the sofa where Laura lay, dead still. Megan walked carefully into the room. Laura lay on the sofa, pale as snow, beautiful, frail . . .

"Peter?"

"She's dead," he sobbed.

And she realized that Laura's condition had worsened in the night, and that she had died while she and Peter had hunted the killer. Laura had died alone. Perhaps, if he had been with her, she might have been saved. At the very least, she would not have died alone and abandoned.

"Oh, Peter!" she whispered, and tried to soothe him.

But he would not forgive himself. "I am cursed! Again, I awakened with blood, and God has punished me for the lives I have taken with this most precious of lives!"

"Peter, no! For the sake of your immortal soul, you mustn't believe such a thing—"

"What do you know of the immortal soul?" he demanded brokenly.

"Only that it is the most precious part of us," she told him evenly. "Peter, Laura is with God, and you must realize that you are not at fault, and you must continue to help others."

He shook, still clinging to his wife's body. "Megan . . . you've been so good to us both. She loved you so dearly, you know," he said, speaking as if confused, broken. "Megan, would you get me a brandy? For the love of God, I need some help now, oh, God, oh, my Laura . . ."

"I'll get you brandy," Megan said quickly.

She hurried to do so.

As she left the room, she heard a shot.

She froze, and turned back.

Peter had taken a pistol to his head. He'd fired one clean shot into his temple.

He died upon his wife's breast.

The following day, the ghastly and gruesome news of the murder of Mary Jane Kelly, a twenty-five-year-old Irish prostitute, eclipsed the news about the Lord Mayor.

She was killed in the room she rented in Miller Square. The murderer had taken his time with her, savagely mutilating her face beyond recognition, slashing out her organs, arranging them about her, skinning parts of her body to the bone.

Megan heard the news as she went about the business of telegraphing the families of her friends about their tragic deaths. She was furious with herself for not realizing Laura's condition, and furious with both Peter and herself—that he had not had the strength to keep from killing himself. Deeply saddened by their deaths, she was still shaken by the death of the young woman she had never known.

That night, broken, lost, lonelier than she had ever been, she found herself walking toward Miller's Square.

The streets were filled with the frightened and the curious. Yet, as she stared at the house where the terrible event had happened, she felt as if she was being watched, and she spun around.

He was there. In a deerstalker hat and black cloak, standing in a deserted yard a few hundred feet away, in the shadows. He lifted his hat to her. She walked over to him.

"What are you doing here?"

"Watching the results of my handiwork."

She inhaled sharply, staring at him with a fury deeper than any emotion she had ever known. "What?"

"Oh, come now! Surely you were aware the torsos in the river were my handiwork! And you are ever talking about innocence and the quality of human life! You are the one who is so righteous, feeding on those condemned for murder and the like. These women were pathetic, rotten, disease-carrying vermin. They were whores. Dying of alcoholism. Dying of despair. I hastened—"

"You butchered them!"

"Ah, well, it looks bad, but I strangled the lasses first. Eased them gently from life—then I chopped them a bit to confuse the police. I mean, I wouldn't have gifted any of them with this life. They were human refuse before I killed them, nothing more."

"You didn't even kill them out of hunger!" she said.

He smiled. And then she knew.

"I killed them because I am a beast. As you are," he told her.

"You killed them to make Peter think that he was a murderer, losing his mind. You lured him away, hypnotized him, and made him think that ... Oh, my God, I don't care what they do to me! I will kill you!"

He never had time to react. She was upon him with a blind

rage unlike anything she had ever known. She ripped with her nails and teeth, battered, tore . . .

And he screamed. And she realized her own savagery. She had nearly committed the greatest sin of her own kind, the only infraction that could bring about her own execution: She had nearly severed his head from his body.

She didn't care.

She would kill him.

At this moment, she would more than gladly die herself.

Arms were suddenly around her, pulling her away.

Lucian. Taking her away.

She felt a rush of darkness and light, time and shadow. Heard his words. ''Don't do it, don't do it! He is badly injured, it could take him centuries to heal.''

She closed her eyes. Life was an abyss. She didn't care. She despised this life. She couldn't bear it . . .

She heard an evil, cackling laughter.

Aaron Carter. He was threatening her . . .

The cackling, like time, faded away . . .

CHAPTER 13

Mamie didn't think a thing about leaving work. She didn't care what Sean or Maggie thought. The killer was no fool. He wasn't coming back where she could recognize him.

And though Mamie knew that everything in the world wasn't always exactly what it seemed, she wasn't sure just how much gris-gris there was in the world, either. She didn't know what she thought about the fantastic story Maggie Montgomery had told her.

She considered herself safe, even in the underbelly of New Orleans. She'd taken several steps into that underbelly, and she was a part of it. There was nothing to scare her there. She'd seen what was frightening in life, and that was poverty. She'd grown up in a four-room apartment with seven brothers and sisters; she'd eaten rice until she'd thought it would grow back out of her head, and she'd heard babies cry all night because they were hungry. No, only one thing could scare Mamie, and that was the possibility of *not* knowing the underbelly of New Orleans. She had connections. No one would mess with her.

Yet, it was late, really late, when she left work. And amazingly, in a city that seldom slept, the streets were absurdly quiet.

People are afraid of the murderer, she thought. All of them staying in. The jazz clubs would be in trouble. And the sex clubs and strip joints. She hoped someone would catch the damned killer soon.

Strange night. Moon riding high in the sky behind shimmery clouds. Gave the place a look of being encased in mist-shrouded gaslight.

She shivered, and walked faster. Heard footsteps. Behind her.

She stopped, turned around. Nothing. No one. She told herself that she had the heebie-jeebies, and that was that. She started walking again.

But just to be safe . . .

If she turned into the alley, she knew a shortcut through one of the old tenement buildings. No one could follow her through it. She happened to know the way because the building had been there when she was a kid.

She turned . . .

And heard the footsteps again.

She remembered her watch, and pressed hard on the face of it. She kept walking fast.

She paused, swinging around, looking back.

She turned again, and froze.

She blinked. She shouldn't have been surprised to see him. Tall, sleek, handsome in black silk shirt and neatly creased trousers. His face was pale; didn't match the darkness of his hair. Dye job? she wondered.

Then she wondered what it mattered. He'd come to kill her.

"Hello, Mamie."

"Hi," she said smoothly. She started walking again. Time. If she could kill time, maybe . . .

"Whoa, Mamie!"

He caught her arm. Pulled her back, irrevocably. Incredible strength.

She opened her mouth to scream.

His hand fit over her mouth before she could inhale.

"You sold me out, Mamie!" he said softly. He laughed, and licked her cheek with the fullness of his tongue. "Umm. Sweet, like milk chocolate. I'm going to enjoy eating you all up, Mamie." She felt his teeth just graze along her throat. "Sweeter than candy. Yeah, lady. You sold me out. Gave the cops a picture right when I was starting to have a really good time, just like the invisible man.''

He smiled at her.

''Yum!'' he said softly, still grinning.

And Mamie knew that she was going to die.

Sean held the awkward electronic tracking instrument out in front of him. He'd called in for back-up and he knew that Jack and others would quickly be on their way, but he knew as well—gut instinct—that time meant everything right now.

He jerked his car to a halt on the sidewalk and sped out of it into the alley.

He rushed down into the dimly lit street, shouting her name.

''Mamie!''

Restlessness and fear had drawn Maggie back to Le Bon Marché. She sat at the bar, sipping the red wine that Sam, the handsome young ebony bartender, had just placed before her.

''It's nice to see you back, but I'm assuming you're looking for Mamie, would that be right, Miss Montgomery?''

''I . . . yes, I guess.''

''I'm afraid she left a few minutes ago.''

''Oh. I'm sorry, too,'' Maggie said, disappointed. Then she realized that her restlessness had been caused by an inexplicable, jagged edge of fear now knotting in her stomach. She slid off her bar stool, drawing bills from her handbag to lay on the bar for her wine. ''I think I'll try to catch her.''

''Wait, Miss Montgomery!'' Sam called.

She paused briefly.

He shook his head. ''Mamie's safe in this neighborhood, you know? I'm not sure . . .'' His voice trailed.

Maggie smiled. ''You're saying that Mamie is black and can take care of herself and I'm white and look like a powderpuff?''

''I . . . well . . . I . . . no . . . yes!'' Sam said frankly.

"I'll be okay, I'll be careful." Before he could protest further, she was hurrying for the door.

"Damn!" she heard Sam swear. "Wait, now, bad things have been happening."

Maggie couldn't wait. She rushed out the door, and down the street.

Sam started after her. As he neared the door, a tall, dark-haired man stopped him.

"It's all right, I'll go after her," he assured Sam.

Sam studied the man. "No offense, sir, but—"

"I'll go after her," the man said, studying Sam intently.

Sam walked back to the bar, suddenly confused. He couldn't remember why he'd been running out to begin with.

"Do you know who I am, Mamie?" the killer whispered softly. He'd forced her back against a wall in the corner of two buildings. They were completely eclipsed by shadow. His one hand remained over her mouth. The thumb of his other hand was upon her carotid artery; he seemed to enjoy feeling the terrified thud of her pulse beat. His fingers rounded her throat.

He continued to lick her face. Graze her throat with his teeth. They were sharp. Needle sharp. Like little knives. Her knees were weak. She'd believed; she hadn't believed.

Now, she'd never known such terror.

"Strange, isn't it? The Ripper has come down throughout time, famous for blood and the mutilations he cast upon his victims! But death itself was never so hard for the ladies— good old Jack! He asphyxiated his victims, half strangled them. He was so careful, he played, he enjoyed . . . but in his way, he was so merciful. Do you know who I am, Mamie?"

She nodded.

Then she heard her name shouted. Lieutenant Canady. She recognized his voice right away, recognized the thunder of his shout.

Naturally, the killer heard Canady as well. He started to smile, his grip upon her throat tightening.

"They never heard anyone scream, Mamie . . ." he hissed, his lips close to her face.

But Mamie was desperate—and she liked life. She bit the hand on her mouth and kneed the bastard in the groin, all in one shot.

The hand slipped away while her attacker swore at her. "Bitch—whore!"

Didn't matter. Maybe none of his other victims had ever screamed, but maybe none of them was quite as good at scrounging the streets as she was. She let out a scream that could have curled the hair on a warthog's back.

He had her again, instantly. And he was powerful. So powerful that she began to see black the minute his hands were on her throat. Just as her vision began to fade, she saw his knife, wielded high above her face. Six inches long, jagged-edged, catching the thin stream of lamplight that hovered just over her head in the shadow-laced corner.

Right when she thought the knife would fall and she would be hurtled into a pit of darkness as the blade pierced her flesh, she heard a harsh command.

"Drop it!"

The knife hovered.

"Drop it!"

The knife started to fall.

A warning shot was fired.

The knife kept coming.

Another shot was fired, catching the killer in the wrist. It seemed like no more than a bee sting. The knife kept falling.

Another shot was fired. Another.

She heard a roar of anger as the knife kept coming, coming, coming . . .

But then, her killer was wrenched away, a split second before the blade tore into flesh.

Gasping for breath, Mamie staggered against the wall. Dizzy, she inhaled, rubbing her throat, trying to gather her senses.

Then she saw them.

Lieutenant Sean Canady, and her black-clad attacker.

The knife had flown; both men were on the ground. She

heard the sounds of terrible crunches as fists connected with faces. As she stared, her attacker seemed to get the upper hand, straddling over the lieutenant who was prone on the old brick roadway. The killer leaned over him, grasping for the fallen knife . . .

Sean bucked. The killer went flying, and landed hard, but he was quickly up, despite the bullet wounds he must have sustained. He reached for the knife.

Sean was up, and came flying for the man, knocking him flat before his fingers could curl around the hilt of the weapon. But the killer jerked his shoulders, and Sean was cast off, landing hard against a wall. He seemed stunned, which wasn't too surprising; Mamie had thought she'd heard his head crack against the wall.

The killer gripped the knife, and started toward Sean.

Flat on the ground, fighting to clear his head, Sean Canady stared at the man approaching him. He was barely breathing hard. His hair was pitch black—*dyed* black, Sean thought, because it didn't fit with his extremely pale features. He was tall and lean and muscular in a wiry way—he surely wasn't built like Conan the Barbarian or anything of the like, which might have explained his uncanny strength—and he looked strangely familiar, though Sean was certain they had never met before.

The killer stopped, staring at Sean, as if he, too, had suddenly recognized him.

He smiled.

"Hello, dead man!" he said softly.

With a burst of energy and pure willpower, Sean sprang to his feet as the killer reached him. He butted him dead on in the stomach, sending him back into the street, buying himself a little bit of precious time. His gun had been lost to the shadows when he'd so desperately tackled the guy to get him off Mamie.

Blood oozed from the man's left shoulder, and from his hand, but it didn't stop him. He recovered quickly and started coming after Sean again. Sean braced for the attack like a boxer, balancing his ground.

But before the attacker could pounce, he heard a furious cry and was amazed to see that someone was hurtling onto the killer's back. "Stop, stop, stop, you bastard!"

Maggie. He was dimly aware that it was Maggie, and there were other footsteps racing down the alley now.

"Maggie! Get the hell away!" Sean ordered her with incredulous fear and fury. Too late. The killer, wearing a mask of pure vindictive anger himself, was reaching behind himself, grabbing her, throwing her from him. Maggie went down upon the pavement, just as Sean threw himself against the killer. With an eerie power, the man struggled from beneath Sean, managing to rise. He started toward Maggie, the knife in his hand. Sean threw himself at the killer again. To his amazement, the fellow just dragged him along. Sean tightened his grasp, at last tripping the man up, forcing him down. He fought his way back to his feet, turned, and caught Sean in the jaw with a right hook that very nearly shattered bone.

Staggering, Sean came up again. He had to. The killer was still going after Maggie. On the ground, she groaned softly. She started to rise, to face the killer.

Sean started to take a running leap after the fellow, but he was suddenly edged aside.

Another man was in the alley. Tall, dark, whipcord lean, wearing a dark silk shirt and neatly pressed black trousers. "Get Maggie!" he cried, and before Sean could stop him, the newcomer had hurtled himself toward the killer, and the two became engaged in a vicious battle of fists.

He was the cop! Sean thought fleetingly. He should be engaged in the damned battle, and the civilian should be taking Maggie away from the fray.

"Maggie!" the killer said, roaring out her name like a battle cry, and lunging toward her. He was stopped by the second man, and Sean realized that he had to get Maggie up and out of the danger zone. He could hear sirens now. Hell, about time. The cavalry was coming at last. But the killer was still raging out Maggie's name, lunging for her. Sean tore pell-mell for her, reaching for her, drawing her to her feet.

Her eyes on his almost made him pause. There was fear

within them. Liquid, shimmering. Not for herself. For him. She loved him, he realized. Really loved him.

"Get the hell out of here, get Mamie, get down the alley!" he ordered her.

"Sean, no, you've got to get out of here!" she pleaded.

"Maggie, go, or else we may have another victim on our hands!"

He shoved her. She tried to fight back, to argue. Then she saw the two men engaged in battle, and she inhaled sharply— and suddenly obeyed. She raced to Mamie, grabbed hold of her, solicitously looking her over for injuries while trying to lead her hastily out of the alley.

The killer was up; the stranger who'd appeared in the alley staggered to his feet as well. The killer was about to escape. The stranger followed him. Sean started after them both. Running hard. The killer slipped around a corner. The second man did the same. Sean followed into the shadows.

But the men were both gone.

Suddenly, police cars were braking everywhere in the narrow confines of the French Quarter. Uniformed officers were spilling from their cars. "He's extremely powerful, use all caution!" Sean warned, wheezing and panting as he approached the cars, shouting directions then, and sending different groups in different directions.

They should catch the killer.

They should.

But he had the sinking feeling that they would not. Hell, the guy seemed to be on enough steroids to pump up an elephant. Bullets barely fazed him. He could probably throw off two or three men. And what about the other man?

Sore, hurting all over, he made his way out of the alley while he listened to the sounds of running footsteps. Jack Delaney, along with Mike Astin in plain clothes, had arrived. Mamie was seated in the rear of his car, shivering. Maggie stood by the car.

Her stockings and skirt were ripped and torn; her ivory jacket was muddied, and her red hair was wildly tossed. Other than that, she didn't look much the worse for wear. Reaching the car, Sean stared at her furiously. "What the hell is the matter with you?"

"What?" she said blankly.

He came to her, shaking her, so unnerved himself that he didn't realize he was a cop shaking a woman on the street. "Damn you, that man's a lethal killer, and you're in an alley throwing yourself at him like Wonder Woman."

Maggie paled, frowning. "I was afraid he was going to kill you!"

"I'm a cop, I'm paid to take risks, I'm trained to take risks, damn you, Maggie—"

"Hey, now, ladies, gents, please!" Mamie ground out hoarsely from the car.

Sean stared at her, then at Maggie. He took her roughly by the chin, moving her face so that he could study it. He wasn't shaking her anymore. He was still shaking himself.

But she looked all right. Really all right.

His hand dropped.

"Maybe we should get Mamie to a hospital," Jack suggested.

"No, no hospital," Mamie said.

"Miss Johnson, maybe you belong in the hospital," Mike Astin persisted, his voice amazingly gentle for a man his size.

Mamie smiled. "No, honey, no hospital. I'm not going to be confined anywhere. I'm going to be sleeping at my own place tonight with guys I've known for years out working the bar and the floor around me."

"Maybe the killer is trapped," Jack suggested, "and you'd be better off in the hospital. Mamie, you're getting some bruises on your throat there."

"I'm fine," Mamie insisted. "No hospital."

"The medics are here; at least let them check you out," Sean advised.

He moved away from the car, still shaking with anger and fear. The streets had come alive with a blaze of lights and the shrill of police whistles. Cops were everywhere. Still, Sean had the eerie feeling that they weren't going to find the killer.

Not the man who had gone after him.

"Son-of-a-bitch!" he exclaimed to the night.

Jack Delaney had come up behind him.

"What?"

"There was a second man—a guy who joined right into the fight—and he's missing now as well."

"Who was he?"

"Damned if I know. He was just suddenly here, racing after the killer, and . . ."

Jack was silent.

Sean spun around to stare at him. "What is it?"

Jack cleared his throat. "We've had another strange happening in the last hour or so."

Still looking around the alley from which two men had cleanly disappeared, Sean arched a brow. "Another prostitute?" he breathed.

"No."

"Another body."

"In bits and pieces."

"Oh, hell."

"The head and torso were pulled in by a fishing boat."

"No ID?"

"Yes, we have an ID."

"Spit it out, damn it, Jack!"

"He was identified as Rutger Leon. You know, he's that tough guy you ran into at the bar, the one egging on the guy you shot to kill the girl? The guy threatening to come back after her."

Sean gave Jack his full attention. "Head and torso?"

Jack nodded, wincing. "They think his extremities might have been munched down by some bayou inhabitants."

It was hard to feel sorrow for Rutger Leon.

It was even more difficult to understand what was happening. A murderer after women in a Ripperesque fashion. A man who was already a corpse beheaded. And now, a bastard like Rutger Leon ripped to shreds.

He looked back around the alley. The damned killer should have been found by now.

"I should just resign," Sean said.

"Maybe we'll find him tonight."

"Oh, yeah. Oh, yeah."

Sean turned away from the alley, his mood even more foul as he made his way back to the car, staring at Maggie. He walked over to where she stood.

"Who was the other man, Maggie?" he demanded harshly. "And don't ask me what other man. You know who I mean. Tell me. Now. Who was he?"

"I—I—do—" she floundered.

"Don't tell me you don't know. He called you by name."

"He's . . ."

"Don't lie to me, Maggie!"

"Hey, Sean!" Jack warned softly.

Sean realized that he was out of control, thoroughly frustrated, and more. He felt like a tiger crawling the walls, he was jealous, irrational—and suddenly scared to death for Maggie.

"Maggie!" he barked out, ignoring Jack.

"An old friend, Sean—that's all. We met . . . in Europe. He's just arrived recently."

An old friend? Or an old lover?

"How did you come to be in the alley, Maggie?" he demanded.

Her beautiful eyes were flickering gold now with anger. She glanced down at Mamie, and to his astonishment, Sean thought that he saw Mamie shake her head slightly.

Maggie set her hands on her hips. "Gut feeling. I was suddenly nervous about Mamie. I hadn't heard from you. I came down to the bar and Sam said that Mamie had just left, so I came outside and then I heard the scuffling and . . ."

"Sean, you're grilling her like a hardened criminal!" Jack said softly.

He tried to ease the stiffness in his shoulders, the steel that seemed to shoot through his back. Something wasn't right. She was lying through her teeth.

"What about your friend?" he demanded.

"I don't know. Ask him!" she snapped.

Sean crossed his arms over his chest. "Well, now, I can't actually do that—since he's disappeared right along with the killer." He swung around suddenly, realizing that one of the officers in charge of the uniformed cops searching for the killer was waiting for his attention.

"Sergeant Meeks."

"Lieutenant, I'm damned sorry, the men are everywhere, but we haven't found him yet. We'll keep it up with all the manpower we can, but . . ."

"Thank you, Sergeant. You're right—we've got to keep every available man looking. Our sketch of the killer is a damned good one. Make sure it's plastered everywhere. But make sure we've got warnings out that the killer is highly dangerous, *highly dangerous,* and that the population is not to try apprehending him."

"Yessir."

"If you need me, I'll be at the station for a while—taking statements!" he said firmly to Maggie and Mamie. Then he turned his back on them, telling Jack and Mike to drive the women to the office while he brought his own car in.

Two hours later, he let Mike Astin escort Mamie back to her restaurant. She'd given her statement. She'd clearly told Sean everything the killer had said, nervously rubbing her neck. There were little scratches, but nothing that had broken the surface. She still didn't want to go to a hospital, and she'd see her own doctor if she felt the need. She told Sean that the killer had been angry with her for selling him out—he had lain in wait to attack her, and he had told her that he liked chocolate, and nearly given her heart failure. He would have killed her if Sean hadn't come along, but she was alive, and grateful. She didn't know anything else, though, there was nothing more she could tell him.

There would be a police guard on her place all night. That didn't seem to mean much to Mamie. She'd insisted on a meal while she gave her statement, and she'd ordered garlic bread, linguini in garlic and olive oil, and a salad—with garlic cloves.

She'd relieved Mike Astin of a tiny gold cross he wore, then smiled sweetly when Sean quizzed her.

"Honey, it's just one of those nights when I want to feel closer to my God, you know?" Mamie said.

"Even God will gag on your breath, Mamie," he told her,

and she'd laughed uneasily. She'd insisted on seeing Maggie, and the two of them had whispered together for a minute before Mamie left, looking at Sean as if he were an evil creature, about to pounce on poor Maggie.

Well, he *was* about to pounce on Maggie. That was for certain.

She sat in his office, irritated now. She'd been restless at first, crossing and uncrossing her legs, pacing. Now she just sat back and stared at him.

"What is it you want out of me?" she demanded.

Even Jack was gone by then. The cops were still searching the streets; they hadn't found the killer.

"The truth."

"I told you the truth."

"The whole truth."

She sighed. "Honest to God, that's the truth. I felt a strange *gut* feeling that I needed to see Mamie."

"You two are awfully chummy all of a sudden. Especially," he pointed out, "since you were the one who reminded me that she did deal in human flesh."

"Mamie seems to be all right," Maggie said with a shrug. "And no matter what she does, she surely doesn't deserve to die at this killer's hands!"

"Right. But you should risk your own life?"

"I didn't mean to risk my own life. I just saw that he was about to attack you and . . ." Her voice trailed. He felt a wave of heat sweep over him, but he fought the desire and the emotion she kept so alive within him.

"Who was the man? Name, address, if you would, please."

He looked downward at the paper on his desk, pencil in hand, and waited patiently.

She didn't speak.

He looked up.

"Lucian," she said after a moment. "Lucian DeVeau. I'm not sure where he's living right now. I hadn't seen him in years before he stopped by the shop the other day."

"An old friend?" he queried, staring at her.

She stared back.

"Or an old lover?"

"Is that question necessary for the police report?" she snapped back.

He set the pencil down.

"It's necessary for me."

She exhaled on a long breath. "May I go home now?" she asked him.

"Old lover. When did it break up?"

"Years ago. Years. Honestly."

"How many years?"

"I don't know!" Maggie snapped.

"Why was Mamie wolfing down garlic?"

Her eyebrows shot up.

"What?"

"Never mind. Never mind." He set his pencil down, rose, and reached for her hand.

"Let's go."

"Together?"

"Yes."

"You've been incredibly rude."

"You need police protection."

"Surely there are other policemen."

"Honey, I'm the cop you're getting. Let's go."

He opened his drawer, reloading his gun, taking extra ammunition. Maggie watched him mutely. Her elbow in hand, he led her out.

Sean wanted to put some distance between them and the killer. Rather than driving to Montgomery Enterprises, he opted for the longer drive out and down the river to Maggie's family's plantation home.

She left him in the foyer.

Fine. He walked around the house, seeing that every window and door was secured.

He looked into the closets, then walked up the stairway. On the midlanding, he paused, looking up at the painting of Magdalena. A strange, hot tremor swept him where he stood. He was tempted to drag Maggie out of the shower and down to the landing.

Very strange. Maybe he really should resign. Have himself committed to a good hospital.

He forced himself to keep walking.

Upstairs, he saw to it that all the balcony doors and windows were secured. It was a time-consuming job.

In her room, he heard the shower running. He lay down on her bed, and closed his eyes, his gun resting over his chest.

In a matter of seconds, he had dozed off.

He had ridden, he had fought. He had slashed at the enemy, he had killed, he had triumphed, and he felt ill. Battle had ended; it was time to go for the wounded, to protect them from the murderer.

And so, he was riding again. The earth tore up beneath his horse's hooves, the breeze rushed by his face. He was dirty, thirsty, hungry, tired. He wanted her. Wanted to ride to her. But this . . .

The killer was before him. Getting ready to strike again. He rode hard, ready to attack—but not kill. God, there had to be mercy somewhere! But the enemy was strong, and still, when he had bested his enemy . . .

Another awaited.

Fleetingly, he saw a face. A face he knew.

Oh, God!

Pain . . .

He felt pain.

The knowledge that death was coming. And she was there, an angel, holding him, tears within her eyes. God help him! He'd had strength, he'd learned both courage and mercy, but he hadn't been prepared, and so now, the world faded away with her tears while the face of the enemy . . .

Sean awoke with a start, realizing that he'd dozed, and that he'd been dreaming of fighting in a war that had ended well over a century ago.

He sat up, carefully placing his gun on the bedside table in Maggie's elegant room.

The killer had been in his dream. The killer he had faced tonight had slain him in his dreams. He was losing it; they were going to take him off the force.

He was never going to have a chance to commit himself. Soon, everyone would see through him, and he'd simply be locked up in a good mental ward.

He stared toward the bathroom door.

The hell with it.

Thoughts played havoc in his head. Mamie's words, Marie's. Voodoo Marie giving him the cross. His strange dreams.

Mamie. Trying to get him to eat garlic.

Mamie, eating enough garlic to choke a horse.

He sat on the bed, shaking his head, then pressing his temples between his hands. He heard his father speaking, laughing. There was a rumor that the Montgomerys threw out a vampire every other generation. Years and years ago Maggie's ancestress had fallen in love with the wrong man. The family had slain him—and she'd gone away.

And every daughter still bore the Montgomery name . . .

All right, he thought, dragging his fingers through his hair, he was really losing it. Maggie wasn't the killer, he *knew* that Maggie wasn't the killer, but what the hell was going on?

He rose, suddenly determined to look around. He pulled open her drawers, searched them. He couldn't believe that he was making a checklist in his mind of all the vampire movies he had seen, all the books he had read. Vampires disliked crosses. Maggie wore them all the time. Vampires had no reflections. Maggie definitely had a reflection. Vampires slept by day . . .

Ha! She walked the streets by day.

Vampires slept in coffins. He'd slept with her often enough; he knew damned well she didn't sleep in a coffin.

Unless . . .

He got down on his hands and knees, and looked under the bed.

He couldn't help it.

Yet Maggie chose just then to emerge from the shower,

catching him redhanded. He sensed her presence as she stood behind him.

"What in hell are you doing?" she demanded.

He straightened, letting the bed skirt fall, rising and taking a seat on the bed. He stared back at her. Hard. Then he shrugged. Something wasn't quite right. Time to get it in the open. Time to find out what?

"Looking for dirt," he said flatly.

She stood very still, apparently realizing exactly what he was about. She arched a brow regally, mockingly. "Why not a coffin?"

"*Do* you have a coffin?" he asked, rising, folding his arms over his chest as he faced her.

"No. Do you?" He didn't answer, he kept staring at her. She exhaled slowly. "We've slept together. You know damned well I don't sleep in a coffin."

He nodded after a moment. "Do you know, Maggie, my dad is always throwing little bits of intriguing historical trivia at me. Here's one for you. There's a curious reason our ancestors started using headstones in graveyards. Do you know what it is?"

"I'm sure you're going to tell me," she said very softly. She stood elegantly tall and straight, wearing a soft white silk gown that emphasized the beauty and perfection of her body and the deep fire-red of her hair.

"Well, in countries throughout Europe—and beyond, I'm certain—there have long been superstitions regarding the dead. A heavy stone on the head could keep a corpse from rising."

"I don't have a headstone, Lieutenant," she assured him. The tone of her voice made him feel like a fool.

He shook his head, sinking back down to the bed. God, he was losing his mind. She was flesh and blood, a living, breathing woman. And he was a cop! For the love of God, he was a cop. He didn't believe in the supernatural, in ghosts, zombies, hobgobblins . . .

Or vampires.

She walked across the room to him. Her white silk gown fluttered about the perfect formation of her body. The nightgown was soft gauze, completely see-through. Her breasts rose high, round and firm, her nipples were hard, enticingly large, and the dark shadow of the triangle between her thighs was hauntingly inviting. She stroked his cheek, lifting his chin, and he met her eyes.

"Do you think I'm a vampire?" she asked him.

"No, don't be absurd," he told her. On the one hand, it was the truth. On the other . . .

Was it an awful lie?

With a soft whisper of silk, she moved away from him. He was torn between the sway of her firm buttocks beneath the telltale silk and a longing to hear her talk, to emphatically deny that anything at all was different about her.

She took a seat in a high-back chair across the room, by the fireplace. The windows were closed and tightly locked, but a blast from an air-conditioning vent drifted by her, lifting her hair and the gauzy material around her. She curled her feet beneath her and sat hugging her legs to her chest. She seemed even more alluring. He was a madman, searching around her bed when they were in the middle of forming a tenuous relationship.

She exhaled. "Sean, I warned you not to get involved with me."

He couldn't be a madman. He loved her; he couldn't lose her.

He rose, going to her. "You could warn me from here to eternity. It wouldn't matter. I'm in love with you, Maggie."

"The truth is," she whispered, "that you barely know me."

"You're wrong. I feel I've known you forever. As if you're a part of me. Like living, like breathing. You're in my blood."

"Really?" she whispered.

He reached down for her hand, drawing her up against him. He held her tightly to him. Her flesh seemed on fire beneath the silk. He rubbed his hands down her back, over her buttocks, pressing her tightly against his arousal, growing hard against the restriction of his pants. She smelled sweetly of her soap. He nuzzled her neck, feeling the urgency of desire she awakened spiraling within him. He kissed her lips lightly, then the length of her throat. She stood pliant in his arms. He kissed her earlobe, the hollow of her collarbone. He buried his face between her breasts, then took a nipple into his mouth, bathing it through the fine white silk, sucking until the rouge peak pebbled to a hard point and he heard the sharp intake of her breath. Her body arched to his. He dropped slowly to his knees, mouthing her flesh, teasing it with his tongue. He slid a hand beneath the hem of her gown, between her legs. He pressed his thumb deep into her, pressed her closer to his face, bathing her intimately through the silk while he rotated his thumb deeply, erotically.

Her fingers knotted into his shoulders. She stiffened, arched, nearly raked the flesh from his shoulders through his shirt. She climaxed with a gasping breath, slumping against him as if she would fall. He stood, sweeping her up into his arms.

And not knowing why, but not giving a damn, he carried her to the stairway. He didn't bother to shed his own clothing, but came down upon her in an agony of desire, and made love to her there. When it was over, he lifted her, and carried her back to her bed, stripped at last, and lay down beside her.

Smiling, she turned to him. "What was that all about?"

"I don't know."

"I thought you were really angry with me."

"I was. I am. And if you ever do anything so recklessly foolish again, I swear I'll take a paddle to you like a child."

She didn't reply. He rolled over then, straddling her.

"Promise me that you won't."

"Sean, tonight was sheer accident. Things just happened."

"Like this Lucian fellow arriving."

She shrugged. "I knew he was in town. He had stopped by to say hello. And we are old friends."

"Yeah, right. So tell me—is it really over?"

"Is what really over?"

"Whatever you had going with this Lucian fellow."

"It was never serious."

"That wasn't my question."

She blinked. "It's really over."

Staring down at her, he felt a forceful shudder tear through his body. He'd never known a need like this, such fierce desire.

Her eyes met his, gold-flecked, exotic. Her hair spilled around her naked shoulders. He looked at her, and wanted her again.

He leaned lower, taking his weight off her, but leaving a leg lying over her. Her fingers trailed over his shoulder and she inched lower against him. She took his sex into her hands, instantly causing it to spring back to attention.

"It better really be over," he said. Tough guy. Yeah, sure. What could he do?

She smiled. "Oh?"

"We've been playing around rather carelessly here. We have to get married."

Her smiled faded. "Sean?"

"Umm?"

"That's one of the reasons you shouldn't love me. I—I can't have children."

The look on her face captured his heart. He drew her closer to him.

"Then we won't have children," he said softly.

"You want children."

"I want you."

"But—"

"We can always adopt if we both choose. Doesn't matter. I love you. Nothing means anything without you."

"Sean—"

"Still . . . don't stop what you were doing."

She managed a smile again. Then she eased down against his body, taking him in her mouth.

Sometime in the night, they slept.

Despite the fact that he was deeply in love, Sean awoke with a terrible weight of responsibility hanging over him.

The killer was still out there. Growing more bold; growing more dangerous.

His eyes half closed, he watched as Maggie awoke. She, too, seemed to wake with a heavy heart despite the night they had shared.

She sat up, staring out at the morning sun through a slit in the drapes, watching as it slowly began climbing higher in the sky. Apparently, she knew he was awake, and she was aware he was watching her.

"Sean?" she said softly.

"Yes?"

"I *am* a vampire," she told him quietly.

CHAPTER 14

"What?" Sean demanded. By morning's light, his suspicions seemed ridiculous. Her words were absurd.

She nodded, looking at him. "It's the truth."

He smiled, feeling that, by day, the whole thing was foolish. "No coffin, Maggie, I looked. No dirt in your bed. You have a reflection, you eat and drink normal food, and you don't burn up in the sunlight."

She didn't laugh. "We aren't destroyed by sunlight, we're simply weaker during the day. Our greatest strength comes at dusk. I don't need a coffin, Sean, and I have a lot of human tendencies because . . ."

"No, don't tell me!" He sat up at her side, smiling, willing to play along. "I know the story. You have human tendencies because you're only half vampire, you're the child of Magdalena and her vampire lover, and so you're a mixed breed? Kind of like a mulatto or a half-breed Indian?"

She stared at him seriously in return.

"I don't need a coffin because . . . we don't really need coffins. They're just dark and comfortable. Besides, I don't seem to have as many weaknesses as some vampires because . . . because my father gave me blood before I passed into darkness. He had friends who were familiar with vampires, and I think that somehow he kept me from actually dying and coming back, the way it is with most. Think about it, why should it have to be a coffin for any vampire? People choose to sleep in different ways, beds, futons . . . any place of rest is fine for vampires. What is a coffin but a box? Secluded, protected. And as for light . . . well, it has taken me decades to adjust to where I'm really comfortable in the daylight. And trust me—you'll seldom catch me at the beach.''

''Maggie, come on, how can you be a vampire if you don't live up to legend?''

''Legend is only hearsay, and that embellished,'' she said sadly. ''But then again, legends are most often based on fact. Many vampires do rest in their coffins, because they died before they were reborn. They awoke in their coffins. A coffin remains home to them. At times, don't we all need to go home? I was never buried. I live here—always returning to my home, which is my native soil. I don't need to carry dirt around with me here. If I go to Europe, yes . . . I bring native soil with me, and it rests beneath my bed. We draw strength from the earth. But think about the city of New Orleans, Sean, and about our cemeteries. Our above-ground tombs are referred to as 'ovens' because they *are* ovens. In a year and a day, the remains of the dead are more or less baked, you know that. The body, per se, no longer exists—bones are pushed to the rear of a coffin to make room for the next deceased in a family. In cooler places than New Orleans, where a tomb bakes in the sun, some vampires do sleep in their coffins. In crypts, in family vaults— in bedrooms. All vampires have reflections—it's a myth, a good story, that they don't. And we thrive on good food, just as others do, we just . . . we just need a little more. That's the curse of our 'gift,' as so many choose to call it. We have a hunger, a thirst . . . and it must be appeased. And as to my genetics . . .'' She paused, shaking her head as she looked at him. ''There was no baby, Sean. Magdalena didn't have an illegitimate child with her French lover. My father knew that I might well live for centuries. So he invented the story that I was having a child. Every twenty years or so, I could come back to New Orleans. As the new heiress. I look like Magdalena, Sean, because I am Magdalena.''

She was lying, of course. Maybe she even believed just a little bit what she was saying. God knew, the legends abounded in her family.

''Maggie, please . . .''

''Sean, you have to listen. It's the truth.''

''Oh, come on, Maggie, I can't believe you!''

''You must believe me.''

He shook his head impatiently.

Vampire. It could really mean so many things. Someone who simply sucked the essence of life out of others. A tyrant of a husband, a shrew of a wife. A psychological vampire, stealing heart and soul.

A hemophiliac, physically needing blood.

An insane man or woman, believing he or she needed to drink blood to survive. Why not? Killers listened to voices, demon dogs who told them how and when to take a life. The world was full of madness. Bloodlust came in many guises.

And Maggie was eccentric, she had listened to one story too many . . .

''All right. You say you're a vampire. So is it your thirst for blood that has brought about these recent murders? Are you trying to tell me that you're the killer, that you had to drink blood?'' He shook his head. He loved her, and he knew the truth. ''Maggie, I've *seen* the killer.''

She shook her head impatiently. ''Yes, you've seen the killer, and no, obviously, I'm not the killer.'' She hesitated, looking down at her hands. ''But you don't want to accept the truth— even though you've seen it. You know that something isn't right, that there's something different about these killings, that blood doesn't disappear. Vampires can and do exist, and I am one. And a long time ago, I did kill. When I—when I was first bitten, my father was desperate to keep me from becoming a heedless predator. He acquired blood for me from different places, he studied vampire lore, he learned. He bought blood from local doctors, the hospitals, even the morgue. I've chosen to . . . well, in the last few years, I've relied on blood banks—

and small mammals. Birds, upon occasion. I never wanted to kill. But I have done so. Condemned men mostly. Once, I finished off a Yankee soldier who had been tainted with bad blood.'' She hesitated. ''Vampire blood. There are subtle degrees to vampire bites; some kill, some taint,'' she murmured. ''That particular man was going crazy. I wish I hadn't had to kill even him. Of course, I did mean to kill that poor retarded child who was to hang—''

''What?'' Sean snapped, remembering his father's story. Was Maggie totally insane—or was he?

She shook her head. ''Long time ago. I had a very good friend and her son was retarded and he was accused of an awful crime he didn't commit. So—''

''You made him a vampire?'' Sean said mockingly.

She shook her head. ''I've never created another of my kind. We're only allowed two per century—''

''Two per century,'' he repeated, but she didn't seem to realize that he was mocking the incredulity of her story.

''But I wouldn't, you see. I'd never do this to anyone.''

''Why not? You seem to be doing well.''

''At the cost of my soul, Sean. I'd never do that to anyone else.''

She was so grave. So straightforward. She thought she was telling the truth.

He just stared at her.

''I wouldn't, Sean.''

''You were talking about the war,'' he said harshly. ''What war? There have been a number of wars throughout time, you know.''

''The Civil War,'' she said with a sigh of aggravation. ''And I killed the man who brought about the death of your ancestor, the other Sean,'' she said on a whisper. ''His name was Wynn, Colonel Wynn. What happened wasn't really his fault, and I was sorry for him as well when I discovered what had happened.'' She hesitated again and Sean realized that he was still just staring at her—very blankly. ''Sean, there's an evil vampire—''

''In contrast to a *good* blood-sucking vampire, right?''

She sighed with great impatience. "Sean, believe it or not, most of us are like any other predator, man included. We have moved into our times, the last days before the millennium! Most vampires limit their blood intake to what's absolutely necessary. There are those who are very old, and who have sickened of killing, who have learned that killing is what gets us killed in return. There are a number of my kind who have learned a way to subsist on the blood of lesser animals as well. Men eat meat, vampires eat the meat and drink the blood. Animals bred on ranches, sometimes other predators when they're in abundance—"

"Is that what you do? Get your blood supply from killer 'gators out in the bayou?"

"Don't be absurd; I told you, I subsist on mammals. Reptiles are cold-blooded. They can stave off hunger for a while, but not fulfill it. And there are blood banks everywhere these days."

"Oh," he breathed. Oh, yes, so matter-of-fact!

She was losing her mind.

He loved her so much.

Suddenly, he drew her against him, rocking with her. "Maggie, listen to yourself. You've got to realize that what you're saying is a delusion. It can't be true. This is the real world. There are very bad men. Yes, they are monsters—God knows, we have human monsters. They aren't ghosts and vampires or werewolves, just monsters who are men, who are human beings. Maggie, I love you. You've got to know that. I love you so much. I know you believe this, but it can't be true. We can talk to someone—"

"Sean, you came in here last night, searching under my bed! You've suspected something since you met me. Now, when I tell you the truth, explain what you're questioning, what you're seeing, you won't believe me!"

He lowered his eyes quickly, not wanting her to see that her words had suddenly made him uneasy. God, yes, he'd seen too much. And there was more. He'd been haunted far too often in the night lately. He'd had so many strange dreams!

He'd dreamed about the Civil War.

He'd dreamed about the killer.

But he was a sane and rational man. He had to deny what she was saying, or someone would lock them both up and the killer would be free to go on an even greater death spree.

"Maggie, I can't possibly—"

"Sean!" She took his face between her two hands, looking earnestly into his eyes. "This isn't as absurd as it seems. Why not? Why can't it be? Perhaps it's like a disease, one we know nothing about. We pass it from one to another. I don't think that any of us really knows exactly where or when it all began, but hundreds and hundreds of years ago, at the very least. Sean! Do you believe in a God, in a Supreme Being? Do you believe in goodness? If there is good, then there is evil, if a man's soul can rise to heaven, it can also be trapped on earth. If there are angels, then there are devils. I am a vampire. There are others."

"But, if such creatures were real, Maggie, the entire world would be peopled with vampires!" Sean proclaimed.

She shook her head, still trying so hard to sway him. "No. Because vampires can be killed. And because, like I told you, there are rules, there are laws. In ancient days, men did hunt us down, kill us, sometimes almost annihilate us. We've learned to co-exist, just as men co-exist with tigers, wild dogs, mountain lions. The rules among us are strict, so that we can survive. We're not allowed to create more like ourselves more than twice during a century. If we did just strike out heedlessly, our numbers would have become so vast long ago that, as you said, there would have been something like a duel to the death— annihilation between humanity and . . . and whatever we actually are! If we destroyed our food supply—that supply which so many of our number still crave too desperately to deny— we would all perish as well. Most of us live quietly. Some are more concerned in their choice of victims than others. I was telling you the truth before—that many of us exist, go about a day-to-day life, and no one ever knows what we are, because we have learned to live without killing humans. We're not living in the past. It's a technical day and age, a new world, you know."

He shook his head. "Yeah, a new world."

"Sean, you've got to believe me. I swear, I'm telling you the truth."

"I don't believe any of this. I can't believe any of this."

"Sean, please, please, you have to listen to me. Because it's the only way you're going to catch your killer."

He frowned. "You know who the killer is?"

She looked at him gravely. "Yes."

"And the killer is a vampire?"

She drew determinedly away from him, rising. She looked down at him. "Yes," she said softly.

He threw up his hands. "My God. You're losing your mind. I'm losing my mind. It's that simple."

"Sean—"

"No, no, I've got a few questions now. We'll go right back to step one. You're telling me that you're really a vampire."

"Yes," she said evenly.

"So, actually, you have incredible strength. In many ways. You could have killed me at anytime."

"Yes," she whispered. "And . . . no."

"What?"

"I could have . . . but I couldn't have."

"Damn you, Maggie, which is it?"

"I have the strength, but . . ."

"You have the strength!" He rose then as well, arms crossed over his chest as he stared at her, shouting, "Prove it. Do something. Take me, then. Do it. Prove this." He advanced on her, a hand on her chest as he shoved her back. He pushed her, hard. Once, again, again.

"Sean, stop it."

He caught hold of her shoulders and shook her. She made no protest. She continued to stare at him, her head falling back. God, she was so beautiful! All that he wanted to do was hold her.

But everything suddenly seemed so insane.

"The killer is a vampire?"

"Yes."

"That's why he's so incredibly strong. Why he doesn't fall when he's shot."

"Yes. Exactly."

He nodded after a moment. "A vampire ... so killing is quick and easy for him."

"It always has been," she reflected.

"You've known him before?"

She nodded.

"Another lover?"

She shook her head emphatically. "I hated him from the time I met him."

"But he's incredibly strong, *because* he's a vampire."

"Yes."

"So—that would make you incredibly strong."

"I told you—"

"No, you still haven't really told me anything. So, I repeat— you could kill me. Quickly. Easily."

"Sean—"

"Answer me. You could kill me. With a twist of your fingers."

"I could, but I couldn't."

"Why not?" he demanded fiercely, his incredulity at a situation that still seemed to bear a certain truth causing his temper to soar.

But she still stared back at him evenly. "I can't kill you, I can't hurt you, because ..."

"Because?"

"Because I love you," she said very softly.

He fell silent, then turned away from her. He sat down on the edge of the bed, staring at her, still refusing to believe. It was insane.

And yet ...

He felt as if he were on fire. With confusion. There were things that he felt ... that couldn't be. He was a sane man. He dealt with madmen at times, but he was a cop, a good cop, and he had faced evil before, but evil came in flesh and blood.

Normal flesh and blood.

"So, you really do love me?"

"Yes. You know that I do."

"I'm sure this is something you've said before. Over the years, of course. Just how old are you?"

"Very."

"When were you born?"

"As a vampire?"

"As a human!"

"Eighteen twenty-one."

"You must be using one hell of a night cream."

"You know that vampires don't age at the same rate—"

"How can I really know anything? I need help here," he said dryly. "Eighteen twenty-one. A lot of years gone by. So, in that time, how many men have you loved?"

She was still staring at him with such level eyes. As if this were a regular, real conversation. "Two before you," she told him, "except that the second one doesn't really count."

"Oh? And why not?"

"Because I think that he *was* you."

Sean groaned and sank down on the bed. "He was me?"

She nodded very gravely, rising and walking to her dresser where she shook a snow globe of a Disney prince and princess and set it down, watching as the glittering particles within the globe settled once again. Then she met his eyes in the mirror. "I've been around a very long time, Sean. Honest. I've seen a lot that was bad, but I've also come to believe in some good. I think that sometimes, perhaps when lives are cut short, people come back. In close and similar situations. I think that you are the Sean Canady I knew and loved during the Civil War."

He looked at her, his throat dry, as he thought of the strange dreams that had been plaguing him lately. Dreams of riding into battle, seeking glory . . .

Last night.

His mad desire to make love on the stairway.

No.

"Who was your first lover?" he demanded harshly.

"Comte Alec DeVereaux. We met when I was very young."

"You loved him—and he did this to you?"

She hesitated, uncertain for the first time. "I loved him, and I believe that he loved me. And I think he foolishly believed he could make things right between us. There is a saying engraved on an ancient tombstone in France: 'And love shall set you free.' I think that Alec believed that my love for him would change things. That he could regain his immortal soul through me. Lucian believes that Alec was convinced of the truth of the saying.''

''Ah, yes, Lucian!'' Sean spat out. ''So—this Lucian is a vampire as well?''

''Yes.''

''And he's survived all this time?''

''Much longer than me. Lucian is ancient. As for Alec . . .'' She shook her head. ''My father killed Alec. He was with one of your great, great—however many greats—grandfathers, and some other men. They thought they knew what Alec was.''

''From what you say, they did know. He was a vampire.''

''He was a vampire, but not evil.''

''What he did to you was apparently evil.''

''I've already told you—''

He groaned with sudden impatience. ''Don't tell me anything else! I don't believe any of this.''

Maggie walked back over to him, sitting Indian fashion on the bed before him. ''Sean, you have to believe me. It's the only way you can fight the killer.''

''I shouldn't have a gun. I should have a stake,'' he queried skeptically.

She ignored his tone, anger flickering in her eyes as she watched him.

''Well,'' he told her, ''I do need a stake, right? We have established that the killer is a vampire.''

She hesitated, watching him. Then she let out a long sigh. ''Yes, he's a vampire. A practiced killer who has made an art of murder through the years. He's also Jack the Ripper.''

Sean's eyebrows shot up. ''Oh, Jesus, Maggie—''

''Don't 'Maggie' me in that tone. I'm going to start at the beginning and try to be concise, and try to get all this through your stubborn head. When I was very young, I fell in love. My father wanted to save his child, so he killed Alec, then spent his life trying to save me. He invented a child—and a way for me to come back to New Orleans every twenty years or so. I met Lucian because—''

''Yes?''

''Lucian is the king.''

''King!'' Sean reiterated through clenched teeth.

''Well, that's what he is. But that's beside the point now. He was my mentor; he taught me the rules. How to survive, how to have a life, how to keep my property. I have always been M. Montgomery in some manner or another. During the Civil War, I met Sean Canady, and I didn't have the nerve to tell him what I was, but I had promised that after the war I would explain why I couldn't marry him. At a party we met a man, and I knew he was one of my kind, except he was cruel. Incredibly cruel. I knew from the beginning that I wanted nothing to do with him, but he pursued me. He killed carelessly, and worse, he enjoyed tainting men.''

''Tainting them?''

''I told you about tainting people. Slicing into their necks with the blood teeth; they don't die, they don't become vampires. If a vampire takes too much blood from a victim this way, the victim dies—or he or she goes mad and starts killing others.''

''Oh, of course,'' Sean murmured.

''Anyway, this vampire slowly killed Colonel Wynn's daughter, then started on him. He destroyed the colonel. Wynn started butchering wounded Confederate soldiers, convinced that a soldier had seduced and killed his daughter. Sean Canady went after Wynn, I came after Sean . . . and Aaron Carter came after me. I was so desperate that I would have kept Sean alive as a vampire, except that it was too late.''

Sean thought that his face must be fixed into a permanent mask of disbelief, like a plastic mask.

''Then the war ended, time went by—Aaron became Jack the Ripper?'' he inquired. ''And Aaron is the killer I struggled with last night.''

She nodded. ''I met him again in London. I had to travel around Europe as well as the States, you see. I didn't age, and I had to allow for each new child to grow up.''

"Of course," Sean murmured.

"I was in London, and I became good friends with a doctor and his wife—remember how I said that I think that people come back when their lives are cut short?"

"What?"

"Well, I think that the doctor was your partner, Jack, by the way, and that Angie was Laura."

"Sure, why not?" Sean said. "If we're going to believe in vampires, we might as well believe in reincarnation."

"I know that there are vampires. I don't know if reincarnation is true or not. I just know that the world is full of souls, good, evil—and I think, old and young."

"And you believe in God, Maggie?"

"Yes."

"And are you damned?"

"I don't know. I pray not. Maybe, even among us, it all has to do with the concept of free will and making choices. And I pray that you won't be such a fool as to not pay attention to what I'm saying, because I'm telling you, if Aaron isn't stopped, more people will die. More and more. Peter—the doctor who was my friend in London—was an incredibly gifted man determined to help out in the slums of Whitechapel. We were out one night when I saw Aaron. We got into a fight; Lucian intervened and ordered us both to leave off. Anyway . . . Laura, Peter's wife, was pregnant, so I kept working with Peter so that she could rest, and stay home, away from the filth and disease and crime on the streets. Then the Whitechapel killings began, and Peter started having blackouts. He was convinced that he was the killer, and I began to wonder myself, because he disappeared each time there was a murder and I couldn't find him. And he'd be covered in blood. Then . . ." She inhaled deeply. "Laura had been sick. Peter found her dead after one of his blackouts. He blamed himself, and . . . he shot and killed himself. It was the morning after Mary Kelly was murdered so brutally. I was dazed, walking around . . . I saw Aaron. And when I confronted him, I found out that he'd been killing the prostitutes and purposely making Peter think he was a killer. He thought it an incredible joke that the police were so mystified, and he loved the lists of suspects. I don't know how to explain Aaron except that he thinks himself a hunter . . . like a cat, perhaps, a killer who likes to taunt and torture his prey. I was so angry that I attacked Aaron, and I hurt him, really hurt him. I would have killed him then except that Lucian stopped me, because, if I had killed him, I would have faced execution from my own kind. Even if Lucian hadn't sanctioned a formal execution, other vampires would have found me and a way to kill me. They might have despised Aaron and agreed with me, but that is the ancient law. We are not allowed to destroy our own kind. Still, Aaron was hurt, really hurt. The kind of hurt that probably took nearly a century to heal. But he's better now. And he's back—strong, evil, vicious. Jack's back!'' she said very softly, and looked at him. ''Don't you understand what you're up against, what kind of evil? Jack is back, and that's the truth. My God, look at the killings, look at your victims! How many men could copycat that well? If you allow yourself to think about it all, you'll realize I'm telling you the simple, indisputable truth.''

The truth. Surely, she saw the disbelief in his eyes.

''Maggie . . .''

''Oh, God'!'' she groaned. ''It's true, Sean. It's true. What will have to happen for me to convince you?''

She sat before him, somehow appearing very innocent and young, even in her nakedness. Her eyes were liquid, glittering a beautiful gold, her hair was still wild around her shoulders; she was so perfect and so lovely, it seemed incredible that she could be telling him such a story, much less believing it.

He cupped her cheek, kissing her lips lightly. ''I'm going to take a shower. Get dressed. Get into work,'' he told her. He rose, walking toward the shower. He felt as if he stumbled like a drunk. He paused at the bathroom door. ''With any luck, they might have caught this madman by now,'' he said.

Her back was to him. Long, sleek, beautiful. She shook her head. ''They won't have caught him. You know that. If they had found them, they would have called you by now.''

She was right; he knew it. Even if he hadn't said where he'd be, they'd have known.

He stepped into the shower and let cold water pour over him. He was in a nightmare, and he needed to wake up.

When he emerged, Maggie was dressed, ready for a day at work. She wore a navy business suit with a white silk blouse and tie. Masculine apparel had never looked so feminine, yet she was the sophisticate now, long red hair swept up into a neat chignon.

"There's coffee in the kitchen," she told him, leaving the bedroom as he dressed.

As it happened, her housekeeper, Peggy—plump, rosy-cheeked, Mrs. Santa Claus look-alike—was in the kitchen as well. She greeted Sean pleasantly, poured him coffee, and offered him a fresh, just-baked muffin.

Maggie was there, too, drinking coffee and reading the news-paper.

"The papers say you nearly caught the beast, Lieutenant Canady!" Peggy said. "You'll get him yet, you mark my words."

"Thanks for the vote of confidence, Peggy," Sean told her. "And the muffin. Maggie, you ready?"

She looked up, nodded, set down her cup, and thanked Peggy as well, telling her she wasn't sure whether she'd be back that night or not. Peggy warned her just to keep herself safe.

As they walked to the car, Sean asked sarcastically, "Is Peggy a vampire, too?"

She shot him a regal glare. "Of course not. She's my house-keeper, she looks out for me, and she's wonderful. Someone has to look after a vampire, right?"

"Ah! So she protects you at your weakest moments!"

Maggie ignored that, sliding into the car beside him. "Peggy's family has looked after Montgomery Plantation for ages," she said. "No, she's not a vampire. But her father worked for me before, and before that, her grandmother, and before that—"

"I get the idea. Does she lure in the unwary for you?"

"Don't be absurd."

"So it's no *House of Dark Shadows,* eh? You do all your own stealing from blood banks?"

"I buy my blood, thank you."

"Pick it right up on a trip to the mall, eh?"

She smiled sweetly. "I should bite you right in the neck."

He shrugged. Why was he hounding her? Was he afraid that she could make him believe? Was she serious, or was he the worst fool of all men, was this a massive joke?

They were stiff, not speaking much, until they neared the city. Then he felt compelled to warn her again. "Maggie, I don't know what is and isn't real anymore," he said, catching her eyes in the mirror. "But I don't want to have to worry about you in all this—please."

"You have to think, Sean. You have to promise me that you'll give some real thought to the things I've said to you!"

"All right. But promise me you won't try to save me or anyone else. You have to stay away from the killer—whether he's a man or a monster."

She sat silently, looking down at her hands. He was almost at Montgomery Enterprises. He pulled the car over as tightly as he could to the curb, throwing it into park to turn and take her hands as he talked to her.

"Sean, I'm trying to help you—"

"Maggie!" he protested, shaking his head and hesitating just a minute. "Maggie, I love you. Whatever is going on. Whether you're nuts, I'm nuts—or we're all nuts. If you want to help me, stay safe."

She stared straight ahead, stiff and angry. Then she looked at him. "I'm telling you the truth, Sean."

"Maggie, this whole thing is so insane. Prostitutes are dead, a pimp is dead—and a corpse is beheaded. It doesn't make sense at all—"

"Yes, it does. I did the corpse," she said quietly.

"What?"

Her eyes locked with his. "I went to the morgue, and beheaded Ray."

"You?" He tried to imagine her—taking a bone saw to a man's neck.

Her lips were a tight, white line. "Frightening image, isn't it? Are you still so sure you love me? Or are you trying not to believe that it could be true? I went after Ray. He was tainted.

That should have been obvious. You shot him, and he didn't fall. Aaron had been at him, and his blood was diseased. Enough so that he would turn. Ray was coming back. I couldn't let a man like him loose with immortal power.''

He sat silently, remembering how he had seen her in the bathroom doorway the morning after Ray was killed. It was possible . . . No. Maybe. Had she come and gone?

''I don't believe you,'' he said hoarsely.

''You don't want to believe me.''

''But—''

''Yes, Sean, I can travel like mist, I can shape-shift. It's mind over matter, almost like telekinesis. It takes a tremendous toll on me, and can't be done often, but then, I haven't needed to do much changing lately. Think about it. Remember waking, and I wasn't in bed with you? I left you, I went to the morgue. Ray was out on a gurney—they were getting ready to cut him open. He was getting ready to consume the blood of every young med student and every old doctor and med tech out there. Aaron had been making sure to behead his victims—but he hadn't killed Ray. You killed Ray, but his blood was infected enough to bring him back. A man like Ray loose in the city . . .''

''Fine,'' he challenged her. ''You think back. London, 1888. The Ripper's victims had their throats severely slashed—a few of them to the bone—*but their heads weren't actually severed!*''

''You think about it. Aaron was trying to make Peter think he was a madman. There were plenty of murders going on at the same time—just nothing so vile as the Ripper murders. Ask your father, the historian. There were torsos found in the Thames near the same time. You have to sever the arteries. I'm telling you the absolute truth, and you have to believe me. You know that men can be monsters, you've seen killers. You've seen men kill out of passion, in anger. You've seen the results when a killer has a sick mind. Combine it all with an ungodly strength and a creature who can come and go at will—and you have Aaron. He's smart. He's leaving these bodies displayed so horribly on purpose. If he had wanted his crimes hidden, they would be hidden. Aaron knows how to dispose of his leftovers.''

Sean shook his head. ''All right, we have prostitutes dead— and a pimp. Aaron—so you say. But Anthony Beale was a man—using those poor women, from the best we can figure. You say you decapitated Ray. Did you also murder Anthony Beale? Tiny drops of his blood did lead to your door.''

''I didn't kill Anthony Beale,'' she said evenly. ''I didn't *murder* anyone. Ray was already dead. I just kept him from coming back to life.''

''So, who killed Beale?''

She looked down at her hands again, shaking her head. ''It must have been Aaron. Beale either annoyed him, or got in his way.''

''And what about old Rutger Leon? Did you do him in— or was Aaron in the middle of a humanitarian streak?''

She frowned, looking at him. ''Rutger? Rutger's dead?''

She was honestly surprised, Sean determined. ''Rutger Leon's body was found yesterday. His torso and head, at least.''

Her frown remained. ''Were they found—separately?''

''Yes.''

''I can't imagine Aaron killing Rutger—he would have enjoyed him being alive too much, tormenting Callie.''

''Well, someone killed him.''

''I didn't do it,'' she said, sounding exasperated. ''I'd tell you at this point if I had done so, don't you think? Especially since you're not believing a word I say to you anyway.''

He reached over and opened the passenger door so that she could get out. ''I've got to go to work. I'm going to have to go and see what's left of Rutger's body. Then I'm going to have a meeting with the task force. By the way—should I buy all my guys crosses?''

''Yours is very nice,'' she murmured tartly.

''It doesn't bother you?''

''I've always loved religious art. And I adore churches. Lucian is always making fun of me. I pray a lot.'' She hesitated, then said, ''Some vampires are weakened by crosses. They won't stop them . . . but a cross can buy some time. And holy water can cause burning . . . especially during the daytime. Vampires are weakest by day.''

''What about garlic? Truth or myth?''

He saw the muscles in her jaw tighten. She didn't know if he was mocking her or not, but she wanted to give him what she considered to be truthful answers. ''Eat a lot of garlic. Garlic in the blood makes vampires sick as dogs.''

''And I can kill one with a stake through the heart?''

''If you get the chance to get a wooden stake through his heart.''

''Or decapitation?''

''Yes, decapitation kills vampires.''

''Great,'' he muttered. ''Just so I have something I can give the guys on the force when I tell them we're after a vampire. Right before they haul me away.''

Maggie stared at him coolly. ''I've bared everything to you,'' she said. ''I've risked my existence. And all you're doing is mocking me.''

''I'm not mocking you.''

''You're not listening to me.''

''Maggie, think about what you're saying!''

''Sean—''

''Maggie, I'm not mocking you, I swear. One way or another, there's a terrible killer out there. I just have to go to work.''

''But you still don't believe me. And going to work isn't going to do you any good if you don't believe me.''

He hesitated, looking out the front window. ''I don't know, Maggie, think about how fantastic it all sounds.'' He stared back at her. ''I do know this.''

''What?''

He smiled crookedly. ''I still love you. And whatever this guy is, I have to go catch him. For you, for me, for New Orleans Parish. Because I'm a cop, and I couldn't live with losing this one. And again, because I love you. And we're going to have some kind of a future.''

Maggie shook her head very sadly. She touched his cheek. ''I love you, Sean. But no, there is no future. Not unless you can trust me enough to believe me.''

She got out of the car, and immediately started walking away from him.

"Maggie!"

But it was too late.

She didn't look back.

CHAPTER 15

He walked into the office, barely aware of the ringing of phones, the hustle around him.

He plopped into the chair behind his desk, hands folded in his lap, staring blankly before him.

"The night continued bad, huh?"

He looked up. Jack Delaney was staring at him sympathetically.

"Have we had a good night lately?"

Jack shrugged. "Well, that's a matter of separating our professional lives from our private lives—"

Sean shook his head, leaning forward. "You've done your Ripper research, Jack, what do you know about vampires?"

Jack shrugged. "The old *Nosferatu,* really great movie. Then there were Bela Lugosi, Christopher Lee, Gary Oldman—and Lauren Hutton. That one was a kid's kind of coming of age movie where she was after high school virgins. *Fright Night,* the first, I loved it. Getting into the whole concept, you can look at *Omega Man* as a vampire movie, then there's *Army of Darkness—*"

"I'm not talking about movies, Jack."

"Real vampires? The basis for the legends, Bram Stoker's

research? Naturally, there was a real Vlad Dracul, a Romanian prince, a bloodthirsty bloke if there ever was one. Records indicate that he killed tens of thousands of his enemies—and his own people—by impaling them and leaving them to die. He supposedly dined among the stench of the dying on the hills, which leads to the idea of drinking blood. But in all seriousness—''

"Yes?" Sean arched a brow, shaking his head. "You are up on your vampire lore."

Jack grinned. "Can't help it, I love a good movie, a good mystery, Jack the Ripper—and weird legends. I'm an Arts and Entertainment channel junkie. When I was a kid in high school, I thought about going into film for a living, and I studied up on vampires because I wanted to make a really good horror film based on the bloodsuckers. Don't really know why. Seems I've always had a fascination with vampires and Jack the Ripper. As if they actually affected me in a personal way, somehow."

Staring at him, Sean arched a brow. Maggie thought Jack was her doctor friend Peter, living another life. Could it be . . .

No. Too, too weird. He shook his head.

"Jack the Ripper was insane. Historians past and present know that to be true. And with modern technology—"

"Ah, but they didn't have modern technology. Hey, and look what we've got—it hasn't stopped crime, has it?"

Looking at his hands, clenched tightly on his desk now, Sean shook his head.

"I think the most interesting thing to me," Jack went on, "is the way that the legend of some kind of blood-drinking creature has appeared throughout different cultures all through history."

"Oh?"

Jack nodded. "Down to Adam, Old Testament. He supposedly had a wife before Eve. Lilith. She sinned, she was thrown out, she ate her own children, and for years, Jewish wives protected their offspring from her, because she was supposed to come back and eat other children. Because all men have descended from Adam and Eve, naturally, we are all prey to the cannibalistic Lilith. Lamia existed to haunt the people of ancient Greece—they were blood-sucking winged women, they seduced handsome young men and, well, you know the rest. All the Lamia were named after *the* Lamia, who was once beloved of Zeus, but found out by the vengeful Hera. Even in China, the people believed in a demon called the giang shi, another bloodsucker. In ancient Sanskrit there were *baital,* creatures who fed on blood; the Germans had a *blutsauger,* and so on. Pottery found in ancient Syria and Babylonia before the time of Christ depicts demons in various acts of bloodsucking or vampirism, and—''

''Hell, what did you do, take classes in this—Vampirism 101?'' Sean asked.

Jack shrugged. ''I told you, I was going to be a great movie maker. Why all these questions about vampirism? You think we've got a vampire in the city? Dead corpses, no blood.''

''I don't believe in vampires,'' Sean said.

''Well, there *has* been a mysterious lack of blood,'' Jack said. ''We don't have any old castles, and it's damned hard for us to dig up our baking dead, but—''

''But someone is killing in a copycat mode, someone who thinks he is a reincarnation of Jack the Ripper, or a vampire.''

''You know, Sean, a copycat can be just as dangerous, just like someone deranged, thinking he is a vampire, can be just as frightening as the real thing.''

''What if . . .'' Sean began.

''Yeah?'' Jack said.

''All right, what if a vampire did exist?''

''We'd have to call in Van Helsing,'' Jack joked. Then he saw Sean's eyes. ''I . . . I . . .''

''Don't have me committed yet, I'm being hypothetical. Dealing with an imitator or the like. After all, this is New Orleans, Lestat's playground, home of voodoo, vampire tours, and more. So, help me out here, huh?''

''In the old Hammer films,'' Jack said thoughtfully, ''vampires slept by the light of day, sunlight could fry them, Holy water was like acid, a stake through the heart was a sure killer, decapitation . . .''

His voice trailed away. He cleared his throat. "Decapitation," he repeated. "But ... it's the victims who are being decapitated. Ahh ... let's see, a victim couldn't become a vampire if he were decapitated, right?"

Sean didn't answer him. "I'm heading back out to the morgue. I need you to do some research for me. Old New Orleans history. I especially want to check into a man known to be in this region during the Civil War. Aaron Carter. See what you can find out for me."

"Sure thing," Jack said. "Maybe I should start wearing a cross, huh? Chewing on garlic?"

"Lots of garlic," Sean agreed, smiling.

"Should I get hold of some holy water?"

"Not yet. I'll let you know."

Maggie had barely made it into her office when she heard the phone ringing. She picked it up.

"Montgomery Enterprises."

"Ah ... and could this be Ms. Montgomery herself?"

Maggie felt her skin crawl.

"Aaron. Damn you."

"Honey, we are already among the damned."

"What do you want, Aaron?"

"Blood, murder, mayhem—the usual."

"You've managed that, Aaron. Why are you calling, what do you want from me?"

"Why, my dear, that's just it. You're what I really want."

"Really? How interesting, Aaron. We despise each other."

"Oh, no, Maggie. You're under the mistaken impression that you don't like me. You're a nasty, self-righteous little bitch, but a darned good-looking one. And a challenge, you know. I want you under my power, Maggie. You've owed me for a long time. And who knows? I might be adoringly obsessive enough to be good to you ... after proper punishment for all you've done to me, of course. But hell, Maggie, maybe I do just want you."

"If you were to have me, you'd stop all these killing sprees?"

His laughter was husky, and seemed to cut deep to the bone. "Not on your life. I'd teach you how to live. I'd teach you to have the power I have, because I'm not afraid to be what I am. A predator, my love. A bloodsucking creature of the night, if you would. You'd revel in life."

"Were you ever human, Aaron?"

"Interesting question. In truth, I was, I certainly was. And this is my territory, honey, more so than it is yours!" he said, a note of anger in his voice.

"And were you a killer when you were human, Aaron?"

"Ahh, another interesting question! Are we killers when we feed on cattle? No, we are simply higher animals, a greater intelligence, cattle are there to serve our needs. Rumor has it that you've always been especially fond of them. My dear, I have always been stronger, more intelligent. I've always loved a good game. I am the highest on the scale of creation; those I've killed have been my cattle, at all times. Human beings are so stupid, you must agree. They just don't believe. They see themselves as higher creatures, too intelligent to realize that there might be more beyond what the eye can see! Even when tales are told again and again, when the truth all but slaps them in the face, they are just so blind. Poor Sean, I'm out to get him, you know. Another Canady. And he'll be easy prey, because he doesn't believe. Just like always. They're too damned bright to believe—until the moment death closes their eyes for good."

Maggie twisted the phone wire tightly in her hands. "Leave the Canadys be, Aaron. I'll come to you. Where? When?"

"Oh, Maggie! No way. I'll come to you, when you least suspect it. Maybe we'll talk again. Maybe I'll give you a few chances."

"Aaron, if you hurt Sean, I'll kill you. I mean it."

"Maggie, my love, I've gotten stronger. A lot stronger. Maybe I won't let you kill me. There is that big chance that you *can't* kill me. Maybe I'll just see to it that you do exist . . . forever and forever, just to entertain me!"

"Aaron, whatever—"

"Good-bye, Maggie, my love."

"Aaron—"

"Remember back, Maggie? Five little whores . . . that's the way they counted it, anyway. If they'd only known. Oh, well, over the centuries, not even I could keep count. But what happened after the first two, Maggie?"

"Everywhere you've gone there has been deception, trickery, and death, Aaron."

"Nature of the beast, and I will teach you that, in time. You've denied yourself too long, Maggie. I know you feel the hunger. One day . . . but I get ahead of myself. What happens after the first two, Maggie?"

"First two? You're already responsible for at least five deaths."

"I had nothing to do with Rutger Leon. But that doesn't matter. The pimp didn't matter; the others didn't matter. Two little whores, Maggie. It should have been three. That Callie bitch. But she's gone and I haven't the interest in tracking her down. Maybe later. Maybe we'll find her together."

She told him what he could do with himself. He laughed.

"A threesome, Maggie. But I'm getting ahead of myself. Damn you, what comes next?"

"Aaron—"

"A double hitter, Maggie. Two little whores in the same night. Remember?"

"The cops are combing the city for you, Aaron. And you're not indestructible—"

"Cops die, too. I definitely plan to kill another Canady. Another Sean Canady. We don't want that bastard riding along into immortality with us, do we now? Double hitter, Maggie. Two little whores. Watch me. Watch me, watch me . . ."

"Aaron—"

The phone line went dead.

Pierre and Sean stood back, staring at the gurneys that held the corpses—Jane Doe and Bessie Girou, their sad lives cut short. Anthony Beale. He'd dealt in human flesh. Did that mean he'd deserved to die such a death? Then there were Rutger and Ray.

"Well?" Pierre asked.

"I'm looking for more puncture marks."

Pierre hesitated. Sean felt the man watching him.

"Puncture marks?"

"Like we found before, Pierre, on Beale," Sean said.

Pierre nodded. "All right," he agreed reluctantly. "But, Sean, I don't get—"

"I believe our madman might think himself a vampire, all right?"

"Yeah, sure, all right," Pierre said.

"Okay, we know that Beale has 'em—I'll take a look at Rutger, you get Ray. Then—"

"I'll take Bessie, and you can look at our Jane Doe." Sean stared at him. "Jane Doe was never in water. Bessie was. I probably know what I'm doing a little better, huh?"

Sean nodded. He stepped forward. The morgue seemed so damned quiet. He'd meant to get over first thing, right after he'd talked with Jack, but Chief Daniels had wanted a report, then he'd listened to a missing persons report on a promiscuous teen who had turned up several hours later. Now, it was dusk. There was a night crew at the morgue, but it was skeletal. Most of the staff had gone home. Not too many people to witness his hunt for puncture marks.

Four corpses, heads not attached, yet there, just a distance away. Death. Sean saw it frequently enough. As people were so fond of saying with a simple shrug, it was New Orleans. Blending pot. A place with magic, and a place with violence brought on by the blending through the centuries. Clashes of culture, of religion . . . of the preternatural?

He concentrated on the corpses. What had been human flesh. His heart surged with pity. What was so cold had once meant life. But there, yes . . . above the cut . . .

Puncture holes. Two of them.

He suddenly felt as if he were on a stage set. As if he stepped back, and the room grew bigger. Yes, this was it, the moment . . . from the corner of his eye he thought he saw mist filtering into the room from the doors, closed since he and Pierre had come to view the five corpses set up for their examination. He needed sleep. Mist rising, the way mist rose from the Mississippi when the temperature cooled and the day drifted to night . . .

Not mist. Someone was with them. He spun around. Gave himself a shake. One of Pierre's assistants had joined them; a man stood next to and slightly behind Pierre. The fellow was young—a student?—and wearing a lab coat over ebony jeans. Sean hadn't heard the doors open. Pierre hadn't even noticed the man yet. "We didn't ask for help," Sean said.

Pierre looked up, studied the newcomer, frowned. "Yes, I'm sorry, what is this interruption? We didn't call for any assistance. Who are you, young man, and who—"

Who or *what?*

Sean recognized him at that moment. The black dye was gone from his hair. He was tall, light, with sharp, striking features and a slow smile that was purely vicious.

"Shut up, old man!" he told Pierre, and with a single back-handed blow, he sent Pierre flying across the room, crashing into a wall of morgue drawers. Two flew open with the impact. A slender, fair-skinned hand fell from a sheeted corpse, and rested lightly upon Pierre's head as he slumped to the floor, unconscious.

"If you've killed him—"

"He isn't dead. I don't like dead meat. Cold blood is like a good wine gone sour. But that's for later. Look at you, Lieutenant Canady! This is just like déjà vu," the man said. He wasn't even breathing hard from the blow he had dealt Pierre. He crossed his arms over his chest, shaking his head as he studied Sean. "Sean Canady. Here we are together at last in an intimate moment. Aaron Carter, sir, at your service, just in case you weren't aware that I was back. I've been called various things throughout the years, of course. Jack the Ripper, the Axeman, the Grim Reaper. La Morte. That was in Paris. Great city, Paris. The French are so emotional. Such sweet, hot blood they provide. That's one of the reasons I always loved New Orleans! Why, we are just full of the hot-blooded here, don't you agree? Sweet little things like Bessie. Satan's spawns, like old Ray over there. Those torn between the darkness and the light, like our irresistible dear Maggie. But I intend to let her see the light—or the dark, as it may be. Ah! Then we have the great would-be heroes—like you, Canady. Hell, I killed you once, my friend. You should have stayed dead.''

Sean studied Carter as he spoke. Was he a centuries-old vampire? Or was he simply an incredibly strong man, made more so by some drugs either craved or taken to combat his form of insanity.

One way or the other, he was a killer.

''Welcome to the morgue,'' Sean said. ''You should take care. You might just find that you stay here longer than you anticipated.''

Carter laughed. ''Nice touch of bravado. Well, you boys were always full of yourselves. The South shall rise again! And all that rot! No, I don't think so. I like the dramatic. I wanted Maggie to see you die again, to realize what you are, and what she is . . . but then, when I followed you to the morgue, I simply couldn't resist the temptation of slicing you up right on the autopsy table!''

Could this man really be an immortal, blood-sucking aberration? Sean was about to find out. He slipped his hand beneath his lab coat, drawing his .38 special.

He saw Carter move—and yet he didn't. He was fast, but before he could pull the trigger, Carter was on top of him, and they were struggling for the gun. Carter's strength was uncanny. Sean could imagine his fingers breaking one by one. Before the first bone could crack, he pulled the trigger, not at all certain where he was aiming.

He hit Carter; for a moment, the man paused. Sean figured he had struck him somewhere in the gut. Maybe it was all a hoax; maybe Carter would fall, screaming, his insides pouring from him.

But then, Carter started to laugh. He jerked the gun from Sean's hands, sent it flying. His hands were around Sean's throat, squeezing. Sean found himself lifted from the floor. Desperately, he grabbed at Carter's hands, trying to wrench them from his neck.

His oxygen was nearly gone. Carter was smiling. He smacked

his lips. In his dazed view, Sean expected to see yellow, fetid teeth, reeking of death . . .

Carter's teeth were white, the fangs now approaching Sean's throat were shining and perfectly snow-colored. He could have been an advertisement for the wisdom of good dentistry.

And yet the man's breath, now circling around what little consciousness Sean had left, had a scent of . . . decay. Distant decay. Not so terrible; oddly enough, almost inviting.

He was dying, Sean realized.

With his last ounce of strength, he banked on a feeble effort, drawing all his effort into his legs. He struck out, managing to land a staggering blow with exacting precision on Carter's groin.

Carter howled, dropped Sean, doubled over. When he started to rise, his eyes now glittering like those of a snake, his pupils appearing horizontal, he was in a rage. ''Lieutenant, I'm going to remove your sex organs with a bone saw and stuff them down your throat while you die in a pool of your own blood!''

And it might have happened.

Except that Sean caught Carter's chin with a sturdy right just as he threatened him, sending him staggering back several feet. Sean used those few moments to grab a broom from the corner, slam it against the steel drawers, and turn it into a pike with a jagged end. Not exactly a well-honed weapon, but the raw splintering of the wood might be just as effective.

Carter made a lunge toward him; Sean raised his weapon, aimed at the vampire's heart.

Carter paused, staring at Sean. And at that moment, the double doors to the room burst open and Jack Delaney came through. ''Hold it!'' he called sharply to Carter.

Carter swung around. He looked from Sean to Jack. He smiled, and started toward Jack. ''Want to fire a few warning shots, Doc?''

''Stop now, or I'll shoot to kill!'' Jack warned.

Laughing, Carter took another step forward.

Jack started to fire.

Carter paused, backing away. He stared at Sean again, then at Jack. Filled with bullets, he bowed politely.

"We'll meet again, gentlemen!"

He started out toward Jack again. Jack reached for another clip.

Carter slammed past him.

Sean chased after him as he started down the hall. Carter rounded a corner. Sean did the same.

Carter was gone. A faint trace of mist remained.

"I didn't see that," Jack said.

Sean didn't reply.

"Maybe I did just see that. Shit, what did I just see?" Jack asked. "Why do I hate that man so much?"

"He's a vicious, cold-blooded murderer," Sean said.

"Yes, but . . ." Jack's voice trailed.

"Good timing, by the way, partner," Sean murmured, still staring down the hall as if Aaron Carter might suddenly reemerge. "What brought you?"

"They said you were at the morgue. And I think I have some interesting information for you."

"Yeah?"

"I found your historical Aaron Carter."

Maggie had tried calling Sean all day.

Gyn at his office had politely fielded her every call, whether she had ranted or cajoled. Sean was out; he was busy. He'd see her that evening.

She was terrified, afraid he might not live to see the evening. If only he believed her, he might stand a chance, but he didn't believe her. He wouldn't protect himself, he wouldn't be prepared. He'd think himself a crack shot, and that he could stop the killer with a bullet.

She sat in her office, her head bowed over her desk, when she felt a stirring in the air. Before she could lift her head, she felt fingers moving lightly through her hair. "Bad day? I've warned you against mortals. Of course, you can save your beloved Canady. You know that."

She looked up at Lucian. He wasn't mocking her. In his typical black silk shirt and chino pants, he appeared the handsomely dressed man about town, arrogant, assured, earnestly sympathetic.

"Aaron is a monster!" she told Lucian. "Why can't we kill him?"

"We're all monsters," Lucian told her. "Remember? How do we condemn him for being a predator, when it is what we are?"

"No, we're not all predators like he is—"

"Ah, Maggie, Maggie, my sweet Magdalena! Don't you remember what it was like? Before the advent of blood banks? Don't you remember the pain, the agony of the hunger when it went deep? I know that you remember the kill, as much as you wish you did not."

"Yes, but men go to war, people do kill, there is anger, there is passion . . . but there isn't such ruthless cruelty in men or beasts that exists in Aaron! Lucian, please . . ."

He sat on the corner of her desk, smoothed her hair back again, smiled sadly. "What is it about you? I should snap my fingers and say be damned with it all! You're not even my lover anymore, and yet . . . but I'm sorry. You know that I can't kill him. Nor can you. And yet . . ."

"And yet what?" Maggie asked, inhaling sharply.

"Part of our code has to do with the lines between life and death, Maggie. Vampires are found and killed by men, and that is why we are not to destroy our own kind."

"Meaning?"

"Meaning, that, of course, though *we* may not kill him, Aaron can be destroyed. Some things are myth, and some are not. All creatures have their weaknesses. We all know too well, we can be killed. A stake through the heart will do it. Cremation. Decapitation. Aaron was not my creation; I never knew who made him, because I believe his benefactor was killed soon after Aaron was made. I had not come to the States often when I followed you here, and I knew little about him. But think, Maggie, you come back here, because here is home. When you travel to Europe, you must bring native soil. I believe that Aaron's roots are here as well. He is comfortable here, he walks freely here—you met him here. And though it's a fallacy that we burn to ash with simple daylight, he must rest somewhere. We must all rest somewhere. If he can be found while sleeping . . .''

She felt as if her heart quickened. That was it. Do some research on Aaron Carter. She closed her eyes. Yes. He had claimed that he was ''distant kin'' to the Wynns. They had accepted him. He had been welcomed as a suitor for Lilly Wynn, all those years ago. Then Lilly Wynn had died . . . and been reborn. She hadn't heard anything about Lilly Wynn since that long-ago time. Since Colonel Elijah Wynn had gone mad and begun to kill his own soldiers, looking for the lover who had cost him his daughter . . .

''Lucian—''

''You mustn't kill him. Remember that.''

She shook her head. ''Lucian, he is a thing of evil beyond any of us. I will rid the world of Aaron, one way or another. And if you must condemn me for the act, Lucian, then so be it!''

''Maggie, Maggie, Maggie . . . you must not be a martyr to the world!''

She had so seldom seen Lucian tender. Passionate, yes. Arrogant, demanding. Not tender. He very gently held her, kissed her forehead, released her. ''This thing I do for you!'' he said softly.

And then he was gone.

CHAPTER 16

Pierre went from the morgue to the hospital, protesting all the while. He was fine, he was embarrassed that he'd been knocked out so easily. He ruefully joked that most people went from the hospital to the morgue, and not the other way around.

"How did that bastard get into my morgue?" he wanted to know. Sean opened his mouth to explain. Closed his mouth, having given up. There was no rational explanation.

When Pierre was gone, he returned to headquarters, telling Jack, who remained behind with some of the uniformed officers to retrace the events, to meet at the office as soon as he could.

Sean walked into his office and slammed the door, totally unnerved and glad to see that Gyn had left coffee on for him, with a note not to stay in his office too late. He sipped his coffee, running his free hand through his hair.

He turned around . . . and saw that Lucian DeVeau was sitting in one of the chairs before his desk.

"Good evening," DeVeau said.

Sean sank into his swivel chair behind the desk. "You startled me."

Lucian shrugged. He was a good-looking man with patrician

features, strange, hypnotic, yellow eyes, and a casual elegance to his movements. "Sorry."

"Well, I'm glad to see you. We've been looking for you, you know."

Lucian smiled and leaned forward, folding his hands on Sean's desk.

"Has she told you yet?"

"Told me what?"

"What she is."

"I don't know what you're talking about."

"You're lying," Lucian said. "But that's all right. We seldom let the truth be known—self-preservation, of course. And people don't handle the information at all well."

"Well, can you beat that?" Sean murmured sarcastically.

"If you don't want my help—" Lucian began.

"On the contrary. I'm anxious to hear anything you have to say."

Lucian's smile broadened. "I'm sure there's a whole lot you want to know. Well, I'm not going to tell you too much about the past. It doesn't matter."

"Because it's over?"

Lucian nodded. "Yeah, it's over. And this is all so charming. I think you really love her. And I think she loves you."

"Are you still in love with her?"

Lucian laughed softly. "Am I in love with her? As much as I'm capable of being, I suppose, but that doesn't matter. I'm here as her friend."

"You're not sleeping with each other?"

"We haven't slept together in years."

"How many years?"

"Decades, old boy, decades."

It all had to be a macabre joke.

"I'm sorry. I don't believe any of this."

"Don't you? I think you do, but I can help you on the road to belief as well. You're not in great shape at the moment, Lieutenant. Another encounter with Aaron? What can I say to convince you—beyond what you already know but don't want to see? Ah, yes! I'm willing to bet that the police have recently discovered body parts. Belonging to one Rutger Leon.''

Sean started. The news hadn't hit the papers yet. The front pages had been filled with the aborted attack on Mamie.

''Fine—what about Rutger Leon's body parts?''

''Well, I'm the one who made them into parts.''

''You?''

''I was very hungry. I'm sure that Maggie informed you there are many of us trying to form a higher society. We indulge in small mammals and the Red Cross most frequently. Still, when I hit one of those terrible urges myself—in keeping with our higher society—I try to abate my cravings with those most deserving. Rutger came to the hospital to torture the girl. I decided not to let him.''

Sean concluded he was definitely losing his mind. ''Why are you here?'' he asked.

''So that you can save Maggie's life.''

Sean frowned. ''What do you mean?''

''She's going to try to kill Aaron, of course. She's going to try to trap him, and kill him. No matter what I say to her. She can't do that. For one, he's very powerful, and he could kill her. She's bested him before, so she doesn't realize just how powerful he's become. And if she managed to do away with him, I'd be required to order an execution. It's a law more ancient than any of us. We are not to kill our own kind. No matter what I think of Aaron, or how I feel about Maggie, if she destroyed him and I didn't order her death, there would be rebellion and chaos among our ranks.''

''Then why are you telling me this?'' Sean demanded harshly.

''Obviously, you, as a mortal, have to kill him.''

''How?''

Lucian smiled. ''Good response. Not 'don't be ridiculous, I'm an officer of the law, I can't kill him.' Get to him before Maggie. And carry a sword.''

''Get serious. I can't walk around with a sword—''

''Then get a really big knife. When you get your chance, you've got to cut off his head.''

"I can't even find him! How the hell am I going to get his head off?"

"Ah . . . now I have your attention. If you want this to end, you have to figure out how to kill Aaron. As to how you're going to manage to do it . . . well, hell, I don't know. I believe he comes from this area—"

"Believe? You don't know?"

"No, I don't know everything. As I said, Aaron has gotten strong. He'd like to be me. But he wants revenge against Maggie more than anything, so he'll go after her first. They met here. And at some time, he must sleep. All vampires must rest. He won't necessarily sleep by day—like Maggie and me, he has learned to abide the daylight. Still, in the day, we haven't the strength we have at night. Find him by day, find him when he's at rest. Don't give him any warning shots, officer. Find him, kill him. Stake him through the heart, take his head."

"If I were to suggest such actions at a task force meeting—"

"No task force is going to help you, Canady. Look to the past. If you dare, be sane. Refuse to believe all this. But if you love Maggie, you'd better kill Aaron."

The private line to Sean's office started blinking. Sean kept staring at Lucian.

"Your phone," Lucian said politely.

"Right. Excuse me," Sean said, swiveling around as he picked up the receiver.

Jack was on the line.

"I'm on my way in right now. You know what, Sean? No one saw this character enter the morgue. No one at all. It was like he disappeared into mist, and arrived from mist. What do you think?"

"I think it's all nuts. Get here as fast as you can."

He set the receiver down and turned back to finish his conversation with Lucian.

But Lucian was gone.

Into thin air.

* * *

Fifteen minutes later, Jack came into his office carrying his notebook.

"You all right?" Sean asked him carefully.

"Oh, yeah. A guy disappears in front of me, bullets don't kill him, but I'm just fine. How about you?"

Sean lifted his hands, giving nothing away with his expression. "I'm interested in what you found out about Aaron Carter."

"Well, there's one hell of a history on a fellow with that name," Jack said. He showed Sean printouts he took from his notebook. "The Carters owned a plantation just upriver from your place. The first generation was fine. The original Carter, Grayson, was a popular man with all ethnic groups; he hired free Negroes, Spaniards, French, English, pirates—he was a magnanimous man who gave many a head start in life. He died in 1747; the place went to his son, Aaron. Aaron was sixteen when he inherited the holdings. He inherited over his older brother, Steven, because Steven was retarded, or slow, or mentally deficient. Still, when Aaron was away on business, Steven remained. Screams were heard in the night, travelers disappeared, and so on. Then, the young and reputably beautiful daughter of a neighbor's black servant disappeared and a group of townfolk broke into the Carter place and guess what they found?"

Sean lifted his hands. "I don't know—Aaron Carter sleeping in a crypt?"

Jack shook his head. "No, Aaron Carter was human enough then. They didn't find him at all. They found slaves and servants hideously killed, their body parts strewn about the basement. In a room kept perpetually dark, the people found a group of terrified young women, a harem of them—black, Asian, white, Anglo, French, Hispanic. He kidnapped them, and entertained himself with them until he tired of them. There were rooms in a wing of the house, supposedly Steven's domain, where dozens of murders had been committed."

"What happened?"

"Well, naturally, Steven was blamed. He was shot dozens of times by the people, then hung by his heels and set afire.

Most of the place burned. Aaron Carter, supposedly returning from abroad, grieved for the people and his brother. He donated money to the families, and had a large chapel built in the ruins of the property. He said he was going away, to Europe, far away from the horror for which he felt so responsible.''

"End of the story?"

"No. There are two endings—the rational story has it that he went to Europe, returned with a wife, a toddling son, and an infant daughter, and was then murdered by the mother of the last girl to disappear into his family homestead. Some say, however, that the girl's mother was heavily into the occult. Not just voodoo, but all kinds of black magic. They said she could summon the devil, and could make people disappear. The story has it that she believed Aaron himself seduced her daughter, and, in turn, she had a very beautiful woman seduce Aaron— and take his life. Whatever the story, he disappeared, but, supposedly, his great-grandson arrived from an island planta- tion during the Civil War and nearly married into the Wynn family—they were distant cousins, since Mrs. Wynn was a descendant of the baby girl Aaron Carter had brought back to the States. She had married a man named Dixon, and rebuilt the house. The Dixons, however, died out at the turn of the century.''

Sean stared at him, feeling a strange sensation rise within him. There was a stretch of land north of Oakville that had been vacant ever since he could remember. The taxes had been paid on the property; the grounds were overgrown, but occasionally tended. Because of the old plantation ruins on the property, it had been fenced off about twenty years ago to keep out tourists—the curious, and the cultists who liked to conduct seances and have services during the full moon.

Sean was quiet.

"What are you thinking?" Jack asked him.

Sean lifted his hands. "I'm thinking that we'd look really ridiculous waiting for daylight, gathering together a duffle bag of stakes and holy water, and hunting through the old Carter/ Dixon property.''

Jack shook his head.

"And what are you thinking?" Sean asked him.

Jack looked at him steadily. "I'm thinking I saw a man today who seemed evil in a way I could touch—and then he disappeared. And I'm envisioning all those old movies. Professor Van Helsing and his helpers, moving quietly through the tombstones and crypts . . . opening Lucy's grave, seeing her beautiful face, and . . ."

"And?"

"Which movie was it when everyone got spattered in a sea of blood once the stake was stuck into the vampire?"

"I don't remember," Sean said.

Jack shrugged. "Then, in the darkness and the mist, the vampire rises—they always wait until it's too late, and somehow the vampire wakes up before they can stake him. And he kills everyone and flies away into the spooky mist of the coming night."

"Jack, these vampires don't have to sleep by day."

Jack just stared at him. *"These* vampires?"

He nodded awkwardly. "If there are vampires. Maybe they're real, maybe they're madman. Anyway, our killer is— one way or another—a psycho named Aaron Carter. Or a psycho using the name of Aaron Carter. He thinks he was Jack the Ripper and a dozen other mass murderers throughout time. I don't know if we can catch him on his property, but if so, at the very least maybe he'll believe that we can best him with the right weapons."

Jack kept staring at him. Sean drew his fingers through his hair. "Look, I know this sounds nuts. I know I can't go in front of a task force meeting and say any of this. But I don't know where else to go or what to do. Whatever he is, he is a monster, human or other, who will strike again. We've got to stop him. I don't have many leads. Investigating the old property seems to make sense to me. Well . . ."

"I just have one thing to say," Jack told him.

Sean paused defensively. "What?"

"Daytime. We're going by daytime. Crack of dawn daytime. We're not going to hunt, find the guy, and have it turn into night right when we find him, before we can impale him. And we're going about this intelligently. We can't have vampires in the cemeteries—we know bodies bake. Live bodies, dead bodies—they'd bake. If the Carters and Dixons were buried in vaults, they must be baked as well—''

''You said that Aaron Carter ordered a chapel or a crypt to be built.''

''What would the temperature be in a chapel?'' Jack asked.

Sean shook his head. ''I don't know.''

Jack nodded. ''All right. We go to the property at the first sign of daylight. We search the ruins, and the chapel. And we are gone by nightfall. I don't believe any of this, of course. I can't believe I'm saying this. I'm going to go home and make stakes out of all my old baseball bats—''

''Brooms will work just fine.''

Jack hesitated. ''Ash. Ash is a good wood. Find anything made out of it. And remember, the chapel must be in ruins by now as well . . .'' Jack began, then fell silent. He was staring out the door to Sean's office.

Sean swung around. Maggie had come. He jumped to his feet, looking at her.

She looked pale; she smiled wanly. ''The chapel isn't in ruins.''

''How do you know?'' he asked her sharply.

''I tried to trace Aaron Carter myself,'' she said softly. She glanced at Jack with an apologetic shrug. ''Then I went to the courthouse and spent some time at the office of public records. A check arrives from an A.D. Carter, Rue Royale, Paris, twice a year for the upkeep of the building of the old chapel on the Carter/Dixon grounds.'' She stared at Sean. ''I'll be going with you.''

''No!'' Jack and Sean said simultaneously.

''Jack, you don't understand, I can help you—''

''Maggie, you know what? We can talk about this tomorrow—'' Sean began.

''Can we? What happened tonight? Your officers are good at public relations, and they're careful what they say to the press, but they did use the word 'disappeared.' What happened at the morgue? The broadcasts are saying that you and Pierre were attacked by a man dressed as a medical assistant who then *disappeared?* You and Jack both fired shots—but he disappeared. That's what they're saying on the news, Sean.''

''The guy got away, Maggie.''

''The guy was Aaron!'' she said angrily. ''The murderer.'' She stared sharply at Jack. ''And you know that he just disappeared into thin air!''

Jack shrugged. ''It wasn't thin air,'' he said defensively. But Maggie kept staring at him. He swallowed. Moistened his lips. ''Maggie, come on. People don't just disappear.''

''He disappeared, Jack,'' she repeated.

''How can you know, Maggie? You weren't there. I think, he, uh, well—'' He broke off, looking into her eyes. His voice faltered. ''It wasn't thin air—it was kind of a mist he disappeared into. But, Maggie—''

''He is a vampire, Jack. You can doubt it, you can question your sanity, but it's true.''

''And you know him?''

''Yes.''

''So the blood drops from the pimp on Bourbon Street that led to your door—''

''Were done by Aaron on purpose. To implicate me.''

''Why?'' Jack asked.

''I'm a vampire, too,'' Maggie said.

Sean groaned.

Jack smiled. His smile was weak. ''Maggie, you're wearing a big, beautiful, gold cross, and you're—''

''I go to church.

''I haven't accepted the fact that I'm supposed to be damned. I go, but Aaron doesn't. You really can hurt him by many traditional means. He's going to be hard to kill, but sometimes, every little edge helps. He won't evaporate or sizzle or melt like a wicked witch from Holy water, but it may slow him down. Garlic will honestly help—''

''Garlic. Maybe we should have a big Italian dinner and refrain from brushing our teeth,'' Jack murmured.

''Yes, we *should* have a big Italian dinner. We'll go to my house. I'll cook.''

"With garlic?" Jack asked, half teasing her, half afraid that his question was entirely rational.

"I won't eat it, I'll just cook it. We'll all stay at my house tonight. And I'll be with you in the morning."

"No, Maggie," Sean grated.

Maggie shook her head sternly. "Yes! And we'll stay together as of now. Aaron wants to kill you, Sean. And he'll kill you, Jack, too, with every pleasure in the world."

"I shot him," Jack said. "Sean shot him. He's got to be in pretty bad shape."

"He's definitely hurt," Sean said, daring her to deny that much.

Her eyes fell. "If he ran, then he was hurt. But if he disappeared on you, he wasn't that hurt. He'll be back."

"But we should have some time," Sean insisted.

"Maybe," Maggie said.

Sean came to her, set his hands on her shoulders, kissed her forehead. "Okay, Maggie, we'll both come to dinner. We'll load down with garlic. But I need to tie up a few things, and Jack needs to go shopping. Give me an hour or so."

She hesitated. "You're really coming?" she asked.

"I swear it."

She stared into his eyes, then nodded after a moment, turned and left them.

Jack looked at Sean. "Maggie's a *vampire?*"

Sean shrugged.

"Maggie?" Jack repeated.

"So she says."

"All right. So—what are we really doing?"

"You're going out for ammunition. Brooms, holy water, blessed crosses. Matches, lots of matches. Or lighters. Or both."

"We would be put away for this, you know."

"There's not going to be any task force meeting about it, Jack."

"No, I guess not. And while I'm out buying brooms to pare into stakes, what will you be doing?"

"I'm going to the drugstore."

Jack arched a brow.

"Sleeping pills. Maggie can't come with us."

"Sean, she can't really—"

"I don't know what's real. But she can't be with us."

Jack turned, shoulders squared, and left the office.

Sean sat back when they were gone. He unlocked his bottom drawer, drew out ammunition. Bullets at least slowed the sucker down. He swung around on his chair and happened to notice the wall. One of his Civil War ancestor's swords hung there. He hesitated, then stood on the chair to lift it down. "Revenge?" he murmured quietly, carefully handling the sword. It was a traceable antique—priceless.

It felt far too familiar in his hands.

He gave himself a shake, dug into a cabinet for a duffel bag, packed his sword and extra rounds of ammunition, and left the office.

He walked down Royale Street. Jewelry dealers, tourist shops, antique stores were just beginning to close for the evening. It was nearly ten o'clock, he realized. A mule-drawn carriage clip-clopped by. Across the street was the pharmacy, an old building, the second floor graced with a beautiful wrought-iron railing. His city. He loved it.

There wasn't room in it for both him and Aaron Carter.

He shifted the duffel on his shoulder and entered the drugstore. Old Trent Bickery, more ash-colored than black, was behind the counter. Trent owed him. Sean had kept his grandson out of prison on what could have been a case of grand theft auto. The boy, given the break, had cleaned up his act and gone on to Duke. Not that what Sean was asking was such a terrible thing, but dispensing narcotics without a prescription was still illegal. And Trent was a man of the law. A Christian to the core, as moral as they came.

"Lieutenant Canady!" Trent greeted him. "I was just about to close up. You caught me just in time."

"I need some help, Trent."

The gnarled old man arched a brow. "You asking me for some kind of uppers or downers, Lieutenant? Ain't like you. Don't be asking me to do anything illegal, now—"

"Trent, you know me. I'm clean. And you know that the

docs down at the medical examiner's office could give me a prescription for anything I wanted. I don't have time, that's all. I need a sleeping pill. Now. Not some over the counter may-or-may-not-work sleeping pill. Someone could get killed. I have to keep her out of danger.''

Trent stared at him a long moment. Shrugged. Turned around and came back to him. ''No taste, no smell. Break one capsule into a drink and she should be out in twenty minutes. Break two . . . and she'll sleep the clock around.''

''Thanks, Trent. Give my regards to your wife, the kids, and *their* kids, huh?''

''Yessir, Lieutenant. You make sure to let me know if everything works out all right, you hear?''

''Sure, Trent. Sure.''

He drove out to the Montgomery Plantation, thinking that the night seemed blacker than usual. There were no stars. The full moon had begun to wane. Storm clouds covered what light it might have offered. The weatherman on the radio advised that there would be wind, rain, and squalls tomorrow from a formation in the Gulf.

When he reached Maggie's, she opened the door for him herself. She kissed him quickly, her eyes surveying his intently.

''You do believe?'' she whispered.

He cupped her chin in his hands. ''I'm going after a vampire by first light,'' he told her.

She nodded, assured, and turned toward the kitchen. ''One hell of a late dinner, isn't it?'' she inquired.

He followed her. Water boiled on the stove, sauce simmered, the unmistakable smell of garlic filled the kitchen. Something in a strange clear hue bubbled on a burner. Sean smelled it, stepped back, wrinkling his nose. ''Whoa, Maggie, are we supposed to eat that?''

She managed to flash him a smile. ''No, that's my personal skin lotion. You and Jack have to rub it all over you tomorrow, especially the neck and breast area . . . wrists . . . anywhere Aaron could sink his teeth into you easily.''

''Oh,'' he murmured.

"Stir the sauce?" she asked, reaching into the refrigerator for salad components.

"Sure. Maggie, where's Peggy?"

"I sent her to see a sister in Atlanta."

"Why?"

She hesitated. As she did, the doorbell rang. "Must be Jack," she told him.

"All right." He went and answered the door. Jack had arrived with two large khaki police-issue duffel bags.

"Got everything?" Sean asked.

"Everything. I had to promise to show up for Mass every Sunday for the next year, since I couldn't quite manage to explain why I needed all the Holy water."

"That will be good for your soul. Come on in the kitchen; dinner's almost ready."

Jack followed him into the kitchen. "Hi, Maggie."

"Hey, Jack."

"Maggie was just about to tell me why she sent Peggy to her sister's house."

She hesitated again, then shrugged. "Well, I hope you really hurt Aaron tonight because he called and threatened me. He wants to kill you and torture me for the next century." She was breaking pasta into the pot as if they were discussing a rational issue. "But he's in the middle of copycat killings in imitation of what he sees as his greatest crimes. Discounting Anthony Beale—"

"He's killed two whores," Jack said.

"So, going by the accepted Ripper numbers—" Sean said.

"Double-header next," Jack finished.

Sean felt a tic in his cheek as his muscles constricted. His hands were clenched into fists. "Jesus, we should be after this sicko tonight."

"Not at night!" Jack said. "He's strongest at night."

Sean stared at Jack. Was his partner *believing* all this?

"We go tomorrow to see if we can't find him licking his wounds," Maggie said firmly. She turned, her hands on her hips, staring at them. "You're sure, though, really sure, that you pumped a major load of bullets into him?"

"Sure," they said in unison, then glanced at one another.

"Yes, we're sure," Sean reiterated.

Maggie nodded. "Well, then, I'm not a bad cook at all, really. Sit down, dinner's ready as soon as I drain the pasta."

Moments later, linguini with a rich red sauce was served along with garlic bread.

Maggie, Sean noted, was having salad. Hers was plain, their salads were filled with fresh chopped garlic.

Maggie served red wine as well. As she opened the bottle, Jack whispered to Sean, "Think there's garlic in the wine as well?"

"No, I think it's a bottle of red wine."

"No blood, right?" Jack was surely joking, but he sounded a little worried.

"No blood."

Maggie poured the wine and went to the refrigerator for some grated cheese.

Sean started to empty the sleeping pills into her glass, then hesitated. He'd wait. He couldn't admit it, but he was afraid. Not so much of dying. He was a cop; he'd gotten used to that kind of fear.

He was just afraid of being without her again.

Jack cleared his throat. "Do we say grace?"

"Hell, yes!" Sean muttered. "God, bless this food, and allow us to kill a monster. Amen. Jack, eat."

After a few moments of strained silence, Maggie asked them to tell her exactly what had happened at the morgue. They both tried to explain. Jack asked at the end, "Did he just disappear into mist, Maggie?"

She nodded. "He can shape-shift. It isn't easy. It's mind over matter. You've seen similar phenomena, even if you don't want to admit it—telekinesis, second-sight, all that. I imagine, somewhere down the line, they'll figure out the scientific reasons why all this can be. But shape-shifting takes a terrible amount of energy, so if he was riddled with bullets and disappeared, as you say, he must be trying to regain his strength now. And don't forget, he might well be awake and waiting, even by daylight. He's weaker by daylight. His vision is impaired, he's far more vulnerable.''

"And so are you," Jack commented.

"So am I," Maggie admitted.

They had eaten all they could eat. The food had been delicious, though heavily laden with garlic. "Maggie, may I have some more wine?" Sean asked.

"Of course."

"Join me."

She turned for the bottle. He slipped the pills into her glass.

"Jack?"

"Sure," he said, and when their glasses were filled again, he raised his. "And here's to our fearless vampire hunting!"

Maggie lifted her glass. "But we must be afraid, and careful!"

"Very careful," Sean agreed.

They drank. Then Sean stood, reaching a hand down to her. "I need some sleep."

"I'll be right up—"

"No, Maggie, you go on. I'll pick up after dinner and turn the broom handles into stakes," Jack told them. "I don't believe I'm saying this. Doing this. Hey, Sean, have we just encountered one bad man too many?"

"Maybe. I don't know."

"No, Jack, you're perfectly sane," Maggie told him.

He nodded, grimacing. "And you're a vampire. And I'm sleeping in your house. 'Night Maggie, 'night Sean."

Sean led Maggie up the stairs. Despite himself, he paused beneath the portrait, feeling again as if a strange sensation stole over him. "So, you're a vampire," he murmured softly. "And you think I'm the reincarnation of my own distant relative."

She touched his cheek. Her hazel eyes seemed gold in the light. "I know I'm a vampire. I simply think that I've loved you for far more than a lifetime."

She stumbled slightly, frowning. He swept her up into his arms.

"Must be the garlic," she murmured.

"Am I unbearable?"

"You must be unbearable."

He walked on up to her bedroom, laid her on the bed, drew the drapes. Propped on an elbow, he lay down beside her. He stroked her cheek. Her skin was so beautiful. Almost translucent. Her breath feathered his fingers. Vampire. Creature of the night. Monster. She should have been hideous. Her breath should have smelled of the rot and death and decay of the ages. She was simply beautiful.

She reached out, knuckles stroking his cheek. "Make love to me," she said softly.

"Ah, my love, the garlic . . ." he murmured.

"Just don't breathe on me!" she teased, and she reached out, curling against him, hands upon his shirt, her lips teasing his flesh. The searing moisture of her kiss against his flesh was a liquid fire. He found himself desperate to lie with her, be with her, as if this might be the last time. Forever. His hands wound into her hair; he avoided her lips, kissed her everywhere else, strewing her clothing as he did so. Her touch feathered him, erotic, sweet; kisses explored until they were both in a frenzy and he blanketed her with his body, far too quickly coming to a climactic explosion. Her fingers curled into his hair and her eyes were on his, gold, cat-like. "I love you, Sean," she said, and her eyes closed.

"I love you, too, Maggie. God, but I adore you!"

She didn't hear him. The sleeping pills had done their work.

He cradled her body against his.

Her mouth was closed; he dared to bend and kiss her, and her lips tasted sweetly of the wine they had shared. What if she were staked, killed as such a "monster" should be? Would her flesh wither, would her breasts sag into leathered brown folds, would her face shrink into the pockets of her skull? Would she turn to ash, and blow away with the wind? He'd never know. He'd die a thousand times before he let harm come to her. If it was true, or if it wasn't, he loved her.

Yet . . .

If it was true, what could they do? Live and love during his short time on earth? Would she wait for him then, to come back as another man, in another century? Yet, what if he were bitten, tainted, and became one of their number? Did they stay here, disappear in a few years, return in a quarter of a century, and play out their lives again and again?

No, he didn't believe it, couldn't believe it.

He laid his head down beside hers and drew her tightly against him. Tomorrow, he was going vampire hunting with a bag full of Holy water and stakes.

He had to believe . . .

CHAPTER 17

Jack came to him at the crack of dawn.

Sean rose, kissing Maggie on the forehead, drawing the covers over her. Then he left her, glad to see that she remained in a deep, deep sleep.

Thinking that they were either ridiculously silly or smart as whips, he and Jack covered themselves with the garlic lotion Maggie had made for them.

Together, they packed Jack's Pathfinder with the duffel bags of stakes, swords—Jack had found a cutlass for himself in the bedroom where he had slept—holy water, steak knives, matches, lighters, flashlights, and hair spray—to ignite a good blaze, should they need to do so.

Finding the property was not difficult; finding a trail that led through the overgrown foliage to the ruins of the old plantation was another matter. Once they reached the center of the property, they climbed from the Pathfinder, looking around.

In many sections, the old house was missing a roof. Vines covered it inside and out.

Even as they stared at the house, the sky darkened.

Jack looked at Sean. "Can you beat that? Daylight—and it just has to be *stormy* daylight!"

"Let's go," Jack said.

They entered the house, each with his gun at the ready,

stakes and swords slipped into their belts, duffel bags over their shoulders.

"I was wondering what weapon I'd be using first. Never imagined it would be the flashlight," Jack muttered.

Sean stepped through the door first. Ahead of him lay the remnants of an elegant curving stairway. Vines curled around it. Portraits covered the walls. Just as Maggie's painting rested on the wall of the midlevel of the stairway, so did Aaron's. It startled him, almost causing him to totter down the steps when he first flashed the ray of light upon it.

"Jesus!" Jack whispered, and Sean knew he was making the sign of the cross on his chest.

"It's him!"

"It's him. Look around downstairs. I'm going to try the bedrooms."

He heard Jack moving downstairs. He carefully moved up the stairs, avoiding the areas where they had rotted through.

His footsteps sounded louder than cannon fire. His movements created creaking sounds that seemed to echo through the ruins.

He reached the top landing. Moving slowly, not for silence but to avoid falling through the faulty flooring, he started to the left of the landing. There were three doors here, no roof above the hall or the rooms. He opened the first door. He was glad he didn't step in. The door led to a gaping black hole. The second door offered the remnants of a woman's room, bed with tattered coverings, filmy traces of drapes on the windows, rotted dressers. He closed the door. The third room offered no more.

He crossed the landing again, and found another series of doors. Odd that someone had closed the doors of a house so decayed. But here, the roof remained. The first room was pitch black. When he waved his light toward the ceiling, he nearly screamed aloud as a hundred bats suddenly came to life, flapping and squalling and diving all around him.

"Sean!" Jack called from below.

He walked back to the landing. "It's all right. Just bats."

"Just bats!" Jack muttered. "Yeah, yeah, we're looking for

a shape-shifting vampire who just might be awake by day, and it's just bats! Yeah, right!''

''Keep looking!''

Sean started back down the hall. He paused, certain he heard movement in a room. Then a sniffling sound. He gritted his teeth and moved as silently as he could.

He threw open the door.

Despite the fact that he had his gun drawn and ready, he was startled by the impetus of the attack upon him. The moment the door opened, someone was flying at him. He could have, should have fired.

For some reason, he didn't. Instinct?

It was a woman, terrified, who had come flying out at him. She was sobbing, striking him, as he braced himself, holstered his gun, and got a grip on her shoulders. Footsteps pounded on the stairway. Jack was with him; more light flooded the room.

The woman was trying to bite him, kick him, free herself.

''Hey, hey, it's all right—'' he began. Jack's flashlight illuminated her face.

''Shit!'' Sean swore. Jeanne! Jeanne Montaine, Bessie Girou's friend, the one who had taken Bessie's son to be her own. ''Jeanne, it's Sean Canady. It's the cops, Jeanne—it's all right—''

''No, no, it's not all right!'' Jeanne swore hysterically, still trying to strike. Her dark hair was in wild tangles, her pretty face was dirty and streak-stained with tears. ''You may be the cops, but it doesn't matter, don't you understand? He'll kill you. He'll kill me, he told me he'd kill me if I didn't protect him. And the boy, the boy is here, he likes really young blood. He'll kill him, then what he'll do to me, oh, God, I have to kill you—''

''No, no, Jeanne, we'll protect you—'' Sean began.

''Oh, God, you don't understand!''

''Who is she?'' Jack asked, trying to set his hands soothingly on Jeanne's shoulders.

''Bessie Girou's friend, the one keeping her little boy,'' Sean explained. ''Jeanne—'' he began again, about to swear that they would protect her. But could they really protect her? They had to.

He was a cop, he reminded himself. That was what he did. Serve—and protect.

''Jeanne, where is he?'' Sean demanded, giving her a serious shake.

Jeanne didn't answer. He heard the sniffing sound again. It was coming from the other side of the bed. Even with both powerful flashlights shining, the room was filled with eerie shadows that seemed to waver and find solid form with each movement. Jack stared at Sean; Sean nodded. Jack moved carefully to the side of the bed.

He stood there very still for a long moment. ''It's the kid,'' he said softly. He reached down. ''Come on, Son. Come on, we're here to help you.''

''His name is Isaac,'' Sean said.

''Come on, Isaac,'' Jack coaxed gently.

The little boy's head and huge, trusting eyes appeared. ''Come on,'' Jack encouraged.

Suddenly, the child sprang. Like a Doberman on alert, like a great cat suddenly uncaged, he sprang at Jack, growling, hissing, scratching, clawing.

Sean pressed Jeanne from him, striding across the room. He caught hold of the child, wrenched him from Jack. The boy turned with the wiry strength of a boa, mouth now open wide, lips tautly pulled back, teeth dripping, aiming for Sean's neck.

But then the boy went limp in his arms. He started to sob and groan. ''My tummy!'' he said pathetically, a little boy again.

''What the hell?'' Jack asked.

Jeanne had fallen to the ground. She clutched her own stomach. Her hair hung over her face. ''He said that he'd given him a good-night kiss. Just a little kiss. A touch. He said he took a little blood. He'd take it all next time. That we'd both live just so long as we served him and pleased him.''

Tainted. Wasn't that what both Lucian and Maggie had said happened when just a little blood was taken. Could the child be saved? If Aaron was killed . . .

And if not, could he really thrust a stake through the heart of a child? Cut off his head, burn him to ash?

As he pondered the question, they all started at the sound of the front door banging shut.

"Oh, my God!" Jeanne started to whimper.

"Shush!" Sean said firmly. He caught Jack's eye. Jack reached for the now softly sobbing little Isaac Girou. Sean dragged Jeanne to her feet. In silent accord, they moved into the hallway.

Far down the stairs they saw a man. In the darkness created by storm clouds and shadows, they could see nothing of his face. Sean heard his heart begin to beat far too quickly. Or was it Jeanne's heart?

He turned his flashlight downward in a sudden determined motion. The light caught on something metal and reflected so brilliantly that Sean had to shield his eyes. He moved the flashlight.

"Mother Mary and Joseph!" Jack swore.

Sean exhaled. Far down the steps stood Pierre LePont, medical examiner. Out of the hospital, ready to go. He carried a huge silver crucifix, which was what had caught the flashlight's reflection so brilliantly.

"Damn, Pierre, you're going to blind us with that thing!" Sean told him.

"Well, we are hunting vampires, right?"

"Maybe," Jack said defensively.

Pierre stared at him. "Don't you think I know a really dead man from a half-dead man when I see one?" he demanded.

Sean didn't have an argument for him. "Get up here, help me finish with these rooms. And give you some quick information. He may be awake. He won't turn to dust in the sunlight. You can hurt him with Holy water. The cross may or may not work. Have you any garlic on you?"

Pierre reached under his shirt. He was wearing a necklace of garlic cloves.

"Good, get up here."

As Pierre ascended the stairs, the ruins were illuminated by a flash of lightning.

It was immediately followed by an earth-shattering clap of thunder.

"We've got to hurry," Jack said, following along as Pierre reached the landing. Together they looked into the remaining bedrooms. Two were almost completely floorless. The last was empty except for the torn gauze curtains that fluttered in the wind of the coming storm.

"What happens if this kid gets hungry again?" Jack asked. Isaac was now clinging to him like a drowning man.

"The garlic kept him from you; we'll hope it keeps working," Sean said.

"I'll take him; let me take the boy," Jeanne said.

"Miss Montaine, you're not doing so well yourself—"

"I love him; I'll be stronger now. Honestly," Jeanne said, smoothing back her hair.

Jeanne held the boy then; Sean and Jack led while Pierre sandwiched the woman and the child between them.

On the ground landing, Sean turned on Jeanne. "Do you know where he is?"

She shook her head vehemently. "No."

"Where now?" Jack asked.

"We find a back door to the family crypt."

Once, the house had been beautiful. A plantation with a dazzling foyer, regal stairway, huge ballrooms, kitchen, dining room, library. Now empty, broken, falling away, it was a haunting memoir to the past. Ghosts surely milled here. Rotted draperies drifted everywhere; chairs awaited dancers who would never return, books lay water-stained upon love seats and day beds.

Going around the rotting stairs, they came through the dining room and kitchen and, at last, to the double doors leading to a rear porch and the rest of the grounds.

Sean threw open the doors.

The storm was coming fast. It was noon; the day should have been bright. Angry gray-black clouds covered the sky, and the day was the color of dusk. It was a perfect backdrop for the family graveyard that lay before them.

Angels stood high on pedestals, their wings clipped and

broken by time and the elements. Madonnas in prayer looked over lichen-covered tombs. Great oaks were spread throughout, casting a cooling shade over the grounds. The land had been built up. Here, farther along the Mississippi, they were on higher ground than in the city of New Orleans. And the long-dead, original owner of the property had planned his family cemetery well; he'd brought in dirt and built it up, so that an incline formed from the rear of the house. Gravesites dotted the landscape.

All the way up to the crypt.

"Let's go, shall we?" Sean said lightly.

They started through the graveyard. Pierre began saying a Hail Mary.

Jeanne joined him.

Jack stumbled and nearly fell as they walked over a broken angel, fallen to the dirt. The wind rose; they heard a strange keening, and realized it was the sound of the air rushing around the many tombs and their funerary art.

They stopped at the crypt. Once it had been protected by iron bars, but the bars had been ripped away. Double oak doors protected the inner realm.

Lightning lit the sky; again, it seemed that thunder shattered the very earth.

Sean pushed open the oak doors and played his flashlight over the interior of the tomb.

There were eight coffins there, all on open shelves, four to each side of the door.

"Shall we?" Sean murmured.

Jack set his duffel bag down and searched in it for crowbars. Pierre stepped forward, taking one. "Jack, guard the lady and child, please. I'm far more familiar with corpses."

Jack looked at Sean, who nodded. He took a crowbar himself and lit into the first coffin.

This fellow had already turned to dust.

He heard Pierre working behind him, heard Jack breathing hard, heard an awful pounding. Their hearts.

The second man retained just a bit of flesh, stretched tightly over his bones. His clothing was elegant, mid-eighteenth century.

The third man had already been decapitated. And a stake lay where the heart had been. Sean shivered, but said nothing.

"Pierre?"

"Nothing but the truly dead, so far," Pierre said.

Sean broke into the fourth coffin. He was startled, stepping back, when he found a young woman there. He'd seen her, somewhere, some time. He didn't know her, but . . .

Yes, she'd worked in Jackson Square. He'd seen her reading tarot cards when he'd talked to Marie Lescarre.

"Who—" he began.

Her eyes flew open. She stared at him with huge, soulful eyes. "Oh!" she breathed. "Oh . . ." Staring at him, she slowly smiled. He backed away, caught by the look in her eyes. "Lieutenant, thank God!" she said. She lifted her arms to him. "Help me, help me . . ."

"My God!" he muttered. Another woman Aaron had taken and made a prisoner. A future kill. A stockpile for his hunger. He had to get her out.

"Sean, no!" Pierre warned sharply.

And then he knew. Knew before she raged upward, fangs brilliantly white and visible. Yet, as her hands caught his shoulders, her mouth closed. She doubled over, screaming in a rage.

He threw her back into the coffin.

"Don't hurt me," she whispered. "I'm old, really old, I've been around forever, I don't kill—" she said forlornly, her voice tremulous.

"You were about to take a good bite out of my neck," Sean said.

"He wants you dead. I'd happily kill you!" she hissed suddenly.

Sean gritted his teeth. She looked so alive. So natural.

Like Maggie. Was this murder? Was he killing the already dead?

"I will kill you!" she charged suddenly, starting to rise again.

Jack swept by him with a stake, lunging to set it against her heart.

And push it through.

She let out an unholy scream, loud, more shattering than the crack of thunder.

They stared at her. She must have been old, as she had said. She seemed to crackle and fade to dust as they stared at her. Her flesh leathered, stretched taut over her bones, cracked. Soon, she was little more than gray skin over bone.

None of them could pull their eyes away. They just stared.

Until they heard the sound of clapping.

They spun around.

Aaron Carter had emerged from the last coffin on the other side of the crypt. He was smiling, amused. ''The great vampire hunters have killed a debutante. Bravo!''

''The tarot reader? Oh, yeah, poor girl. How many corpses can we accredit to her?'' Sean asked.

''Oh, this century, she's not been here very long. She rids the streets of the homeless and runaways. Ah, but you *have* seen her before. Years ago, she was one of the freshest, sweetest little things you might have imagined. Rich, quite a catch. Ah, well . . .''

''You're heartbroken, I can see,'' Sean said, his own heart slamming against his chest, his breathing coming fast and furious.

''She protected me; she adored me, you see. She served me well. She is another debt that you will pay. She never did understand about Maggie . . . but you understand now, don't you, Lieutenant?''

''Yes, I understand.''

''By tonight you'll be dead, and she'll be mine.''

''I don't intend to die,'' Sean told him.

''I think I'll get rid of the old geezer first,'' he said, referring to Pierre. ''Then the young man. The emotional young Jack Delaney, your Irish lackey there. I think I've seen the boy before, and I think he's seen me, and he's been a fool at every go 'round—''

"Murdering asshole!" Jack responded, staring at Carter with a violent rage.

"Watch it, Jack," Sean warned. "He wants you angry."

But Jack was watching Aaron as if he were staring into the face of pure evil. "This time, you die. We're prepared for you, you fool—"

"You're the fool!" Aaron thundered, his anger suddenly showing. "You're prepared, you're prepared! You know nothing."

Jack had done away with one of the undead; he was feeling confident—and acting from an uncontrollable anger. He raised a stake, flying heedlessly at Aaron with a cry of rage.

"No, we take him together—" Sean cried.

Jack never reached Aaron. The vampire ducked the blow, rose, and lifted one arm, sending Jack flying across the crypt. Jack cracked against stone, fell to the ground. Sean pulled his .38 and started firing, knowing that it slowed the vampire down. Aaron turned, coming at him. Sean dropped the gun, and raised a stake. Aaron grasped the weapon before Sean could drive it home. They struggled. Sean saw Pierre coming at Aaron; Aaron saw him, too. He turned enough to strike Pierre so hard that he flew against the old coffins and crashed down to the floor with wood splintering down on him.

Then Aaron turned his full attention back to Sean. The stake was a shaft between them. Sean felt ridiculously like Robin Hood fighting with Little John to cross a bridge.

But this bridge meant life or death.

Grinning, Aaron used his superior strength and slowly pressed the stake downward. He opened his mouth. His fangs dripped. Still having to struggle with the stake, he was taking his time, but he nearly reached Sean's throat. He began to laugh; the sound was deep, husky, amused.

Then the laughter faded. Aaron Carter stopped. Sean felt the strength against him suddenly wane. Aaron was weakening. It was the garlic. Sean took the advantage, thrusting backward with the stake.

Aaron staggered backward against the wall of the tomb,

shaking in fury. He started to cough, gagged, choked. Then he inhaled deeply, staring at Sean.

"By God, you'll pay, she'll pay! You don't know just how you'll pay!" he swore, shaking.

Then he turned, stumbling from the tomb. Sean pushed himself from the wall, following Aaron Carter out into the day. The clouds had come closer to the earth. The very air was gray. The rain began.

"Carter!" he cried.

But the vampire was gone.

Or so he thought.

The wind suddenly picked up. Like a massive hand, it whipped against him. "You will die, Canady bastard!" he heard. A voice? A hiss on the wind.

And that was all. He was slammed back against the stone of the tomb. His head struck. He felt the intensity of the pain for just a moment.

Gray surged around him.

The sky grew darker, darker into an ever-deepened shade of gray.

And then it was black.

The phone was ringing. Maggie heard it, as if it were a long, long way away. She was so tired. She fumbled around to find the receiver.

"Hello?"

"Maggie, my darling."

Instantly, she was awake. Aaron's voice. She sat up. Looked at the clock. It was day. Sean was gone. Panic filled her.

"Aaron—"

"Maggie, my love, yes."

"Where's Sean?"

"Lover boy?"

"Talk to me. Quit mocking me, or I'll hang up on you."

"If you do, another Canady dies."

She clutched the phone tightly, biting into her lower lip. "Do you have a Canady with you now, Aaron?"

"Umm, maybe."

"Do you have Sean?" she almost screamed.

"I have a Canady."

"Which Canady?"

Maggie felt herself shaking. She didn't know where Sean was; he had tricked her to save her. Aaron wasn't dead. He sounded strong and well, and vengeful.

"Where are you?"

"Where am I? Well, I was resting nicely at my own home until I was disturbed by your friends."

"What happened?"

"To your friends? Why, nothing, as yet. They destroyed my beautiful young creation, Lilly Wynn. But then, she was always a substitute for you."

"She was your own descendant, you fool! Where is Sean?"

"Oh, I imagine he's hurrying back to you. But that will do him little good."

"Why not?"

"Because you're coming to me. Now."

"How are you going to make me do that?"

"You'll come—when you figure out where I am. And who I have with me."

"Where are you?"

"Surely you've realized. I'm at Oakville. The Canady Plantation."

Maggie felt as if she turned to ice. "You haven't—"

"Ah, what have I done? Well, so far, not much. I stopped by Montgomery Enterprises to pick up a few of your friends. Chocolate and spice. One is Angie, the other . . . Cissy, I believe. Black is beautiful. I told you there would be a double-header. And as to Canady, for the moment, I've just knocked the old man on the head. Daniel, that's his name, right? If you're not here, alone, in half an hour, I'm going to do the girls first. My finest imitation of my Jack the Ripper days. Then I'm going to use my pinkie nail to slit a deep hole in the old man's carotid artery. I'm going to drink him dry. Then I'm going to leave a piece of him in every single room for his son to find. Naturally, as soon as I can, I'll kill Sean the cop as well. Maybe Sean's younger sister will show up as well with her little ones. Yum. She can become my last kill in the Jack the Ripper mode— she can be my Mary Kelly.''

Maggie listened in cold horror. She gave herself a shake. Damn Sean! He had given her something to make her sleep. She had to shake it off.

And she had to reach Aaron.

She swallowed hard.

"Aaron, I will kill you," Maggie told him.

"No, my love. This time, I think you will do whatever I say. Your thirty minutes have started. All right, well, I'll give you thirty-five. I'm going to be kind enough to allow for traffic."

The phone went dead in Maggie's hand.

CHAPTER 18

Mamie was desperate.

She felt safe enough, and it had actually been fun—being guarded by the police for a change rather than being hounded by them. Every eight hours, the shift changed. A different muscle-bound, handsome young officer came to look over her.

But early this morning, the call came. Tough old Libby Warren who ran a house of top-notch girls out on the highway, twenty miles due west of the city, had disappeared. Her bar man had seen her with a tall, handsome fellow with pale skin and Ray-Bans, and then she had disappeared with him. But not before she had told her bartender to call old Mamie, since Mamie had said she had just the right girl for the fellow.

Well, she shouldn't have done it. She shouldn't have listened to Maggie, telling her that she was a vampire, too, that she could fight him when no one else could. It was obvious. Libby was dead. Libby hadn't reached her, and it was a good thing, because if she had sent Maggie after the fellow, Maggie might be dead now, too.

But she had to tell Sean Canady. She tried calling the station; they wouldn't tell her where Sean was. They wouldn't tell her where his partner, Jack, was, either. She tried Sean's home in the city, and his father's fine plantation. She tried his beeper number, but he didn't respond. Finally, she decided she just had to move herself.

The boy watching over her then was maybe twenty-five. Tall as Mike Jordan, handsome as Lucifer. Copper-colored, with the most gorgeous eyes she'd ever seen. She asked him to take her down to headquarters.

"Mamie, I was told to keep you here at the restaurant. We're in a controlled environment here, there are more officers patrolling just outside—"

"Well, honey, what would you have at police headquarters if not a whole bunch more police officers?"

"I've been told to watch you here. You're to stay here unless Lieutenant Canady tells me differently—"

"That's just it! I need to reach Lieutenant Canady!"

"You just need to be patient, Mamie."

She sniffed loudly, turned her back on him, and began to plot. She tried all the numbers Sean had given her again, then she decided to call Maggie.

She was surprised when Maggie actually answered the phone. Her voice was tense, sharp, as if she expected someone else. "Mamie! Mamie, what is it?"

"Why, honey, I just had to let you know that I think Carter has killed an old madam out on the highway. He suspected something right away, I'm sure. I was trying to find Lieutenant Canady—"

"Mamie, I know where Aaron Carter is. I'm going after him now."

"But—"

"Mamie, tell Sean I loved him, please."

"But, honey—"

"Mamie, I don't know where he is. I was supposed to be with him . . . he and Jack went out to the old Carter/Dixon ruins. I think he's still alive. But Aaron Carter has some friends of mine and Sean's dad and . . . and I've got to go, Mamie. Stay safe, stay with the police."

"Wait, wait, you're going after this madman alone—"

"Not a word, Mamie! You'll get someone else killed! This is my disaster, and I've got to end it!"

"Wait, honey, wait—"

"I can't talk. I don't have time. I answered the phone because I thought it might be Aaron again. I've got to go, Mamie."

"Honey, I've got to help you—"

"Then pray for me, Mamie."

"But I can send the police—tons of them!"

"No! He'll kill someone immediately if I don't go alone."

The line went dead.

Feeling sick, Mamie stared at the phone. The old ruins, she mused. She was suddenly afraid. Well, Sean was at the ruins; the killer was not. She had to find Sean as fast as possible.

Mr. Good-Looking wasn't going to let her out of his sight.

"Officer?" she called softly.

"Yes, ma'am?"

"I've Lieutenant Canady on the phone."

He walked toward her, nodding. When he had nearly reached her, she creamed him across the temple with the receiver. Big, broad, and beautiful, he fell without a whimper. "Sorry, honey," Mamie said softly. "But give me a normal man, and I can deal with him every time!"

She slipped out of the restaurant the back way, glad of the rain and the ceaselessly gray day. The cops were trying to keep dry. Still, she carefully avoided the police on the streets. With her coat high around her face, she made off in her bartender's car.

Once out of the French Quarter and on the highway, she gunned it.

He felt . . .

The rain. Light, soft, touching his face. He was sleeping, his head was heavy . . . hurt . . .

Someone was touching him. Maggie. No, not Maggie. Not a gentle touch. Someone was slapping his cheeks.

"Honey, honey, you have got to wake up! Lieutenant Canady, it's me, Mamie."

Mamie!

The grogginess vanished. He sat up, feeling his head. He groaned aloud; the pain was still there, but his mind was sharp and he was feeling a growing sense of alarm.

They had found Aaron.

And Aaron was gone. Pierre and Jack were on the ground beside him. Jeanne was sitting with the boy, sobbing. The boy was staring at them all as if . . .

"I think the white girl there has lost it, Canady," Mamie said. "She's been clinging to Bessie's kid—and don't that boy look spooked!—and crying away. Jack is out cold, but don't fret, he's alive, and the old geezer over there is breathing, as well. But you've got to move, get some kind of help. Maggie was on her way to Ashville—"

"Ashville!"

Sean leaped to his feet, nearly knocking Mamie over. He automatically reached for her. His head was still spinning.

"Be smart now, Lieutenant—"

"Yeah, I'll be smart. Shit!" He looked around at the others, then at Mamie. "You've got to take charge here. I'll call for help on the radio—watch out for Bessie's kid. He's like a rabid dog."

"Lieutenant—!"

"He's at Ashville. And Maggie is after him. Alone."

Mamie didn't try to stop him again. Sean grabbed a duffel bag and started running around the graves to reach the cars at the front of the house.

Mamie looked at Bessie's little boy. Such a precious little thing.

He hissed at her.

"Don't you mess with me, young Isaac! I'll slap you clear to China, little man!"

The hissing stopped instantly.

Mamie felt good. Then she looked around herself. At the dark graveyard. At the tomb. At the open coffins.

"Oh, shit!" she said aloud.

And she prayed that help would come fast.

* * *

The rain had stopped.

The darkness of the day remained, a warning that the rain would come again.

The massive front doors to Ashville stood open.

Maggie jumped out of her car, running up the steps, not taking the caution to slow down until she reached the doors themselves. She'd been so afraid, she'd been tempted to will herself here, to come in mist, and yet, she knew she would need all her strength.

Lightning slashed across the sky, eerily illuminating the doors that stood open like a gaping entry to a black pit of hell. There was an ominous rumble of thunder on the air. The storm clouds billowed in shades of gray, darker gray, and black. All blue was gone from the sky.

She stepped through.

She nearly tripped over a body, and panic tightened her throat. She couldn't see, because the darkening sky outside provided no light to the interior of the house. Blindly, she stumbled down, praying that she had come upon Daniel or her friends while they were still alive, and not mutilated corpses.

The body was cold. She almost cried out, but in the pale daylight filtering through the door, she was able to see at close range that the corpse did not belong to Daniel Canady, Cissy, or Angie. She gasped out loud, feeling tears spring to her eyes as she saw Aaron's greeting: Another woman. The only blessing was that the woman was a stranger.

She had been savagely killed. She was dressed in elegant, bloodstained undergarments—stockings, garters, spiked heels. Her legs were at an awkward angle. She lay in the entryway of the house with her throat slit ear to ear, nearly beheaded. A note lay upon her stomach. "Practice, Maggie. This one's a meal, I'll have to dispose of the body later, since I needed her to greet you while she's not part of my artistry. The next killings will truly be my experiments in terror. You were scared, weren't you? Where are your pretty little friends, chocolate and vanilla? I love a black-and-white shake. They are beauties. I can scarcely wait to taste them.''

Her mouth and throat were bone dry. Where *were* the girls?

And Daniel? Did she dare cry out? Was Aaron watching for her, waiting?

She shed her shoes to walk through the grand entry hall and past the stairway. She looked into the kitchen and dining room, the parlor, and then the library.

Daniel Canady was there, slumped over his desk. The desk where he had drawn his books out when she had come here. She remembered how she had sat with Sean at a window seat. It had been so wonderful. A night with him, a normal night. Falling in love again, seeing his eyes, hearing his laughter, having his fingers brush her, touch her. But this was where it had brought them now!

She swallowed hard, thinking that she couldn't bear it if she had brought about the deaths of Daniel or her friends. How could she ever face Sean again if she had caused the murder of his father, and how could she ever live with herself if Cissy or Angie were to die, and so horribly, because of their association with her? She closed her eyes suddenly. Her father had loved her; he had refused to believe that she had been damned. Had she wanted some kind of forgiveness so badly that she had damned all those around her?

''Please!'' she prayed silently, and she wondered if her prayers could ever be answered as she moved on her stocking feet into the library. Daniel's back was to her. She was terrified that she'd touch him—and discover he was slumped over because his head was nearly detached from his body.

But his head was still attached. Shaking, she fell to her knees by his side, trying to see him in the shadows brought on by the coming storm. A jagged streak of lightning lit up the sky beyond, and she saw that a trickle of blood streaked down his face from his temple. But his flesh was warm, and she frantically touched his throat, looking for a pulse, and she found one.

A whimpering sound came to her, and she turned. There they were as well, Cissy and Angie, both still alive, tied together and slumped against the far wall. Cissy's head was down; Angie stared at her with wide, terrified eyes that pleaded for help.

''Oh, thank God!'' she breathed. Coming to her feet, Maggie

started across the room to free them, praying that Cissy was conscious, and that she'd be able to run.

But suddenly, a cold draft seemed to burst into the room, ruffling the drapes, stirring papers on the desk.

"Maggie . . ."

She heard her name called out in a low, slow, haunting whisper. "Maggie, Megan, Meg . . . Ms. M. Montgomery . . . come, Maggie, what will you do now? Where am I, Maggie? Can you see me, can you find me? Ahh . . . do you dare come for me, fight me? If you win, they live. If you lose, I do as I choose. And you suffer until you wish you were dead anyway, Maggie, Maggie, *Magdalena!*"

She kept walking across the room, searching the shadows, trying to discover where he was.

"Aaron, this is between us—"

"Canady is between us. Did you like the present I left you in the foyer?"

"Who was she, Aaron?"

"Maggie, I don't even know. The Avon lady, maybe. A poor misfortunate who stumbled into my path. I told you, I was rudely awakened by Lieutenant Canady. Then I was just so awake, and I knew what I had to do . . . I hurried right over to Montgomery Enterprises and watched your friends. Pretty, pretty girls, Maggie. I was just on fire! I didn't want to do anything premature, so I slipped into a local strip joint for a bite before collecting the girls and bringing them here. I didn't have much time. I needed to get you to this old homestead as well, and I'm imagining that even Canady might figure out where we are soon. It was just that once I picked up your lovely friends to bring them here, I was so tempted to drink . . . and I wanted you here for the finale, of course. You shouldn't feel too badly. This one didn't hurt at all. She died crushed in my embrace, loving every minute of it."

"I hate you, Aaron. I hate you because you're a cold-blooded killer—"

"No, Maggie, we're all cold-blooded killers. You can't change nature, not the nature of the beast."

"No, you're wrong, we don't have to be cold-blooded killers—"

"What a lying, self-righteous little beauty you are, my sweet. You've killed. You know you've killed."

"Only when—"

"When you judged a man, and determined he should die? Oh, Maggie, you're a spawn of Satan, and you want to give yourself the power of a god! You think you can set yourself up as judge and jury?"

She shook her head. "Go to hell, Aaron, where you belong. I still believe in God."

"Fool, for God has forsaken you! Do you think you can find forgiveness because the blood you crave comes from the Red Cross?" he mocked.

"Aaron, you're the fool. What will this prove? I hate you for your brutal cruelty, for the vicious sickness that's so apparent in your eyes. Aaron, you were a monster long before you were ever diseased."

Deep, haunting laughter filled the room, seeming to come from everywhere.

"Diseased? You consider us diseased, my dear?"

"Yes! Exactly!" she said in a soft whisper.

He shook his head. "We are magnificent creations! We are the culmination of the power of evil, or so we can be! We are predators, like sharks, like crocodilians—black widows, Maggie, if you will. We are born to kill, to rip, to tear, to weed out the human population. You are a blind little fool to deny it, to try to be what you are not!"

"I refuse to be a monster, Aaron!"

"You refuse to do so, alas! Perhaps you'll change your tune. All for a noble cause, of course. Come to me, Maggie. Ask for my forgiveness. I think I'd like you on your knees. Beg me, promise me—poor, damned creature that I am!—a taste of heaven. Do all this . . . and maybe I'll let the girls and old Canady here live."

"I'll do anything you want, Aaron. Just let me untie them so that—"

She had reached Cissy and Angie. They were bound with

their own stockings. Tightly. So tightly that she struggled with the knots. Her gaze met Angie's, and she tried desperately to reassure her with her eyes, and make her understand that she must free Cissy as well, and that they must get out.

She screamed, startled when a heavy blow fell across her shoulders, sending her flying across the room. "Get up, Maggie. I didn't decide to free anyone yet."

She stood.

"I just told you that I'd do anything—"

"Lip service, Maggie. Come to me."

"Where are you?" she demanded harshly, coming to her feet, alarmingly aware of his strength. She realized that she'd beaten him before because she had always fought him with a heedless rage—he had killed all that she had loved, and she hadn't cared anymore. He had gotten smart as well as strong. Taunt her, make her think that she could save her friends, and he had power over her.

"Where are you?" she repeated. She needed to get him out of the library. Perhaps that would give the others a chance to free themselves.

She started walking slowly back toward the door to the library. When she reached the doorway, she heard his laughter again—coming from behind her. She spun around.

Now he was there, in the flesh—standing beside Daniel Canady.

Tall, lean, handsome features as ever distorted by a cruel grin.

He had picked up Daniel's head by the hair. He held his knife, one with a blade over six inches long, against Daniel's throat.

"Remember all that I've done, Maggie? With a knife just like this one . . ."

"I remember, Aaron." She lifted her chin and waved a hand in the air, indicating his head. "But when you started all of this, here, now, were you trying to make me think that Lucian was the one doing the killings?"

He shrugged. "Sure . . . I didn't intend to fool you for long, but I thought that perhaps, seeing me from a distance, hearing what I looked like, well, you might think that your precious

Lucian had come back to basics and was truly being a king of our kind.''

''No one would ever mistake you for Lucian, Aaron.''

''Oh, and why is that? Do you think that our mighty Lucian has never ripped mortals to shreds? You fool yourself, if you believe such fantasy.''

''No one would ever mistake you for Lucian,'' she repeated.

''Come on, get into the spirt of this. What will you do for me, Maggie, if I let Canady live? He's so close to death at this moment, I can almost taste it.''

She exhaled on a long breath.

''Aaron—''

''Psychology, Maggie? I'd be so careful if I were you. No matter how powerful you think you are, you couldn't possibly reach me in time to stop me from killing him.''

''You're asking me what I'll do for you. What do you want, Aaron?''

He reflected on the question for a minute, smiling.

''I've made myself pretty clear, I think. Kneel, Maggie.''

Slowly, keeping her eyes on him, she did so.

''Tell me you're sorry, Maggie. Come to me on your knees, and tell me that you're sorry for the way you've hurt me over the decades.''

She inched toward him, realizing that she had no choice. Aaron didn't bluff.

Time. She had to think . . .

She came toward him slowly on her knees. Very slowly. ''Let him go, and I'll leave this house with you.''

''Oh, Maggie! How you lie.''

She shook her head. ''I'm not lying, Aaron. I'll do anything if you'll let him live, and let the girls go.''

''How noble. But let's see if you're telling me the truth. Come . . . keep coming. Come all the way over here . . . Now stand. Slowly. Now kiss me, Maggie. Make it good. Make it a promise of everything to come.''

She stood before him, and yet he hadn't moved. He still held Daniel's head by his hair; still held a knife to his throat.

She touched his cheek. On her toes, she brushed his lips

with her own. His mouth was cold. He tasted of blood. It should have whetted her own hunger. That was what he had intended.

"Thirsty, Maggie?" he whispered against her lips.

"Yes," she said.

"Why don't you kill Canady?" he suggested.

"Because I have learned not to kill."

"Not good enough, Maggie," he whispered against her lips, moving the knife slightly. "Try another kiss. Taste my lips. Taste what you are."

"Let Daniel go. Get that knife away from him."

"All right." He let go of Daniel. In a split second, the knife was pressed hard against her throat, and she realized he had the strength to sever her head from her body with little effort if he chose to do so.

"Come on, Maggie, now," he whispered softly, sensually.

With his free arm, he pulled her closer.

"If you kill me, others will kill you. Lucian—"

"Lucian's reign is ending. Can't you see that? Has your precious Lucian come here to intervene? Lucian has no blood lust, and no power. Don't you understand yet? I've spent all this time, nearly a hundred years, Maggie, learning greater power, greater strength. I'm not afraid of Lucian judging me. If I kill you, I'll kill Lucian as well, and my reign will begin. Don't make me do it, Maggie."

She exhaled on a long breath, meeting his eyes. Then true terror filled her, for she suddenly heard a voice.

A mortal voice.

"Let her go, *asshole!*"

Sean had come.

CHAPTER 19

Despite being a cop, despite everything he'd witnessed in all his years on the force, tripping over the corpse had nearly caused him to scream. *Who was it, Jesus Christ, who was it, who lay there dead?*

He fell to his knees.

Examining the poor dead woman had nearly made him ill.

Then the fear had set in, colder than any he had ever known, deeper than any pit of hell. His father. What if this had been done to his father? To Maggie. The house was so silent. Silent and dark, while outside, the storm clouds seemed to whirl in a strangely purple sky.

He staggered to his knees, inhaled deeply.

Prayed for courage, as he'd never prayed before.

He wanted to shout out, call his father, call Maggie. He didn't dare. His only chance was the element of surprise.

Nearly blind in the dark shadows of the house, he used his memories of a lifetime to inch his way through the rooms. The dining room was empty; the kitchen ominously silent. He went to the parlor, and then . . .

Then he heard the voices. Heard the husky depth of Carter's

voice, taunting Maggie. He paused, dead still, as he listened to Maggie.

Bargaining for his father's life.

He moved closer. He was as prepared as he could be.

Yet, fear moved him, and he came to the library door, and he saw Aaron with his knife at Maggie's throat.

And he shouted out, raising his .38 special.

"You heard me! Let her go."

The killer pushed Maggie aside, holding her with one arm. He leaned his other arm upon Daniel Canady's head. With his eerily glowing eyes strangely alive in the shadows, he laughed at Sean.

"Let her go . . . or what, big boy? Look, Maggie, sweetie, the cop has come. Why don't you tell him that his bullets can't kill me."

Maggie, staring at Sean, swallowed hard.

"Tell him, make him understand!" Aaron said angrily. "Or I'll rip his throat out!"

"Sean, you've got to go. You've got to turn around and go, please—"

"You heard her, big boy. Get out of here. If you do, when I get my hands on you—I'll just kill you. Short and sweet and simple. Give me trouble, big boy, and you'll just wish that you were dead."

Maggie was at Aaron's side. So was his father. Sean had to do something.

He heard noise to the side of the room. He didn't dare glance away, but with his peripheral vision, he saw Cissy and Angie huddled against the wall. Angie was barely moving.

But her hands were on Cissy's wrists; she was untying her friend. Aaron Carter meant to have a field day here. A glut of murder.

He was a cop. A crack shot. He couldn't kill Carter with a bullet, but he could sure as hell hurt him. Buy some time for the others. Sean raised his .38 and aimed at Aaron's head.

The shot sounded like a cannon. His aim was true. The bullet plowed into Aaron's forehead.

Maggie screamed; Aaron cursed as he floundered backward. Sean felt one moment's wild elation.

Then he realized that Aaron Carter, white faced and snake-eyed, was coming forward.

Maggie moved like lightning, taking one of his father's massive old historical volumes from the desk. She slammed it against Aaron with a savage force. Aaron doubled over, gasping. Sean started forward, firing his gun again and again.

But when he reached the spot where Aaron had stood, he was gone. "Maggie! God, Maggie!" he cried out, clasping her in his arms, trying to see to his father at the same time.

"Your father probably has a concussion," Maggie said quickly, touching his cheek, her hazel eyes shining with unshed tears. "Oh, Sean, you shouldn't be here—"

"The girls, my father. Help me!" he said simply. He lifted his father's dead weight from the chair at the desk. Maggie ran to Cissy and Angie. Angie was free. Her fingers fumbled with the ties that held Cissy. "Come on, come on, up, are you all right?" Maggie asked anxiously. Cissy nodded, swallowing hard. "Maggie, for the love of God, what is he? His strength . . . we were helpless. We—"

"You've got to get out of here, fast, and send help, please, while Carter is weakened. Go! Can you drive, can one of you drive?"

"Yes!" Angie exclaimed. "Cissy, let's go. Maggie, you've got to come with us—"

"No, we need to stay with Sean's dad! Go, please, go, get to the police station, quickly!"

"Go!" Sean thundered, and the pair fled.

Sean had his father in his arms. He carried Daniel to a sofa, laid him down. He looked at Maggie. "Where has Aaron gone?"

"I don't know."

"Will he die yet?" Sean demanded. No. He thought back to his encounters with the vampire. He hadn't died in the morgue, and he hadn't died in the cemetery.

She shook her head. "No," she said softly.

Deep, eerie laughter seemed to fill the whole of the house.

Maggie's beautiful gold eyes were on his. His features were taut. She was afraid. Not for herself. For him. He wanted to stroke her cheek. Assure her. How in God's name could he do that?

"He's not gone at all!" Maggie breathed. "Barely hurt!"

From outside, Sean heard the gunning of a motor. The girls, at least, had escaped.

Then he felt Carter.

Though he was crouched down by the sofa, Sean was suddenly picked up by what seemed to be a gust of black wind.

He struggled, trying to strike the force that held him in a death grip. Arms were around him, arms so tight he couldn't breathe. He couldn't see at all. He could only smell something foul, something like decay. He was stifling.

"Dead man, you're a dead man!" Carter roared. "But I'm going to take you apart piece by piece!"

He was thrown then, thrown hard. He landed with a cracking thud against the wall. Desperately, he tried to clear his head, to rise.

He saw Aaron then. Form and mass rather than shadow.

"Aaron! I'm the one you want to hurt!" Maggie cried. She was backing away from Aaron, trying to lead him away from Sean.

Then she changed tactics. She cried out suddenly, throwing herself against Aaron. But he started laughing again, the sound rising to mingle with an explosion of thunder from outside. "Do you think you'll destroy me again, my love? Do you think I went away to heal for all that time without making sure I was stronger than you could ever hope to be? I've gorged on blood, Maggie, bathed in blood, *swum* in blood. I have a power you'll never take, never in a thousand years . . ."

He was lifting her. Her fingers were around his throat and she was screaming and tearing into him. But her cries were fading away, and all her fury seemed fruitless.

Sean managed to get to his feet, took aim, and fired again. Rapidly. Careful not to hit Maggie. Damn, but he couldn't get a clear shot at the head or heart . . .

Maggie screamed again, clawing at Aaron as the bullets jerked their way into him.

He dropped her.

And suddenly, once again, he was gone.

A rush of foul, evil darkness swept around Sean. Arms encompassed him, bony fingers tore at his flesh, icy, cold, they lifted him . . . threw him again.

He thudded to the floor. In pain. Arms wrenched, back, head, shoulders . . .

He lay in darkness. He saw Maggie trying to stagger up. With tremendous force, he crawled his way to her.

"Where is he?"

"I don't know. But he'll be back."

He dragged her into his arms. Met her eyes.

"Maggie, you have to do it. Make me one of you."

She shook her head wildly. "No, Sean, let him take me, let him take me out of here. Maybe you'll be safe then!"

"No, Maggie. Don't you see? Nothing you do will change him. If he beats us, he'll just be stronger."

"Please, Sean, I couldn't bear it if I brought about your death . . . again. I love you, Sean, please—"

"Do it, Maggie."

"You can't kill him as a vampire, Sean. You'll have lost your soul, and when you die that way . . . there is no forgiveness, no escape from eternal damnation."

They heard the laughter again. Soft at first, growing louder. Looking beyond Maggie's shoulder, he could see a huge shadow beginning to form on the wall.

"Do it, Maggie! I beg of you!"

"No, Sean—" she pleaded, kneeling before him.

"Damn you, do it, or we're dead, and dozens more will pay, as well. Maggie, for the love of God!"

He drew her against him, hard. He felt her tears fall on his flesh.

"Now, Maggie!"

"No!"

"Maggie! Don't drain me, just taint me. I'll have the strength, but I won't be a true vampire."

''Sean, I don't know. When men have been tainted, they go insane. They become killers themselves—''

''It's our only chance!''

Then he felt her teeth. Cold, hard, like steel needles, sinking into his throat. He was filled with a rush, like ice water cascading through his veins. He held her, and held her, as he weakened at first, as he felt his life force washed away in a cold, rushing river . . .

Then suddenly, there was a strength in him. A strength like fire. And when he felt himself plucked up again, he strained hard against the force, bursting free of it.

A moment later, shadow formed to substance. Aaron stood before him, whirling his deadly knife. He beckoned to Sean with both hands. ''Come on, big boy. Come on, copper, come on, pig!''

He whirled toward Sean, and leapt up. His feet caught Sean in the head, sending him flying once again. Sean quickly staggered up, refusing to lose the fight when he had equal power.

Aaron came toward Sean again.

Maggie rose, flinging herself on Aaron's back. Her nails ripped down his back, tearing his shirt and his flesh, but he swung her off, hard, and kept walking. He stood in front of Sean and threw a backhanded blow against his cheek that sent him reeling again.

But Sean was quickly up, praying that his own power would come.

Again, Aaron came at him.

This blow sent him flying all the way out to the hall. He landed against the wall, right beneath a painting of the Sean who had been slain during the Civil War. He heard Aaron's laughter in the distance.

Someone was beside him. Lucian hunkered down by him, fierce and determined. He had pushed Sean's duffel bag into the hall where they now stood.

''Your sword. You've got the strength now. End it. Use your sword, Canady.''

Lucian pressed the duffel bag toward him. Sean nodded,

reached into it, and took out the Confederate-issue cavalry sword.

Aaron called to him from the library. "Come on, big boy, come on, come on!"

Sean rose, the sword at his side, and walked back to the library. Aaron was staring at him, smiling, tossing his knife from hand to hand as he approached him. "I'm tired of playing, pig. Time to dine on pork."

Sean waited. Until Aaron was almost upon him.

Then he raised his sword.

And . . .

Swung. With all his newfound strength.

There were seconds, just seconds, when he saw the alarm in Aaron's eyes.

Then steel bit into flesh and muscle, blood and bone.

And Aaron's head went flying, severed from his body.

"Sean!" Maggie cried out, racing toward him. She pitched herself into his arms. He held her. Tightly. Nearly smothered her. Encompassed her. Weakness pervaded him. They sank to the floor together.

"Oh, God, Sean!"

"Well, we have the murderer!" he whispered.

"Oh, God, Sean, but you don't understand . . ."

"Maggie, we're alive now. We've the killer in the house; there will be no more slayings. We have to live the best we can now, and be ever wary!"

He staggered to his feet. He could hear police sirens. Mamie hadn't been able to sit tight after all. He went out to find Lucian.

But Lucian was gone.

Within a moment, officers were filing in. Jack, a bandage around his head, was among them; even the chief. Sean tried to talk, to explain. His head suddenly seemed to kill him.

He pitched forward, blacking out.

Maggie had never told him that vampires could pass out.

* * *

Time passed quickly.

Daniel was fine after a few nights in the hospital—he did have a concussion.

So did Sean. He shared a room with his father.

The papers—and the police force—hailed Sean and Maggie as heroes. They had stopped the New Orleans Ripper.

The case ended more bizarrely than it had begun. The killer's corpse was taken to the medical examiner's office. Someone, however, stole it—and replaced it with a decapitated skeleton. But then, Pierre LePont, the most fierce and fastidious of the medical examiners, had been in the hospital with a concussion as well. Strangely enough, he wasn't furious that the real body had been stolen.

The incident was intensely investigated, but there seemed to be no answers as to what had happened.

The real corpse was never found.

The bones, when investigated and carbon dated, proved to be well over two hundred years old.

Still, New Orleans was a strong city. Days passed, then weeks. The murders and the bizarre incident of the disappearing corpse no longer appeared on the front pages.

Sean looked at himself in the mirror every day. He didn't seem to change.

He still liked garlic.

And yet . . .

He had to admit to being slightly afraid that he would soon become a madman. He was only able to function at his job because he knew that both Maggie and Jack were watching him.

Maggie moved into Sean's apartment little by little. They spent a lot of time at Ashville, and Montgomery Plantation as well. They healed.

They waited.

One afternoon, about a month after Aaron's death, Sean met Maggie at Montgomery Enterprises. When he entered the shop, Cissy was on duty, and told him that Maggie had had an appointment and he should wait for her upstairs in her office.

He was sitting in her swivel chair, idly looking at her handsome sketches on the wall, when he suddenly turned around to discover that he had company.

Lucian DeVeau sat relaxed and composed in one of the chairs before the desk.

Sean felt a cold sweeping over him. He had killed a vampire after Maggie had drunk his blood. Had Lucian come to tell him that he was about to face a fight he couldn't win?

"Lucian," he managed to say.

Lucian grinned. "Ah, yes, Lieutenant! You look well."

"Am I well?"

"You look just fine to me."

"Damn you, Lucian, if you're here to tell me that I am a vampire, or that I was a vampire when I killed Aaron and there's a death sentence decreed on me, get it over with. And whatever is going to happen, so help me God, I'll take you with me if you think you can make Maggie pay for anything—"

"Ah, Lieutenant! First of all, I made you pick up the damned sword. The bastard was after me. High treason, no matter how you look at it. But think. Do you feel any different? Any different at all?"

"I don't understand you."

Lucian sighed with exasperation. "No one is coming to kill you, Canady. There's no death sentence."

"On me or on Maggie?" he demanded hoarsely.

Lucian smiled. "Lieutenant, you aren't a vampire. Or even tainted. You might be a fool, but then, under the circumstances, that's forgivable."

"I'm not a vampire? All right, I didn't go all the way. Or Maggie didn't go all the way. But I was tainted!" Sean leaned forward. Was he insane? There had been many times during the past weeks when everything had been so damned *normal,* he'd begun to think that he and Maggie had simply faced down a brutal, heinous, *mortal* killer.

Lucian leaned toward him, shaking his head. "I don't think you understand. At all. I'll explain. You never were a vampire—and you were only tainted for a short time. Maggie was always different, because her father fought to keep her alive.

She never officially died; she was never buried. She never before attempted to taint anyone; when she killed, it was usually for mercy, and she did so completely, by the rules of our kind. I don't completely understand what happened myself, but I realized quickly that I had no power over you; I couldn't summon you. That being the case, you're not tainted, and you're definitely not a vampire. Maybe there really is a God. Maybe, in the end, he does make the rules. For all of us. Maybe there's magic in faith. I remember when Alec first met Magdalena.''

"Alec? Alec who made Maggie a vampire?''

Lucian nodded. "Alec was head over heels in love with her; he risked his life every second of that affair. But she was deeply in love with him as well, and he was convinced that he could make things right between them. On one of the ancient graves I've seen in Europe, that of a reputed vampire who survived the plague in the thirteen hundreds, there is a saying engraved deep into the mortuary stone: *And Love will set you free.* Alec believed there was forgiveness in love. The age-old tale of beauty and the beast. We are only monsters when we see ourselves as such. Perhaps it's true. Perhaps it's not simple. And maybe the power of the human spirit is stronger than any other, and perhaps even another silly saying is true—Love Conquers All.''

"I do admit that there is a Higher Power as well. There is a hell, and a heaven, in our souls, and beyond. Maggie never lost her faith. How many vampires have you heard of who regularly go to church? I've tried to summon you—I've tried to command you both to my presence. You never heard my call. You were not compelled to obey it. I don't have all the answers. But I came to tell you this. You are not tainted, you are not a vampire; and perhaps Maggie has found peace, for she doesn't hear me anymore.''

"I wish—I wish I could believe that. If it's the truth, what are you doing here?''

"I came to say good-bye—and wish you well. I don't want to see Maggie. Hurts too much. I did—well, almost—love her once. So, good-bye, good luck, and take my advice. Don't dwell on the past, don't wonder about what might have been real and what might have been imagined or remembered from dreams. You've been given life. You bested Aaron Carter with the strength of your own will, and your love for Maggie. For a mortal human, you're all right. So, forget what happened. Forget about me: I've never been your enemy. Go live your life. Have the sense to cherish what you have.''

Sean hesitated, studying the man. Lucian stared at him with his golden eyes, his striking features grave.

Sean nodded, and after a moment, slowly offered Lucian his hand. ''For a vampire, *you're* all right.'' He grinned. ''Sir, you are a gentleman and a scholar, as my father might say.''

Lucian looked slightly embarrassed. It might not look so good for the king of the vampires to be admired and befriended by a mortal.

But he accepted Sean's hand, almost as if remembering a different world, and a different phase of his own existence. They shook hands. Then they rose together.

Lucian grinned suddenly, making a Star Trek symbol with his fingers. ''Live long and prosper!'' he quoted. ''Damn, but I do love movies!'' he told Sean. ''Living through centuries of technical advances does have its advantages.''

Sean laughed, returning the hand sign.

''Good-bye, Canady, and good luck.''

Sean nodded. He suddenly heard his name being called. He looked toward the stairs. Hearing her voice as she called him, he knew that Maggie was back.

He turned to say good-bye to Lucian, but no one was there. Leave it to Lucian to make another such exit.

''Sean!''

He hurried down the stairs. She was waiting for him in front of the register desk. She was breathless, eyes alight with a glittering skim of moisture, her smile stretching from ear to ear.

''Maggie, what is it?''

''It's unbelievable!''

''What?''

''I mean, impossible, but true—''

''What, Maggie, what?''

"Sean, I'm pregnant!"

"What?"

He slipped his arms around her, somewhat startled. She'd never even mentioned the possibility. She had told him that there *wasn't* such a possibility. Well, with so much going on, naturally . . .

But she nodded vehemently now, so happy that her very warmth seemed to flow into him like sunshine.

"I'm pregnant." She was trembling.

"But I thought that you couldn't—"

"I know! Now I can! I'm so happy, I can't believe it. Sean, something has happened. I don't know what. I'm different. I've no strength, no powers. And I'm pregnant. I made them do four different tests! It's for real. Oh, Sean, we're going to have a baby! Somehow, we've more than survived this, Sean. We're . . . we're both . . ."

"Mortal," he suggested softly.

She swallowed hard, nodding. "Oh, Sean . . ."

He held her close.

"How can it be?" she asked softly.

"Faith," he told her. "Love."

"I'm still so afraid to believe—"

"Don't be afraid. We can't be afraid. We have to take each moment and simply be thankful for it."

"Are you glad about the baby?" she asked him.

"Delighted. Nothing in this world has ever made me happier. Except just being with you."

She drew away from him, searching out his eyes, then burrowing against his chest again.

"Now, as for you—are you happy?" he asked her seriously.

"Me? Of course. Oh, God—"

"Maggie, you're going to age now. We're both going to get old. And we're going to die."

"I know. Isn't it wonderful? Sean, I want to get old with you. And death . . . death will be fine. Just as long as they bury us together."

He laughed softly, taking her hands.

"Certainly. We have a family vault right on the property. But first . . . we do have a lifetime to live."

"A baby, Sean." She was trembling. "Oh, Lord, I can't tell you, I couldn't believe it, I was so pleased myself, I just hope that you—"

He lifted her chin. "I'm thrilled beyond measure. I'm not a kid, you know." He smiled. "I'm going to be a dad. I owe you more and more."

He kissed her lips tenderly. Then he slipped an arm around her shoulders.

"Oh, Sean, do you think—"

"Maggie, let's not wonder. Let's just marvel about our good fortune."

"My love," she murmured.

"Let's go home."

Outside, he looked up at the night sky. The moon was full and golden. Maggie was warm in his arms. They were going to marry and start their family.

A prayer fluttered out toward heaven, straight from his heart.

Thank you, God.

Life was good.

Life was a gift.

He meant to live it to the fullest.

Books by Shannon Drake

COME THE MORNING
CONQUER THE NIGHT
THE KING'S PLEASURE
TOMORROW THE GLORY
BLUE HEAVEN, BLACK NIGHT
ONDINE
LIE DOWN IN ROSES

Published by Zebra and Kensington Books